# THE COVE

# THE COVE

BOOK TWO OF THE LOST BOYS TRILOGY

# RILEY QUINN

For permission requests, contact:

pr@rileyquinnofficial.com
www.rileyquinnofficial.com
www.westbaypublishing.ca

ISBN 978-1-7753730-9-4 (pbk) — ISBN 978-1-7771298-0-4 (epub)
ISBN 978-1-7771298-1-1 (mobi) — ISBN 978-1-7771298-2-8 (pdf)

394 pages
Text set in Baskerville

Cover design by Dan Van Oss
Map design by Sofia Soria

First Edition
1 2 3 4 5 6 7 8 9 10

For Fiona, who kept me laughing from the first page
to the last.

To haunted books and multilingual dictionaries!

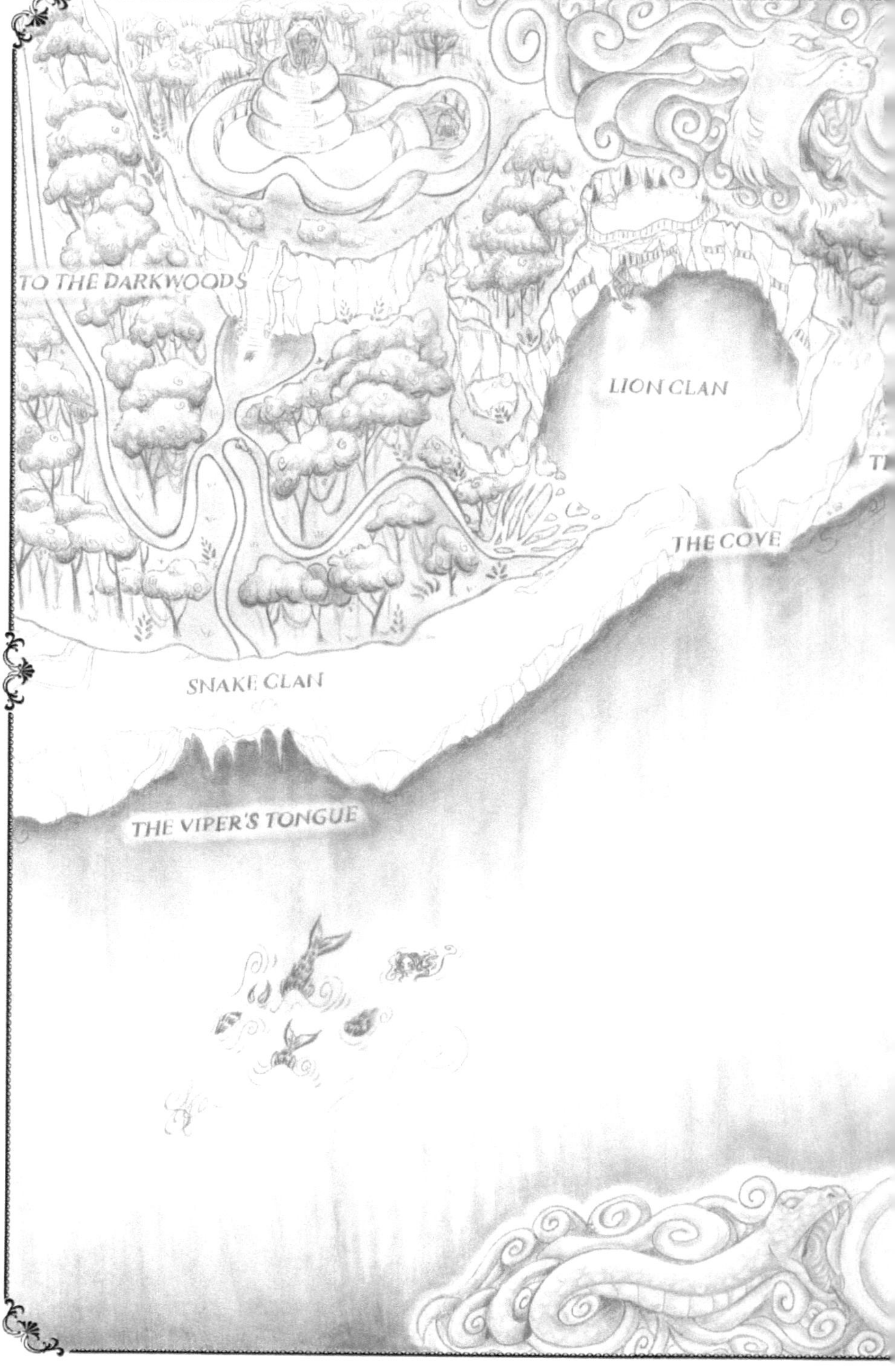

TO THE DARKWOODS
LION CLAN
THE COVE
SNAKE CLAN
THE VIPER'S TONGUE

TIGER CLAN
CRED CAVE
THE FOG WATERS
THE TURQUOISE ISLE
DRAGON CLAN
N
W
E
S

"I am not young enough to know everything."

—*J.M. Barrie*

# TWELVE HOURS AGO

Leonardo sprinted down stone steps, the rapid breathing of thirty other kids echoing through the stairwell behind him. Others rushed in front, swords swinging at their hips, shields clanging off the walls, and the leather straps of slingshots clutched tight in their fists. Dying sunlight flashed in stripes across their faces as they passed long slitted openings in the stonework.

Leonardo nearly missed a step and swore, grabbing an opening for balance as three Lion Clan girls shoved past him. He glanced through the tall window, watching black sails billow as a ship crossed the Cove.

Pirates.

"Let's go!" shouted Strato. He yanked Leonardo's shoulder on the way past. "I ain't fighting pirates alone."

Leonardo pushed away from the window, dusting salt off his hands. He gripped the handle of his sword as they reached a landing and hooked around a corner, then down another staircase.

Voices crashed in the confines of the tunnel, breathless and sharp with adrenaline.

Then the steps ended in a wide passage, only a few meters above sea level and cut with ornate openings that gazed out across the Cove.

Kids rushed to the openings, weapons sliding from their belts. A pair of girls released slingshots as another whipped an arrow from its sheath, fitting it to a bowstring. Leonardo watched the stones arc through the air and fall well short of the ship, then the arrow loosed with a snap, sailing out over the waves.

"Hold your fire," snapped Mishti, the girls' leader. "They're not even close yet."

"Sorry."

"Wait for my order. Is that too difficult to remember?"

Next to them, the boys under Leonardo's command leaned through the openings, staring as the ship approached. They hadn't been here an hour, and they were already under attack.

*What else is new?* Leonardo pushed through the crowd of girls, ducking past swords and arrowheads.

"Mishti," he called, dodging a girl with a spear. "Mishti, who's on that ship?"

"Pirates," she replied, without looking at him. She stood in her own opening, the wind of the sea snapping at her robes.

*I know. You already said that.*

"Are they other kids?" he pressed. "What are they doing here?"

"Yes, they're other kids," she snapped. "Were there anything other than kids in your corner of the woods?"

Leonardo stepped around two more girls and stopped behind Mishti's shoulder, both of their eyes on the ship. He hadn't realized quite how wide across the Cove was; in all the time it took to run down here, the pirates were only halfway across.

"They're like a clan," said a girl nearby, with strawberry blonde ringlets and a feather on a string around her neck. Unlike everyone else, she didn't carry a weapon or seem at all prepared to fight.

"They kidnap kids from other clans," she continued, her gaze darting out to sea between words. "The youngest, usually. They're here for Pompey and Charley."

"Charley just got here," said Leonardo. "How could they possibly—"

"You'll find the magic here is…different than anywhere else in the woods," said Mishti.

A splash sprayed up from the sea, and Leonardo turned as kids crowded toward an opening.

"Back up!" shouted Puck. "Back up!"

"What is it?" said Leonardo. No one answered, and he wove through the throng of kids, heart racing. Water sloshed and voices rose in pitch. Leonardo struggled to see anything past all their heads. He pushed his way to another opening in the wall and leaned out over the water, just in time to see Puck and Strato lean down, desperately grabbing for Bates, who treaded water an arms-length out of reach.

"Bates!" snapped Leonardo, "What are you doing?"

Bates neither replied, nor seemed to notice the boys trying to reach him.

"Halfwit just jumped in!" said Strato.

Then Leonardo froze as a faint breath of music carried on the breeze.

"Shh," he hushed the kids around him. He strained to listen, but the voices of everyone else drowned it out.

"Everyone quiet!" yelled Leonardo. This time both clans fell silent as a long note carried across the water. A second voice joined it, then a third, weaving and rising to chilling heights.

The song originated from somewhere near the pirate ship, and when Leonardo squinted, he thought he could see something in the water.

Sirens. Only moments ago, Leonardo and his clan encountered them upon reaching the Cove. He had no interest in doing so again.

"Get back from the edge," he ordered. "Puck, Strato, now."

"But Bates!" said Strato.

Leonardo kicked off his boots, tossing his sword on the ground. "I'll get him."

"Wait." Viola placed a hand on Leonardo's shoulder. "Look."

As the song grew louder, the ship began to turn; the bow swinging dramatically until the hull faced sidelong to the fortress. Kids crowded the rails aboard the ship. It continued rotating until it pointed back out to open sea, gold-framed windows peering out from the stern as it began to retreat across the Cove.

Silence filled the stone passage as the last wisps of music faded in the slosh of the waves.

"What just happened?" asked Leonardo.

"The sirens did their job for once," said Mishti. She glanced pointedly at Bates, still in the water. "The pirates can't stay, or they'll lose all their boys overboard. Now come on, get him out of the water. I've decided to let you stay tonight."

# CHAPTER 1

The clatter of boots on stone steps woke Leonardo. A spike of alarm jolted him as he grabbed for his sword. He pushed himself up, blinking at dawn-lit limestone walls. Sunlight flooded through square-cut openings, and a sharp breeze carried in off the sea, tinged with the smell of salt. Around him, seven other boys and two girls stirred, rising through the webs of sleep.

Near the far wall, Nym sat wide awake, still as a cat, eyes on the big wooden door as the footsteps drew closer. He'd likely been up for hours already, lost in his own thoughts as he waited for the rest of them to join him.

The footsteps stopped and the door pushed open a crack. A small girl's face peered into the room, then lit up with relief when she saw Leonardo and Nym were awake. He recognized her from last night. *Isabella,* Mishti called her.

Leonardo released a breath, uncurling his fingers from his sword.

"Morning, Isabella," said Leonardo.

"Mishti said to wake you all for breakfast," said Isabella. "She says she won't wait and…um…" She glanced down.

"It's ok," said Leonardo. "Let her know we'll be right up." He'd experienced enough of Mishti last night to anticipate she wasn't the patient sort. He didn't intend on making Isabella repeat whatever choice words she had about his clan sleeping in.

"Ok," said Isabella. She cast a quick, curious glance around the room, then turned and darted away. The heavy door fell shut.

Everyone was awake now—except for Pinch, though Moth was attempting to rouse him by kicking him repeatedly in the side. This produced little effect, except for triggering a muffled mantra of, "Fugh you, fugh you, fugh you," from under the ratty tricorn resting atop Pinch's face.

Meanwhile, the rest of the clan rose painfully from their sleeping rolls, stretching and plodding stiffly to the door.

The youngest of their strange bunch—and seemingly least affected by sleeping on the stone floor—was Charley, still in single digits, and one of only two girls in Leonardo's clan, unlike Mishti's. She bounced up and ran for the door on bare feet, determined not to waste another second that could be spent playing with her new friends.

Leonardo straightened, wincing as his muscles protested. He vowed to find a better sleeping arrangement by the end of the day.

"Great choice bringing us here," said Strato, half-awake and heavy with sarcasm. "This is *way* better than the Darkwoods."

"Want to go back?" asked Leonardo dryly. He swore, rubbing his back. "I'm sure Ajax won't hold a grudge."

"Are you going senile already?" Strato shook sand out of his baseball cap and pulled it on backward. "I knew you were getting old, but—"

"Careful. You're a year younger than me, tops."

"Yeah but look at you."

Leonardo stopped massaging his back.

He guessed himself at something around sixteen, though none of them knew their exact ages. Or their real names. Or where they came from. Or where they went when the woods discarded them.

"I hope it gets better than this, though," said Robin. "At least back home, our beds weren't on rock."

"*Back home*," said Pinch, lifting his tricorn off his face. "In Raven Clan. With Ajax. Who would kill you. If that's what you want, you're a bigger halfwit than I thought."

"I know," said Robin, combing his red curls with his fingers.

"It doesn't have to be a bad thing," said Leonardo. "We'll make a new home here."

"And for the record, Strato," said Pinch, jamming his thumb at Leonardo. "This halfwit was the last one to agree to come here."

"No, I was," said Strato. "Because you invited me last."

"Ok, boys," said Viola. She came from the Native tribe that watched over the woods. She was the same age as them, and Leonardo's clan took her in when her people left her behind. She'd been with them long enough to know that if no one stopped it, it would go on forever.

Viola followed Nym to the door, one eye narrowed as she

waited for the bickering to resume. When it didn't, she smiled at Leonardo.

"Good morning," she said, working her dark hair into a braid. Her brown eyes gleamed in the dawn light as she slipped out of the room. Leonardo's gaze lingered on the door as her footsteps tapped lightly up the stairs and out of earshot.

"Aaaand, the queen has spoken," said Strato.

"You know what, Strato—" started Leonardo.

"What?"

"Give him a break, Strato," interrupted Bates, his dark skin a sharp contrast next to pale, pasty Pinch. "He likes her."

"Really?" said Pinch dryly. "I haven't noticed."

"Apparently she kissed him once," said Moth. "I still don't believe it."

"*Wow*," said Leonardo. "So you're one of them now?"

Moth shrugged, his curls in his eyes. "Haven't seen it, don't believe it."

"Then pay better attention," said Leonardo, starting for the door.

"Are you claiming it's happened more than once?" asked Strato.

"I'm leaving now," said Leonardo. He let the door fall shut to a chorus of "Ooh," and "Liar."

Leonardo grinned as he ascended the stairs. These boys were the only friends—the only family—he remembered. Everything before the woods was a blur, and the blind trust of a clan was like a life-raft in the sea of jumbled and forgotten memories that surged just out of reach.

Leonardo jogged up the stone staircase to a circular landing with a domed ceiling. Two more wood and iron doors cut into the curved wall, engraved with lion heads, and another chiselled staircase continued up to his right.

He recalled the impatient instructions Mishti gave them last night and took the door to his left, which opened to yet another flight of limestone steps, leading down, down, and further down, to sea level. The entire fortress was built into the side of a cliff, belonging to Lion Clan, a group of girls whom Leonardo's clan had met upon arriving at the Cove. There lay a small dilemma in the fact that Leonardo's new clan had chosen the same name, and now two Lion Clans occupied the chiselled passageways.

They were lucky. Raven Clan would not have been so accommodating.

He wondered why Lion Clan was. He'd tried to ask last night, but Mishti answered all his questions with, *'we'll talk tomorrow.'*

Patience was not a virtue Leonardo possessed in any great quantity.

He reached the bottom of the stairs, breathing in a heavy mist, saturated with minerals and seawater. The racket of falling water echoed up ahead, and Leonardo rounded the corner into a vast sea cave.

Freshwater ran from dozens of overhead ledges, spilling out of an underground river and splashing into the saltwater pools in great sheets. Rivulets trickled down the rock walls, keeping the stone dark with moisture.

The roar of crashing water echoed around the massive cave system, craggy with winding tunnels and deep pools. Tiny lights gleamed from high in the ceiling; glowing fairies nesting in the warm, humid environment.

Leonardo stared around in awe. Raven Clan's old camp consisted of one-room treehouses, connected by rope bridges and crude ladders. He couldn't comprehend the scale of disparity.

Mishti had assigned Leonardo and the boys to a tunnel that swung out to the left, and Leonardo moved across the wet rock toward it, his footsteps smacking through puddles. Hundreds of fairies whirred over his head, flitting from roost to roost. The whine of their wings was just audible over the crash of water.

The underground river stemmed from a hot spring and caused an explosive reaction of steam when it fell from the ceiling and met the cool seawater. Leonardo stripped off and plunged into the water, staying under in the refreshing cold for a few seconds before he surfaced, raking his hair off his face and swimming to where it was shallow enough to stand on the bottom.

Leonardo moved to one of the cascades, closing his eyes and letting the hot water crash over his head. It was a strange sensation; the cold seawater numbing his feet, while the fresh spring water poured hot and steaming over his head.

Leonardo scrubbed his hands over his arms and chest, then dunked underwater once more and swam back to the edge. A pile of rolled woven towels filled a natural shelf, and Leonardo shook one out. Back in the Darkwoods, all they had were the clothes on their backs and whatever was left behind by the boys who'd vanished. Sometimes they got supplies from Viola's Native tribe, but not often.

Here, they had everything they could ever need. He'd pressed Mishti for answers last night, and while her responses were vague, he'd gotten the definite impression that the woods itself provided Lion Clan with this extravagance.

*The woods* were a presence, a watchfulness. *The eye of the dream-world,* where over-imaginative children could find themselves trapped if they weren't careful. The ocean was also part of 'the woods', as were the cliffs, the islands out to sea, and everything within their reach, for miles and miles into the fabric of imagination. The girls here called it the Lostwoods, but whatever the name, Leonardo had never seen it show so much favour for one clan.

*Why?* he wondered. *Why them?*

They were the only girl clan he'd ever heard of, but that couldn't be enough to earn this type of favour.

*Do all the clans of the Cove get it like this?* He couldn't believe that either. The clans of the Darkwoods lived in the dirt while in another corner of the woods, these clans were living in fortresses? *It can't be that unbalanced.*

He wondered how many clans there even were in the Cove. So far, they'd met three; Snake Clan, Lion Clan, and the pirates. He anticipated more. The Cove was bigger than the Darkwoods, and the Darkwoods had four clans, plus Viola's people—*the guardians of the woods.*

He wished he could have pushed them for more information before they all left. He'd met the chief twice, and his answers were even more cryptic than Mishti's.

Leonardo tossed his towel in the corner and dressed in one of the robes the girls had provided them, shrugging his arms through the cowled sleeves. It felt like a religious garment, made of silky gold fabric with a tie-string around the waist. His other clothes were filthy from days of travel, so he'd accepted the ropes gratefully, though the loose garment wasn't quite to his taste.

"Be quick," said Leonardo, as he passed Pinch, Strato, and Bates on the way out. "I don't want you late to breakfast."

"Who cares about breakfast?" said Pinch. "I'll eat when I'm ready. All this fancy—"

"Is how they do things here," interrupted Leonardo. "And we will respect that since we have nowhere else to go. Understood?"

Pinch grunted, but Leonardo let him be. Back in Raven Clan, Leonardo, Pinch, and Moth had been best friends. Now Pinch was Leonardo's second-in-command—or *se-com*, as the boys abbreviated it—and despite the face he showed to the world, Leonardo knew Pinch would follow his orders to any end.

Straightening the cowl of his robe, Leonardo started up the steps to the terrace high above, preparing himself for a tense breakfast with their hosts.

# CHAPTER 2

The terrace sat atop a natural ledge, wide and deep and overlooking the sparkling waters of the Cove below. A stone balustrade ran along the open side, and heavy blankets hung over doorways along the back wall of the cliff.

A table of lashed bamboo stalks sat atop two stumps in the centre of the terrace, covered in platters of food and surrounded with smaller stumps where most of Mishti's Lion Clan already sat. A few pulled their robes closer around themselves, cool in the shade of the clifftop. Leonardo predicted it would heat up quickly; not a single cloud marred the pure blue sky, and the cracks in the cliff alluded to a baking sun.

Nym, Robin, Puck, and Moth had taken their seats as well, and Moth was deep in conversation with Juliet, Lion Clan's shaman. They'd met last night after the pirates' failed attack.

She didn't look how Leonardo would expect a shaman to look.

Quiet and pretty, strawberry blonde and entirely uninterested in attention. She dressed simply, in the same gold robes as the rest of them. The only difference was a tiny iridescent feather that she wore on a string around her neck. Moth said it was a hummingbird's tail-feather, and it symbolized her connection to the magic of the woods.

"Moth can hear the fairies," she was telling Mishti as Leonardo walked up. "They can talk to him."

"Yes," said Mishti carefully, her Hindi accent lilting over the word. "So you said."

"You don't believe me," said Juliet, more a fact than a retort. She sighed and turned back to Moth. "Have they said anything else today?"

"The same as last night," said Moth. "Pirates. Pirates, pirates."

"Right," Juliet chewed her lip. "But that was after the pirates left?"

"Morning," said Leonardo, joining the table.

"Morning, Leo," said Moth brightly.

He tried to scuffle his stump-chair over to make room for Leonardo and ended up elbowing Juliet in the process.

Juliet drew a sharp breath.

"I'm sorry!" Moth whipped around and almost fell off his stump. He grabbed the table for balance, causing a bamboo carafe to wobble, filled to the brim with fresh orange juice.

Everyone around the table froze, but only a single drop of juice ran down the green shell of the carafe. One of the girls reached out and steadied it.

"Crisis averted," said Puck jovially.

Leonardo released his breath and placed a hand on Moth's shoulder.

"I'll just sit here," he said, taking a seat at the foot of the table. Around the gathering, Lion girls eyed Moth with not-quite-hostility, but something close. Leonardo bit his tongue. He hated to see Moth viewed in the same light as Raven Clan used to see him. He wanted to tell the Lion Clan girls about all the positive traits that Moth brought to a clan, but he knew his interference would only make things worse.

At least Juliet seemed to see past his shortcomings. She brushed off his apologies and plunged right back into questioning him about the fairies. It was nice to see Moth get the attention for once.

Leonardo nodded a greeting to Mishti at the far end of the table. She'd tied her black hair into something slightly less wild for breakfast. Her bindi dot stood stark and red against her dark skin, and gold jewelry glinted alongside the sharpened throwing rings on her wrists. All of it lent to a blade's edge balance of grace and violence.

She nodded back, slow and careful. They'd been engaged in a strange dance since Leonardo's clan traipsed into her camp, believing incorrect information that it had been abandoned.

Mid-table, Charley sat in a tight-bunched cluster of young girls, all of them talking at high speed. Her pet wild hamster, Lion, wobbled his basket on the seat beside her, and she steadied it automatically, never breaking from whatever was so important they couldn't even take turns speaking.

He grinned a little, happy she'd found friends. Aside from Viola, who was older than her, she'd been the only girl in Leonardo's

Lion Clan. She was telling a story now about the many dangers they'd faced on their trip south. He'd heard her bragging about it last night as well. He made a note to curb that later. Charley was a good kid, but her enthusiasm got away from her sometimes. *Most times*, if he was honest.

"Leo." Puck leaned over, interrupting his thoughts. "Strato wants me to tell you he apologizes for earlier. You were right about us coming here."

Leonardo stared at him. "He what?"

"He wants you to know he was wrong."

"And why are *you* telling me?"

"Because," said Puck, "He bet me ten bragging points you'd buy it."

Leonardo closed his eyes. *Of course.*

"What's a bragging point?" he asked.

"Beats me; something he and Bates do. Anyway, I don't think you bought that, did you? I win if you didn't believe it."

"Sure," Leonardo swatted a bug away from the food. "But how does me not believing your lie make you win?"

"Because it's not my lie, it's Bates's." Puck tapped his head. "Lie by proxy."

Leonardo drew a slow breath. Sometimes he underestimated his clan's capacity for pointlessness.

"Don't worry about it," Puck slapped him on the back and turned to join Nym's conversation.

Then Viola rounded the stone outcropping that hid the stairs, her hair split into its customary twin braids, her tan skin still shiny from the steam caverns. Beaded leather moccasins poked out from under the hem of her gold robe.

She took the seat to Leonardo's right and slipped her fingers into his under the table.

"Am I late?" she asked him under her breath.

"No," said Leonardo. "She hasn't started yet."

"Oh good. Do you know what's happening yet?"

He shook his head. "Last night, she just told me to make sure everyone was present. I'm hoping she'll finally tell us something useful."

He glanced back for Pinch, Strato, and Bates, who still hadn't surfaced.

"They should be here already," said Viola.

Leonardo nodded, glancing down the table at Mishti. She, in turn, eyed the three empty seats, an eyebrow raised.

Finally, Strato and Bates jogged around the outcropping, followed by a deliberately slow Pinch.

*Get over yourself and sit down,* Leonardo snapped at him silently. On the outside, he kept cool in front of the Lion girls. Moth's pointed glare conveyed the message clear enough anyway, and Pinch rolled his eyes as he sat down across from him.

Then Moth tilted his head in exasperation. He reached down and shoved something under the table, then turned to Leonardo.

"He put his foot on my knee."

"I sprained my ankle," retorted Pinch. "I ran up all those steps to get here in time."

"Right," said Leonardo. "Now sit up like a proper person."

"Fine." Pinch dropped his foot to the ground with a smack that startled kids down the table, then sat as straight as sarcastically possible. At the far end, Mishti cleared her throat. "If everyone is present, we'll begin."

# CHAPTER 3

The Lions linked hands around the table. Leonardo hesitantly followed suit, taking Moth's hand with his left and squeezing Viola's on his right. Moth's palm was clammy, and Leonardo frowned at him before realizing Juliet held his other hand.

Leonardo smirked and glanced away as Mishti stood, straightening her robes. Pinch made a face, trapped holding hands with Viola and Puck.

"We thank the Lostwoods for providing us with this food," started Mishti, head bowed and eyes closed. "For this sunshine, and for the peace we continue to experience in the Cove. We thank the Lostwoods for its gifts and its favour, and for guiding our hand when we are uncertain."

Pinch glanced at Leonardo and rolled his eyes. Leonardo gave him a sharp look and Pinch grinned.

"We thank the Lostwoods for the sirens, who guard our waters from seafaring enemies, and the fairies, who warn us of intruders in camp." She opened her eyes partly on this line, looking down the table at Leonardo.

Now Leonardo fought the urge to roll his eyes. He'd explained to her several times already that his clan thought this camp was abandoned.

A pack of fairies whirred past, drinking from the trailing flowers along the cliff face. Others made attempts at the food on the bamboo table, but the Lions swatted them away, temporarily breaking their hand-held circle.

"Finally, we thank the Lostwoods for the future, for writing our destiny in gold and sunlight. *Our steel is yours, our hand is yours, our hearts are yours.*"

The Lion girls repeated this mantra.

*Is this why the woods—or* Lostwoods—*favour them? * Leonardo wondered. *Because they worship it?*

Charley mouthed the words hesitantly, one eye on Leonardo. She was trapped in a strange juxtaposition, surrounded by her new friends, devout to whatever this was, while her clan sat in silence. Leonardo gave her a reassuring smile, masking his unease. He'd seen Mishti watching Charley last night, and he had a feeling she planned to poach her into the 'real Lion Clan.'

He didn't intend on letting that happen.

Then Mishti left the table and walked to the balustrade as a redheaded girl pushed back her seat and followed her. Sophie— Mishti's second-in-command.

"What are they doing?" whispered Leonardo.

Viola shook her head, brow furrowed.

Sophie procured a slingshot from her robes and fit a pebble-sized ball into the pouch. She drew back the slingshot as Mishti pulled a smooth, bent piece of wood from the folds of her own robes.

"What the hell?" whispered Leonardo.

Mishti gripped one end of the boomerang as Sophie fired her shot over the rail.

Leonardo watched the tiny yellow ball arc skyward, then Mishti raised the boomerang over her shoulder and hurled it into the air. It looped wide, spinning faster and faster as it curved to meet the ball. They collided in an explosion of yellow powder and the girls around the table let out a sharp, collective shout.

Leonardo jumped at the volume of it.

Pinch grabbed the edge of the table. "'the fuck?"

The boomerang spun back around the cloud and Mishti caught it. She wound up for another throw as Sophie fired a second ball of hard-packed powder. This one exploded in a red cloud, and the girls shouted louder.

Viola twisted at the same time and shouted, "Boo!" at Leonardo.

He flinched and she grinned.

"Stop that!" he said, grinning despite himself. His heart still raced from the shock of the first shout.

"You're too jumpy." She poked him with her foot.

The boomerang cut through the middle of the colours, a tail of tinted smoke following it. The third ball was packed with vibrant green, and Mishti's boomerang sliced through it as the final cry punched the air. Leonardo braced himself for another, but she caught the colour-stained weapon and returned it to her robes as she and Sophie walked back to the table.

"Do you do this every morning?" Moth asked Juliet.

"Of course," said Juliet.

"Why?" asked Leonardo.

"To worship the woods," said Juliet, looking slightly baffled.

"Or scream at it," Strato said to Bates, less quietly than he meant to. Leonardo suppressed a grin as the girls around them scowled.

"Let's eat," said Leonardo, to gloss it over.

Mishti paused, now scowling as well, then she lowered herself to her stump chair.

Every vessel and utensil on the table was made of bamboo, hand-carved, and Leonardo filled his cup from the carafe of juice. It was a blend of citrus fruits, hand-squeezed, and the scrambled eggs on their bamboo plates came from the coop of wild chickens Lion Clan kept somewhere in this fortress.

His clan revelled in the luxury. While travelling, their meals had been even less glamorous than normal.

Near Mishti, a girl bit into an apple and blinked, puckering her face. She tossed it backward, over the rail and out of sight.

"A fish will eat it," said another girl, when some of the boys frowned.

"The fish are violent here," confirmed Juliet.

*Wonderful.*

"Mishti," said Leonardo.

"Hm?" Mishti bit into an orange wedge.

"You allowed us to stay last night——"

"I'm wildly aware."

"Why?" he asked. "At first, you said we could stay if we helped fight off the pirates. But the pirates never attacked."

Mishti glanced at Sophie, her expression mildly amused. She tossed the orange rind onto her bamboo plate. "You'd rather be kicked out?"

Leonardo crossed his arms.

"Then I don't think you're in a position to be questioning me," said Mishti. But her eyes darted in a way that made Leonardo frown. Next to her, Sophie chewed her lip, studying the table intently.

*They want us to stay,* he realized. *Why?*

"Leo makes a good point," said Pinch, his tone equally skeptical. "We show up at your camp, using your name, and you let us stay for free? What's in it for you?"

"Careful how you speak to me," said Mishti, the amusement gone from her face.

"No," said Leonardo. "You act like letting us stay is some big favour, but I don't think it is."

"Excuse me?"

"What would you do if we left?" Leonardo stood up. "Our boat is right down those stairs. Say the word and we'll leave right now."

Silence fell over the table. Mishti narrowed her eyes. Leonardo didn't blink.

The only sound was the scrape of vines, rubbing against the cliff, and Leonardo made no effort to break the silence. He had no desire to get back on the water, but he needed answers, and he had a feeling Mishti wouldn't test his bluff.

The seconds dragged on. Leonardo's clanmates darted looks at him, but he never took his eyes off Mishti. Finally, she glanced at Sophie. Sophie nodded, ever so slightly.

Mishti took a forkful of scrambled eggs and swallowed before speaking.

"Fine. We're allowing you to stay because of Pompey. And Charley."

Charley paused, half an apple in her hand, then she slowly lowered it the rest of the way into her hamster's basket. A boy her age sat to himself across the table. Pompey was the only boy in Mishti's Lion Clan, just like Charley was the only girl to show up on the banks of the Darkwoods.

*Ok. Here we go.*

"They're tied together," said Juliet. "I'm sure of it."

Moth nodded, and Leonardo realized the two of them had already been discussing it.

"There are two Lion Clans," said Moth. "One all boys and one all girls. Then—at about the same time—a girl shows up in the boy clan and a boy shows up in the girl clan—"

"There's one Lion Clan," said Mishti. "Just because you want to name yourselves—"

"The Lostwoods named them," interrupted Juliet, drawing a surprised look from Mishti.

Leonardo lowered himself back to his seat. This was taking a direction he didn't expect. Or necessarily want.

*Are they deliberately changing the subject?*

"Moth told me," continued Juliet. "He saw a lion in their old camp. *A lion.* In the *Darkwoods.* Then it disappeared. Afterword, he carved a sculpture of it—they have it with them here—and it fell on Pinch when their camp burned down. He had dozens of carvings, and it's the only one that survived."

She raised an eyebrow pointedly.

"Maybe the Lostwoods were telling them to come to us," said Mishti. "There can't be two Lion Clans."

"Who cares if there are fourteen Lion Clans?" said Leonardo. "What's your point about Charley and Pompey?"

"My point is," said Mishti. "If the Lostwoods switched them, we need to understand why."

"The natural answer is, 'to bring us together'," said Viola. "The woods left me behind when it took my people to fight the Dark. I think that was so that I'd join Lion Clan—er, Leonardo's clan. What if the woods need us to all join forces to fight the Dark?"

"The Dark?" asked Sophie.

"It's a thing from up north," said Leonardo. "It's like...a presence."

"And it's hunting us," said Nym.

Alarm spread across the faces of the Lion girls.

"It started with some dead trees," said Leonardo. He relayed their encounters with the Dark, carefully avoiding any of the secrets Viola had revealed to them. The dreamworld, their imagination, his brother's involvement. All of that was valuable knowledge that he didn't intend on sharing for free.

"So this *Dark* of yours," said Mishti, when he'd finished. "I have yet to see it. The things you just told us...the dying trees, the attack on Nym. His hands look fine to me."

Nym self-consciously glanced at the backs of his hands. Ever since they'd arrived at the Cove, the blackness spreading through them had completely vanished. Leonardo was relieved for Nym, but it didn't exactly put him at ease; he didn't trust anything that gave up so easily.

Mishti waved around at the splendour of the Cove, rich with fruit trees and lush groves. "Nothing is dying. If what you're talking about begins here, then I'll consider your theory, but I can't believe the woods would bring you here to fight something that's miles in the other direction."

Viola pursed her lips. They couldn't argue with that logic, but Leonardo knew what she was thinking. *If the Dark is coming, we need to be ready for it.*

"We had no warning before everything went to shit back home," said Pinch.

"No, we didn't," said Leonardo. "In the space of one day, we were attacked by three clans, our camp burned down, my brother Aleksander—"

"Our leader," interjected Moth.

"Yes, our leader, disappeared; and his successor, Ajax, tried to kill us all for challenging him."

"Then the Dark came," said Viola. "The woods took my people away, but I was left behind. The Dark destroyed our camp."

Mishti tapped her fingers on the table while they spoke. She glanced impatiently at Sophie. "Then perhaps the Lostwoods led you to us for safety. Clearly, you need it."

"Hey," snapped Strato. "We were the fiercest clan in the Darkwoods."

"Yeah," said Bates. "We don't need help from any—"

"And there's your problem," said Mishti. "The clans of the Darkwoods are only boys, yes?"

"Yes," said Leonardo brusquely.

She tsked her tongue. "Disaster waiting to happen. You'll find we're far more civilized here in the Cove."

"Yeah?" said Pinch. "And tell me how you'll use your *civilization* to fight the Dark. Will you invite it to breakfast? Spoiler alert, you'll *be* breakfast."

"Watch your tone," snapped Sophie.

"Can we get back to Pompey and Charley?" asked Leonardo.

"Ok, ok," said Juliet. She stood up, palms out placatingly. "Idea: I'll ask the Lostwoods about all of this. Moth can ask the fairies."

Moth started to say, "It doesn't work that w—" but Juliet placed a hand on his arm.

"We'll see what we can learn," she continued. "And then we can make an educated decision."

Mishti studied them, throwing rings jingling on her wrists. Sophie leaned over and whispered something to her. Mishti nodded, then thanked Juliet.

"We'll adjourn this debate until Juliet receives an answer. Tomorrow is the full moon. It will be the perfect time to ask."

Leonardo drew a deep breath, reaching for the carafe of orange juice. His fingers shook and Viola came to his rescue. She grabbed it first, smoothly filling her own cup, then offering to fill his. Leonardo nodded in appreciation, steadying his hands. His last days in Raven Clan were fraught with conflict—the eight boys barely came out of it alive—and he wasn't in a good state of mind for more fighting yet.

Under the table, Viola took his hand again and squeezed his fingers.

After breakfast, Leonardo rose and crossed to the balustrade, caught in the first beams of sunlight creeping over the clifftop, heating the stone rail enough that Leonardo's arms warmed pleasantly when he leaned on it.

Tan sea cliffs surrounded the Cove, looming over a sandy beach across the water from Lion Clan's cliffside fortress. Dense jungle backed the beach, parting over the mouth of a river. A week's travel up that river lay the Darkwoods and Raven Clan. It felt like a different world, but he knew it wasn't. The river tied all four corners of the woods—or the *Lostwoods*, as the Lion girls called it—and if Leonardo's clan could get here, then the Dark could too.

But the Dark wasn't the only threat. Leonardo gazed out to sea through an opening in the cliffs.

"Do you think we're in danger here?" asked Juliet, stepping up to the balustrade beside Leonardo. The hummingbird feather around her neck gleamed in the sunlight. Moth moved up on her other side.

"I don't know," said Leonardo, pulling himself from thoughts of pirates. "Viola says the Dark is coming everywhere." He looked around for Viola, but her back was to him, in conversation with a Lion Clan girl. "According to her," he finished, "nowhere is safe."

Juliet drew in a breath. Her strawberry blonde ringlets lent to her innocence, and Leonardo felt guilty for saying it so bluntly. He hadn't meant to scare her, but he needed these Lions to comprehend the severity of the situation. Maybe if Juliet understood, then she could change Mishti's mind.

"The fairies should have warned us," she said, her voice edged with the slightest skepticism. "They always try to when danger is coming."

"Maybe they *have* tried to," said Leonardo.

"Maybe." She studied the horizon. "If that's true, I expect they'll try again, now that we can speak to them." She glanced at Moth admiringly.

"I can't speak *to* them," corrected Moth. "Only hear them."

"Still," said Juliet. "It's incredible to be able to know what they're thinking."

"Yes. Incredible," said Pinch, walking up behind them. "'Pirates', right? That's what they said today?"

"That's correct..." said Moth warily.

"'Pirates, pirates, pirates'," quoted Pinch. "Well I don't know about you, Leo, but I for one feel enlightened."

"Shut up, Pinch," said Moth.

"I'm serious," Pinch leaned on the stone rail, long fingers tracing the carved edge. Then he grinned. "Actually, no I'm not. It's a useless talent, Moth."

"*Pinch*," said Leonardo, just as Juliet said, "You don't know what you're talking about."

"It's ok," said Moth, smirking as he regarded Pinch. "It's hard to take anything serious from...this." He waved a hand at Pinch.

Leonardo snorted, stifling a laugh as Pinch glared at him. The robes were somewhat comical to begin with, gold and silky and elegantly cowled. But to make matters worse, Pinch insisted on wearing his giant black tricorn hat atop the ensemble. And his long frame lifted the hem of the rope a few inches off the ground, revealing a pair of weathered combat boots.

From the boots to the robe to the hat, Pinch looked like a dress-up trunk gone wrong.

And he knew it. Pinch made a face, plucking at the rich fabric.

"That's it," he declared. "I'm changing. Where did you put my clothes?" he snapped at Juliet.

"Me?" asked Juliet.

"Your...*clan.*" Pinch said the word with unveiled contempt, waving vaguely at the Lions around the terrace. Or the terrace itself. Or the breakfast table. It was hard to tell what exactly annoyed him the most.

"Oh. I'm not sure," said Juliet. "Probably the laundry baskets. Which means they should've been cleaned first-thing this morning. They're probably on the line now. I'm sure they'll be delivered to your room as soon as they're dry."

"Yeah, Pinch," said Moth, hands on his hips. He was notably shorter than Pinch, even with the extra inch of curls. "Just be patient. Besides," he added, grinning. "Don't you feel free in these—"

"Dresses?" said Pinch. "Oh yes. Free as the wind."

"Someone woke up on the wrong side of the..." Moth frowned, "...stone floor?"

"Yeah Pinch," said Leonardo. "Snap out of it already."

Pinch opened his mouth for a retort, then he shut it. He'd promised Leonardo that he would dial back the lone-wolf attitude.

"Come on," said Leonardo. "Let's go find our clothes."

"About time," said Pinch, but his tone changed. Pinch was a simultaneously complex and exceedingly simple creature. Accept him for what he was, and he'd be loyal forever.

Leonardo rolled his neck as he followed Pinch across the terrace. Becoming leader on the run had been a challenge. Now that they'd reached safety, a whole new batch of fires had begun to burn. Leonardo was growing tired of putting them out.

*We need some rain,* he thought. Overhead, the sun burned in a cloudless sky.

# CHAPTER 4

Leonardo and Pinch found their clothes hanging dry on a line in one of the open-air passages, along with a dozen spare robes.

"Where do they get so many supplies?" asked Leonardo.

"Beats me," said Pinch, dragging his black tee-shirt off the line. "Could be like the swords and shit back in the Darkwoods. It's just *there*. No explanation."

"Could be," said Leonardo, brow furrowed as they traced their steps back into the fortress, and the endless stairways. They hung a left at the first landing and Leonardo glanced up an adjoining staircase at the echo of laughter and rapid, high-pitched voices.

"Here comes the stampede," said Pinch dryly.

"But if that's the case, then why?" he pressed. "We need the swords to defend ourselves. They're important for our survival, so the woods gives them to us. But robes and towels and sleeping gowns?"

Pinch shrugged. "Girls have different priorities."

"I don't think Mishti's priorities are much different from the leaders of the Darkwoods," said Leonardo. He remembered her girls in their gold armour when his clan walked into their camp.

Behind them, the voices grew closer, pared with running footsteps. They rounded the next corner and moved to the side of the passage so as not to be trampled.

Down the passage, Pompey glanced up, hearing the noise too. From the dart of his eyes, he appeared to briefly consider making a break for it, then he drew himself up as Charley and half a dozen other girls rounded the corner.

"Hi Leo," said Charley as they sprinted past, gold sleeves flying at their elbows and robes tangling around their ankles.

Pompey shifted back and the girls ran past him, barely glancing his way. Their voices disappeared down the passage ahead, and he put his head down, hurrying past Leonardo and Pinch.

Pinch twisted to watch him go.

"Weird kid."

"He's completely ostracized here," said Leonardo.

"Still a weird kid," said Pinch.

"How would you feel if you were treated like an outsider in your own clan?"

"Ahem..." said Pinch. "Raven Clan?"

"That's different. You were weird from the beginning."

Pinch opened his mouth to argue, then cocked his head. "True."

Then Pinch stopped walking. "Mishti didn't imagine these robes."

"What?" Leonardo turned back, frowning at him.

"You said Mishti's priorities are no different than ours, but she's not the one who imagined all this."

Leonardo looked down at his robe, realizing Pinch was right. "No. It would've been—"

"The first 'Lost Girls', if Viola knows what she's talking about."

Pinch was referring to the secrets she'd told them on the river, just days earlier. Alongside the revelation that the woods were inside their imaginations, she'd explained that every treehouse, sword, and stream originated from the minds of the first children to get lost in their imagination. In the years since, a more stable and natural ecosystem had developed, but if Leonardo understood Pinch correctly…

"You think the first Lion Clan girls imagined an endless supply of luxuries?"

"According to Viola's rules, only the first kids could imagine things into real life."

"And the woods keep replenishing it," said Leonardo. "Because endless is endless. I wonder…" His mind shifted beyond the robes and towels. Their weapons, the baskets of arrows he'd seen. *What if they're self-replenishing too.*

"Maybe girls *are* smarter than boys," said Pinch, chewing his lip.

"This fortress certainly beats the treehouses in the Darkwoods," agreed Leonardo.

"The first halfwits in the Darkwoods could've imagined whatever they wanted," said Pinch. He scratched his chin. "The fuckers gave us a bunch of sticks and ropes."

Leonardo chuckled. "And meanwhile, the girls here made all this."

An elaborate gold-etched Lion glared at them from the door to their room.

"And you wonder why the woods favour them?" said Pinch. "The other option is a bunch of halfwits hacking at each other in longboats. What do you think their boat even looks like here? I bet their sails are made of silk." He stretched the sleeve of his robe.

"I wouldn't be surprised," said Leonardo.

Inside the room the girls had given them, Pinch changed into his regular clothes while Leonardo gazed at the sea through the square opening in the wall. Far below, waves crashed against the cliff, and seabirds screamed as they wheeled in the wind. A creeping vine hung over the corner of the window, growing from a crevice somewhere overhead. Small purple flowers bloomed along its length, and a tiny fairy flew up as he watched. She ducked her head inside a blossom, drinking the nectar, then flitted down to his hand, landing with bare feet on his knuckles. She wore a bell-shaped flower as a dress, her chestnut hair tied up in a fountain atop her head.

She smiled up at him, wide and cheesy, her eyes as green as Charley's.

Leonardo grinned back. The green-eyed fairy had taken to him while they were travelling. Sometimes she'd ride around on his shoulder, other times she'd simply touch down for a few seconds before flying off again. Viola said fairies were very attached creatures and formed strong bonds with humans. He'd seen them hovering around the Lion Clan girls, and last night, he'd found Charley covered in so many that she was almost unrecognizable. She liked to feed them while she talked to them, even though she never got a response. At breakfast, Leonardo witnessed her smuggle a handful of orange wedges into her pockets.

He grinned again, thinking of his clan's youngest member. He didn't care how or why she'd been switched into his clan. She was one of them, and that was all that mattered. He'd seen Mishti watching her, the gears turning behind her eyes, and it put him on edge. Especially after seeing how the girls ostracized Pompey.

If Mishti had a trade in mind, his answer would be a resounding *No.*

*We need to make a plan,* thought Leonardo.

Pinch tossed the gold robe in the corner as Leonardo stepped away from the window.

"Mucho better-o." Pinch now stood in his regular clothes—albeit cleaner than Leonardo had ever seen them—and Leonardo rolled his eyes.

"Happy now?" he asked. Pinch's discarded robe landed partly on top of Lion's basket and Leonardo crossed to fix it.

"Mucho," said Pinch. "Why are you still wearing your dress?"

"Because it's nice to have a change of clothes for once." Leonardo pushed the robe off the basket with his foot. The hamster inside peered up at him, orange and white face twitching.

"We need to call a clan meeting," said Leonardo.

"Now?"

"Later today. Before dinner. Mishti worries me."

"She's a spooky sort."

"Right," said Leonardo slowly. "In the meantime, let's go make sure the others aren't terrorizing our hosts. Puck is the only se-com up there and that scares me."

"Yes, boss." Pinch butchered a salute.

Life hadn't been simple in Raven Clan by any stretch, but at least Leonardo hadn't felt the need to sleep with one eye open. Actually, that wasn't entirely true, but Mishti's 'sophisticated' Cove unnerved him more than any danger he'd faced in the Darkwoods.

# CHAPTER 5

Leonardo found Bates and Strato up in the clifftop grove, between well-tended rows of fruit trees. They'd cornered two girls, and after approximately five seconds of conversation, the girls stepped around them, rolling their eyes.

Leonardo swore, jogging a few steps to catch Bates and Strato before they went after them.

"Guys," hissed Leonardo. "Can you *please* stop chasing every girl in this camp?"

"What else are we supposed to do?" asked Strato. Just like Pinch with his tricorn, both boys refused to give up their hats, despite how comically they paired with the robes. Leonardo couldn't decide which of them looked more ridiculous; Strato in his backwards baseball cap, or Bates in his fedora.

"Just…lay low," said Leonardo. "I'm trying to figure out where to go from here, but you two harassing the girls isn't helping anything."

"Sorry," said Bates.

"Yeah," said Strato. "Sorry. Can we do anything to help?"

Leonardo started to say no, he didn't even know himself what to do, but then he paused.

"Yes, actually," said Leonardo. "Can you two keep an eye on Charley?"

"Like, babysit her?" asked Bates. His expression said he'd rather do anything else.

"No, more just...keep an eye out," said Leonardo. He glanced around to make sure they were alone in the grove of trees. "I don't trust Mishti," he said under his breath. "I don't like the way she watches Charley."

"Say no more," said Bates. "Ready for duty, Spy Master Strato?"

"Hell yeah," said Strato.

"Hold up," said Leonardo. "*Spy* might be a bit—"

"Don't worry about it," said Bates. "We've got this."

"If Mishti thinks we're—" started Leonardo.

"We won't get caught," said Strato. He slapped Leonardo on the shoulder as they stepped around him. "We'll get to the bottom of this, don't you worry."

"Spy salute," whispered Bates, attempting an uncoordinated sequence of hand gestures. Then they ran off.

Leonardo drew a breath. He hoped he hadn't just created a new problem. But if the boys could find out Mishti's plans, it might be worth the risk.

***

Twenty minutes later, Leonardo walked past a doorway and

38

hesitated, backtracking to find Puck talking to a trio of Lion Clan girls in one of the open-air passages.

"…you have no idea," said Puck. "Three clans, all attacking us at once. We'd captured Fox Clan the day before—they attacked early—but Hawk and Bear freed them. You should've seen it; a hundred slingshots, all shooting at the same time. We were up in the treehouses, and we needed to get to the ladders to keep them from coming up."

"How did you do that?" asked one of the girls, her robes painted with flowers and altered to sit more fashionably. She stood with a hand on her hip.

None of them had noticed Leonardo yet. He lingered in the doorway.

"A lot of dodging," said Puck. He mimed a ducking, weaving run. His general layer of pudge didn't lend to the action-hero aesthetic he was attempting, but he made up for it in drama. Watching him, Leonardo saw a very different picture than he remembered from the attack. In reality, most of the pebbles had ricocheted off the planks of the rope bridges or the boys' shields. A few found their marks, but the slingshot assault was far from the worst part of the attack.

Leonardo couldn't imagine how Puck would describe the sword combat.

"Didn't you have fortifications?" asked another girl, dark-skinned with an elaborate twist of braids behind her head.

"Well, we propped up shields around the ladder platform," said Puck. "That was pretty effective."

"So, your camp was just treehouses and rope bridges?" asked

the third girl, her blonde hair cropped blunt at her jawline. "That doesn't sound very defensible."

"Raven Clan was the fiercest clan in the Darkwoods," said Puck. "Our defences were just fine."

"But they beat you," said the dark-skinned girl. "And burned your camp."

"Only because the Native Chief showed up," started Puck hotly.

Time to interject. Leonardo stepped through the doorway, clearing his throat.

"Oh good, Leo, it's you," said Puck. "Tell these girls there was nothing wrong with our camp."

"It was a bad design," said Leonardo. "I'm surprised no one burned it sooner."

Puck froze, mouth partially open. The girl with the cropped hair laughed, and the other two exchanged a grin.

"If we'd had something like this place," said Leonardo, "Raven Clan might still be standing."

His conversation with Pinch earlier had gotten him thinking, and Leonardo saw clearer and clearer how intelligent the first clans of the Cove had been. How well they grasped the implications of a world in which their wildest dreams were a finger-snap away.

"But…" said Puck, scrambling now. "Tell them how we were the fiercest clan in the Darkwoods."

"Very much so," said Leonardo. At least he could help Puck recover some face, and Puck wasn't wrong about that fact. "Aleksander was the best battle commander the Darkwoods has ever seen."

Then Leonardo saw an opportunity. Puck wouldn't like it, but the chance was more important.

"Unfortunately," continued Leonardo, "Aleksander refused to leave—his willpower alone prevented the Lostwoods from making him disappear—and doing so opened a tear for something to come in. It's called the Dark, and it's hunting for us. The last time we saw it was in the Darkwoods, but it's going to come south eventually."

"Weren't you talking about that at breakfast?" asked one of the girls.

"Yes," said Leonardo. "I know Mishti isn't worried about it, but the reality is, if we're not ready when it comes, we won't stand a chance."

The girls frowned, and he left them pondering in the passage. Puck took advantage of the moment to escape a lost battle. Leonardo felt bad for him, but in truth, Puck's ego could use a good poke now and then. Since he'd named Puck a se-com, the boy's confidence had been off the charts, and Leonardo had full faith he'd bounce back quickly from this.

He returned to the terrace and crossed to a blanket-covered doorway with a feather etched above the door. Inside, he found a room strung with more feathers, bones, and oddities than he cared to understand. A wall of mixed spices assaulted his senses, and he blinked at the pungency. Moth and Juliet stood over a table, dividing a pile of red flower pods.

"Oh hey, Leo," said Moth. "Come see this."

Leonardo approached the table and Juliet stepped back to let him see.

"These are called flame-of-the-forest," she explained. "When they're dried like this, they can be turned into the powders we use to celebrate the Lostwoods."

"About that," said Leonardo. "Why do you do that?"

"Celebrate the Lostwoods?"

"All of it; the prayers, the balls of powder Mishti and Sophie exploded this morning...What does it mean?"

"It's life," said Juliet. "Colour, joy. The Lostwoods are full of life, and we celebrate it by throwing colour in the wind. Lion Clan has been doing it as far back as our stories go."

"And the prayers Mishti says? Do you think the woods are listening?"

Leonardo had known for a long time that the woods watched and listened, but he'd always felt it more of a collector's gaze than a deity's.

Juliet shrugged, smiling patiently. "The Lostwoods are a creator, no? Everyone prays to a creator; we choose the one we can see. And the Lostwoods reward us for it."

*Interesting.*

"Juliet is teaching me how to listen to the woods," said Moth.

"Yeah?" Leonardo raised an eyebrow.

"He could already hear the fairies," said Juliet. "This is nothing compared to that."

"Maybe for you," said Moth.

Juliet shook her head, bright with admiration. "Moth is a natural shaman."

"I'm sure he is," said Leonardo.

He wasn't entirely sure what was happening here, but Juliet seemed trustworthy. Leonardo got the impression she wasn't quite as opposed to their presence as Mishti.

"It's hard work," said Moth, grinning at the praise. Both cheeks dimpled in his slight layer of pudge. "She makes it sound easy."

"I'll take your word for it," said Leonardo, then, "I should leave you to your...listening. By the way, Moth, we're having a clan meeting later today. Nothing serious," he added for Juliet's benefit.

He left them among the feathers and beads, ducking out of Juliet's quarters.

*The Lostwoods reward us for it.* He wondered what exactly that meant.

By the time he corralled everyone for the clan meeting, Leonardo found himself exhausted from an afternoon of putting out more fires. His clan was lively at the best of times, and brazen and thoughtless at the worst. Leonardo collapsed onto a rock in the underground cavern, legs burning from the hundreds of stairs he'd climbed that afternoon.

"Where have you been?" asked Viola, perching on the rock beside him. "I've been looking for you all day."

"Have you?" asked Leonardo. "I'm sorry. I've been—"

A few feet away, Bates tried to push Robin into a pool. Robin, violently red-haired and skinny as a twig, slipped out of his reach.

"Dealing with that," she finished for him. "I can help, you know."

"You shouldn't have to," said Leonardo. Then, quieter, "Mishti won't let us stay here forever. All of you should enjoy the downtime while we have it."

"And watch you run yourself into the ground?" asked Viola. "You can't lead if you're too tired to stand."

She was right, of course.

"So, what's up, boss?" asked Strato. A cloud of steam swirled behind him, burning off the underground pools.

"We need to make a plan," said Leonardo.

"You all heard Mishti," said Puck. "She's only letting us stay until she figures out Charley and Pompey."

"Hey, that rhymes!" said Bates, rejoining the group.

"Focus," said Leonardo. "If that's true, then we need to figure it out before they do. Nobody's told them about the imagination stuff, right?"

"Right." His clanmates nodded. Moth hesitated a second, thumbs kneading, then he nodded as well. Leonardo studied him. *You'd better not be informing Juliet.*

"Good," he said finally. "Let's keep it that way."

"Can we talk about last night?" said Strato. He leaned on an outcropping of rock, baseball cap twisted backward. "Did anyone else notice a certain…amateur-ness with the slingshots and arrows?"

"What do you mean?" asked Leonardo. He'd made his own observations, but he wanted to hear Strato's thoughts first.

"They were wasting ammo before the pirates got halfway across the Cove."

"They have a lot of weapons," agreed Puck. "But they don't look very confident with them."

"We should have a fighting contest," said Bates. "Like we did back in Raven Clan."

Leonardo shook his head. "We need to lay low right now. No fighting, no bragging, no giving them any reason to kick us out."

"Why?" asked Robin. "Like you said at breakfast, if they kick us out, we'll just find a new home."

"We barely survived the last journey," said Leonardo. "I was trying to get information at breakfast. Like it or not, we need to stay here until we get a better grasp of the Cove."

"*And*," said Strato, "They're all girls. I, for one, am not ready to leave yet."

"Amen," said Pinch.

Viola rolled her eyes.

"So we're in agreement," said Leonardo. "We keep the waters calm, and we figure out what Charley and Pompey's switch means. The Dark too. If it's coming, we need to start preparing."

"How do we do any of that?" asked Robin.

Leonardo started to answer, then he frowned. *How* do *we do that?*

"Well," said Puck. "We can…um…"

"The river kept the Dark away," said Nym. He swallowed, a glazed look in his eyes. It wasn't hard to imagine the nightmare replaying through his mind.

"Temporarily," said Leonardo carefully. "We need a permanent defence."

"What about Charley and Pompey?" asked Viola. She shifted on the rock to face Leonardo. "Maybe they're the key to it."

Leonardo regarded Charley, feeding bits of lettuce to her hamster.

*Nothing's impossible*, he thought. But some things were highly improbable.

"Here's what we do," he said instead. "We listen and we observe. The Lion girls know more about all of this than they're telling us."

"What makes you think that?" asked Robin.

He didn't *think*; he knew. Because Mishti reminded him more of Aleksander than anyone he'd ever met. Their kind thrived on secrets.

A voice reminded Leonardo that he, too, was keeping secrets from Mishti.

*Right*, he told himself. *Because that's what good leaders do.*

"Trust me," said Leonardo. "Nothing about this is what it seems."

# CHAPTER 6

That night, Leonardo woke to a pair of silhouettes crouched over him, shaking his shoulder.

"What the—" Leonardo grabbed for his sword.

"Hey boss, it's us," said Strato. "We got some info for you."

"Spy report," whispered Bates, attempting his complex salute.

Leonardo closed his eyes and stifled a groan. "Now?"

"Come on," whispered Strato. "I don't want to wake the others."

Leonardo swore under his breath and climbed to his feet, following them across the dark room to the heavy wooden door.

As soon as it fell shut, Leonardo folded his arms. "If you two are caught—"

"We know, we know," said Strato. "But you're the one who had this idea. Do you want to hear or not?"

"Ok," said Leonardo, blinking sleep from his eyes. "What do you know?"

"Well," said Bates. "I've been listening around—super casual-like—and I found out how they got Pompey."

Leonardo straightened, suddenly alert. "How they *got* him?"

"Yeah. They normally only get newbies at the full moon. That's what this big full moon thing is tomorrow—"

"Wait," said Leonardo. "*That's* what it is?"

"Apparently," said Bates. "And get this: all the clans get together and have some kind of bargaining, auction-thing to determine which clan gets the kid."

Leonardo's chest tightened. "Seriously?"

"I tell you," said Strato. "They do things different here."

*An auction. For a kid.* The idea turned his stomach. Showing up in the woods, nameless and confused, was traumatic enough, let alone this. Add a bunch of strangers bartering over the kid, *buying* them…it sounded like a nightmare.

"What about Pompey?" he asked, forcing the thought aside. "You made it sound like they got him a different way."

"They did," Bates nodded dramatically. "A week ago, he showed up in the 'sacred cave', totally off schedule."

"What's the sacred cave?"

"Hell if I know."

"Tell him the other part," said Strato, swatting at a moth circling his head. "About the robe. They found him in a Lion Clan robe."

"Apparently, they normally show up wearing white robes," explained Bates, "which only turn the right colour after the auction."

"*Turn* the right colour?" asked Leonardo.

"You've seen the magic here," said Strato. "It's way more intense than it was in the Darkwoods."

Leonardo nodded. He needed to learn more about this ceremony, and soon.

"So the clans are all meeting tomorrow?" he asked.

"Today," said Strato. "It's past midnight."

"Right. Good work," said Leonardo. "Keep listening. But—"

"We know, we know," said Bates. "'Be careful'."

"Careful is our middle name," said Strato.

"Yes, sir," said Bates.

Leonardo drew a breath as they backtracked into the room and returned to their sleeping rolls. He couldn't shake the dread creeping up on him. Pompey, Charley, *the auction*. Something bad loomed just out of sight, and he needed to be on high alert today.

Leonardo lay awake for the next hour, turning over the new revelations in his mind. He couldn't sleep; thinking about what would come at daybreak.

He tried to place himself in a new kid's shoes. In the Darkwoods, new children were found along the riverbank, confused and often terrified. Raven Clan had taken them in, accepted them, named them, understood them. And the kids quickly found a home in Raven Clan. For all of Aleksander's faults, he was good at making new kids feel welcome.

In stark contrast, the kids here were apparently subject to some bizarre cave-turned-market, among hundreds of strange faces, where they were treated as a prize to be bought.

Eventually, he straightened and crossed to Viola's sleeping form, wrapped in a silky nightgown the girls had lent her.

Leonardo himself chose to sleep in his regular clothes—one day in robes was enough.

"Viola," he whispered, shaking her shoulder.

"Hm?" she rolled over, blinking up at him.

"Bates and Strato just told me…" He trailed off, seeing the sleepy lack of comprehension on her face.

"Has something happened?" she asked, suddenly more alert.

"Not exactly—"

"What's going on?" She pushed herself up on one arm.

"It's about Pompey."

Viola glanced around the shadowy room, the snores of the boys rising and falling. "Let's go down to the caves," she whispered.

"The Caves?"

"It's too loud for listening holes."

Leonardo stared at her a second. "You really think they have—"

She nodded again.

Leonardo thought back to his conversation with Strato and Bates, out in the passage.

*Shit.*

"I'll go first," said Viola. "Follow me in ten minutes."

"Why?"

She rolled her eyes, gently impatient. "If we're caught, I can claim I got lost, and you can say you came looking for me."

"Couldn't we just say we both got lost?"

Viola shrugged. "My way is more believable. These girls are smart, Leo. Both of us choosing the wrong door is suspicious."

"I suppose."

"Ok, I'll see you soon." She pecked his cheek and rose to her feet, stifling a yawn. Her ghostly form swished to the door, white silk caught in the moonlight.

*Listening holes, getting caught…*

Viola was a step ahead of him. He made note to ask her opinion more. She'd been quiet in the clan meeting, but he suspected she might have a better grasp of the situation than any of them.

Ten minutes later, Leonardo jogged down the steps into the foggy humidity of the sea caves. Fairy lights illuminated great clouds of steam, and the roar of falling water somehow seemed louder at night.

Viola was nowhere to be seen, so he picked the nearest tunnel and started toward it, breathing in the heavy sulphur steam. Every footstep echoed off the cave walls, sharp and wet.

A few feet into the first tunnel, Leonardo called Viola's name, softy out of some absurd fear that someone up in the fortress would hear him. Through meters of stone and crashing water. She had him paranoid now.

He received no answer from the empty tunnel and started to turn back when something splashed behind him. Leonardo whipped around, hand going to his sword.

A shape drifted across the pool, blonde tangles framing a porcelain face.

"Leonardo," said Adriana, turquoise tail flicking under the water.

"Hello, Adriana," said Leonardo warily. He'd met the siren once before when her pod crashed his clan's boat upon entering the Cove.

"You haven't forgotten my promise," she asked, blinking rapidly. "Have you?" Every movement a siren made was faster than a human'.

*Come down to the water one night and I'll sing for you.* No, he hadn't forgotten. But now he knew how dangerous a siren's song could be.

"What are you doing in here?" Leonardo asked instead.

Disappointment flashed through her eyes, impossibly blue even in the dim light.

"We sleep in here," she answered. "These caves continue far underwater. Lion Clan lets us use them in exchange for protecting their waters."

*Odd.* If the sirens wanted to use the caverns, he found it hard to believe the Lions could stop them.

Adriana read his confusion. "They may not be able to swim down, but the Lions have much sway with the Lostwoods. If they wanted us out of their territory, the caves would quickly get a lot less hospitable."

"I see," said Leonardo.

"And these are the only hospitable caves as it is. The other ones are full."

"Full?" asked Leonardo. "Of what?"

"Sea monsters," said Adriana, making her hands like claws. "Anyway, I couldn't sleep. The full moon tomorrow makes the tides all weird—"

"Sea monsters?" said Leonardo.

"Figure of speech," said Adriana. "Kind of. Not really. Anyway! I had a feeling I should come up here, and now I know why." She smiled, drifting closer to the edge of the pool.

*So…are there sea monsters or not?* He shuddered. He'd already had one encounter with bloodthirsty sea creatures upriver. He wasn't keen on another.

Leonardo glanced around the cave. *Where is Viola?*

He was grateful for the darkness, rendering the surface of the water black and mostly opaque. He knew the sirens didn't wear any sort of clothing, and Adriana drew closer by the second.

"Did a girl come down here?" he asked clumsily.

"What girl?" Adriana folded her arms on the rock ledge. "One of the Lions?"

"No, Viola. She was in the boat when you—"

"Yes, I remember her." Adriana's tone turned cold. "No, I haven't seen her. I just surfaced."

"I should find her," said Leonardo. He took a step back toward the main cave.

"So soon?" asked Adriana. She swam alongside the path as he started walking. "Don't you want to hear a song?"

"No," said Leonardo. "Sorry."

"Come on," coaxed Adriana. "A lullaby. My mother used to sing it to me."

"No singing," said Leonardo. "Whatever you did out in the water, I'm not letting that happen again."

She smiled. "It's intoxicating, isn't it? Sometimes I wish I could experience it; it looks so peaceful."

"It's not," said Leonardo. The memory tugged at his thoughts, reminding him what a lie that was. Her humming had a narcotic effect on the mind. After her pod of sirens crashed his clan's boat, she'd given him a sample, and Leonardo still felt traces of it now, clouding the edges of his thoughts as she blinked up at him.

"Goodnight," said Leonardo, stepping around the end of the pool and into the other cave. He moved out of sight and closed his eyes, drawing a steadying breath. There weren't any sirens back in the Darkwoods. He didn't understand their magic yet, and until he did, he intended to keep his distance.

Something splashed in the pool to his left and Leonardo opened his eyes, heart sinking.

Adriana shook her tangles out of her eyes.

"Miss me? All these pools are connected underwater."

"Please leave," said Leonardo.

"Ok, ok," she started to turn, then peered over her shoulder with an expression that was somehow both impossibly sweet and endlessly provocative. "Last chance. You've never heard anything like it, I promise."

"I'm not interested," said Leonardo.

"Fine." She jutted her chin and dropped below the surface. A cluster of bubbles broke in her place, then she vanished with a flick of teal fins.

*Jesus.* He was going to find Viola, then they were getting out of here.

"Leo?" Viola's voice sliced through his thoughts. She rounded the edge of a tunnel diagonal to the one he'd gone down, her borrowed nightgown shimmery in the steam.

"There you are," said Leonardo, moving quickly to meet her.

"Were you talking to someone?"

"I..." Leonardo almost lied, then he stopped himself. "Adriana," he said.

Viola's eyebrows shot up and she paused, peering around the water.

"I sent her away," said Leonardo. *Like I should have done last time.*

But last time he'd been unprepared, stranded in the middle of the Cove, in her element.

Viola nodded. "That's good. She's dangerous, Leo. What is she even doing in here?"

"Apparently they sleep down there." Leonardo pointed into the unseen depths, where the pools dropped off from shallow ledges.

"I see," said Viola.

"But she's gone now," said Leonardo. "Forget her."

"Happily." Viola smiled, her brown eyes deeper than the sea pools. The humidity made her nightgown cling to her curves, and Leonardo swallowed as she swayed closer.

"You look like you again," she said, regarding his regular clothes. She pressed a hand to the rough, patched stitching of his shirt, nothing like the smooth gold robes they'd all been wearing lately. "A *Lost Boy*, not a prince."

"I feel like me again," said Leonardo. "But it's not the clothes."

He kissed her, pulling her to him as she raised up on tiptoes. Viola was a creature of the woods, tangled intrinsically with its magic, and he felt the fairies in her, the vines, the crashing water around them. He slid his hands along the silk arms of her dress and held her shoulders. She bunched her fingers in the fabric of his shirt, shifting closer and stepping on his foot with the toe of her moccasin.

Her lips parted for his, soft and searching. Distilled energy charged his senses, sparking where his fingers brushed the back of her neck.

When they pulled apart, Viola didn't release her grip on his shirt, as if anchoring him so he couldn't drift away. He kissed her forehead and she folded against him, silent but pulsing with life. Her heartbeat thumped against him, racing as fast as his own. Back in the Darkwoods, her tribe strictly forbade contact with the Lost Boys, and Leonardo's brother Aleksander reciprocated the sentiment. Everything about this was forbidden; but now, here in the paradise of the Cove, there was no one left to say anything.

The biggest of the cave's waterfalls splashed noisily behind her, and he watched the weaving streams of water as he hooked a finger in her left braid and slid it through, freeing the dark waves. She smelled like jasmine or ginger.

He tipped her chin up and kissed her again. It was like plunging back into the rock pools after climbing out and forgetting how it felt. He let himself fall into her now, his head swimming with the clarity of it—her, the fairy lights twinkling through the mist, the crash of the water, powerful and exhilarating.

They separated again and Viola took his hand, leading him to the edge of the water. Her right braid hung intact, the left loose and untamed. He liked the lopsided visage.

Viola caught him staring and made a face.

"Fine," Leonardo reached out and unravelled her other braid. "There, now you're a total mess."

If anything, it only distracted him more, as Viola with her hair loose was almost a stranger. And the stranger was just as attractive as the girl he knew.

"Shut up," said Viola, not unkindly. She slipped off her moccasins and dipped her feet in the water. Leonardo kicked off his boots. The warm mixture of fresh and saltwater swirled around their feet.

She lay her head on his shoulder, and Leonardo gazed at the lion head carved high up on the stone wall. A long candle burned in place of each of its fangs, and he wondered who lit them.

*Maybe the woods do.*

"We should talk about the full moon thing," said Leonardo.

"I don't want to," said Viola, her voice calm and lazy.

Leonardo squeezed her hand, watching the flaming lion fangs. "It *is* why we came down here," he reminded her.

"Fine." Viola sighed, tugging a loose thread on her dress. "But I thought this was about Pompey."

"It is," said Leonardo. He told her what Bates and Strato had learned.

Viola shifted on the pool edge, frowning at him.

"Did Mishti plan on surprising us with all this?" she asked when he'd finished.

"Apparently."

"I don't like her," said Viola.

"I don't trust her," agreed Leonardo. He trailed his foot in the water. "But she's protecting her clan. I'd do the same."

"What do you think it means? Pompey showing up between moons."

Leonardo watched the flames dance, high on the wall. "Charley showed up at the wrong place, he showed up at the wrong time. I think it's more evidence to everyone's theory."

"That they're tied together. But why?"

"I don't know," said Leonardo. "Maybe we'll find out at the ceremony."

"Do you think we'll be invited?"

"I hope so."

"What happens if we aren't?"

Leonardo shrugged. "Then we find a way in. Earlier, you were talking about listening holes…"

They talked for another hour, analyzing every 'if', 'maybe' and 'possibly', until they finally lapsed into silence, no further ahead than they'd been when they started.

"We should probably get some sleep," said Leonardo, reluctant. "I want to be sharp tomorrow. Especially if we have to sneak in."

She flicked a puddle of water. "Sure."

Leonardo slipped a hand behind her loose hair, drawing her in for one more kiss before they pushed themselves up and started for the stairs.

"What did Adriana want?" asked Viola as they left the cave.

"To sing," said Leonardo. Those two words conveyed enough.

"I wish she'd quit it," said Viola. "She's dangerous. Everything's dangerous here."

"Everything's dangerous everywhere," said Leonardo. He thought about the Dark, creeping through the woods, killing everything it touched.

Viola slipped her fingers into his. "We'll survive it. We'll find a way to fight all this danger, just like we did on the river."

"I know," said Leonardo. "I know."

But he didn't, and he recognized Viola's tone enough to know that neither did she.

# CHAPTER 7

Leonardo cornered Mishti after breakfast. He followed her down the steps to a big stone passage, the same one he and his clan had entered through when they first arrived. Giant stone columns stood along the open side, overlooking the Cove. A breeze whistled through the passage, barren and hostile to visitors, with a row of arrow holes in the back wall. At the far end, a staircase wound down to the dock, but Mishti stopped before that.

She stood in the space between two columns, her gold robes stirring in the breeze. She ran an ink-stained rag over the polished surface of her boomerang, removing streaks of colour from the morning's worship.

"Hello Leonardo," she said, never breaking her gaze from the cliffs.

"What is this ceremony today?" asked Leonardo. "I heard something about a new kid arriving."

"Who told you that?" asked Mishti.

"Does it matter?"

She shrugged, studying her boomerang. She wiped off one last streak of colour, then slipped it inside her robes.

"We receive new kids during the day of a full moon. I assume this isn't the case in the Darkwoods?"

"Every full moon?" asked Leonardo.

"Then it's less frequent up north."

"What about Pompey?" Leonardo stepped up between the columns, following her gaze to the break in the cliffs, where the sparkling sea stretched out to the horizon.

"What about him?"

"I heard he didn't show up like the others."

"Sounds like you've heard a lot," said Mishti. She regarded Leonardo now, turning so the wind flipped a strand of black hair off her face.

"Is it true?" Leonardo pressed. "I heard he showed up in the sacred cave between moon cycles."

"How do kids show up in the Darkwoods?" Mishti asked.

*Deliberate deflection.* He'd forced her onto her heels.

"On the riverbank," said Leonardo. "There's no specific time."

"And they're always boys."

He nodded. "They're always boys. The only girls are from the Native tribe, like Viola. Now, I don't think you answered my question."

Mishti made a derisive noise, and Leonardo crossed his arms. The harder she deflected, the harder he'd press. But before either of them could speak, Sophie burst into the passage.

Leonardo silently swore.

"Mishti, Leonardo," said Sophie. "Come quick. You need to see this."

Leonardo glanced at Mishti. She furrowed her brow, shoving the ink-stained cloth into her sash. "Let's go."

They followed Sophie back up the steps to the terrace, then across to Juliet's shaman quarters.

Inside, they found Moth and Juliet leaning over the same table where they'd been sorting the flowers yesterday. They stepped back to let Leonardo and Mishti in, and Leonardo drew to a stop.

The bright red flowers still littered the table, but the petals had been arranged into a pair of exceptionally complex lion heads, surrounded by an unbroken circle of petals.

"Who did this?" asked Mishti.

"The Lostwoods," said Juliet. "It has to be. Last night, I asked for answers. This is the clearest answer I could have received."

Beside her, Moth nodded. "Leo, look at the detail. It's amazing." He reached out to run a finger along the perfectly rounded edge of the flat picture. Juliet batted his hand away first, light and quick.

"I told you not to touch it," she said under her breath. "It's the work of the Lostwoods."

"What does it mean?" asked Leonardo.

Mishti answered, surprising him. "It means our clans are supposed to unite."

She let the words hang in the air, heavy with implications.

Leonardo exchanged a look with Moth.

"I agree," said Juliet.

"What am I missing?" asked Leonardo. "Sure, it's two lions in a circle but—"

"The circle is the Lostwoods' symbol for unity," said Moth suddenly. His use of the girls' name for the woods caught Leonardo's attention. "Right?" he asked Juliet.

"Right," said Juliet. "It's unmistakable. The two lion clans must unite."

"Ok," said Mishti, with icy acceptance. "I'll tell my clan. Leonardo, you tell yours."

She spun on her heel and pushed through the doorway.

"Hold up," Leonardo jogged after her. The heavy blanket swung across the door behind him. "You want to merge our clans, just because of some picture?"

*Something's missing.* Some vital detail that benefited Mishti's clan.

*What do they gain?*

"Yes," said Mishti.

"Because of a bunch of flowers?"

*Does she think it will be easier to poach Charley if we're one clan?*

That wasn't terrible logic.

Mishti stopped, annoyance radiating off her. "I don't know how you did things up north, but when the Lostwoods tells us to do something, we listen. Whether we like it or not."

She tried to walk away again.

*If we're one clan, does Charley and Pompey's switch even matter anymore?*

Of course it did. Mishti couldn't expect anyone to actually buy this 'one clan' idea.

"Who will lead?" asked Leonardo. If Mishti intended to stick with this absurd story, he wasn't giving her time to regroup.

"Both of us," said Mishti, surprising him again. "Your 'Lions' will never follow me. Not while you're here. The Lostwoods has to know that, so if it wants us to unite, there's only one way to do it."

"You're kidding, right?" Leonardo cut in front of her. "Do you expect me to believe this?"

"Believe whatever you want," said Mishti. "The Lostwoods are ever-changing and we must change with them. But we're wasting time. The other clans may be on their way already—"

"They're coming *here*?"

"...and we need to display a unified front. Go tell your clan."

"Tell them what? You think they'll believe this any more than I do?"

"I don't care what you tell them, but—"

"Ok, fine," said Leonardo. He'd play her game, whatever the hell it was. This conversation was destined for nowhere, and maybe Viola or Pinch or one of the others might have some insight. He and Mishti parted on the stairs and Leonardo took them double-time. He ran into Charley halfway down, with a group of young girls.

"Leo!" said Charley. Her blonde hair was braided in one of the complex styles he'd seen the Lion girls wear. The paperboy hat she normally wore was nowhere to be seen.

"Charley," said Leonardo. "Find the others and tell them to meet me at our quarters."

The other girls frowned, glancing at one another. "Why?" asked Charley.

"I'll tell you at the same time as them," said Leonardo.

"Ok..." said Charley slowly. "Now?"

Leonardo nodded. "You should probably find Mishti," he told the girls. "She's calling a meeting too."

Twenty minutes later, Leonardo had tracked down the rest of his clan and gathered everyone in their sleeping quarters. Puck closed the heavy wooden door behind him, frowning around at the group.

"What's going on?" asked Robin. "Is something wrong?"

Pinch crossed his arms, calculating from under his tricorn. He was usually the quickest to disregard danger, but even he looked worried. It spoke to the position of the entire clan—no one felt safe here.

"Moth and Juliet found a...message?" Leonardo glanced at Moth. "From the woods."

He wanted to cut straight to his suspicions, but he wasn't entirely sure where Moth stood on the matter. That alone caused a fresh wave of annoyance in Leonardo. If he couldn't even trust his closest friend, Mishti was winning on a larger scale than he'd realized.

"What kind of message?" asked Viola.

Leonardo's annoyance wrestled with guilt. Did he really think Moth could be brainwashed so easily? Maybe he was being too—

"Two lions," said Moth. "Made of the flowers they use for the sacred powders."

"So?" said Strato. "There are two Lion Clans. Nothing new there."

"They were surrounded by a circle." Moth's voice sparked with excitement. "That's their symbol for unity," he added when no one grasped the weight of this.

Leonardo's heart sunk.

"Ooh, unity," said Pinch.

"How do you know the woods made it?" Strato scoffed. "Anyone—"

"Who else would?" asked Moth, his tone sharp. "Juliet said she didn't, and no one else goes in there."

"Moth, stop being an idiot," said Pinch.

"You think she's lying?" Moth crossed his arms.

"You only just met her!"

"I trust her," said Leonardo, just to assuage Moth.

Pinch snorted, rolling his eyes.

Leonardo lowered his voice. "But I don't think we can write-off the risk that they're trying to manipulate us. I…" he glanced at Charley. "Has Mishti said anything to you?"

"Me?" asked Charley, surprise on her face. "No. Why?"

*Then what the hell do they gain by merging with us? Or pretending to?*

"Never mind," said Leonardo. He didn't want to worry her unnecessarily. "Just let me know if she says anything to you. Anything at all. Ok?"

"Ok…" said Charley, brow furrowed. Her green eyes studied him.

"I don't like it," said Viola. "I don't trust anything here." As she said it, she glanced at the wall near the door, but Leonardo didn't care about listening holes. Mishti knew he didn't trust this. In fact, he wanted her to know how suspicious he was.

"Mishti thinks the woods want us to unite," said Leonardo. "Become one Lion Clan."

"Batshit," said Bates.

"They hate us," said Strato.

"Some of them, maybe," said Moth, still haughty. "But—"

"None of my friends hate us," said Charley, her troubled gaze still fixed on Leonardo. "They want us to stay."

"We need to be careful," replied Leonardo. He said the next part pointedly, one eye on Moth. "They might be acting friendly on Mishti's orders."

Charley chewed her lip. Moth wouldn't look at him.

Leonardo hated all of this. In a day and a half, Mishti's girls had already blurred his clan's loyalties.

"They've been all girls since the beginning," said Bates. "Doesn't it seem odd they'd change so easily?"

"Exactly," said Strato. "It's weird."

"Guys," said Puck. "There's a perfectly reasonable explanation for this."

"Yeah?" said Strato.

"*Yeah*," echoed Pinch, before Puck could. "They're scared. Have you seen them? Praying, worshiping, exploding those coloured balls in the morning. They're fucking terrified of the woods. And the woods are fucking terrifying, but we don't dance around trying to keep it happy."

"So, any message," said Leonardo, "no matter how vague..."

"Would be enough to make them do something drastic," finished Viola. "Like joining with us."

Next to her, Puck shrugged. "Close enough to my theory. Maybe a detail or two off, but—"

A chunk of rock fell from the opposite wall, cracking hard on the stone floor. Everyone froze. The sound echoed around the room as a small cloud of dust drifted from the impact.

Leonardo gripped his sword handle, scanning the crags in the wall.

Then another rock fell, and everyone's gaze snapped to a ledge near the ceiling, where a cluster of fairies stood watching them.

Leonardo's breath quickened.

*It's a warning.* Viola's theory about listening holes jumped to the front of his mind. He glanced at Moth, who frowned, squinting one eye as he listened. Then his gaze darted around the walls.

"What's going on?" asked Nym.

Moth raised a hand to scratch his cheek, shielding his lips as he mouthed, *act natural.*

*Dammit.* It was one thing to acknowledge Mishti's girls *could* be listening, another to *know* they were.

"You didn't have a theory, halfwit," said Pinch, as if they'd never been interrupted.

"Yes, I did," said Puck. "In fact—"

*Like hell.* "Guys," said Leonardo. "Let's go down to the caverns."

They eyed him with surprise, but Leonardo wasn't going to tiptoe around Mishti. "I want to speak with my clan in private," he told the room, heart racing as he crossed to the door.

***

Down in the steam caverns, masked by the racket of falling water, Leonardo addressed his clan. "Them spying on us is all the more indication they're scared. And if they're scared, it means they're not an immediate threat to us. If they actually believe this, and it's not a trap—"

"Many animals attack when afraid," countered Puck.

"Yes, but these are people, and smart ones," said Leonardo. "If Mishti's afraid of the woods, she's not going to touch us. So long as she thinks the woods want us together, she'll honour that."

"Plus, if the woods do want us together," said Moth, "we should listen to that."

"Whose side are you on?" asked Pinch.

"He's on our side," said Leonardo quickly. "Just because he's friends with Juliet doesn't mean he's forgetting the dangers here. Right?"

He fixed another pointed look on Moth as he said this. Moth nodded, slightly sheepish. "Right."

"Our main enemy is the Dark," said Viola. "If Mishti wants to join forces, that might not be a bad thing. Maybe she'll start listening to us, and we can convince her it's a real threat."

"I agree," said Leonardo. "So, we merge with Lion Clan." He lowered his voice. "Or at least, that's what we tell them. And we watch, and we listen, and if anyone senses anything suspicious, they tell me. Good?"

Heads nodded around the room.

"Good," said Leonardo. "Be careful, everyone."

# CHAPTER 8

Snake Clan arrived first. Every member of the clan wore a grey cloak, hoods pulled up and shading their faces. Leonardo and Mishti stood in one of a dozen arch-cut openings along the cliff, down a long passage to the left of the main fortress.

If he leaned out to his right, he could see the front of the fortress, just visible in the curve of the cliffs. Below his current position, the Snake boat sailed into a sea cave. Supposedly, the cave wound back to a large chamber where all the clan boats would be beached. The rest of Lion Clan—the unified Lion Clan—had gone ahead to receive them, under the command of Mishti's and Leonardo's se-coms. Viola wanted to join Leonardo and Mishti up top, but Leonardo didn't trust Pinch and Puck to keep things in order without her.

The entire ceremony took place in the cave below, away from the fortress. Lion Clan left a small guard behind, but otherwise, the fortress stood empty and vulnerable. Leonardo eyed the short dock and the stone staircase that ascended to the undermanned entry passage.

"Mishti," asked Leonardo. "What happens if one of these clans decides to attack?"

"We left some girls behind," said Mishti. "They'd hold them off until we got back."

"It took ten minutes to walk here," said Leonardo. "You think six girls would hold them that long?"

"Lion Clan has held this camp since the beginning. We know what we're doing."

*Do you?* Leonardo recalled the arrow holes in the entrance passage, but six girls surely couldn't hold that passage against an entire clan. Even for the Lion Clan of legend, the outcome would be dicey.

*Something's missing.*

"Besides," said Mishti. "None of the clans would attack on a full moon day. It's a sacred occasion."

"Are all the clans here as...devout, as Lion Clan?" asked Leonardo.

"Of course," said Mishti. "But we're the Lostwoods' favourite."

"Why?"

"Because we are." She gave him a quizzical look. "We always have been."

"But there has to be a reason," said Leonardo.

Another longboat sailed into the Cove now, flying a red sail emblazoned with a tiger's head. The rowers wore red robes, just like the gold ones Lion Clan wore. The hem of Leonardo's own robe swished around his ankles in the breeze. Mishti insisted they all wear them for the ceremony. He felt like an idiot.

"Tiger Clan," said Mishti, as if she'd just tasted something bitter. A carved tiger's head jutted out from the bowsprit, painted red and gold.

"There's your reason," she added as they rowed across the Cove.

"I don't understand," said Leonardo.

"You will, after today," said Mishti.

Tiger Clan was made up of all girls. Like Lion Clan was until very recently. All of their faces were powdered chalk-white, painted with red lips and bold black detail as they peered over their shoulders at the Lion fortress. Their leader, standing at the rear of the boat, gazed up at the openings where Leonardo and Mishti stood. Her face shone stark white like the rest, her robes shimmering red in contrast. Last night, he'd thought of Adriana's face as one of porcelain, but that was before he'd seen Tiger Clan. In their matching robes and heavy oriental makeup, they resembled a boat of carefully painted china dolls.

A cold dread welled in his stomach as the Tiger boat glided below them, into the cave and out of sight. Something about those perfectly painted faces left him deeply disconcerted.

Last of all came a longboat with a white silk shade canopy and a giant dragon head curving up from the bowsprit.

"Dragon clan," guessed Leonardo.

"Less late than usual," said Mishti. "What a nice surprise. Come on, let's get this over with."

She led the way down another tunnel and several stone staircases, lined with flaming torches, until they bottomed out in a sandy cave. Voices echoed from the far end, and Leonardo and Mishti followed the sound to a huge circular cavern, with sunlight pouring in through a jagged hole in the ceiling. The rest of their merged clan stood in a cluster, gold robes glinting in the filtered light. To their right, across a wide swath of sand, the cave opened to the sea. If Leonardo's sense of direction held true, this was the backside of the cliffs which formed the Cove.

Off to their left, Snake Clan, Tiger Clan, and Dragon Clan stood distinctly apart, a careful tension resonating between them as the leaders called greetings to one another. The swath of sand between them might as well have been a canyon for the way they toed it.

Each clan had at least forty members, and they all paused as Leonardo and Mishti emerged.

Grey cloaks, red robes, and deep blue turned as one, and silence fell over the cavern. Not a friendly pair of eyes met their gaze, and an uneasy pit settled in Leonardo's stomach.

"Your clan's gotten bigger, Mishti," called an older boy at the front of Dragon Clan. He stood boldly before the rest of them, robes stretched over his sizable girth. Leonardo assumed he was the leader.

"We've gained members, yes," said Mishti, starting across the sand to join Lion Clan. She sounded tense. "The Lostwoods sent them to us."

"Boys, nonetheless," continued the Dragon leader. He raised an eyebrow at Caliban, the leader of Snake Clan and the first face Leonardo had met in the Cove. A face he hadn't trusted from the second he saw it.

"Leonardo," said Caliban. He smiled from under his grey hood, one eye blue and the other green. "I see you found what you were looking for."

"Yes," said Leonardo. "Although, we were unaware that Lion Clan's camp was already occupied."

Caliban shrugged. "It wasn't my place to ruin the surprise. I met Leonardo several days ago," he explained to his peers. "When his clan first arrived."

Leonardo and Mishti stopped a few meters from the other clans, maintaining the same barrier of sand that divided them all.

"Where did they come from?" asked the Tiger Clan leader. She was young, but her gaze was level. Unflinching.

Their makeup was even eerier up close. Forty pairs of dark-lined eyes blinked at him, and the hairs stood on the back of his neck.

"The Darkwoods, in the north," said Leonardo. "The woods—er, *Lostwoods*—guided us here."

"Indeed?" said the Dragon Clan leader. Tight, dark curls spilled across his broad forehead, shiny with perspiration in the humid cave.

"Look at her feet," whispered Robin, just behind Leonardo.

"Who's?" whispered Bates.

"The Tiger girl," hissed Robin.

"Juliet received a sign this morning," said Mishti, darting an annoyed glance at Leonardo's clanmates. "The Lostwoods told her that we are supposed to merge with these northerners."

"I can't see her feet," whispered Bates. "What about them?"

Leonardo half-turned to quiet them.

"Shush," hissed Puck.

*Thank you.*

"Why?" asked the Tiger girl.

Leonardo frowned. A thin gold chain dangled from her right hand. It disappeared under her robe, swinging slightly as something stirred the red silk near her feet. A second later, a small head poked out from under the hem. A tiger cub gazed around the cavern, a gold collar around its neck.

Leonardo's mouth fell open.

"Shit!" whispered Bates. "They have a tiger!"

A few feet away, Charley shifted backward, clutching something tighter in the folds of her robe.

Leonardo resisted the urge to groan. *She brought the hamster.*

"We don't know yet," said Juliet. Leonardo tried to remember what they were talking about.

*The merged clan.* From the crossed arms and skeptical faces, he guessed the other clans bought it with the same grain of salt his clan had.

*Interesting.*

"But our stance is unchanged," said Mishti. "We believe in peace in the Cove."

This received a mixed reaction. The perspiring leader of Dragon Clan nodded in agreement, the painted faces of Tiger Clan exchanged careful looks, and hooded Caliban worked out a kink in his neck.

"Shall we make introductions then?" he asked, his hood sliding back a bit to reveal the snake's-eye scar on his forehead.

"This is Demetrius," said Caliban, nodding to the Dragon Clan leader, who bowed in grand fashion, then fixed the folds of his robe with deft precision. Leonardo didn't trust him an inch

more than the other leaders. His curls were perfectly shaped, his expression carefully arranged. A wrinkle remained near his shoulder and his fingers flicked to fix it.

"Obsessive much?" whispered Robin.

"Tell me about it," whispered Bates. He mimicked the motion in Leonardo's peripheral. Most of his clan tried to stifle a laugh, except for Strato, who snorted outright. Leonardo shot a look at them.

"Ruler of the Turquoise Isle," continued Caliban, his one blue eye on them. "I don't know how much Mishti has told you, but the only Clan living here in the actual 'Cove' is Lion Clan. The rest of us run our little kingdoms in the jungle, on the island, etcetera."

"And Caliban has always had some sort of problem with this," said Mishti.

"I just find it interesting that we call the whole place 'The Cove'," said Caliban. "That's all. Darkwoods; whole place is dark. Redwoods; full of red trees. Highlands; it's up high. Cove; different story altogether."

"Huh," whispered Puck. "That's true."

"That's the way it's always been," said Mishti.

"I know, I know," Caliban raised his hands. "Not trying to ruffle feathers. Now, where was I? Right, Tiger Clan."

He gestured dramatically to the clan of face-painted girls. "Leonardo, meet Cleopatra."

Cleopatra gave the slightest of nods. She couldn't be older than fourteen, though she carried herself with staid seriousness.

The tiger cub at her feet peered up at her, flicking the gold chain with its ear.

"Don't let her name fool you," said Caliban. "Our Cleo is not the Queen of the Nile, but rather the Empress of the most ethnically pure and prejudiced clan in the Cove. We children of Lostwoods come from everywhere, but Tiger Clan only accepts girls from a mystical land called the *Far East*. Far East of where, I'll never know; my recollection of the places before these woods is exceptionally foggy."

Silence filled the cavern again. Every Tiger Clan girl fixed her gaze on Caliban, who either didn't notice or didn't care. "I suppose it's impossible to *prove* that a child comes from where they appear to, but—"

"We are not prejudiced," said Cleopatra. She spoke softly, but it didn't take the sting out of her tone. Her slight accent rolled over the words with unquestioned authority. Leonardo's clan, who'd kept up a whispered narrative since the meeting began, fell silent.

"Oh, yes you definitely are," said Caliban, a painfully fake grin on his face. "But that's not the point."

"The Lostwoods has little patience," said Mishti, heavy brows drawn together. She placed a hand on her boomerang. "We should not keep it waiting."

Demetrius flicked his gaze to where her hand lay. "Indeed."

Leonardo noted the fresh bead of sweat on his temple.

"Damn," whispered Pinch. "I wanted a fight."

Leonardo shot a look at him, then to the rest of his clan. *Enough.*

Pinch and Strato rolled their eyes.

Then Viola gripped each of their arms and both boys flinched.

"Ow!" hissed Pinch. "Your nails——"

"Quit it," she whispered, and Leonardo turned forward again, suppressing a grin.

Mishti eyed him sideways. From her stony expression, he deduced she wasn't particularly impressed with his clan's discipline. Leonardo tried to care, but her annoyance gave him a petty satisfaction.

Meanwhile, Demetrius waved his Dragons forward, temporarily interrupting Cleopatra's dagger-eyed view of Caliban as the blue-robed kids passed between them. An ankle-deep tidepool occupied the centre of the cavern, and Demetrius moved around the edge of it. Based on the wet sand spanning out through the cave opening and down to the shore, Leonardo guessed that the cavern filled up at high tide.

The four clans spread out to surround the pool. Mishti started for the wet sand on the open side of the cave, as Pinch and Strato yanked their arms out of Viola's grip. She smiled sweetly at Leonardo, a proud jut to her chin. He chuckled, following Mishti across the cavern.

Not a word was spoken, but the porcelain painted faces of Tiger Clan watched the Snakes with unveiled contempt, and Demetrius surreptitiously fixed his robes. The clans formed a complete circle, broken only by a five-foot buffer where one ended and the next began.

As Leonardo stopped next to Mishti, his boots sunk a few inches into the silt. The rest of the Lions fell in behind them, and a charged anticipation settled over the clans. The crash of waves echoed around the cavernous ceiling, breaking against the shore

outside. The minutes dragged on and Leonardo glanced at Moth, frowning. Moth worked his thumbs, studying the tide pool. Viola tilted her head.

Another minute passed and nothing changed. Over a hundred kids stood motionless, staring at the empty pool.

Leonardo started to wonder if something had gone wrong. Then, as if sliding into focus, he realized that a girl stood in the pool, the hem of her white robe dragging in the water. He blinked, startled.

"How long has she been standing there?" hissed Robin.

"She..." Strato trailed off, frowning.

As impossible as it seemed, Leonardo was certain she'd been in the cave for some time before he noticed her.

"At least a minute, I think," said Bates, scratching his chin.

"That's impossible," said Puck. "I've been looking at the water the whole time—"

"Greetings," said Mishti, cutting them off. "Welcome to the Lostwoods."

The girl turned in a circle, chest heaving. She drew a breath as if to scream, then bit her lip hard. A ring of kids in colourful robes stared back at her, painted and hooded faces talking fast as they sized her up. The girl looked oriental, ten years old at the most, with long dark hair that flowed over her shoulders, stark against her white robe.

"Care to make first claim, Cleo?" Caliban asked the leader of Tiger Clan.

*They're not even going to explain anything to her?*

Leonardo opened his mouth but Mishti silenced him with a severe look.

*Fine.* He'd see how it played out, *then* he'd interrupt.

Cleopatra regarded the girl, her expression unreadable under the white powder.

"Ok," she said finally. "I will start this."

The girl shrunk back from the ranks of Tiger girls. Leonardo couldn't imagine how she must be feeling. *Confused, terrified…* surrounded by a downright alarming group of kids…

"And I will offer a counterclaim," said Demetrius immediately. "You owe seven favours. I'll trade one back for her."

"At last count, we owed you six," said Cleopatra.

Demetrius clicked his tongue chidingly. "You must keep better records, Cleo. Remember last month—"

"What?" said Moth under his breath.

"It's an auction," Leonardo replied, disgusted. The girl's fear-stricken gaze flicked from face to face. Leonardo fought the urge to intervene. *The least they could do is tell her where the hell she is.*

"We trade in favours," Juliet explained quietly, slipping up between Leonardo and Moth. "It's like a currency in the Cove."

Leonardo couldn't care less if they traded in seashells.

"Usually they just get stockpiled until the next full moon," continued Juliet. "There's no real set value. It depends on what people need…or want."

Moth asked her something, but Leonardo wasn't listening anymore. The girl in the water locked eyes with him. Behind her, Cleopatra and Dimitrius continued to argue, while Mishti and Sophie consulted a scroll of paper. Leonardo suspected he might be the only person in the circle who wasn't caught up in the auction.

"Where am I?" asked the girl, her voice barely a whisper.

"Four favours for the girl," said Caliban, joining the auction. "Two to Dragon and two to Tiger. Think about it, Cleo...you need them."

"Where am I?" she repeated, louder. Her gaze clung to Leonardo like a lifeline. No one turned.

"You're in the Cove," said Leonardo.

The leaders broke off mid-argument.

"What are you doing?" snapped Mishti.

Leonardo ignored her.

"We all came here the same way as you," he told the girl. That wasn't entirely true, but it didn't need to be. "None of us remember anything. Even our names."

The girl blinked, brows drawing together, and Leonardo recognized the moment when she realized that she had no idea who she was.

"Why—" started the girl.

"Leonardo," snapped Mishti. "This will be her new clan's responsibility."

Leonardo turned to face her. Angry red flushed her cheeks. His intervention was embarrassing her in front of her peers.

*Good. It's about time she got knocked down a peg.*

"She's terrified," he replied, addressing all the clans. "Does no one give a shit about that?"

"Leonardo." Mishti drew a breath, tightening her jaw and visually restraining her anger. She calmly fixed a strand of black hair. "If you don't shut up now, we will have to ask you to leave."

"Yeah?"

The girl in the pool stepped back, hands shaking, and lost her footing. She fell into the shallow water with a gasp. Everyone glanced at her, then immediately back to Leonardo.

Steel hissed around the cavern as swords were drawn.

Leonardo's clan instantly drew their own blades, but Leonardo halted them with a hand. His anger pressed him to keep arguing, but he knew when to stand down. He pursed his lips and stepped back.

# CHAPTER 9

"Can we get back to business?" asked Demetrius.

"Of course," said Caliban. The grin under his hood left no doubt he was enjoying the confrontation more than anyone else. "I believe I made the last offer."

"Snake Clan doesn't take girls," said Mishti. "Your offer shouldn't count."

"And Lion Clan doesn't take boys," countered Caliban. "Yet look behind you. Times are changing. Or maybe I'll just give her to the pirates. They're always looking for new recruits."

"Fine," said Mishti. "Six favours. Two to each of you."

Caliban opened his mouth, a wicked glint in his mismatched eyes, but Mishti cut him off.

"I won't bid higher and Cleopatra can't afford to. If you gamble again, she's yours."

"Eight favours," said Caliban, as if he hadn't heard her. "Three to Lion, three to Dragon...and two to Tiger."

The Tigers bristled and Cleopatra swore. "If you think my clan will be cheated—"

"You owe everyone favours." Caliban shrugged, spreading his cowled arms like a showman. "You're in a cheatable position."

One of Cleo's clanmates rushed up behind her, whispering something in her ear. The girl clutched the scroll of paper they'd consulted earlier.

Cleopatra never broke eye contact with Caliban. A vein pulsed behind her white powder. After a long minute, she swore again and nodded.

"Fine. She's yours."

Caliban bowed theatrically.

Horror spread across the girl's face. She pulled her knees up, shrinking smaller as she stared down the prospect of being taken by Snake Clan.

"Why does Tiger Clan owe so many favours?" Leonardo asked Juliet, still standing beside him.

"They are...selective about their recruits," replied Juliet. He followed her gaze to Tiger Clan's carefully painted faces. "Suitable girls don't show up often."

"And the other clans exploit that," guessed Leonardo bitterly. He held his breath, waiting for another clan to outbid Caliban. The thought of that girl, scared and confused, ending up in a clan like Caliban's turned his stomach.

Juliet nodded. "Tiger Clan pays a lot for their girls. They almost reached the owing limit getting their last girl. No clan can owe another more than ten favours."

"Nine favours," said Demetrius, with the grand cockiness of someone who knew he couldn't be outbid. He took a deliberate pause to pat dry his sheening face with a silk cloth. He licked his lips, studying the other clans. His Dragons stood in precise formation behind him, impeccable in royal blue. "Four to Tiger,"—he acknowledged Cleopatra with a slow nod—"and two-and-a-half each to Snake and Lion."

"The fuck do I do with half a favour?" demanded Mishti.

Demetrius ignored her. "Anyone care to outbid me?"

"How does he have so many?" asked Viola.

"Dragon Clan takes everyone," said Juliet. "Boys, girls, it doesn't matter. They can take gambles because—"

"They never have to worry about going months without a new recruit," finished Moth.

"Exactly," said Juliet.

Demetrius stepped to the edge of the tidepool and opened his palms to the girl. "Welcome to Dragon Clan. Please, join us here, you must be getting cold."

The girl glanced back at Leonardo, causing Demetrius to frown. Leonardo looked away. He'd caused enough friction already, and he was just grateful she didn't wind up with Caliban.

The girl took a hesitant step, wading toward Demetrius, then her robes began to shimmer. She froze as colour ran like dye down the white silk.

"Relax," said Demetrius, helping her onto the sand. "You're a Dragon now. The Lostwoods know it."

"Come on," said Mishti, her voice frigid. "The ceremony is over."

She started for the stairs, robes flapping behind her. Leonardo cast one last look at the other clans and the new girl, then followed her, his clan falling in around him.

"They're all insane," whispered Strato.

*Yes, they are. Lion Clan included.*

"Later," replied Leonardo, glancing at Juliet.

# CHAPTER 10

That night, long after the other clans had returned to their boats and sailed back to their own territories, Leonardo found himself on the terrace, in the middle of one of the most chaotic experiences of his life.

Drums pounded a feverish tempo near the balustrade, sweat sheening on the girls' faces as they beat out rhythms in the torchlight. The rest of Lion Clan staggered around, some girls singing, others downing a blended citrus drink from wooden punchbowls, splashing bamboo cups into the orange liquid.

Apparently, they mixed it with the extract of some 'sacred cactus'. Leonardo tried it and grimaced, swallowing the bitter aftertaste. He glanced around, then tipped the rest of his cup over the side of the cliff.

As the night wore on, Leonardo began to question the exact function of the cactus in the punch. With every cupful, both his clan and Mishti's slipped further into a bizarrely joyous state.

"Is it like alcohol or something?" Leonardo asked Moth, covering one ear to block out the drumming.

"Or something," agreed Moth. He staggered and gripped the edge of the bamboo table.

Leonardo raised an eyebrow and Moth blinked hard, focusing on his face. "I thought it was just orange juice," he confessed. "Like in the mor—whoa."

Moth ducked, shielding his head. Leonardo whirled around, throwing his arm up to block—nothing. Only a fairy zipped past, several feet above them.

Moth watched it pass with big eyes.

"The fairy?" asked Leonardo.

"Hm?" Moth straightened.

"Moth," said Leonardo, incredulous. "Are you serious?"

"Oops," Moth chuckled. "Looked closer."

*Good God,* thought Leonardo.

Then someone pounded Leonardo hard on the back. Leonardo coughed and staggered forward.

"Leo," said Pinch, bamboo cup in hand, tricorn resting cock-eyed on his head. "Try to tell me the parties back in Raven were better than this, I dare you."

"We didn't have parties in Raven Clan," said Leonardo.

"Exactly!" said Pinch. "Fucking dull clan. We should've come here years ago!" He slurred most of the words, then punctuated the statement by downing the rest of his drink.

"Ok, you stop," he snatched Pinch's cup from his hand, "and you sit down," he said to Moth. "Before you fall over the railing."

"Boo," complained Pinch. He swiped vaguely for the cup, and Leonardo handed it to Juliet as she joined them.

"Keep this away from Pinch, please?" he asked, batting Pinch's arm down as he reached for it again.

"Done," said Juliet. "I can get something to counteract it, if you want?"

"Please," said Moth, relief in his voice. By appearances, it took most of his concentration to stay upright. "I thought it was orange juice."

"Easy mistake." Juliet shot an exasperated smile at Leonardo and took Moth's arm. "Come on, let's get you fixed up. Pinch, do you want—"

She trailed off and Leonardo turned to find Pinch waving a clove of garlic at arm's length. "Stay away, witch!" he slurred, very pleased with himself. "Been waiting all day for that one," he informed Leonardo.

Juliet frowned at the garlic.

"Take Moth," said Leonardo. "I'll deal with Pinch."

"Is that garlic?" asked Viola, stepping around Juliet as she guided Moth away.

"Yup," said Pinch. "Hunting vampires." Then he paused. "Witches. Leo, did I call her a witch or a vampire?"

"A witch," said Leonardo dryly.

"Right. Shit." Pinch eyed the garlic, then tossed it over the cliff.

Viola rolled her eyes. "Whatever's in that drink," she told Leonardo, "I'm not going anywhere near it." She glanced over her shoulder. "I gave mine to Bates. He and Strato are half a bowl in, just so you know. I told Charley not to go near it."

"Thanks, I'll find them," said Leonardo.

"Leo," said Viola. She caught his arm. "Leave them. It's clearly not dangerous, and you need a break."

"Yeah," said Pinch. "Relax, enjoy the party, have a drink..." His gaze shifted over Leonardo's shoulder and he tailed off. Leonardo turned to see three Lion girls dancing to the drums.

"Duty calls," Pinch straightened his hat and moved around Leonardo.

"Pinch—" started Leonardo, but Viola squeezed his arm. "He'll be fine. *They'll* be fine."

"I suppose they're as drunk as he is," said Leonardo.

"He's right, you know—not about the drink—but about relaxing. There's a lot we don't understand here; maybe a night off will help us all get a clearer head."

"Maybe," said Leonardo, watching Pinch stagger over to the girls.

"And besides," said Viola, mischief sparkling in her voice. "If you're not chasing the boys around, we might get a chance to slip away from this party..."

"Yeah?" Leonardo focused back on her and she slid her fingers into his, swinging them as she fixed her deep brown eyes on his. Then Mishti sauntered up like a gold-robed battering ram.

"Leonardo!" she slurred, grinning. "Violet!"

"Viola," Leonardo and Viola corrected in sync.

"Do you understand now?" Mishti demanded, alarmingly jovial.

"Understand what?" asked Leonardo. He darted a glance at Viola. She raised an eyebrow with an expression that said, *she's clearly enjoying the cactus punch.*

"Why we're the Lostwoods' favourite!" said Mishti, slow and exasperated. "You asked me earlier today—"

"Yes, I remember," said Leonardo. "And no, I still don't understand."

Mishti rolled her eyes at Viola.

Viola crossed her arms.

"Tiger Clan is too prejudiced," Mishti started, loud and carefully articulated. "Snake Clan is just…creepy. And Demetrius is too greedy. And too smart for anyone's good. The Lostwoods seek perfection, ok?" She waved around at the party. "This is pure. We celebrate the woods, we trade our favours to keep the peace. Lion Clan has not fought a war in decades, but we keep our weapons sharp."

"Lion Clan hasn't fought a war in decades?" Leonardo echoed.

"Correct." Mishti jutted her chin.

Leonardo furrowed his brow.

Then the drummers started up a new beat, louder and faster with every ear-shattering crack. Leonardo twisted to see them, crouched in front of the stone balustrade. Viola edged away, plugging one ear. He marvelled that the girls didn't sprain their hands.

"Come on," shouted Mishti. "Why aren't you drinking? You two need a drink."

"Sure," said Viola. Leonardo frowned at her and she shook her head. He grinned.

"Good." Mishti spun on her heel and they followed her into the crowd. Bodies pressed around them, spinning to the music and sweating in the warm night. A pack of jumping, hooting kids— including Puck and Strato—moved on a collision course for their path. Leonardo and Viola glanced at each other, then sidestepped behind the horde.

Free of Mishti, Leonardo pulled Viola away from the party. Flames crackled atop torches, faces blurred past, and fairies dipped overhead as they wove their way to a recess in the cliff.

"This is kind of fun," said Viola, her face flushed. "You have to admit it."

All Leonardo could think about were Mishti's words.

"Everyone's always said Lion Clan was the greatest clan that ever lived," he told her.

Viola sighed. "Do you ever stop thinking?"

"In every story," continued Leonardo, "they conquered the Cove and fought off hundreds of attacks."

"Maybe that was before," said Viola. "They've probably changed. New members, new leaders…"

"If Raven Clan stopped fighting, even for a day, the other clans would've struck before we could blink," said Leonardo. "Something doesn't add up here."

"A lot doesn't add up," Viola agreed. She glanced around, then leaned closer to him, her voice hushed. "Can we talk about that ceremony today?"

"I have no idea what that was." Leonardo kept his voice low.

"That poor girl," said Viola.

"The part I can't understand is, if they all go through that, why has no one changed it?"

"They seem very stuck on tradition."

"Interesting." Leonardo watched the feverish chaos around the terrace. The drums pound-ed a relentless beat and he shook his head. "How are they still going?"

"They're taking turns," said Viola. "Watch; a new girl is swapping in now."

Sure enough, a girl drifted over to the drums, swaying to the rhythm. She nodded to Sophie, Mishti's se-com, and Sophie rose from her drum, grimacing as she flexed her fingers. The other drummers didn't break pace, and the new girl slipped effortlessly into the beat.

The dancing and singing and celebrating roared on. A cloud of yellow smoke exploded overhead and Leonardo caught a glimpse of Mishti's boomerang as it spun through the colour. A red burst exploded a moment later, to the cheers of the revellers. Anyone who'd dipped into the punch seemed to be coursing with energy, including most of Leonardo's own clan.

The punchbowls were never empty, as Isabella, Mishti's young aide, carried bamboo pitchers out to refill them throughout the night.

After one such refill, Charley and a trio of young girls appeared near the table. The girls pushed Charley and she shook her head, laughing. She looked so different in the Lion Clan robes, her hair braided like theirs, that Leonardo didn't even recognize her at first. She eyed the orange drink in the punchbowl and Leonardo crossed his arms.

"I told her not to drink it," said Viola.

The girls seemed to be egging her on, and finally, Charley took a bamboo cup and filled it from the brimming bowl. She hesitated and the girls bunched around her, laughing and encouraging her.

Leonardo set his jaw. He took one step toward them, but

Charley made a funny face at the girls first, then downed the entire glass in one gulp.

She staggered, extending her arms for balance, and the girls laughed.

"I *told* her not to," said Viola. She marched past Leonardo as Charley pinwheeled her arms and mimed a clumsy curtsey.

Then Charley spotted Leonardo and Viola. She said something urgent to her friends and they all glanced over, joyfully afraid. The whole pack took off, sprinting through a gap in the Lions.

Leonardo and Viola shoved after them, ducking and elbowing through the haze of noise and bodies. They burst into an opening near the balustrade just as Charley, unsteady on her feet, stumbled and dropped the empty bamboo cup. It bounced and rolled over the edge of the terrace, vanishing into the night.

Charley staggered after it, stopping herself hard against the rail. She gazed down, over the sheer side of the cliff, and started to tip forward. Too late, Leonardo realized she was going to fall. Viola gasped and they both lunged forward.

Charley's scream was cut short as one of the drummers twisted, grabbing her ankle before her weight could take her over.

Charley gripped the low stone rail, shaking, and straightened unsteadily as Leonardo and Viola ran up. Her whole body trembled.

Leonardo took one look at her big green eyes, afraid and dizzy with the effects of the drink, and clenched his jaw. Anger flared in him; at Mishti, at this celebration, at the godforsaken 'sacred cactus'.

"Viola, take her to Juliet," he said. "Get her the antidote."

"When I tell you to do something, you listen," Viola said to Charley, taking her shoulders and guiding her away. Fear tinged her words, and Leonardo eyed the rail.

"Thank you," he said to the drummer who'd grabbed her ankle.

"We're one clan now," said the girl. Sweat gleamed on her dark skin as her hands pounded out rhythms on the drum. He thought her name was Celia.

*One clan.* Maybe that wasn't such a loathful thing to contemplate.

Charley's trio of friends still lingered nearby. They scattered when he glanced at them, disappearing into the crowd.

Nearby, Strato and Bates stumbled over themselves, intoxicated and laughing hysterically. He caught a sudden movement in his peripheral, then something whipped over his head. Leonardo ducked, watching Mishti's boomerang curl up around the terrace. He whirled to find her standing ten meters away.

"Ha!" she said, then turned her attention to tracing its arc.

Leonardo drew a slow breath. *This is a madhouse.*

Puck jumped up on a chair, singing in full voice along with the chaotic music.

Leonardo needed out. He spotted the staircase at the end of the terrace and cut toward it, angling around Strato, Bates, and half a dozen Lion girls. He jogged down the steps, into the peaceful solitude of the open-air passage, then crossed to the second staircase that wound down to the water.

His clan's boat was still tied to the dock, bumping against the wooden posts. Leonardo stood on the dock for a long moment, the sounds of the celebration echoing high above, then he climbed into the boat and settled on a rower's bench. The wet slap of waves under the dock kept an irregular counterrhythm as the raven-turned-lion carving gazed out to sea from the bowsprit.

Since arriving in the Cove, Leonardo had struggled with the question of whether they'd made the right choice.

*There was no home for us left in the Darkwoods,* he reminded himself. *But is this a home?*

It felt more like the kind of place one didn't escape alive.

This celebration, the ceremony earlier, all of it felt *wrong*. And aside from maybe Viola, Leonardo felt like he was the only one who saw it.

Moth and Juliet, Charley and her friends, everyone else...they were trapped in the web. He wasn't sure quite what that meant, but it scared him.

# CHAPTER 11

A splash pulled Leonardo from his thoughts. He looked around, knowing who was coming before he spotted her. Adriana pushed a lock of wet hair off her face, smiling as she swam toward the dock, rippling a sash of moonlight on the waves.

"You're missing the party," she observed.

"Correct," said Leonardo. "Has Lion Clan always been this…"

"Loud?" asked Adriana. "Reckless?"

"It seems excessive," said Leonardo, gazing up at the flickering torches and hooting voices.

"Two things," said Adriana. "One; yes. They do this every full moon, and they rely on us to make sure no one sneaks in and attacks them while they're at it. The pirates are just around that rock," she added, pointing.

"They are?"

"Don't worry, we live to serve." She mocked a two-fingered salute.

"What's the second thing?" asked Leonardo.

"You," said Adriana. "You need to relax. The Cove is about having fun and not asking questions. Paradise is only paradise until you figure out why it's not."

"What does that mean?" asked Leonardo.

Adriana clicked her tongue. "No questions, weren't you listening?"

The breeze shifted, carrying the heady taint of seaweed and brine.

"I know what the woods are," said Leonardo. "I know we're inside our imaginations, or the dream world, or whatever you want to call it."

Adriana tilted her head. "And how would you know that?"

"Viola told—"

"Ah, Viola," said Adriana. She made a face. "She's been busy, hasn't she?"

"What does that mean?"

"No. Questions." Adriana flicked water at him. It splattered on his face, surprisingly cold.

"Look at it this way," she continued. "If you know what this place is, you have all the more right to enjoy it. Dream until the woods throw you out."

"How do *you* know what it is?" asked Leonardo. "Did the Natives tell you too?"

Adriana rolled her eyes, vivid blue even at night. "You're a stubborn one, aren't you? No, the Natives didn't tell us. Everything *from* the Lostwoods knows the Lostwoods. It's only you tourists who get left in the dark."

Leonardo paused. *Left in the* Dark.

"But if we *tourists* stop visiting," he countered, "the woods will cease to exist."

"Oh indeed," said Adriana. "And besides, it's much more fun with you here. Have you rethought my offer at all?" She blinked rapidly, blue eyes shining in the moonlight.

"No," said Leonardo. "And I'm still not interested."

"Oh, come on." She hummed a few notes, and Leonardo stood up, causing the boat to rock.

"Sailor and a siren," said Adriana, grinning. "Story as old as time."

"Go away, or I will," said Leonardo. He stepped out onto the dock.

Adriana sang a note, clear and warbling. It sent a chill through his bones, wild and uncontained and haunting to its last wisps.

Every muscle froze in Leonardo's body.

"Stop," he demanded.

She sang another note, so high that it whistled like the wind.

Leonardo ripped his mind from the sound and forced himself to walk toward the steps. His heart pounded, fear chasing his pulse as he realized just how easy it could be for her to sing him into the haze that already clouded the edges of his vision. And then...what? Drown him? Wasn't that what sirens did?

Another splash and her singing broke off. Leonardo turned to find that she'd gone. He furrowed his brow, moving back down the dock and leaning over the surface. Dark water sloshed against the boards, but Adriana was nowhere to be seen.

Then Leonardo heard the faintest of melodies from under the waves, growing louder but muffled by the water. The notes looped slow and melodic, otherworldly and captivating and rippling like a ribbon in the water.

The sea obscured everything below, yet the song carried on, beckoning him into the depths to find its source. A wave sloshed and a few droplets hit Leonardo in the face. He reeled back in shock, scrambling to his feet and trying to remember when he'd gotten on his knees. He'd been leaning out over the water, his face only a foot from the surface.

He stumbled back toward the steps, eyes locked on the surface and blood pounding in his ears. Just before he reached them, Adriana surfaced, flicking her hair out of her eyes.

"I'm getting impatient," she snapped. She took in his location, one foot on the first stone stair. "Oh. You're leaving."

Go away, Adriana," said Leonardo.

For a few seconds, she looked as though she wanted to push it further, then her eyes flashed. "Fine."

She plunged below the surface, and Leonardo took his chance to get away. As he ascended the stairs, he spotted her streaking out across the Cove, much faster than he'd realized the sirens could swim. She reached the opening between the cliffs before he summited the steps.

*Why did you even talk to her?* He should've known better. Next time he would. He still recalled the water hitting his face, a few inches from falling in.

Leonardo looked up at the roughhewn ceiling of the passage. The pulsing beat of the celebration above carried down through it, and he contemplated just staying here until it ended. He'd had enough insanity for one night.

He walked to the gap between two columns, a warm night breeze stirring his hair as he gazed across at the dark cliffs. Then he froze.

*Dammit.*

A ship rolled into the Cove, black sails flying against the night. Adriana's form streaked alongside it, like a dolphin just below the surface. As the ship plowed toward the fortress, Adriana suddenly cut across its path. The bow rolled over the line of her wake and the entire ship vanished as if it had never been there.

*Oh shit. Oh* shit.

He took three steps toward the stairs to the sea, then changed his mind and ran back to the gap between the columns. Panic shot through his nerves, pulsing in time with the drums over-head.

Adriana surfaced in the middle of the Cove, a small head in the dark water. He was too far to see her expression, but her face was turned up toward the fortress. He'd seen enough magic by now. Wherever the ship went, he doubted its reappearance would be anywhere good for Lion Clan.

He broke into a sprint, up the steps to the terrace, which was unchanged from when he'd left it. The celebration raged at full boil.

Leonardo remembered Mishti's words the first time the pirates came. *They kidnap the youngest members of other clans to grow their own.*

He needed to find Charley and make sure she was somewhere safe. Then he could focus on warning Mishti and the others.

*Did no one see the pirate ship?* Not a single kid on the terrace seemed concerned.

Then he spotted Sophie, red braids dishevelled as she shouted desperately over the music. Leonardo rushed over to her in time to hear the word, "—pirates."

"HEY!" she yelled at the drummers. "Stop playing!"

The drummers didn't hear her.

"Go over and stop them," said Leonardo. "Then get your sword."

She nodded, curt and grave, and sprinted toward the drummers.

Leonardo rushed to Juliet's quarters. The last time he'd seen Charley, Viola was taking her there for the antidote. He threw aside the curtain and swore. Only Moth and Juliet occupied the space, studying a crocodile's skull on a shelf.

"Where is Charley?" asked Leonardo, his pulse thumping.

"She and Viola went downstairs," said Juliet. "Why? Is something wrong?"

"The pirates are here. I think they might be inside the fortress."

Moth blanched and Juliet stared at him. "*Inside?* How?"

"Later," said Leonardo. "I need to find Charley."

And now Viola. He had no idea how violently the pirates conducted their kidnappings, and as far as he knew, Viola was unarmed.

Leonardo rushed back outside and raced for the stone outcropping that hid the end of the terrace. The drums had stopped now, and a new chaos was replacing the party. He shoved around a girl on the stairs and rounded the steps to the armoury.

Puck and Nym stepped out, swords and shields in hand.

"Give me that," shouted Leonardo, grabbing for Puck's sword as he tore down the stairs. Puck gave it up without question, and Leonardo descended past the armoury to a dome-ceilinged landing, with heavy doors splitting off in three directions.

A boy he didn't recognize stood in a doorway, dressed in rags and carrying a sword. Leonardo ran at him and their swords rang out in the confined stone space. The boy hacked. Leonardo deflected, throwing a punch that connected square with the pirate's jaw. The boy reeled and Leonardo drove his sword through him. The boy vanished. Leonardo swallowed hard. So, death worked the same in the Cove as it did the Darkwoods. No one died in a dream, but neither did they ever return.

He hooked left, down the steps to the room the Lion girls had assigned them. He found it empty, sleeping rolls laid out in their places and their few possessions piled in the corners. Charley's hamster basket sat where she'd left it for the party.

*Shit. Shit shit shit.*

He ran back up the stairs and met Puck, Nym, Pinch, Mishti, Sophie, and a dozen other Lions on the landing.

"This way," said Mishti, a knife-edged throwing ring in each hand. She led the way through a door and down a torchlit corridor. "Sophie said the sirens let them in." Her voice carried a strange quality. *Betrayal.*

"That means they're down here," she finished.

*Not the sirens,* thoughts Leonardo. *Just one.*

A shape materialized around a corner, and Mishti hurled one of her throwing rings at it. The girl ducked out of sight and the ring clanged harmlessly off the stone wall.

Mishti grabbed it as she rounded the corner and led the way down another flight of steps. At the bottom, a corridor stretched out into the darkness. In the glow of the wall torches, the pirate girl sprinted away as a second figure struggled from the ground.

Mishti wound up to throw her ring, but Leonardo spotted twin braids and the gold sheen of a Lion Clan robe.

"Stop!" he shouted, grabbing Mishti's arm.

Mishti threw him off, her face incredulous. Then Viola turned to face them, staggering against the wall.

Leonardo pushed around the others and ran to her. Blood ran down the side of her face and she blinked hard, a bruise blossoming on her cheekbone.

"They took Charley," she said, wincing. "And Pompey. Go!"

"Are you ok?" demanded Leonardo.

"I'm fine, *go!*" She shoved him weakly, bracing one hand on the wall.

Lions pushed around him, sprinting down the tunnel.

"Get up top," said Leonardo. "Find Juliet and Moth." He squeezed her hand. "We'll get them back."

He raced after the others, down two more flights of stairs and another corridor, until they rounded a corner and burst out onto the edge of an underground lagoon, glowing with fairy light.

Like a massive, hunkering shadow, the pirate ship loomed in the centre. Masts soared to the jagged ceiling, bound with heavy rolls of black sailcloth.

A long rowboat pushed through the still water toward it, filled with pirates. Leonardo's heart plummeted. They were too late.

Charley and Pompey sat tied up in the stern, desperation on their faces as they watched their rescue stop short on the lagoon edge.

# CHAPTER 12

W atch out!" shouted Charley.

Leonardo twisted just in time to block a pirate's sword as he leapt off a rock. Two more pirates sprang off the rocks and three more came running along the edge of the lagoon.

*No. No no no.* They couldn't afford to be slowed by a fight.

Leonardo deflected a flurry of blades, his stomach in his throat. He ducked as Mishti hurled one of her rings at the newcomers, barely missing him.

He twisted, incredulous, as she fumbled to grip a second ring. *She's still drunk.*

Sophie swung around a gold-embossed shield, her sword flashing out from behind it, and Puck, Nym, and Pinch hacked at the pirates, swords ringing out in the cavern. More pirates leapt over the side of the ship, splashing into the water and swimming toward them.

Leonardo threw off his assailant, and Strato put a sword through him. The boy vanished, his sword clattering to the rocks. Leonardo glanced back at the water. They were almost to the ship. Charley and Pompey leaned over the stern, terror on their small faces.

A shout made him spin. He ducked a blur of steel…

… and the pirate's sword went directly through Strato's back, just as Bates and Robin burst from the opening to the stairs.

Shock flashed through Strato's eyes. Time froze for a split second, then he vanished. Leonardo stood reeling, staring at the spot where he'd been.

*He's gone.*

Bates yelled something; he couldn't hear what. Then reality crashed violently back. Bates slashed clean through the pirate who'd taken down Strato. The pirate vanished, just as the ones in the water stumbled ashore, whipping swords from their belts. The rocky edge of the lagoon grew crowded and Leonardo struggled to maneuver, staggering as he blocked swing after swing.

He stepped in the crack between two rocks and swore, stumbling sideways. A soaked pirate jumped at him, but Robin leapt in the way, fighting off two blows before the pirate struck him across the jaw. Robin faltered, the pirate's sword flashed, and before Leonardo could react, Robin was gone. Just like Strato.

Time spun at a cockeyed angle. Leonardo struggled to push down his horror.

*The kids are still in danger.*

Something whizzed past his head and the pirate cried out, grabbing his jaw as Mishti's boomerang clattered to the rocks. She ducked under an attack and slashed one of her throwing rings up, hand-to-hand style, across another pirate's chest. He reeled back, blood welling on his shirt.

All at once, Leonardo's rage boiled over. He lunged at the pirate who'd vanished Robin and beat him backwards until he stumbled on a rock. Leonardo put a sword through him, staggering into empty space as the pirate's sword clattered off the rocks.

His breathing came fast and heavy.

*They killed Strato and Robin.*

Out in the lagoon, the rowboat pulled alongside the ship and the pirates hoisted a kicking Pompey and Charley up a ladder, over the side and out of sight.

*Shit.*

Leonardo shoved a pirate out of his way and secured his sword in the sash of his robe, pulling it as tight as he could, then he dove into the water.

The folds of his robe tangled around his limbs as Leonardo kicked out, fighting through the water to the giant blackened hull. He looked up between strokes, salt stinging his eyes. The pirates in the rowboat scaled the ladder and heaved the rowboat up on ropes, then a dozen panels in the side of the ship slid open and a row of cannons jutted out. Two rotated to fix on Leonardo, a pair of faces just visible over the iron barrels.

Leonardo's blood went cold, then something slammed into him underwater. Leonardo's body twisted under the force of it, plowing him under the surface and driving him hard across the lagoon. Bubbles streamed past his face as the air was violently forced from his lungs.

He surfaced, coughing and gasping, near the far edge of the

lagoon. A redheaded siren blinked at him, her eyes as blue as Adriana's.

"Stay here," she ordered, then she plunged back underwater.

Leonardo coughed again, grabbing the slippery edge of a rock and dragging himself out. Everything around him spun. Swords clashed from the far bank, and Leonardo struggled to his feet and started toward it, yanking his sword from his drenched sash.

More pirates emerged from the tunnel. Leonardo prayed Viola had gotten somewhere safe. The pirates outnumbered the Lions for a moment, then the rest of Lion Clan staggered out of the tunnel, still unsteady from the party, but overwhelming the pirates two-to-one.

Pirates pressed and Lions gave ground, then Lions pressed and pirates gave ground, driving each other toward the water on the narrow edge of the lagoon. The pirates fought harder and quicker, and Leonardo watched in desperation as two of Mishti's girls vanished, joining Strato and Robin. If not for the sheer imbalance of numbers, the pirates would've destroyed the Lions in minutes. Leonardo doubled his efforts, scrambling over rocks to rejoin the fight.

Fairies swarmed overhead, diving and weaving in panic. *Pirates,* Moth had heard them say yesterday. *Pirates, pirates, pirates.*

The cannons exploded with a boom that shook the cavern. Leonardo dropped flat, covering his head. A line of shots hit the lagoon and water sprayed into the air. More panels slid open and more cannons rolled out, firing at the water in quick succession.

Teal fins streaked past under the surface as sirens circled the ship.

Keeping low, heart racing so fast it hurt, Leonardo climbed

and clawed over wet rocks. The sword piercing Strato's chest replayed over and over in his mind. Heavy, pulsing guilt ripped at him. He'd been distracted by the kids; hadn't seen the attacker until it was too late. In ducking to save himself, he'd left Strato helpless.

And Robin. Robin tried to save Leonardo and was killed for it, too. Both boys' deaths slammed squarely on his shoulders.

He forced himself to keep moving. The battle crashed on, and he wouldn't let more vanish because of his absence. He was almost upon it when it suddenly ended. One pirate lost his sword, then Mishti disarmed two more in rapid succession. Pinch punched a pirate in the face and threw him to the ground. Puck and Bates dragged another down. In seconds, all the pirates on the edge of the lagoon were weaponless, frozen at sword and knifepoint.

Then the pirate ship rotated in the water with a great groan, the old boards creaking in protest.

*No.* Fresh dread flooded Leonardo's limbs.

Its prow swung toward a cascading waterfall that crashed into the far end of the lagoon, and four kids stepped up to the rail. Two of the boys were Leonardo's age, one dressed extravagantly in a purple coat and a feathered pirate's hat that put Pinch's to shame. The other dressed simpler in a white cotton shirt, long blonde hair tied back. A girl stood with them, light brown hair spilling out from under a black trilby hat with a skull-and-crossbones on the band. The fourth kid was younger, maybe twelve, chubby and round-faced with a pirate's tricorn jammed on his head.

Leonardo straightened on the rocks, gripping his sword. Adrenaline alone kept him standing.

The kid with the purple coat and feathered hat raised a hand,

and four more pirates dragged a kicking, struggling Pompey and Charley up to the rail.

Leonardo clenched his jaw.

"We have no need to keep them," said the pirate with the blonde hair. "Do not gamble on our desire to spare them."

*He's bluffing.* Pirates had been killed too in the fight. This couldn't all be for nothing.

"Instead," said the chubby kid. "You will put down your weapons and set free those wastes of pirates you currently hold captive. We will be allowed a clean getaway, and the sirens won't follow us. No one gets hurt."

Leonardo glanced at Mishti. She licked her lips, gripping a throwing ring in each hand, pressed to the throats of two captive pirates.

"We treat our recruits well," said the blonde pirate on the ship. "If you comply, I personally guarantee they will be happy and comfortable and a part of the crew as soon as they're willing."

Pinch, Puck, and the rest of Leonardo's clanmates glanced at Leonardo. Leonardo glanced at Charley, her face screwed up as she battled her captives. The four pirates at the rail stood with cold disregard.

*They* have *to be bluffing.* But what if they weren't? He knew nothing about these kids, and he'd already witnessed the heartlessness of the Cove, back when the new girl arrived in the sacred cave.

Leonardo wrestled with the gamble. Finally, he nodded to his clan.

They dropped their swords and the pirates staggered away. Mishti looked around, mouth open. She swore, fingers clenched white on her weapons. Death radiated from her gaze as she slowly lowered them.

"There," said the chubby kid, adjusting his tricorn hat. "Not so hard, was it?"

Meanwhile, the kid in the purple coat still held his arm in the air, frozen in dramatics from when he'd called forward Pompey and Charley. He lowered it now and they were dragged back out of sight.

Leonardo felt sick.

The girl pirate still hadn't spoken, and she crossed her arms, surveying the lot of them until she stopped on Leonardo. The smallest frown creased her brow, and she shifted her gaze back to the rest of the Lions.

The chubby kid said something to purple coat, and purple coat nodded, then raised his arm again with a flourish. The boat began to move again, and the pirates on shore staggered to the edge of the lagoon. They stopped, and Leonardo realized they wouldn't be able to swim fast enough to catch it.

The pirates on deck appeared unruffled, their faces cast warm in the fairy light. The girl turned her gaze on Leonardo again, silently piercing. The ship slipped through the waterfall and vanished, as magically as it had in the Cove.

All at once, the pirates on the edge of the lagoon turned and sprinted for the stairs back into the fortress, shoving desperately past the Lions.

"Stop them!" shouted Mishti.

Leonardo reacted a second late, unable to tear his eyes from the spot where Charley and Pompey vanished. On his orders.

He forced himself into motion, jumping down the last boulder and stumbling after the Lions as they chased the pirates up the steps. He doubted his decision with every step.

The pirates fled all the way to the terrace, led by a girl who navigated the torchlit corridors with fleetfooted ease. Leonardo and the Lions chased them past the abandoned drums and punch-bowls, down the steps to the open-air corridor and finally to the dock where the old Raven Clan boat was tied.

The pirate ship had reappeared right where it first vanished, and it sailed now for the mouth of the Cove. The marooned pirates piled into the Raven Clan boat and sliced through the tie ropes, shoving off from the dock before they were even all on-board.

The last pirates to reach them dove into the black water, swimming hard and heaving themselves over the side as the oars sloshed into motion.

"That's our boat, assholes!" yelled Pinch.

All of Lion Clan stopped on the dock and the steps. There was no point swimming after them. Under oar, they were moving too fast to catch.

The sirens surfaced around the Cove and Mishti shoved her way to the end of the dock, breathing heavy.

"Let them through!" she shouted. "Do not follow them! I repeat, *do not follow them*!"

The sirens parted for the longboat, and the pirates closed on their ship. Ropes were tossed down from the deck, and they shimmied up, abandoning the longboat to drift lifeless near the mouth of the Cove.

Full crew aboard, the sails billowed and the ship quickly plowed out to sea, a swath of silver moonlight rippling in its wake.

Unable to pursue, a few sirens swam to the abandoned longboat and began dragging it back to the dock.

"Fuck," said Mishti.

"Where is your boat?" demanded Leonardo. It sounded like someone else's voice.

"They said not to follow them," said Mishti, marching back to the steps.

Leonardo whirled around. "So, what, we just give up?"

"No, obviously," snapped Mishti. "Sophie, meet me in my quarters."

"I'm coming too," said Leonardo.

"Fine. It's a party," snapped Mishti. "God, I hate pirates."

# CHAPTER 13

Leonardo summited the last of the steps and staggered across to Juliet's quarters, with the feather etched above the doorway. He pushed through the curtain and Viola, Moth, and Juliet looked up anxiously.

He released the breath he'd been holding, closing his eyes in relief. Viola sat on the table—bruised and weak, but alive—while Juliet tended to her wounds in the glow of fairy light.

"Well?" asked Moth.

Right. They didn't know yet.

"The pirates took them," said Leonardo, the words dropping like lead. "And…Strato and Robin…we lost them in the fight."

Horror painted across all three faces, and he set his jaw. "We'll get them back. The kids, I mean."

Heavy silence followed his words. Moth swallowed hard.

"We'll avenge them," said Leonardo, his chest tight. "I'm going now to meet with Mishti and Sophie to make a plan."

"You're bleeding," said Viola.

Leonardo reached up and touched a slick patch on his forehead. Juliet already had a wet rag in her hand, and she crossed to him, wiping it away while Leonardo grit his teeth.

Viola drew a deep breath and let it out. "We have to get her back, Leo. Both of them. They must be terrified."

"Juliet said the pirates treat them well," said Moth, his expression strained. "New recruits, I mean. That's what she's heard, at least."

"Some get away," said Juliet. "They tell stories, and it sounds like the conditions are ok. Most of the crew stays by choice, not force."

"But they were kidnapped," said Viola. She slid off the table, steadying herself on a shelf of dried herbs. "Right? All of them, from their clans."

"Before they had time to establish any clan roots," said Juliet. "Before long, they'll have spent more time with them than us. New loyalties form fast. Pompey is an outsider here; there are other boys in the pirates."

She finished cleaning his cut and crossed to a shelf of supplies.

"So that's why they go after younger kids," remarked Leonardo. "So they can brainwash them."

Viola chewed her lip, and Moth shook his head. "We need to get them back before that happens. The Lostwoods switched them for a reason, and if it has anything to do with the Dark, we can't have them way out there on some pirate ship."

"We will," said Leonardo. He stopped Juliet as she approached with a jar of green paste. "I'm fine," he told her. "Thank you."

"But—"

"I have to go meet with Mishti. If it gets worse, I'll find you."

"It's still bleeding," she argued.

Leonardo wiped his hand across it. "There, problem fixed. Thank you, Juliet. Use it on Viola, she needs it more than me."

"I'm fine," said Viola.

"I'm glad you are." He held her brown-eyed gaze. He'd lost two friends today, and he was grateful to still have Viola and Moth in front of him. "I'm sorry I couldn't get Charley back."

"We will," she said. She tried a weak smile.

"Leonardo," said Juliet carefully. "Have you considered that this might all be by design?"

Leonardo paused, one hand on the door curtain. "What are you talking about?"

"What if the Lostwoods want Pompey and Charley to go with the pirates?"

Leonardo dropped the curtain. "Why would the woods want that?"

"Maybe it's part of the big picture." Juliet placed the green jar back on its shelf.

"No." Leonardo looked to Moth and Viola. Their faces were grim. "No, that doesn't make sense."

It did make some sense. But that would mean…Strato and Robin…was their disappearance part of the design too? What about everything else? *Do we have a say in any of it?* Everything they did, everything they said…He couldn't believe that.

Juliet's eyes were pitying.

*That's exactly what she believes. That's what all these girls believe; that whatever happens is ok because the woods allowed it.*

"I have to go meet Mishti."

Leonardo pushed out of the room.

Outside, he spotted Pinch and Puck in the adrenaline-laced crowd, ready for a fight they weren't allowed to pursue. Raw anger and loss burned in the ex-Ravens' eyes. Leonardo looked for Bates, but he was nowhere to be seen. He and Strato had been particularly close.

"You two, follow me," he ordered his se-coms. "Everyone else, start cleaning up this terrace."

The order came out before he could think. He paused, unsure how Mishti's Lions would react to his authority, but not a sideways glance was cast. Ex-Ravens and Lions alike set to emptying the punchbowls and carrying away the drums.

Leonardo, Pinch, and Puck descended the steps to Mishti's quarters, a spacious room just below the terrace, with big bell-shaped windows cut into the rock, overlooking the Cove. Mishti and Sophie sat in bamboo chairs, pouring over a hand-drawn map in the lamplight. They looked up and Mishti pulled her lips in a thin line.

"Do we need your entire clan in here?"

"Pinch and Puck are my se-coms," said Leonardo. "If Sophie's here, they're here."

"Fine, we don't have time to argue. Here, drink this." She tossed a corked bottle at them.

Puck caught it, eyeing the dark liquid inside.

"It'll clear the effects of the punch," said Sophie. "Just a swig each."

Puck uncorked it, took a sniff, and screwed up his face. He held it out to Pinch. "Here, you first."

"Just drink it, halfwit," Pinch's voice was especially terse. Bitter emotion glinted in his eyes. He grabbed the bottle and threw back a mouthful. "Fuck. That tastes like mouldy hell. Here."

Puck reluctantly accepted the bottle and swallowed his share, coughing violently. "Here." He offered it to Leonardo.

"I didn't drink the punch," said Leonardo.

Both Pinch and Mishti stared at him, then rolled their eyes.

"Is that a map of the Cove?" asked Leonardo. He didn't have much patience left.

"Yes, and it tells us nothing," said Mishti. "Clan boundaries are pointless; the pirates could be in any single spot on this map."

"Pirates always have hideaways," said Puck. "Caves, and grottos, and—"

"This isn't Blackbeard and the seven seas," snapped Mishti. "This is a bunch of kids in a god-forsaken magic boat that sails itself."

"They have to go ashore somewhere," said Leonardo. He moved closer to the map. "Are these all caves?" He traced a finger along a row of dark, spiraled openings in the cliffs.

"Yes," said Sophie. She grabbed the corners of the map to turn it, then glanced at Mishti for permission.

Mishti sat back, crossing her arms, and Sophie rotated the big sheaf of paper.

Leonardo eyed Mishti, his own emotions pressing at the seams. *This whole thing is her fault.* If not for her 'full moon celebration', they wouldn't have been caught off guard. If she hadn't gotten so intoxicated, he could've talked sense into her and ended it before the pirates even arrived. If it wasn't for her…Strato and Robin would still be—

*Adriana let the pirates in,* a voice whispered in his head. *Not Mishti. And who's fault is that?*

"...this is our camp here," Sophie was saying. She pointed to a lion's head sketched over a horseshoe of cliffs. "These are the cliffs you see there." She pointed out the window at the moonlit Cove outside.

*If you hadn't been so harsh with Adriana, Charley and Pompey might still be here.*

Leonardo studied the dark lines of the map. A wall of cliffs ran for miles along the sea, from a depiction of a coiled snake in the western jungle, to Tiger Clan's camp in the east, beyond a hazy stretch labelled *The Fog Waters.* Dragon Clan's territory lay on an island out to sea, and Leonardo's hope sunk as he realized how vast this corner of the woods truly was.

"How many sea caves are along these cliffs?" he asked.

"Countless," said Mishti.

"Are they patrolled? Whose territory is this?"

"No one's," said Mishti. "They're uninhabitable."

"Why?" asked Leonardo.

"Sea monsters."

That confirmed Adriana's claim.

Dread clawed at him, picturing Charley and Pompey out there.

"What's the Viper's Tongue?" asked Puck, pointing to a marked cave.

"It leads through the cliffs to Snake Clan territory," said Sophie. "It's the only patrolled cave aside from the Sacred Cave here in Lion Clan territory."

"We're wasting time," said Mishti.

"Then let's get on the water," said Leonardo. "What are we doing in here?"

Puck grabbed the door handle, then paused. "Wait. What do you normally do when a girl gets kidnapped?"

The ice in Mishti's glare dropped the room a degree.

"Nothing. They're too fast to catch."

Leonardo stared at her. Juliet's words played through his mind; *maybe it's all by design.*

"So what, we just give up?"

Every story he'd ever heard about Lion Clan painted them as the greatest clan of all time; undefeatable in battle and never backing down from any challenge.

Mishti rolled her eyes. "I *just* said, we have to get them back."

"When?" asked Pinch. "Puck, did you hear her say that?"

"Enough." Mishti half stood.

"No." Leonardo slammed his hands down on the other side of the table, startling her. "You're our best shot at finding these pirates, and so far all you've done is hide in here."

"So, what would you do?" countered Mishti. "Chase them? They'll kill the kids. But I suppose brute force is all you know in the Darkwoods."

"You're the one who said we need to unite," he retorted. "You're the one who said we need to be co-leaders. I'm trying to work together, but if you insist on treating us as the enemy, we'll go and find the kids ourselves. Hell, we might actually find them."

"And how would you do that?" Mishti shoved her chair back. "This is *our* home, *our* waters. You think that you can waltz in and find them before we do?"

Leonardo thought about the display in the lagoon; an entire clan of drunk Lions struggling to hold off a handful of pirates.

"Yes," said Leonardo. "Frankly, I do."

Mishti laughed, cold and tasteless. "If that happens, I'll show myself out of this clan."

"Good," said Leonardo. "From what I've seen, that should have happened years ago."

Silence stretched over the room. Mishti blinked and Sophie raised an eyebrow. Puck's eyes darted from Leonardo to Mishti and back again.

"Damn straight," said Pinch.

Mishti didn't speak a word. A strange expression tugged at her face.

Leonard shoved the map across the table at her. "You keep looking for them in here. I'm going out in the real world."

He turned and yanked open the heavy wooden door, just as Juliet, Moth, and Viola came rushing down the steps.

"They're going east," said Viola.

"What?" Leonardo stepped back to let them in. "The pirates?"

"She saw them," said Moth. "In a vision."

"It's not a vision," said Viola. "I just..."

"You *saw* them," said Leonardo.

He'd seen her do this once before, back when they were trying to escape the Darkwoods and she divined the location of Hawk Clan, allowing them to skirt around their enemies.

"What are you talking about?" asked Mishti.

"She can see things," said Juliet. "The Lostwoods show her."

"Ok, so they're going east," said Leonardo. He grabbed the map again. There was a lot of coastline to the east. If any sea cave along it was more hospitable than Mishti said, they could be tucked out of sight and Lion Clan would never find them. But with Viola's abilities...

"How much can you see?" he asked her.

"Not much, and it's..." She frowned, closing her eyes. "It's fading, the further away they get."

"Get her in the boat then," said Pinch. "Let's go pirate hunting."

"Stop." Mishti moved around the table. "We'll take our boat. It's faster."

Leonardo gave her an appraising look. That wasn't the response he'd expected.

"Ok fine, but move it," said Pinch. "We've gotta go."

The eight of them rushed out of the room and up the stairs to a narrow stone corridor, then down another staircase to the door they had chased the pirates through only minutes ago. They returned to the lagoon, where a big, gold-tipped longboat drifted at the end of a braided rope. A gold sail bunched at the top of a short mast, and a gleaming gold lion's head stared out from atop the bowsprit.

"Where did this come from?" asked Puck.

"Everything here is magic," said Sophie. "You didn't realize that when a pirate ship vanished through the waterfall?"

"The Lostwoods hid it for us," said Juliet. "We don't have cannons like the pirates. They would have destroyed it."

Leonardo helped yank in the rope until the boat bumped along the rocky edge. He jumped over the side and moved quickly to an oar, settling back on a bench behind Moth. He gripped the smooth wood, bracing his feet. He'd been a rower for a long time before the rapid series of promotions that left him in charge of this dwindling fraction of ex-Ravens.

Mishti took the rudder, while Puck, Pinch, Juliet, and Sophie went to the other oars. Viola moved to take the oar behind Leonardo, but he stopped her.

"Rest. We need you sharp."

Viola started to argue, and he gave her a look. "You're barely on your feet as it is."

Her dark eyes burned, but the fire faded as he pressed his hand on top of hers. "You have a job to do. We need you searching."

"Fine." Viola crossed her arms, but she looked partly relieved. The dried blood on her head and the blossoming bruises cast her in a weary light. Leonardo vowed to make the pirates pay for everything they'd done tonight.

Sophie untied the bowline, and Mishti called the order to row. Leonardo dug in with the other Lions, driving the longboat for the waterfall. He twisted to watch over his shoulder as they plowed into it.

The mist sprayed his face and he braced for the impact of the water, but right when it should have hit him, Leonardo realized they were in the middle of the Cove, outside under the midnight sky.

Spray spackled his clothes, but otherwise, he'd stayed dry, and only a few rivulets of water ran through the footwell. Puck, Pinch, Moth, and Viola peered around with the same bewilderment, then Mishti tugged a cord and the sail unfurled with a great swish.

"Let's move," she ordered. "Double time. To the east."

Leonardo cut his oar into the waves, and the boat pushed through the choppy waters. By the time they reached the mouth of the Cove, they were slicing through the troughs. Mishti controlled the rudder with one hand and the sail with a rope in the other. As they passed between the massive twin peninsulas which formed the mouth of the Cove, a gust of wind caught them and the sail billowed to full capacity.

The boat jumped forward, leaving the towering walls of limestone behind. They hooked left out of the Cove and started down the coast.

As the map suggested, the coast was formed entirely of the same tan cliffs which surrounded the Cove. The sea sloshed through dark openings and sheltered inlets, but Viola and Mishti both waved off Leonardo's inquiries.

"They went further," said Viola.

So Lion Clan too went further. They rowed down the coast, the full moon their only light, the only sound the splash-clunk of oars and choppy waves. The sea was an entirely new beast compared to the rivers they were used to. Strained faces grimaced down the length of the boat, and swears under breaths punctuated the creak of wood as the sea toyed with their progress.

Meanwhile, Viola sat stoically on her bench, eyes closed and body shifting with the waves as she searched the darkness with her mind. Leonardo's gaze flicked to her as he rowed, silently thanking the woods that she'd survived the attack.

Strato and Robin hadn't been so lucky. Now that the adrenaline was wearing off, Leonardo felt the reality of their vanishing sharper than before. He drew a tight breath, gripping the oar handle until his fingers turned white.

He'd lost clanmates before—more than he cared to count—but Strato and Robin were the first of the nine who'd travelled south with him. The ten of them shared a unique bond; they'd all chosen each other, escaped together, and Leonardo knew that the boys' disappearance would hit all of them hard.

Robin was always quiet, the youngest ex-Raven in their group. Leonardo realized he didn't know half as much as he should about the boy. He regretted not talking to him more.

Strato, in contrast, was loud and cocky. He'd been the last to join the new clan, but his loyalty was unwavering, and he'd trusted Leonardo when most of Raven Clan turned their backs on him.

Leonardo wouldn't let their disappearance go to waste. Charley and Pompey were still out there, and their rescue was still within reach. He took another stroke, burying his emotion in the rhythm of the oars. Being out on the water put Pompey and Charley's position into new clarity. The isolation was chilling, the waves endless and uncaring. He scoured for any sort of shape on the horizon, any faint silhouette against the inky sky, but only the waves marred the endless flat.

He wondered how far it went. *If this is all made of imagination, then maybe it continues forever.* Although, that same logic could justify any infinity of possibilities beyond the horizon. Impossible wasn't a thing here.

After twenty minutes of rowing, Viola shook her head. "I can't see anything."

Ten more minutes and her clairvoyance was still as dark as the water. Facing backward in the boat, Leonardo eyed the miles of pale cliff face, pocked with dark openings. He recalled Mishti's comment earlier about the inhabitability of those caves. *Sea monsters,* she'd said. He still didn't know if she was serious, but he didn't feel like finding out.

The boat suddenly felt very small, the eight of them scarcely armed and a long way from shore.

"We're turning back," said Mishti.

"What?" demanded Leonardo.

"We have to keep—" started Viola.

"At dawn," interrupted Misti, "we'll sail to Snake Clan territory. Caliban may be able to amplify your abilities."

"*Excuse* me?" said Leonardo.

"Amplify?" asked Puck.

"With magic," said Mishti.

"No way," said Leonardo. He'd seen hints of the Cove's 'magic', and he'd seen enough of Caliban to know he wanted nothing to do with it. Besides, he was skeptical that a clan's magic could even work on her. Viola's people were untouchable to the woods itself. Why should Caliban's powers be any more effective?

"They can do that?" said Puck.

"Of course," said Sophie. "We keep telling you, *this entire place is magic.*"

Leonardo shot a look at Viola and furrowed his brow. "Viola—" He broke off as she nodded.

"We need to get them back, Leo." She drew a steadying breath, her eyes on his. "Whatever it takes."

# CHAPTER 14

At daybreak, Leonardo met Mishti in the lagoon with a mixed party of a dozen other Lions, including Viola, Moth, and Pinch. The rest stayed behind to guard the camp, under the command of Sophie and Puck.

Leonardo wasn't happy about the idea of using Caliban's magic on Viola, but she was willing, and she'd reminded him that it might be their only chance to find the kids. So here they were, setting out to turn in one of the two favours Snake Clan owed Lion Clan.

The dozen armed Lions piled into the boat, strapped into plates of gold armour with swords, shields, and slingshots at their sides. A heavy, charged energy permeated the air. In the light of morning, their clanmates' disappearances and kidnappings were more real than ever. The group before Leonardo was hellbent on revenge.

Leonardo moved past them to the stern, where Mishti stood with her hand on the rudder. He placed a hand on the boat's gold-coated stem, eyeing the old, weathered Raven Clan boat in the water alongside them. They'd brought it into the lagoon after returning last night.

Now, one of the girls on the rocky edge untied the line and a girl up front coiled it in the bow. The rowers pushed off, rippling the water, and guided the boat toward the waterfall.

They passed through the mist and slipped inexplicably into the very center of the Cove. Leonardo craned back at the fortress of Lion Clan and tried to gauge just how far they'd jumped. Two hundred meters, at least. The impossibility of it made him dizzy.

Mishti tugged the rope and the sail unfurled. The rowers dug in and the Lion boat plowed for the west side of the Cove, where the cliffs eased down into the jungle and the river forked through the sand into a tangled fan of distributaries.

The day had barely set in, the back half of the Cove still caught in shadow, but the heat of the morning was already climbing. As they cut across the sparkling waves, the sun beat on his face, countered by the spray of mist off the sea.

Leonardo turned to face Mishti, her black hair and gold robes snapping in the wind. "Those four pirates at the rail..." he asked. "Who were they?"

"The First Four," Mishti replied, never taking her eyes off the approaching beach. Ever since Leonardo yelled at her last night, she'd been strangely cooperative. "They've been here since the beginning."

"The beginning of the woods?" He awaited her impatient correction, but Mishti simply nodded, ever so slight.

"They've never gotten old enough to disappear. Pip hasn't even gotten old enough to stop looking like a fat little kid."

"They're the ones who…*first settled* here," said Viola, eavesdropping from where she sat nearby.

Leonardo glanced at her. She meant *imagined,* but a quick dodge had saved her from accidentally revealing the information to Mishti's clan.

She locked eyes with him, drying her palms on her dress.

"*Some of* the ones," said Mishti.

"There were others, at first," said Moth. "But they all disappeared, just like we do. For some reason, these four can't. Juliet told me," he added, at the frowns from his clanmates.

"Can't?" asked Leonardo. *Or won't?* His brother Aleksander had held onto the woods for years longer than he was supposed to.

"*Can't,*" said Mishti. "They're un-vanishable." She paused. "Even if they tried to do it themselves."

A heavy silence followed her words. Leonardo suppressed a shiver at the thought. He didn't feel like asking how they knew that particular fact.

"And they're all from the Cove?" he asked. He'd never heard of the 'First Four' back north.

They reached the distributaries now, and Mishti steered the boat into the deepest, winding between banks of sand to the main river. The same waters that ran all the way up to the Darkwoods. Leonardo was fairly certain none of their old rivals would come south looking for them—they had their own power-struggle in the Darkwoods to keep them busy—but none the less, his stomach tightened being back on the river.

"One is from each corner of the woods," said Mishti. "Cyrus, with the purple coat and the big hat, is from here in the Cove. John—he didn't have a hat—is from the Highland, Pip—the little fat one—is from your Darkwoods, and Kate is from the Redwoods. Don't ask me where they got their ship or why they do things the way they do. I have no answers for you."

"But *they* might," said Viola. "All the things my people never told me, the things my people never knew…If we could talk to the pirates—"

Leonardo shot her a warning look. Excited or not, she was venturing close to dangerous territory.

"Before or after we steal back the kids they took?" asked Pinch. Sarcasm, bitterness, and annoyance fermented together in his tone. Each member of the clan was processing their losses different, but Pinch had known Strato and Robin as long as Leonardo, and he'd been in a dark mood all morning.

"After," said Viola, unfazed. They passed under a giant waxy leaf, casting her face in shadow. "Once their crew has surrendered, we tie them up and interrogate them."

Mishti snorted a laugh. "You *are* new to the Cove, aren't you?"

Viola placed her hands on her hips. "You don't think we'll beat them?"

"No," said Mishti. "I *know* we won't."

"Then what the hell are we doing?" asked Leonardo.

*How could our stories have been so wrong about Lion Clan?*

"We're getting our kids back," said Mishti. "Without a fight."

"Favours," said Moth, suddenly understanding.

"No," said Mishti. "They don't acknowledge favours."

The boat slid through a swarm of gnats. Leonardo swatted at

them, spitting one out of his mouth. "Then we're kidnapping them back."

"Someone gets it," said Mishti.

"Your life would be much simpler if you just explained things," said Moth.

They rounded a bend in the river, and a line of parrots watched them from a lichen-covered branch.

"I had an interesting conversation with Thaisa this morning," said Mishti, after a pause.

Leonardo tried to recall which of the girls was named Thaisa.

"The leader of the sirens," said Moth.

*Right.*

Leonardo got a sinking feeling.

"Apparently it was Adriana who let the pirates in," said Mishti. "And apparently it had something to do with you, Leonardo."

Everyone in the boat frowned at him, including Viola.

"I needed some air from *your party*," said Leonardo, more aggressively than he probably should have. "So I went down to the dock last night. She showed up and started singing, so I walked away."

"And then what?" asked Mishti. "She just got angry and let the pirates in?"

"Apparently," said Leonardo.

Mishti closed her eyes, pinching the bridge of her nose. "Why did I let you all into my clan?"

"Because the woods told you to," said Viola, uncharacteristically brusque. "We can deal with this later. Right now, can we focus on the pirates?"

"Not if I can't trust that Leonardo isn't making more trouble whenever I turn my back."

They passed through a forest of bamboo, casting all their faces in green-tinted light.

"We lost two clan members in that attack," snapped Leonardo. "How many would you have lost without us?"

"There wouldn't have been an attack without you."

Something rustled through the tall vegetation, thwacking and rattling the stalks. Leonardo flicked a quick glance, but nothing showed itself.

"This isn't Leo's fault," said Viola.

"Then whose is it?"

The air in the jungle grew muggier by the second, driven by the pounding heat from the rising sun. Sweat ran down Leonardo's temple and sheened on his clanmates' faces.

"The sirens are dangerous," said Viola. "If you didn't keep them so close—"

"Two things," said Mishti. "One; every living thing in the Cove is dangerous. Two; girls are immune to a siren's song, so 'keeping them close' has never caused a problem. Until now."

Leonardo squared his jaw, then they rounded a bend and slid past the big white rock that marked the edge of Snake Clan's territory. Everyone in the boat straightened, and Leonardo placed a hand on his sword. Viola drew her slingshot, slipping a pebble into the pouch.

Any conflict within the boat shifted to the backburner as they slipped down the first leg of Snake Clan territory. A troop of monkeys greeted them around the next curve, their fur a flaming orange. They ran along branches to stay with the boat, hooting and screeching and shaking the leaves.

One monkey stretched its jaw wide at them, revealing long incisors.

"Are those things dangerous?" asked Moth, watching the monkeys as he rowed.

"*Are those things dangerous*," mocked Pinch.

"Shut up. I'm serious."

"It's a goddamn monkey, Moth."

Next to Leonardo, Mishti drew an impatient breath. "We're in enemy territory."

"I know," said Leonardo. A school of white fish streaked past and he tensed, remembering the white-finned creatures which had attacked them upriver.

"Can you make them quiet, then?"

"Guys," said Leonardo.

"He's scared of monkeys!" said Pinch.

A monkey screamed overhead, making Moth jump.

"Enough," snapped Mishti. "Both of you."

"You're not my leader," said Pinch.

"Yes, she is," said Leonardo, though the words sounded forced. "We're co-leading the clan now."

"If you believe that, you're dumber than Cato," said Pinch.

"No one in the entire woods is dumber than Cato," said Bates.

"Who is Cato?" asked one of the girls up front. She took a hand off her oar to comb back the strands of hair plastered to her forehead. The humidity was heavy enough that even breathing took effort.

"This half-witted oaf back in Raven Clan," said Pinch. "Good with sword, bad with brain."

"He's gigantic," said Bates. "He's like a monster."

"Guys, cork it," said Leonardo. He separated his shirt from his back, slick with sweat.

"Really?" said the Lion girl. "He must have been terrifying to fight."

"Only Leonardo could beat him," said Bates. "When we escaped, Leonardo fought him and—"

"*Bates*," snapped Leonardo. "Enough."

"Is this how you run a clan?" asked Mishti, rolling back the sleeves of her robe.

"Welcome to the Darkwoods," said Leonardo.

"We're not in the Darkwoods." Mishti threw her boomerang, scattering a swarm of insects ahead of them.

"Put these boys in a boat, and we might as well be," said Leonardo.

"What does that mean?"

It meant that old habits died hard, and as much as Mishti made them dress in golden robes and comply to the ways the Cove, once they were on the river, they became Ravens once again. And Leonardo didn't entirely mind it.

Before he could reply, Caliban's thin, knife-edged voice materialized out of nowhere.

"Leonardo. Mishti. And a pack of Lions. To what do we owe the honour?"

The air rippled over the river ahead of them, and the Snake boat appeared as though a sheet had been tugged off of it. A dozen hooded Snakes manned their benches, moving in single-minded rhythm. Caliban's mismatched eyes glinted from his perch atop the captain's platform.

# CHAPTER 15

S o, you come to us for a favour," said Caliban.

Caliban and his silent, hooded clan led the Lions up a set of stone steps and into a courtyard surrounded by a cracked stone wall shaped like a giant snake's tail. Towering tree roots gripped the wall like long fingers, blooming with legions of mushrooms and creeping vines. The rest of the serpent coiled into a circular pyramid, forty feet tall, with a row of steps fashioned into a forked tongue that spilled from its mouth.

"Yes," replied Mishti. "May we ask it now or must we walk even further?"

Leonardo's clanmates gazed around at what he'd call ancient ruins, if he didn't know the temple was still inhabited.

"A little further still," said Caliban, with a showman's effortless command. "Have patience, Mishti."

A cacophony of birds and monkeys screeched from the jungle beyond the wall; heavy branches and overgrowth nearly bursting through the old stone. Bates jumped as something slithered over his foot, disappearing down a crack in the tiles.

"This way, my good Lions." Caliban ushered them up the narrow steps of the snake pyramid, over each ring of the coiled serpent until they passed between marble fangs into its mouth.

"Nice digs," remarked Pinch, poking his hand on the dull tip of a fang.

An altar-style table stood in the centre of the domed room, knotted with interwoven carvings of snakes. Green gemstone eyes stared at the Lions as they bunched behind Leonardo and Mishti.

"Alonso, go get the favour sheet," said Caliban. One of the younger Snakes ran down the steps of a crypt-like opening in the floor. To Mishti, he said, "Ask away."

"These things must be done with some decorum," he added to Leonardo before Mishti could speak. "You understand. Mishti would not barter with a clan in the middle of the Cove; she would be hospitable and welcome them into her camp. Thus, at Snake Clan, we do the same."

"Inside a giant snake's head," said Viola under her breath.

Leonardo glanced at her. She twisted a bead on her dress, nervous energy radiating from her. He realized she might be more anxious about this plan than she was letting on.

*Of course she is.*

No sane person would contemplate being 'amplified' by Caliban without having doubts. He wondered how many she was hiding just to get to the kids quicker.

His own hesitations rose to the surface again.

"Yes indeed," said Caliban. He gazed around the room.

Dampness darkened the fissured stone. "Inside a giant snake's head."

A centipede crawled out of one the openings, antennae twitching. The Lions edged away from the wall.

"The pirates took our two youngest," said Mishti, crisp with impatience. Leonardo thought he sensed a nervous undercurrent in her tone as well.

"Indeed?" said Caliban. "Two. A story of failure I would love to hear, but doubt I will get to. So, you want revenge?"

"We want them back," said Leonardo. The centipede crawled over the snake carvings as he re-questioned Mishti's plan. "We want to know where the pirates went."

He knew nothing about Caliban's so-called magic. If everything he'd seen so far was any indicator, they should be running as fast as they could the other way.

"Mishti, trying to get back girls the pirates took," mused Caliban. "These *are* changing times."

"A boy and a girl," said Leonardo. "They were at the full moon ceremony yesterday."

"Ah, so you lost a member too. The puzzle becomes clearer. You northerners are not used to having your boys stolen away."

"No," said Leonardo. "We're not. And we want him back."

Moth, Pinch, and a few of the Lions glanced sidelong at Leonardo, but no one said a word. Mishti remained unfazed. There was no reason to correct his natural assumption that the boy was Leonardo's and the girl Mishti's.

"Well," said Caliban, his hood shadowing his angular face. "The question may not be where the pirates *went,* but where they're going. They travel hundreds of miles in that boat of theirs, searching for a way out."

"Out of the woods?" Leonardo frowned at Mishti. She hadn't said a thing about that.

She wouldn't make eye contact with him now, and Leonardo frowned deeper. *What did she think she'd gain by keeping it from us?*

"Tell me," said Caliban. "If you'd been in the woods since forever, never growing old while everyone around you ages and disappears...wouldn't you start to feel trapped? Eventually become obsessed with leaving?"

"Can you help us or not?" snapped Mishti. "We don't have time to waste."

Her face was flushed, but Leonardo couldn't tell if it was from the heat, anger, or her own doubts.

"What favour do you ask?"

"Help us figure out where the pirates are. Or where they're going," said Leonardo.

Caliban tsked his tongue. "Then I can't help you, sorry. Crystal balls aren't our area of expertise. Deception, voodoo, spook tricks; your wish is my command. I've even experimented with teleporting—unsuccessfully. But reaching into a hat and pulling out information like that—"

"We don't need you to do it," said Mishti. "We just need you to amplify another's ability."

*Here we go.* Leonardo's stomach jumped to his throat.

Caliban paused, frowning. "What other?"

"Me," said Viola, squeezing Leonardo's hand as she stepped up beside him.

Caliban's eyes darted to their clasped hands. "And *who* exactly are you?"

The question rang eerily similar to one that Viola's grandfather, Chief Tokala, had asked Leonardo in the Darkwoods. The hairs stood on Leonardo's neck and he gripped the pommel of his sword.

"I come from the Native tribe," said Viola. "I can see..." She paused, trying to phrase it. "Things that are happening. Things in other places."

"Really?" said Caliban. "And you feel that if we amplify this ability, you will be able to see where the pirates are going."

"Yes," said Viola.

"Then we must attempt it," said Caliban, smiling so much like the namesake of his clan that a second shiver ran up Leonardo's spine. Caliban winked his one blue eye. "For a price."

As he said it, the boy Alonso reappeared up the steps, carrying a scroll of parchment. He fixed his gaze on the ground, darting glances at the Lion girls. The Lions edged out of his way, bumping together in the cramped room, as if afraid to catch some contagious disease.

"Consider the favour paid," said Mishti. "Cross it off your sheet and I will cross it off mine."

Caliban smiled wider. "We owe you two favours last I checked. "Call them both paid and I will guarantee success."

"No deal," said Mishti.

"What?" said Leonardo and Viola in sync.

"You're providing one favour: amplifying Viola's abilities."

"And guaranteeing success," said Caliban. "That is a favour in itself."

"Bullshit," said Mishti.

One of the Snake boys took a threatening step toward her, and all of Lion Clan bristled, hands jumping to weapons. Caliban stopped him with a hand on the boy's shoulder, and the Snake reluctantly shifted back, unblinking gaze fixed on them. The Lions edged back too.

Leonardo fought the urge to call off this whole thing.

"You're not the only one who has a relationship with the Lostwoods, Mishti," said Caliban. "For one favour, we will do our best. For two, I will call on the Lostwoods to assist us." He spread his hands. "Guaranteed success."

Leonardo glanced at Viola. She squared herself, steeling her expression. He could read her mind; *we'll never find the kids on our own.*

Moth's eyes darted from Snake to Snake, while Pinch stared down the one who'd challenged them, tricorn pulled low over his eyes.

"Mishti," said Leonardo. "We need to take it."

"They're not your favours to barter," snapped Mishti.

She was definitely nervous, and it only reaffirmed Leonardo's doubts.

"I thought we were co-leaders now," he pressed. The words were foreign; some automatic part of his brain fighting to keep the plan on track while the rest of him wanted to turn and rush his clan out of this pyramid.

Mishti met his gaze, his challenge reflecting in her eyes. The other Lions glanced at each other, their entire bodies tense, and the Snakes watched with blatant intrigue.

"He's not wrong either," said Caliban mildly. "If you want the kids back, you need to pay up. And if I recall correctly, we don't have time to waste."

"Fine," snapped Mishti. "Two favours. But if this doesn't work—"

"Don't worry," Caliban flexed his fingers. "It will work. Alonso, bring the scroll here."

Alonso handed Caliban the scroll and Caliban spread it on the stone table. Alonso's hood shifted back to reveal the snake's eye scar on his forehead. Leonardo tried not to stare.

"Look at that," hissed Bates, barely louder than a breath.

*They're just children.* Some of the youngest in the room were barely older than Pompey and Charley.

*Does Caliban give them the mark?*

*Or does the woods do it?*

He hadn't contemplated that possibility yet. It stopped him in his tracks. The woods inflicting a scar certainly seemed less gruesome than a kid doing it. He'd never heard of the woods doing anything like that before, but it sounded *right* in a way he couldn't explain. Like an invisible piece that fit perfectly in an invisible puzzle.

Mishti procured her own scroll and spread it next to Caliban's. Both sheets were covered in tally marks. Caliban put a thick charcoal line through the two marks on his sheet, and Mishti did the same on hers.

"Good," said Caliban. "Now come, we must conduct this outside. Alonso, take this back downstairs and send up anyone who's still down there."

Alonso nodded, casting one last unnerving look at the Lion girls, then slipped back down the steps into the passage.

*Why would the woods maim its children? Its* captive *children*, Leonardo reminded himself.

That was a question he couldn't answer so easily.

"Everyone out!" said Caliban. As he passed Leonardo, he leaned close. "Do not fear. We'll get Charley back. And Pompey too, of course."

Leonardo's blood went cold, and Caliban patted him on the shoulder. "You can't lie to a Snake. Remember that."

Then he was moving through the giant stone mouth and down the steps outside.

Leonardo made eye contact with Moth and Viola. Both stood close enough to have heard.

"He would've seen Charley when we first arrived," said Moth under his breath. "He must have remembered her."

"Dammit," said Leonardo.

"It's fine," said Viola, her voice tight. "He has to understand why we'd try to hide it."

Leonardo wasn't so sure. Thus far, he'd failed to predict most things Caliban did.

They followed the Snakes out of the pyramid and down to the courtyard of stone tiles, outlined with weeds and grass sprouting through each seam.

More Snakes emerged from doorways cut into the sides of the stone snake, nondescript as ghosts in their grey cloaks.

The serpent's tail curled in a perfect circle around the pyramid, then arched up, as if hooked on a branch, to form the entranceway. Through it lay the stone steps down to the water and Lion Clan's boat, which was tied up in a swampy stand of aquatic trees.

Caliban led them past the arch, to a spot where the tail looped up over itself and formed a smaller courtyard outside the main ring, accessible through a tunnel in the stone wall.

"Mind the hole," said Caliban, as the last of the Lions filed inside. The tiles twisted in a vortex pattern, centred around a foot-wide hole in the ground. Leonardo leaned to see down, then quickly shifted back.

A hiss rose from the pit below. Hundreds of snakes twisted together in a writhing knot of tails and fangs.

"Holy shit." Bates stumbled back.

"They can't hurt you from the pit," said Caliban.

More cloaked boys appeared atop the wall of the courtyard, encircling their party from above, while the boys on the ground formed a tighter ring around them.

Leonardo fought the urge to draw his sword. A few feet from him, Mishti's fingers twitched, throwing rings dangling on her wrists. In the cowl of Viola's silk sleeve, Leonardo glimpsed the edge of her slingshot. Then he noticed the cord from Pinch's, barely visible in the shadows of his own sleeve.

Caliban gazed around at the eerily still faces of his clan, evenly spaced along the back of the snake and in the courtyard below it. Quiet stretched over the jungle. Even the insects and birds fell silent, plunging the canopy into an eerily perfect void.

"Good," he said, steepling his fingers. "Now we begin."

Each Snake brought their hands together, overlapping the sleeves of their cloaks. Leonardo's mind went immediately to what weapons could be hiding in those folds.

The Lions shifted into a tighter bunch, backs facing inward and eyes on every corner of the courtyard.

"Great sentient Lostwoods," started Caliban. "We ask for your assistance today."

A breath of wind stirred Leonardo's robe.

"Ah, you're listening," said Caliban. "Good."

He turned his mismatched eyes on Viola, lit up with an energy that bordered on wild. A pit settled in Leonardo's stomach, buzzing with apprehension.

*What are we doing?* There had to be a way to find Charley that didn't involve...whatever this was.

Caliban reached for Viola's hand. She gave it hesitantly, eyes on Leonardo. He placed his hand on his sword now, and Mishti dropped a ring off her wrist, catching it smoothly.

"We ask for your assistance in amplifying this girl's ability," said Caliban, raising Viola's hand over her head like the victor of a fight. He flicked his other hand in a circle and the Snakes shuffled into motion; the inside ring walking in a clockwise direction while the upper ring moved in the counter direction.

Leonardo and the Lions whipped around, swords half drawn. But the Snakes didn't pay them any attention; pacing in their circles with quiet purpose. Their soft, muted footfalls filled the air with an unsettling percussion.

"Let her see," said Caliban. "As far as she needs to, to find the pirates and find her lost ones."

Viola drew a breath, uncertain. Leonardo tried to give her a reassuring look, but he knew his eyes showed anything but.

In his peripheral, he glimpsed a flickering light. Leonardo frowned, his gaze darting from Snake to Snake as a glow began to emanate from under their hoods. It grew brighter, steadier, and the Snakes paced faster.

"What the hell?" Pinch edged back, bumping shoulders with Leonardo.

Now every Snake cast a brilliant light from under his hood, and Leonardo struggled to wrap his head around it. It wasn't white light, but neither was it coloured. It was like every time his mind came close to understanding it, the answer darted further away. If he had to make a guess now, he'd say the light was black.

Standing with Viola next to the snake pit hole, Caliban flicked his free hand again. The Snakes stopped circling and turned to face inward. As one, they tossed back their hoods. Caliban did the same, and each of their snake's eye scars gleamed with black light.

# CHAPTER 16

O h my god," said Moth.

A jolt shot through Leonardo's limbs.

Before anyone could react, Caliban produced a knife and flicked it toward Viola's head. She flinched away and Leonardo jumped forward, but Caliban was quicker. He lopped off the tip of her left braid and darted away from her, holding his hands up placatingly.

Leonardo levelled his sword at him, and Caliban took a deliberate step further from Viola. The knife gleamed in one hand, a severed inch of braided hair in the other.

Viola's hand went to the remainder of her braid as it unwound itself, twisting loose without the tie to hold it in place.

Still under Leonardo's sword-point, Caliban stepped to the snake pit and dropped the lock of hair through the opening.

For a second, nothing happened. Then a burst of light shot through the opening. Leonardo jumped back.

Then Viola cried out, "I can see them!"

She gazed around, dark eyes blinking at the courtyard but not seeing it. "They're...It's an island...I think."

She frowned, studying something over Moth's head. Moth twisted to see, but only the circle of Snakes stared back at him.

"There are hundreds of islands out to sea," said Mishti.

"This one...it has a...a temple or a palace on it," said Viola. "There's a clan—"

"Dragon Clan?" asked Mishti. "That's the Turquoise Isle."

"Yes," said Viola. "I see their boat."

"And the pirates?" said Leonardo. "Are they attacking the Dragons?"

"No," said Viola. "They're..." She frowned, then her eyes widened.

"What?" Leonardo and Mishti asked in sync.

Caliban smiled.

"My people," said Viola. "They're here, they're...on the island, with Dragon Clan. But not *with* Dragon Clan. They're out in the jungle. Fighting the Dark." She paused. "It's bigger than it was before."

"The Dark?" said Mishti. "What about the pirates? Where are they?"

"I—"

A cold wind blasted through the courtyard. All the Snakes scars went dark, and Viola blinked, rubbing her eyes. She turned in a circle, looked up at the sky, rubbed her eyes again.

She whirled on Caliban. "I need more time!"

"Sorry." Caliban waved for his Snakes to disperse.

"That's it?" said Leonardo, incredulous.

"We still don't know where they are," said Mishti.

"Sure you do," said Caliban. "They're on the Turquoise Isle."

The Snakes atop the wall descended out of sight, but the ones in the courtyard remained surrounding the Lions. The few Lions who hadn't already drawn their swords did so now. Even Moth had his drawn, gripped in two hands.

"For now," said Mishti. "And *where* on the island? It could take days to explore."

"Your problem," said Caliban. "I provided my end of the bargain, plus she found her people. That should be a favour in itself."

"You knew her people were there," said Leonardo.

"Guilty," Caliban bowed deep and dramatic. "But I didn't know the pirates were."

Leonardo stepped toward him. "You knew her vision would go to them."

"And you ended it early," said Mishti, sliding a throwing ring into each hand. "I demand you start it again."

The Snakes surrounding them stiffened.

"I'm afraid that cannot happen," said Caliban, gentle and sickeningly understanding. "It's too dangerous to put her at risk like that again."

"At risk?" said Leonardo.

"How dangerous *is* this?" asked Moth.

"And I'm not the one who ended the vision," replied Caliban, with enough undertone that Leonardo's heart sank.

"Then who did?" asked Mishti. "The Lostwoods?"

Leonardo already knew the answer.

"The Dark," said Viola. She crossed to the snake pit and

peered down, then quickly shifted back. Grim confirmation played across her face.

Leonardo stepped closer, still gripping his sword, and looked into the hole. He caught his breath. A crocodile skull rested atop the nest of snakes, a black, burnt line splitting its eyes.

"What the hell is that?" asked Mishti.

"That's how it sees," said Leonardo, recalling the one other time he'd encountered a skull like this. It was right after Viola's people left the Darkwoods—after the woods snatched them away—and left Viola behind. The Dark struck her old camp, killing everything from the trees to the earth. Viola barely escaped, and when Leonardo and his clan found her, they also found a skull like this in the centre of the clearing.

"How *what* sees?" demanded Mishti.

"The Dark," said Caliban. "The heart of it lies here in the Cove, although it's hiding."

"It's real?" said Mishti.

"Very." Caliban eyed the skull. "It's getting more aggressive."

"How long have you known?" She advanced on him. "Why have you not said anything?"

Caliban didn't budge until she was an inch away. Then he grinned. "Knowledge is power, my dear lioness."

"Don't patronize me. Where is it? It's on the Turquoise Isle?"

"Correct."

"With the pirates, Charley, Pompey, Dragon Clan, and Viola's people," said Leonardo. He glanced around at the rest of his clan; ex-Ravens and original Lions alike. "Come. We have to go."

# CHAPTER 17

Silver fish darted under the boat as they rowed double-time through Snake Clan's territory, bound for the Cove.

"We only stop long enough to get the rest of the clan," said Mishti. "Then we set sail for the island."

"How far is it?" asked Leonardo.

"A few hours," said Mishti. Stripes of sunlight slid across her dark skin as they passed beneath the canopy. "Half a day if the winds don't cooperate. Either way, we'll arrive while the sun is still up. Searching the island, however..."

"If we have to do it in the dark, we will," said Leonardo.

Insects swarmed over the water, hovering in giant clouds. Dragonflies darted through them, weaving in and out of the boat's path.

"We could get the sirens to help," suggested one of the girls.

"Are you serious?" demanded Bates. He twisted around on his bench. "You want to work with those—"

"*Adriana* let the pirates in," said another girl. "The rest of the sirens are still on our side."

"I'm with Bates," said Nym. "I want nothing to do with them."

Leonardo had to agree. So far, the sirens had brought nothing but problems.

He followed one dragonfly's path into the trees and froze. A long, tawny shape detached itself from the shadows, moving just behind the first line of trees.

Pinch saw it too.

"Holy shit." His mouth fell open. "That's a lion."

"What are you…" Moth broke off. "Ohmygod. Ohmygod you weren't joking."

Leonardo gripped the handle of his sword. A gold mane swayed as the lion plodded through the underbrush, leaves crackling under its heavy steps. Then it passed behind a tree, and where it should have emerged, only dragonflies darted through the muggy air.

"Where did it go?" asked Bates.

Leonardo leaned to see, but it was if the lion had passed through a hidden doorway. It was gone.

"Did it turn?" asked Viola.

"It left," said one of the girls up front.

Bates screwed up his face. "Where?"

"Somewhere else in the jungle," said the girl. "Could be miles away."

"So it teleported," said Pinch dryly. "Great. Pits of snakes and teleporting lions."

"It left," repeated the girl. "The Lostwoods let them come and go when they wish."

"Leo, remember the lion I saw?" said Moth. Excitement flashed in his eyes. It was the same expression he'd worn when they realized the fairies were real. "It was there, and then it just wasn't."

"I remember," said Leonardo. He was beginning to understand how unique each brand of magic in the woods was, and that every creature had its own relationship with the woods. Snake Clan's magic was a far cry from the religion that Lion Clan practiced.

"The good old days," said Nym.

Leonardo regarded him, chewing his lip. *The good old days.* Before Nym was touched by the Dark, before they lost Strato and Robin; when the biggest threats in their lives could be met at sword-point.

Shortly after they passed the white rock, a flicker of teal fins marked the presence of sirens. They streaked through the water under the boat, and Mishti called for the rowers to halt.

Oars reversed with a great slosh, and the boat came to drift as three heads surfaced near Leonardo and Mishti.

"Great," said Bates dryly. Leonardo wasn't used to seeing him so bitter. It made him angrier at the pirates and Adriana for letting them in.

He recognized the redheaded siren who'd saved him from the cannon in the lagoon, as well as a dark-haired siren with sharp features whom he'd met upon his clan's arrival. He clenched his fists, reminding himself that these ones fought *against* the pirates.

"Thaisa," said Mishti. "The pirates are on the Turquoise Isle."

"With Dragon Clan?" asked the dark-haired siren, an eyebrow cocked in surprise.

"We don't know yet," said Mishti. "It's a big island. But yes, it is possible Dragon Clan is working with them."

She didn't say a thing about the Dark.

"Do you want us to go?" Thaisa flicked a lock of wet hair from her cheek. "Adriana has been banished; she won't interfere."

Leonardo thought of the pale creatures upriver and wondered if that was where Adriana had been sent. He shuddered.

"Go," said Mishti. "Look for them. But do not let yourselves be seen; if they know we're hunting them, they may decide the kids aren't worth keeping alive."

"Understood," said Thaisa.

Their eye contact lingered a touch longer than necessary. Mishti's expression softened. Leonardo wasn't sure if he should look away. The moment felt strangely private.

"Be careful," said Mishti softly. "The pirates seem particularly hostile this time."

"I'll take half the pod," said Thaisa. "The rest will continue to guard the Cove."

"Good," said Mishti.

They held eye contact a moment longer, then the three sirens dove back underwater, tails flicking as they propelled away.

"Oars down," called Mishti.

Leonardo frowned, watching the trio streak downriver. "What do the sirens do," he asked, "besides serving you?"

Mishti regarded him for a long moment, leaning back as she held the rudder in position. Finally, she said, "Nothing."

*Right.*

That's what he'd suspected.

"Why?" asked Leonardo.

"What?"

Leonardo ducked as a low branch swept past. "They could always choose to *not* serve you. Why don't they?"

Mishti raised a throwing ring, shearing a branch off before it could hit her face. It struck the edge of the boat and slid into the water.

"You ask too many questions."

*And you keep too many secrets,* thought Leonardo.

"Let's find the kids," he said instead. He'd find the answers to everything, whether Mishti cooperated or not. As soon as they got Charley back, he'd turn every stone in the Cove if the last one told him what was going on here.

***

When they reached the Cove, Leonardo shielded his eyes up at the fortress. It hung from the cliff face, marble pillars and sunlit gold awaiting their return. They cut straight across the water toward it, jumping the choppy surf. A wave splashed against the hull next to Leonardo and he flinched, surprised by the cold.

Mishti leaned over the side and shaded her eyes. From deep below, a shape rose through the water, flowing and graceful. The siren materialized through the gloom, swimming for the surface with strong tail-strokes like a dolphin. She skimmed alongside the boat, just below the waves, then abruptly cut across their path.

The boat jumped over her wake and suddenly plowed through the waterfall, straight into the lagoon.

"Halt!" shouted Mishti.

The rowers down the boat forced their oars backward. A wave crashed against the rocky edge. Water sloshed around the lagoon, pitching the old Raven Clan boat where it was tied and nearly knocking Leonardo off his feet. He gripped the stem as Mishti tugged on the rudder and guided them over to the edge.

One of the girls up front jumped onto the rocks, then ran the tie rope up and looped it around a stalagmite.

The rest of them scrambled out, climbing to the bow and over the front edge. The clear water of the lagoon rippled as the boat rocked, but no one came close to falling in. Ex-Raven or original Lion, they'd all spent their fair share of time getting into and out of boats.

Leonardo waited until they'd all disappeared up the stairs, leaving him and Mishti alone on the edge of the lagoon, then he turned to face her. "Mishti, you saw the skull," he started as she crossed her arms. "The Dark is here. We need to start working together if we're going to survive it."

"I saw a lot of things today," said Mishti. "And I've *seen* a lot of things in this Cove. You know what's in common? If it involves Snake Clan, it's probably a trick."

Leonardo shook his head. "I saw a skull just like that back in the Darkwoods. It's connected to the Dark."

"And let me guess, teamwork is the only way to defeat it, right? We'll all hold hands and—"

"I need you to take this seriously."

"I know what you're doing, Leonardo," Mishti pulled the

strings on her armour, letting the heavy plates fall to the rocks. She straightened her robes.

"And what would that be?"

"I'm not stupid." Mishti threw her armour into the boat. "Your clan needs a new home. All this shit with the kids and the pirates and the Dark benefits you, doesn't it? It's a pain in the ass, but it benefits you."

"You're the one who said we needed to unite," said Leonardo.

"And you agreed pretty quick."

"Look, Mishti." Leonardo started untying his own armour. "I don't know what game you're trying to play, but you need us as much as we need you."

Mishti barked a laugh, already moving for the stairs. "I don't have time for this."

"When did it happen?" asked Leonardo. He threw his armour in the boat and jogged after her.

"When did what happen?"

"Lion Clan used to be the greatest clan of all time. You still pretend to be, but you're not."

"Says the leader of a clan that burned up."

"I was never the leader of Raven Clan." Leonardo followed her up the stairs, taking them two at a time.

"Since I've gotten here, you know what I've seen?" he continued. She frowned as he listed items off on his fingers. "You lost the auction, lost Pompey, allowed a strange clan to enter your camp uninvited, allowed the pirates to enter your camp uninvited, barely survived the pirates...oh, and whatever it is you hold over the sirens, you're losing that too."

"Thaisa is entirely loyal."

"And Adriana isn't. Look Mishti, if anyone can defeat the Dark, it's Lion Clan. But you need help."

"From you?"

"Who else is stepping up?" He moved past her and blocked the doorway. "Together, we can return Lion Clan to greatness."

"Move, Leonardo." Mishti tried to push past him.

"No." Leonardo stopped her. "Do you think you can fix this yourself?"

"Fine!" Mishti placed her hands on her hips. "No, I don't. I don't even know what's happening anymore. I've always followed the Lostwoods' wishes. I've never questioned a single sign." She sniffed, forcing back angry tears. "But if this…" she spat out the next word, "*Dark* is here, and the Lostwoods brought you to stop it…" She swallowed hard. "If all that is true, then I'm just…irrelevant."

"Why would you be irrelevant?" asked Leonardo carefully. Angry Mishti was nothing new, but vulnerable Mishti was a person he'd neither expected nor knew how to respond to.

"Think about it." She pinched the bridge of her nose. "I put in years of work, which amounted to nothing but a group of blindly religious girls who can barely survive a fight. Then you suddenly show up, take over my clan, and know more about it than I ever did. And Caliban knows about the Dark too."

Leonardo's irritation grew with every word. They didn't have time for Mishti to throw in the towel. The pirates could be leaving the Turquoise Island as they spoke. If she felt like some sort of failure or betrayed by the woods, then she'd just have to suck it up and soldier on. He never wanted to be leader, but he didn't sit around and complain about it when his clanmates were in danger.

"What do you want, Leonardo?" Mishti asked suddenly. "Did you come here to take my clan?"

"I want to survive the Dark," said Leonardo. He held her desperate gaze for a long moment, forcing himself to swallow his distaste. "I want all of us to."

# CHAPTER 18

Mishti left six girls behind, while the remaining thirty-two piled into the boats, along with the five boys, Viola, and Leonardo. Mishti's boat was bigger, but ten girls joined the boys in Leonardo's boat, to help row and balance the weight.

In the wake of the last attack, they'd put the camp on lockdown. Heavy doors sealed every passage, including the one the pirates had entered through. Leonardo and Mishti nearly got in another argument when he demanded to know why those doors hadn't been closed during the party, but the kids were still in danger and he forced himself to pick his battles.

For now, at least, she seemed to have pulled herself together. Her episode on the stairs left him deeply bothered, and he wanted Viola, Pinch, and Moth's opinion on it, if he could get them alone. Unfortunately, he knew that wouldn't happen anytime soon.

Instead, a different debate sprang up as Leonardo's clan settled onto their benches.

"What's going on between Mishti and Thaisa?" asked Puck. "Did you see the way they looked at each other?"

"Oh yeah," said Nym, climbing over the benches. "Apparently they're dating."

"What?" said Bates. "How do *you* know?"

"I listen." Nym shrugged his slight shoulders. "These girls talk a lot."

"Huh." Puck quirked his mouth. "Fair enough."

"Apparently they've been a thing for a while," said Nym.

*That explains Lion Clan's alliance with the sirens.*

Viola leaned in close to Leonardo. "I'm more curious about what's going on between *them*," she said conspiringly, nodding down the boat as Juliet took her seat next to Moth, showing him a scrap of parchment with something sketched on it. Moth studied it, nodding, and dug through his bag until he procured a chunk of driftwood. His whittling knife glinted between his fingers

"Moth and Juliet?" Leonardo frowned. "She's training him to be a shaman."

"And that's all it is?"

"What else would..." He paused. "Do you mean...you think there's something more?"

He *had* noticed they were close, and Juliet was pretty enough, and Moth was...well, Leonardo supposed he had a certain awkward charm, but he hadn't really thought there was anything going on between them.

"Yes, Leo." Viola rolled her eyes. "She follows him like a puppy."

Leonardo tilted his head, regarding them anew.

"Trust me." Viola squeezed his hand. "In the meantime, let's go get Charley back."

***

The two boats cut between the cliffs and into open water, Leonardo and Mishti at the helms, their crews rowing hard. They had enough people on the benches now that rowers could swap out when they grew tired, and the boat itself would never break stride.

In the blazing heat of the day, that should've happened often, but Leonardo realized within the first half-hour that neither his nor Mishti's Lions intended to bow out before the other.

Fresh rowers sat waiting on the middle of each bench, but not a single kid down the length of the boat dared make eye-contact with them, lest it revealed their fatigue. As if the sweat on their faces and the dark stains on the shirts didn't give it away already.

Leonardo's clan wore their old clothes from the Darkwoods. Last night, Leonardo learned how impractical the robes were for swimming. If this rescue involved getting in the water, he didn't need his clan struggling through sheets of silk.

They had, however, swapped out their old, hardened leather vests for real armour. Gold Lion Clan plates and shields lay piled under the benches. His clan was proud, but they weren't stupid.

Well, not *entirely* stupid. Their refusal to swap out with new rowers made a hard case against them. Meanwhile, Mishti's boat pulled further ahead by the minute, as her all-girl crew swapped in and out efficiently. The endurance competition lived on Leonardo's boat, and Mishti peered back over her shoulder, impatience on her face as they dropped further behind.

"Ok," called Leonardo. "Time to switch. One at a time, starting at the bow and working backward. Let's go."

To their credit, not one of the eight rowers, boy or girl, uttered a word of complaint. With someone else making the call, they could safely retain their pride. Exhausted rowers slumped in the middle of their benches while fresh arms took over. The boat quickly picked up speed again, drawing back even with Mishti.

"Get some water," said Leonardo. Full canteens lay among the armour below the benches. The sea wind and the cool mist off the waves helped combat the effect of the sun, but it did nothing to prevent dehydration.

Only a single cloud inched across the seamless blue sky. A stray—cotton-white and too small to offer any hope of shade.

"Nym," said Moth. "Give Lion some water too. His basket is under your bench there."

"Lion? You mean the hamster?" Nym reached under his bench.

"You brought that rat on the boat?" demanded Pinch.

"What was I supposed to do?" said Moth. "Leave him behind?"

"You're such a halfwit."

"He could've starved!"

"It's fine," said Leonardo. The sun was exhausting enough. No one needed to suffer through listening to them bicker. "Nym, give him some water."

"Already on it." Nym filled a canteen cap and placed it in the corner of the basket.

Leonardo took a drink from his own canteen, squinting at the hard light on the waves. They were in for a long day.

At some point close to the second hour, Leonardo stripped off his shirt and tied it into a sort of turban atop his head. The first throbs of a headache pushed at the front of his skull and his fingers burned red on the rudder handle. Down the centre of the boat, sweating crew members held up shields and pieces of armour as umbrellas.

At one point, while on a break, Bates edged between two rowers and leaned over the side, scooping up a shieldful of seawater and dumping it on his head. It splashed Bates and Juliet, but neither complained, and soon Nym and Moth were doing the same, dousing themselves and their crewmates.

"How close are we?" Leonardo called to Mishti. The limestone cliffs stretched to the east for miles, dry and sunbaked. Dark caves gaped from the craggy face, white foam waves crashing against the sides. He recalled Mishti's warning that they were uninhabitable. *Sea monsters*, she'd said. But they would provide a respite from this heat, and they wouldn't need to stay long. He worried about his crew, and even Mishti's efficient team was flagging in their pace.

"That's it there," Mishti pointed out to sea.

Leonardo squinted at a shadow on the horizon. His optimism darkened.

Bates sagged on his oar. "Why are their territories so far apart?"

"Mishti," said Leonardo. "We need to rest. It's too hot to stay out in the sun like this."

"You want to go in the caves?" called Mishti, snorting. She shook her head. "Not an option."

"Well, neither is rowing for that island," countered Leonardo.

He was hot and sticky and agitated. "We're going less than half the pace of when we started. It'll be nightfall by the time we get there."

"It's better than what we'll face in there," said Mishti.

"What exactly is *in there*," pressed Leonardo. "You said 'sea monsters'?"

"Correct. They have tentacles. They bite. Good enough?"

Leonardo eyed the nearest cave, big and open and not as dark as most of them. Then he regarded his crew. Puck's hands slipped off his oar and he weakly grabbed for it, rotating the shaft in a stroke that barely skimmed the surface.

On the centre of his bench, Moth wavered, blinking hard as he grabbed Juliet's shoulder for balance.

"We'll just go in the entrance," said Leonardo. "We can't stay out here like this."

Mishti set her jaw, but when she glanced at her own crew, she didn't respond immediately.

"Take us over," called Leonardo, pulling the rudder as the rowers on the left flank lifted their oars and allowed the righthand rowers to propel the boat into a turn.

They'd stayed close to the cliffs all afternoon and came upon the cave quickly. Leonardo and Mishti called, "Halt," as they slipped into the shade, and the rowers barely had the strength to force back their oars and bring the boats to a drift.

They glided in a short way past the mouth of the cave, and Leonardo gazed around at a ceiling of stalactites, like hundreds of crooked teeth. The cave bottom was visible too, sculpted with masses of featureless rock and no sand to obscure the water. At first glance, there appeared to be no sea monsters.

The sighs of relief down the boat reassured Leonardo that he'd made the right choice. Regardless, Mishti and the Lion girls gazed around the cave warily.

"We'll leave soon," said Leonardo. "Ten minutes, tops."

Mishti didn't reply, too busy scanning the shadowed corners and dark tunnels that snaked away from the main cave. An inkling of doubt crept into Leonardo's mind.

*What exactly lives in these caves?*

The crystal-clear water was devoid of any life, except for a school of tiny fish that darted around one of the bigger rocks. The boats rode on the swell of waves that rolled in, inching them deeper inside. Leonardo started to tell his rowers to back-paddle a bit, but they looked so exhausted that he decided it could wait another minute.

"What do you normally do?" he asked Mishti. "The Clans can't regularly make this journey."

"Not in the middle of the day," said Mishti. "Or on days this hot."

"When Tiger and Dragon come up for the full moon," said Sophie, "they set out early while the sun is just rising and the cliffs still offer shade. If it's a hot day like this, they'll often stay in the sacred cave until evening before heading back south."

"And you didn't think to mention this?" demanded Leonardo.

She rolled her eyes. "Would it have made a difference?"

As she spoke, Leonardo noticed Bates and Pinch whispering in the bow. Pinch nodded, then they both tossed their hats on the bench, stripped off their shirts, and leapt overboard, plunging into the clear blue in a cloud of bubbles.

"Hey! Get out of the water!" yelled Mishti.

Bates and Pinch surfaced, shaking the water out of their hair, and Mishti yelled at them again. "Get out! Now!"

They looked at Leonardo, still standing on his captain's platform.

"You heard her," he snapped. Mishti returned to scanning their surroundings, and Leonardo did the same, heart racing.

"What are we looking—" he started, then Viola cut him off.

"What is *that?*"

"What the hell?" said Puck.

Between the stalactites, purplish-red creatures emerged, peering down at the boats with bulbous eyes. Tentacles curled around the stalactites; Leonardo slid his sword from his belt.

"Octopuses?" said Nym.

Pinch and Bates scrambled into the boat, Nym and Puck helping heave them over the side. They straightened, soaking wet, and reached for their swords.

Dozens of octopi descended from where they'd been hiding. Leonardo stared, dumbfounded, as the creatures used their tentacles to maneuver on the ceiling.

They weren't large; their heads were maybe the size of his two fists and their tentacles no longer than his forearm. One turned its bulging gaze on Leonardo. He gripped his sword tighter as even more emerged, directly above the boats.

Then one of the octopi hissed, opening a round mouth of needle teeth.

"Fuck that," said Pinch.

"That's no octopus," said Puck.

It dropped, falling straight for the boat. Leonardo jumped on the nearest bench and swung his sword like a baseball bat. He connected with a heavy smack, and the creature flew into the water. Red pooled on the surface around it.

Then the rest dropped.

"Shields!" yelled Sophie. Lions on both boats grabbed the big emblazoned shields, still lying out from where they'd used them as umbrellas. They threw them over their heads while the rest of the clan slashed wildly at the rain of small, tentacled monsters.

Hundreds fell all over the cave, like the loudest, most violent hailstorm of their lives.

Leonardo beat octopus after octopus out of the air, ducking and grabbing for a wooden shield in the nearest footwell.

*Why the hell didn't you listen?*

He'd put his clan in danger again. This time, he refused to lose a single member. He *couldn't* lose another of his dwindling family.

Leonardo swung the shield over his head, just in time to catch one of the creatures. It stuck, tentacles reaching around the edge, and Leonardo smashed it into the side of the boat. A purple, lifeless lump slid off onto the bench.

Another fell straight for his face, and Leonardo hacked it away one-handed. Across from him, Mishti slashed over her head, a throwing ring clenched in each fist.

Puck cried out as one landed on his arm, tentacles wrapping and circular mouth gaping. Bates grabbed it with his bare hand and ripped it away before it could latch on.

He threw it out over the water and Leonardo deflected two more. Shouts and the wet smack of creatures echoed around the cave. Leonardo stared around, chest heaving, as the last ones dropped harmlessly wide. They splashed into the water and jetted toward the bottom.

Blood clouded the surface, and more ran down the arms of the Lions. Most of it seemed to be from the creatures, but one girl pressed her hand to the back of her neck, teeth clenched against the pain of a bite.

Leonardo heaved a deep breath. That was too close.

Then the surface rippled and an octopus came flying out of the water. A dozen more followed right behind it, hurtling for the boats. Leonardo swung his shield and ducked as one slammed into the wood and another shot over his head, tentacles flailing. They came from all sides, crisscrossing and colliding in the air.

"Argh," shouted Puck, as Bates clipped him in the face with his shield. Puck reeled back and kicked over an open canteen. It splashed into Leonardo's ankles and he flinched in surprise, barely dodging a flying octopus.

Juliet gasped as one flew into her, tentacles rapidly searching for a grip. Moth whipped around, sword in hand, and speared it straight through the creature's head. He stumbled as another collided with his back and then a third smashed into his head. Leonardo leapt over the bench and ripped it off, his fingers sinking into wet, glutinous flesh.

He threw it as far as he could, then turned for the one on Moth's back. Moth cried out, and when Leonardo smashed it off with his shield, it took a chunk of flesh with it. Blood ran down Moth's side.

*Good God.*

One smacked into Leonardo's hip, tentacles whipping around his leg. Leonardo flipped his sword around and drove it straight down, throwing his shield in the way of another in his peripheral.

Meanwhile, more began pulling themselves out of the water

and up the sides of the cave. Tentacles searched for purchase as they scrambled up toward the ceiling.

"Moth, Puck, Nym, Bates," shouted Leonardo. "Get to oars and row. Everyone else, shield them!"

The four boys jumped for the nearest benches, and the kids around them shifted their attention to protecting the rowers, angling their shields into a makeshift shell.

Leonardo jumped over the back two benches to the captain's platform and grabbed the rudder, shoving his sword in his belt. He wrenched it around, defending wildly with just his shield as the boat lurched into motion.

Moth, Puck, Nym, and Bates pulled as hard as their arms would let them, handle shafts clanking in the oarlocks. Mishti shouted the same orders at her crew. Painfully slow, the two boats rotated in the water and started for the sunlit mouth of the cave.

# CHAPTER 19

An octopus leaped over the stern and slammed into the back of Leonardo's head. A slippery, wet tentacle smacked across his face and he tore it off. He grabbed behind his head and flinched away as the creature bit his hand. Pain stabbed through his entire arm.

Leonardo swore. Blood ran down his fingers. He gritted his teeth, took his shield in both hands, and swung it back over his head.

The shield hit something rubbery and the creature fell to Leonardo's feet. He stomped on it, nearly slipping and grabbing the rudder handle again for balance.

Meanwhile, Puck had to drop his oar to fend off an attack. The boat skewed crooked for a few seconds until he managed to throw the octopus overboard and regain control of his oar.

The boats staggered drunkenly through the water, but safety

drew closer with every stroke, and the Lions began to outpace the octopi climbing the ceiling.

When they finally burst out into the sun, only a few of the creatures followed. They jetted along under the surface, then launched up suddenly, twisting in the air. But the Lions were ready for them, swords flashing before they ever reached their targets.

"What sicko imagined those?" demanded Pinch, blood running down his sword.

"What?" asked Juliet.

*Dammit, Pinch.*

The secret was their one advantage over Mishti's clan.

"He means, like, who would even think those things existed?" said Moth quickly.

"Oh. Yeah, I don't know."

Luckily, no one pressed it further. They left the dead creatures floating on the waves and plowed away from the cliffs. More kids jumped to the oars, and within minutes, the cave was a distant nightmare.

Leonardo wanted to call a stop to tend to their wounds, but he was equally aware that the sun posed its own threat and they still had a long way to travel. He took quick stock of his crew and ordered those with minimal or no injuries to the oars, while the ones with serious bites gathered down the centre of the boat.

Juliet tended to them, tearing already bloodied shirts into strips which she bound around the ugly wounds they'd sustained—part puncture and part gouge. Leonardo poured water from a canteen over his own bleeding fingers, grimacing at the crescent of razor stabs.

"Juliet," he called. "Are sea monsters venomous?"

She didn't reply, but her grim expression told him enough.

*I suppose we'll find out* how *venomous soon.*

It hurt like hell, but he forced himself to grit through it.

*Would Aleksander complain while his clan was wounded?* Not a chance.

"How can I help?" he asked. He looped the stern rope around the rudder, binding it straight back, and jumped down between the benches.

"Change this water," said Juliet. "Please."

She tied off a strip of torn fabric around Moth's torso and passed Leonardo a basket of red-tinted water. Leonardo carried it to the edge and dumped it over. He eyed the blood welling up between his fingers, then leaned down, set his jaw, and plunged his fist into the saltwater. The pain struck instant and deep. He grunted and flexed his fingers under the water, watching the tendrils of blood swept away by the sea.

"Here, I packed an emergency kit under the bench," Juliet said to Moth behind him. She dragged it out as Leonardo filled the basket and heaved it back up over the side, spilling saltwater into the footwell, still littered with dead sea monsters.

"Remember the numbing leaves I told you about? We need to make a paste out of them to put on your bite."

"I'm fine," said Moth. "It's just—"

"You won't be fine, after your first shift of rowing. And neither will the others."

Moth paused to consider this, grimacing. "Ok, let's do it."

"Better."

"Here's the water," said Leonardo. He set it down in the

footwell and Juliet nodded gratefully, strawberry blonde ringlets plastered dark with sweat.

"Thank you. We need to keep them clean until we get to...you got bit too."

Leonardo looked down at his hand, fresh blood mixed with saltwater, gleaming in the sunlight.

"What?" Viola shifted on her rowing bench to see. "Leo, you're covered in blood!"

"It's not as bad as it looks," said Leonardo.

"Give it to me," said Juliet. She wet a rag in the basket of water and cleaned the bite, then bound a fresh strip of fabric around it. "There. You're as bad as Mishti."

"Thank you," said Leonardo. He did appreciate her effort, if not the spectacle she'd made of it.

"Now go steer this boat," she said. "Moth and I can handle this. Right Moth?"

"Of course," said Moth, busily grinding the leaves into a paste in a bamboo canister.

Leonardo climbed back to the captain's platform and freed the rudder from where he'd bound it.

He set his sights on the hazy island in the distance. *Charley and Pompey had better be there.* If not, he had no idea what they'd do.

# CHAPTER 20

An archway of porous stone and iridescent shells towered over the water, marking the entrance to Dragon Clan's camp. The Lions glided under it, weary and exhausted. Dragons stood awaiting them along marble walls and atop stone steps into the sea. Feathery palms and tropical flowers bloomed everywhere—a pensile paradise in the shade of billowing white curtains on ascending tiered balconies, so densely covered in grapevines and ivy that it looked to be part of the landscape.

Demetrius stood on the nearest steps, robes stretched over his generous girth. He waited for them with hands folded in the deep blue silk. Decorative vases, benches and abundant greenery surrounded the watchful Dragons. They leaned in close, whispering to each other as the boats slipped past.

"Mishti," called Demetrius. "And it's Leonardo, right? You both look terrible."

"We've been travelling all day," said Mishti. Her tone indicated she had no desire for small talk.

"And you got in a fight?" he questioned, studying their crews.

"Sea monsters," said Sophie.

"Ouch," said Demetrius. "But you must have a good reason for sailing here on a day this hot. I'll boldly assume that this isn't an attack."

"It's not," said Leonardo.

"Good," said Demetrius. "Then steer your boats down that tunnel. We'll get you patched up."

Leonardo glanced at Mishti and she nodded, ordering her crew toward one of three stone-bricked tunnels.

"This one leads to the hanging gardens," said Juliet, "If I remember right."

Darkness enveloped the tunnel, just tall enough for the mast of Mishti's boat. When they emerged out the far side, it was into a shaded grove of fig trees, marble terraces, and shallow waterfalls, spilling sheets of water from scooped openings in the stepped landings, trailing with flowers and vines.

Fairies and hummingbirds whisked around, hovering to drink from hibiscus and honeysuckle blossoms.

Viola nudged Leonard on the shoulder, her voice low. "This is the place," she whispered. "This is the temple, or palace, or whatever it is, that I saw."

"So the kids are here?" asked Leonardo.

"No, I don't think..." Viola frowned. "Not *here*, exactly."

Demetrius emerged through the garden, followed by his Dragons. He spread his hands, calmly grandiose. "Welcome to the hanging gardens."

A few Dragons hurried forward and caught ropes tossed up by the rowers in the bow of each boat. They tied them off and the Lions began climbing out onto the half-submerged steps. Moth winced, clamping pressure on the red-stained binding around his side. Leonardo flexed his stiff fingers, gritting his teeth at the pain. The effects of Juliet's numbing leaves had long worn off.

"What attacked you?" asked one of the Dragons, a girl with searching eyes and a chestnut complexion. "What did they look like?"

"Octopuses," said Bates. "Octopuses from hell."

"With teeth," added one of the Lion Girls.

"Clearly," said another Dragon, studying their makeshift bandages.

The Dragons led the Lions across a bridge to a grassy alcove surrounded with low stone benches and lemon trees. Birdsong filled the air and insects buzzed past.

"Rest," said Demetrius. Dragons brought forward cracked coconuts and offered them to the exhausted Lions as they gratefully lowered themselves to the grass. The boys eyed their hosts suspiciously, but they hesitantly followed the girls' lead and accepted the gifts.

"It helps with dehydration," explained Demetrius.

"Do you trust them?" Leonardo asked Mishti under his breath.

"To not attack us?" said Mishti. "Yes."

"I'll go get something for the pain," said the Dragon girl who'd first spoken. Her dark skin was perfectly unblemished, her hands smooth and unlined. Leonardo had thought that Mishti's girls lead a comfortable life, but he wondered if the Dragons could somehow have it even easier, out here on their island paradise.

The girl stepped past Leonardo and hurried over the bridge out of sight. The smell of soap and flower petals hung in the air behind her. More Dragons appeared with supplies and began setting up to clean and stitch the wounds.

"Let them help," said Leonardo, when his clan bristled. He didn't need them making new enemies. He'd learned already that the Cove's politics were a lot more complex than up north, and he trusted Mishti that their immediate safety wasn't at risk.

"Demetrius," said Mishti. "We need to speak with you. Sooner than later."

The light in the garden was beginning to turn a light hue of pink, and Leonardo glanced at the sky as it began its descent into evening shades.

"I trusted you had a good reason for coming here," said Demetrius. "Let us talk then. Come, we'll leave our clans in peace."

Leonardo hesitated. He trusted Dragon Clan, but only to a point. This easy, gracious persona was very different from the bold, obsessive Demetrius they'd met at the full moon ceremony. Demetrius glanced at him, then his hand, mistaking the reason for his reluctance to leave.

"We can wait if it's bad," Demetrius offered. "Bite wounds fester quickly. Especially out in that heat."

*The clan will be fine.* Peace was important in the Cove.

"I'm fine," said Leonardo. "Let's go."

Demetrius eyed him dubiously, but he nodded and led them over the bridge. Leonardo flexed his bound fingers, wincing at the sharp jabs. He realized Mishti was watching, head tilted appraisingly.

*Does she think it's careless?* His right hand was the one he used to wield a sword.

*There's a good chance there will be a fight at the end of this,* he thought. But the trail to Pompey and Charley grew colder with every wasted minute. He'd deal with his hand later.

Demetrius led them to an open-air dais, hung with white curtains drawn back to provide a view of the sea. The sun set in spectacular shades of orange and pink, streaking the water and the sky and painting the white curtains rose.

Leonardo and Mishti both eyed the view with grim expressions.

It looked as though they be searching in the dark after all.

*That's fine.* They could use the cover of the night to surprise the pirates. If they found the pirates.

"So," said Demetrius, walking to a plate of grapes on a table. "What brings you to the Turquoise Isle, in the sweltering heat, covered in sea monster bites?"

He was the perfect opposite of Caliban, genuine and carefully articulate, without a hint of mocking in his tone.

"The pirates attacked us," said Mishti. "They entered our lagoon, kidnapped our two youngest, and escaped. We want to get them back."

"Huh," Demetrius chuckled, an eyebrow raised. He plucked a grape off the vine and studied it. "They stole away with *two* Lion cubs. How fascinatingly rare."

"They attacked during our celebration, after the full moon ceremony," said Mishti.

"Oh yes," said Demetrius. "Your celebration."

"You don't celebrate the…*Lostwoods*, after the ceremony?" asked Leonardo.

Demetrius chuckled. "No. My clan is not quite as…let's say…*fanatical* as Mishti and her Lions."

"We're wasting time," said Mishti.

"Sure," said Demetrius. "You've been in my camp for close to ten minutes and I still don't know what you're here for. You owe us *a lot* of favours, so I find it hard to believe you'd be here for favours of your own."

"We know the pirates are on your island," Mishti. "And the Natives."

Something flickered in Demetrius's eyes. It might have been panic, but he buried it too quick.

"Oh yes, the Natives," said Demetrius. Fresh off a decade in the Darkwoods." He shuddered. "I don't know how they did it. Leonardo, is it really as bad as the stories say?"

"I don't know your stories," said Leonardo. He had no interest in discussing his home with Demetrius.

"They say the trees grow so close that some areas never see the sun, and the clans haven't stopped fighting for an entire generation. I've never been myself; why would I leave a place like this for something like that?" He shuddered again.

Leonardo frowned. Demetrius sure knew a lot about the Darkwoods. And it was accurate. Up North, the little they thought they knew about the Cove had turned out to be wildly off-target.

"The pirates," said Leonardo. He could contemplate the knowledge disparity later. "Where are they?"

"How would I know?" Demetrius frowned from Leonardo to

Mishti. A bead of sweat glistened on his forehead. His fingers darted up to blot it with a square of silk.

"Cut the bullshit, Demetrius," said Mishti. "We know they're on this island."

*Or at least, they were.* A lot of hours had passed since the encounter with Snake.

"If they are, then I don't know about it." Demetrius laughed, but Leonardo caught a nervous edge to it. "And I think I'd know about it."

"Are they in a cave?" pressed Mishti. "A lagoon?"

"She's a stubborn one," Demetrius mused to Leonardo, faking a grin.

"What about a river?" asked Leonardo.

Demetrius sighed. Too heavy, too forced. "Yes, we have caves and lagoons and rivers on this island, but I promise you there are no pirates in any of them."

Leonardo and Mishti made eye contact. Unspoken agreement passed between them.

"We don't believe you," said Mishti.

"Well I'm sorry to hear that," said Demetrius. "But I don't know what to tell you."

"The truth?" suggested Leonardo. He resisted the urge to draw his sword. Mishti's fingers twitched, throwing rings glinting on her wrists in the dying sun. Demetrius's eyes flicked to their weapons, then the trail back to the gardens.

"Look at it from my point of view," he tried. "Why would I let pirates so close to my own camp? What would I gain?"

And now Leonardo was looking at it from his perspective, and suddenly the pieces began to click into place. Mishti allowed the sirens to live in the caves below the cliffs in exchange for protection. What stopped Demetrius from striking a similar bargain with the pirates?

"Fine," said Leonardo. "I suppose you're right."

Mishti shot him a confused look and Leonardo blinked back at her, urgently attempting to convey his meaning in the split second before he turned his gaze back on Demetrius. Demetrius narrowed his eyes.

"No good leader would keep the pirates so close," continued Leonardo. "And you clearly know what you're doing here."

Mishti studied him from the side, chewing her lip as she tried to piece it together.

"We apologize," she added, an eye still on Leonardo. "For questioning you. We have to follow up every lead."

"I can see that," said Demetrius. He dried his broad forehead again with the square of silk, fingers flicking to tame a stray curl. Wariness burned behind his small eyes. "Why? The last time you came to my camp hunting pirates was when you first became leader of Lion Clan. Although I remember that visit being less accusatory."

Mishti blinked slowly, studying the curtains.

"She was young then," he told Leonardo. "Maybe the youngest leader of Lion Clan ever—but who can trust the stories, really? Details get...warped, in the hand-me-down. Is it the same in the Darkwoods?"

"Yes," said Leonardo. Lion Clan specifically was an example of that, although there was no hand-me-down. Aleksander himself had been to the Cove long ago, and his description of Lion Clan ventured far from the truth.

"She decided that no pirate would kidnap a single Lion cub during her leadership," continued Demetrius. "She was determined to track them down, but if I recall, never succeeded."

Mishti swallowed, lips pursed.

"After that, I suppose you accepted the fact that the pirates would always win." Demetrius clucked his tongue. "So why today? Why suddenly care so much to get back a kid? Are you putting on a show for your new guests?"

"One of the kids was ours," said Leonardo. "Up North, we don't have pirates. I'm not so willing to let a member of my clan go."

"I see," said Demetrius. "You'll learn quickly, the same as Mishti did. But I do wish you luck. Maybe this will be the one time the pirates lose."

"We should get back on the water," said Mishti. An undercurrent edged her words, and Leonardo understood it. The more pieces fell together, the more hostile Dragon Clan's camp began to feel, and the quicker he wanted his clan safely back in the boats.

"So soon?" said Demetrius. "Don't you want to let your clans rest?"

"Clan," said Mishti. "And they'll be fine."

"You *are* in a rush." He plucked a last grape off the plate and started back for the hanging garden, blue robes sweeping behind him. "But I trust my Dragons are finished stitching them up, so you can be on your way immediately."

Leonardo and Mishti hurried after him, down the steps of the dais and onto a cobblestone path lined with tall, thin trees. Sunlight filtered through the marble columns and ivy, dappling the trees and the confetti of fallen flower petals that littered the ground.

"Where do you plan to go next?" asked Demetrius, with too much care to make it sound like he didn't.

"Further east," said Mishti. "If you haven't seen them, they must have continued down the coast."

"Maybe Tiger Clan saw something," Demetrius suggested.

"Maybe," said Mishti.

# CHAPTER 21

When they crossed the bridge into the lemon grove, Leonardo and Mishti found their clan gathered around something on the ground.

A pit formed in Leonardo's stomach.

Then Moth glanced back, crouched with Nym and Viola. "Leo, come look at this."

His tone eased Leonardo's alarm.

Leonardo crossed the grass to see what he first took for a lizard, sprawled out on a flat rock. It lay basking in the last rays of the sun, roughly the length of his hand and brilliantly blue.

Then it stretched its wings.

Leonardo stopped in his tracks as the tiny dragon lifted its head and flicked out a forked tongue.

"Oh yes," said Demetrius behind him. "Our lazy blue friends."

"Does it breathe fire?" asked Bates.

"Luckily, no," said Demetrius. "Or else this entire island would've burned up a long time ago."

"How many of them are there?" asked Viola.

"Hundreds. Thousands." Demetrius shrugged. "There are colonies of them in the wilder parts of the island. Down in the caves and out in the jungle."

"How big are they?" asked Puck.

"No bigger than this one," said Demetrius. "They're small, but very efficient killers. Of fish, birds, lizards; nothing our size, of course."

Beside him, Mishti gazed around the lemon grove, a frown creasing her brow.

Leonardo stiffened. *Where are the other Dragons?* The human ones were notably absent.

"It's getting dark," said Leonardo. As fascinating as the dragon was, he had no interest in getting ambushed while they studied it.

"We're leaving already?" asked Puck.

"The pirates aren't here," said Leonardo. "We need to get to Tiger Clan before dark."

"*Tiger Clan?*" said Sophie, just as one of the Dragons returned over the bridge.

"Good luck with that," the Dragon mused, a smug set to his smooth jaw. The smell of soap was strong on his skin. Actually, they all smelled like soap, shiny with the obsessive perfection of a clan run by Demetrius. "It will be well into the night by the time you reach them. They're not fond of visitors at any hour, but especially not that late."

"Then we should leave now," said Mishti. The Lion girls gave her a strange look, but no one questioned anything aloud.

"If we spend the night here, the pirates get further away," said Mishti.

"A valiant hunt, if nothing else," said Demetrius. "Maybe you'll catch them after all."

They returned to the boats, still tied in place and bumping gently against the low stone wall of the canal.

The Dragons who'd vanished earlier reappeared now, emerging from paths and talking in low voices.

Leonardo ushered his clanmates into the boats, one eye on the Dragons. Tiny fairy lights zipped through the air as the garden descended into twilight, and a larger bat-like creature that might've been a dragon launched out of a bush and wheeled away, up into the treetops.

Moth squinted after the fairies, then he drew a sharp breath. He snapped around to Leonardo and mouthed the word *pirates*. Leonardo's stomach clenched. He darted a glance to see if the Dragons noticed. Pinch kicked Moth under the bench. Moth pulled his lips tight.

"Good luck," said Demetrius. "You should reach Fog Waters before midnight. I hope you find the pirates waiting there."

Leonardo stepped down into the boat as two Dragons crouched to untie their lines.

"Thank you for your clan's assistance," said Mishti. The words sounded forced. "We couldn't continue without the stitches and clean bandages."

"Our pleasure." Demetrius scratched his chin. "I assume you

wouldn't object to us adding a favour to the score sheet? A small return for our time and resources."

Mishti set her jaw. For a second, Leonardo thought she would argue. Then she nodded. "Of course. I will have Sophie update our sheet as well."

"Good, good," said Demetrius. "Please do. I hate having to argue over such petty things at full moon ceremonies."

He grinned easily at Leonardo. "Not all clans are as diligent at record-keeping as Lion Clan and ourselves. Snake Clan, in particular, has arrived at some meetings with a rather peculiar memory of how favours are owed. But I digress. One last observation before you set sail; your hand is still untreated."

Leonardo glanced down at his bound hand, the fabric stained with sweat and blood. A throbbing pain pulsed from the needle-tooth punctures, but he pushed it back.

"I'm fine," said Leonardo.

Demetrius's eyes assured him that he wasn't fooling anyone, but Leonardo didn't care. Getting his clan out of this garden outweighed all other priorities.

"Of course," said Demetrius again. "So long, my friends."

They shoved off the stone wall and rowed for the mouth of the tunnel, now lit with fairies. Once they were inside, Leonardo considered having his clan raise their shields overhead as they passed through the mouth of the tunnel, but he scrapped the idea just as quick. If Demetrius wanted to harm them, he'd had plenty of opportunities before this.

They slipped out into the small cove, under a deep indigo sky. Demetrius and his clan stood waiting, just as they'd been when Lion Clan arrived earlier.

Leonardo gripped the rudder and steered them out through the archway into open water.

"So, the pirates aren't here?" asked Viola, once they were safely out of earshot. "I've been trying to sense them, but I can't see a thing."

"The fairies said *pirates*," said Moth.

"Oh, they're here," said Leonardo. "Dragon clan is protecting them."

"What?" demanded Juliet.

"We don't know that for a fact," said Mishti, from the other boat. "But I agree," she added reluctantly. "That seems to be the case."

"So, where are they?" asked Viola. "Are they in that camp?"

"I don't think so," said Leonardo. He suspected Demetrius would've ushered them out quicker if the pirates were that close.

The hulking silhouette of the island loomed behind them, big and dense with a carpet of palms and a steep cliff in the centre. It looked even more daunting in the twilight.

"Leo," said Moth. He pointed at the surface of the water, where long shapes streamed past meters below, vague in the gloom. Leonardo could recognize the sirens by now, and he and Mishti guided the boats around the curve of the coastline, out of sight of Dragon Clan's camp. Leonardo kept an eye over the stern for any boats following them.

The moment they were in the clear, a dozen sirens surfaced around the longboats.

"We found the pirates," said Thaisa, dark hair hanging heavy with saltwater. "Their ship is in a cave on the far side of the is-land."

"Good job." Mishti smiled down at her, admiration in her eyes. The expression was so disconcerting on Mishti's face, Leonardo lost his bearings for a second.

"What about Charley and Pompey?" asked Viola. "Are they still on the ship?"

"I don't know," said Thaisa. "We stayed underwater."

The boats rolled over a wave, temporarily hiding the sirens from view. Leonardo twisted to scan the moonlit water behind them for Dragon boats, but nothing rounded the curve of the island.

"We need a plan," he said, as they levelled out again.

"We don't have time for a plan," said Mishti. "If they sail out—"

"Then we let them go," said Leonardo. "And have the sirens follow them. We have the element of surprise. We can't barge in and blow it."

"Fine." Mishti lashed a rope around the rudder. "Then let's make a plan."

"Thaisa," said Leonardo. "Is there somewhere near the cave where we can stash the boats?"

"There's a river," said Thaisa, sharp eyebrows drawn together. "It opens into the sea a hundred meters from the cave."

"Good. We'll tie the boats up there. How far into the cave is the pirate ship?"

"It's a deep cave," said Thaisa. "They're in the deepest chamber."

"Guards?"

"We never surfaced," she repeated, "but I saw the bottom of a rowboat near the opening."

"Ok," said Leonardo. "Here's what we'll do."

# CHAPTER 22

They tied the boats to a stand of stubborn bushes along the river, which cut through a cleave in the cliffs along the south side of the island. Nym and a Lion girl stayed on the steep shale bank next to the ropes, ready to untie them the moment the rescue party returned.

"It worries me," Leonardo heard Nym telling the girl. "You should've seen my hand before. Ever since we got here, I haven't seen a hint of the black."

The rescue party consisted of only Leonardo, Mishti, Sophie, and Pinch. This was the greatest point of contention from Leonardo's clan, who despised being sidelined in a fight. Viola argued vehemently that four people stood no chance against the pirates.

But they weren't going into a fight. If this worked properly, the pirates wouldn't even know they were there until they'd already left. And for that to happen, they needed the smallest party possible. Two to free Charley and Pompey, and two to watch their backs.

"I don't like this," called Nym from the bank. "Four of you against all of them?"

"We'll be careful," said Leonardo.

"We fight together," said Nym. "We always have."

"Nothing changes now. As I said, it won't be a fight."

Nym crossed his arms, but he didn't press any further. Leonardo studied the dark water, questioning his own plan. If it did become a fight, they would be wildly outnumbered. He held no illusions that they'd stand a chance.

"Leo," said Viola. She waited until he stopped to look at her. "I don't feel good about this either. I can't lose you too."

He knew she'd lost more loved ones than any of them.

"Trust me," he assured her, trying to convince himself at the same time. "This is the only way."

He, Pinch, Mishti, and Sophie lowered themselves into the water. Pinch's tricorn hat rested on his bench in the boat, awaiting his return.

Thaisa and three other sirens swam over and turned their backs so the four Lions could take their shoulders. Mishti wrapped her arms around Thaisa's neck, whispering something that made her smile. Sharp bones protruded under cold, slippery skin as Leonardo took hold of the nearest siren's shoulders. He drew a deep breath, recalling his few close encounters with sirens. The first time, on the river, his life was in jeopardy. The second, in the Cove, his mind was in danger. He made eye contact with Viola, still in the boat, and gave her a small nod.

*We'll be back soon. With Charley.*

Then they were swimming away, downstream and back into the ocean. They slipped through the dark waves, keeping close to the cliffs and out of sight of the cave opening. These cliffs were different from the ones near Lion Clan's camp. Whiter, chalkier, and spiderwebbed with veins of brilliant turquoise which hinted at the island's name.

The cave itself gaped from up ahead, dark and twinkling with the ever-present fairy light.

"Hold your breath," said the siren in front of Leonardo.

*Here we go.* His entire plan hinged on this part succeeding.

The sirens dove and Leonardo plunged underwater. He gripped her slick shoulders, eyes squeezed shut as her tail whipped hard against his legs, propelling them deeper and deeper beneath the waves. The darkness behind his eyelids turned to pitch black, the pressure building in his head as they dove deeper still.

The siren twisted and her tail whipped hard, cutting around a corner and into the cave. Her back rippled rhythmically with the motion and Leonardo fought to hold on as they rocketed through the depths, water streaming past his face. His lungs burned, and Leonardo clenched his jaw, trying to focus on his grip as she hooked around turns.

The seconds dragged on and the blood pounded in Leonardo's head. He needed air. She must have noticed his grip falter because Leonardo felt the muscles in her shoulders twist as she glanced back at him. Then she hooked straight up, corking for the surface, and Leonardo forced himself not to breathe. Air was on the way. Red pulsed at the corners of his vision as he dug his fingers into the siren's skin.

Then she slowed down, losing momentum and delaying Leonardo's access to air. He almost let go and clawed for the surface himself, but she rotated first, throwing him off and clamping a hand over his mouth as they broke the surface.

Leonardo's first gasp was smothered by her hand, and he pulled oxygen in through his nostrils instead. She raised a finger to her lips and pointed up.

Leonardo followed her gaze, water running in his eyes as he struggled to breathe. The pirate ship loomed over them, the stern sheltering them from view. She took her hand off Leonardo's mouth and he sucked in a breath. She winced at the noise. Mishti, Sophie, and Pinch bobbed a few feet away, equally depleted.

The cave was massive, domed with gleaming walls of solid turquoise. Leonardo scanned the ceiling for any matching-coloured sea monsters waiting to drop. But he doubted the pirates would weigh anchor here if there were sea monsters.

As he caught his breath, Leonardo listened hard for any sound of the pirates. The curve of the stern hid the deck from sight, and one of the sirens drifted back enough to see the rail. She watched for a few seconds, then swam back under the curve of the stern, shaking her head. *No one there.*

Leonardo closed his eyes in relief.

*We're in.*

*Now the hard part.*

They wouldn't have the sirens' help for this. Pinch lifted a sodden coil of rope off his shoulders and swam below a decorative claw that protruded from the stern. Two levels of gold-framed windows angled up above it.

Pinch tossed the rope into the air, lasso end flailing for the claw. It missed, and the rope slithered back over the gold scrollwork. Leonardo and Pinch both grabbed for it, but it fell out of their reach, splashing into the water.

"Shit," they swore in unison.

Thaisa swam back far enough to see the railing. She watched for a second, then nodded the all-clear.

Pinch gathered the rope and took aim again. This time, he managed to hook the lasso over the decorative claw. He tugged the rope, then started up, using the knots they'd tied for purchase. Leonardo followed him, Sophie and Mishti on his heels.

Leonardo's right hand throbbed with a sharp, stabbing pain, forcing him to awkwardly climb with his left. He heaved himself over the claw, gritting his teeth, and gasped at the stab in his fingers as he accidentally put weight on his hand.

"Shhh," hissed Mishti.

*I know.* His nerves fired in time with the water running off their sodden clothes.

Pinch glanced down at them, then carefully shuffled out onto a narrow wooden ledge wrapping around the side of the ship. Leonardo followed him, muscles tight as they crept around the hull. The rigging swayed and whispered against the boards, threatening to snag a foot.

A wave rolled through the cave and the ship groaned, creaking and protesting as it tipped sideways. *Shit.* Leonardo clenched the stiff ropes, scrambling with his feet on the wet wood as it nearly pitched him off.

When it rolled back upright, Pinch used the rigging to clamber up to the next ledge, then even higher to the wooden rail that ringed the upper deck. Leonardo scrambled silently after him, trying to use only his left hand.

They stopped just below the rail, hidden from view of anyone on the boat. Leonardo glanced down as Mishti and Sophie moved into position below them.

"Ready?" he whispered.

"Hell yeah," whispered Pinch.

As one, they grabbed the rail and scrambled up and over it, onto the deck. It was empty, aside from a big wooden ship's wheel. They ducked low and shifted out of the way of Mishti and Sophie, who followed a second behind. Leonardo glanced around. Down on the main deck, a single kid stood near the rail, gazing at the turquoise tunnel that wound back to the sea.

Mishti advanced to the rail, slipping a throwing ring off her wrist. The kid twisted just as she sent it flying. It whirred toward him, airborne for a split second, then he vanished on impact. The ring flew into the water, slicing below the surface with barely a sound.

The four Lions crouched, ready for a second pirate to sound the alarm, but the deck remained silent.

"I think he's the only one," whispered Mishti.

Leonardo nodded. The pirates couldn't be expecting an ambush in this cave, especially with the two guards in the rowboat down the tunnel.

"How many more rings do you have?" he whispered.

"As many as I need," she whispered back. "The Lostwoods will return them to me."

Leonardo frowned after her as she descended the stairs to the main deck.

*Of course the woods returns them.* These girls barely had to lift a finger.

Every boot scuff and creaking board echoed in the massive chamber of the cave. The looming shadows of the rigging hung over them like giant spiderwebs, strung from the three soaring masts. A crust of salt crunched under Leonardo's fingers on the rail, and he dusted them off, gripping his sword to stop his hands from shaking.

He'd faced his share of combat in the Darkwoods, but this intrusion was something else entirely. This giant ship, cloaked in the quiet of the cave, felt unnervingly intimate. He'd infiltrated the pirates' lair, and he couldn't stop glancing over his shoulder.

Another set of twin staircases led to an angled deck in the bow, but Leonardo could see that it too was empty. Here amidships, sixteen cannons gazed out over the rails. He leaned back as they passed the main mast, gazing up the dizzying height to where heavy sails lay furled along horizontal beams.

*How do a bunch of kids sail this thing?*

From the main deck, Leonardo counted three possible options for Charley and Pompey's whereabouts. First, an old, weathered door led under the raised rear deck, an oil lamp burning on a hook alongside it. Second, a smaller door opposed it below the foredeck, and lastly, a wooden hatch led belowdecks.

"Do we split up?" asked Sophie under her breath.

"No," said Mishti.

"We stay together," agreed Leonardo.

"It has to be the hatch," whispered Pinch. "Pirates always throw prisoners in the brig."

"The 'brig' is a long way down," said Sophie. "Look how big

this ship is. There have to be decks in between, and I'd bet that's where most of them sleep."

"So, we'll tiptoe," said Pinch.

Whatever they did, Leonardo wanted to do it fast and get out of this exposed position.

"Let's try these doors first," he whispered. If the majority of them slept belowdecks, he wanted to check everywhere else first.

"I agree," whispered Sophie.

Leonardo's gaze flicked from one door to the next. *But which one?*

"It's an equal guess either way," said Mishti. She took hold of a throwing ring in each hand and started toward the door at the front of the ship. Leonardo and Pinch drew their swords, fanning out behind her. Sophie moved around Mishti and took hold of the handle.

She glanced back. "It's locked."

For a second, no one said anything. Thoughts fired through Leonardo's mind as fast as his pulse.

*If the door is locked...* that was a good sign, wasn't it? *But maybe they're all locked. Do we break it down?*

If they guessed wrong, the entire rescue was about to blow up.

"Leo," said Pinch. "Your rock."

"What?"

"Your magic rock."

"Right!" Leonardo fished in his pocket. Back when things fell apart up north, Aleksander had given Leonardo a rock which could turn into a key. Leonardo had used it twice, on two very different locks, and succeeded both times. He pulled it out now; smooth and heavy, the length of his thumb, and pure black.

Mishti and Sophie frowned at the stone. As he'd done the first two times, Leonardo tossed it in the air, watching it spin end over end. When it landed in his palm again, it wasn't a rock anymore, but a gold key. Mishti and Sophie's eyebrows jumped up.

"Where did you get that?" Mishti demanded.

"The Darkwoods," said Leonardo. He stepped past Sophie and gingerly inserted it in the lock. It fit perfectly, and the mechanism clicked when he turned it. Leonardo winced, but no sound came from the other side of the door.

Leonardo returned the key to his pocket, then he drew a breath, gripping his sword. He glanced at the other three, then swung it open. The hinges screeched and they jumped back, swords raised.

The room was lit by a hanging lamp and hundreds of fairies, most of them crowded around a small girl who stood with her hand next to a knothole in the plank wall. A boy sat against the opposite wall, near the V-shaped bow of the ship. He jumped up as they stepped inside, but the girl moved faster.

"LEO!" shouted Charley. She ran across the cabin and hugged him so hard he stumbled back a step.

"We knew you'd come," she said, jumping back. "They locked us in here and they told us we could only come out if we joined the crew but we said, 'No way' because we knew you were coming to save us even though Pompey said no one ever gets rescued from the pirates. Where is everyone else?"

"In the boats," said Leonardo. He couldn't help but grin, despite the danger they still faced. Relief coursed through him. *They're safe. We have them.*

Now they needed to get out.

"Let's go," said Mishti, ushering them through the doorway. As she passed, she leaned down and picked up something from the shadows. A second later, Leonardo realized it was a throwing ring.

*Hell.* The Cove's magic was moving faster than he could keep up with.

They flooded out onto the main deck, just as a sound echoed through the cave. A long, high note warbled through the air, otherworldly and haunting and all too familiar.

*Shit.*

Leonardo spotted her a second later, her blonde waves distinguishable in the mouth of the tunnel. *So, she wasn't banished upriver after all.*

"Adriana," said Leonardo.

Then the door on the far side of the deck swung open. A girl stepped out, drawing her sword, and Leonardo recognized her as one of the four leaders. The same skull-and-crossbones trilby hat rested atop her head, light brown hair spilling out from under it. She smiled, sharp and electric.

The pirate in the purple coat and feather hat emerged behind her. He raised his eyebrows, regarding their rescue attempt.

"I thought we told you to leave us alone," he said. *Cyrus,* Mishti had called him yesterday. And the girl was Kate.

"Apparently, you also thought we would listen," said Mishti. She pointed to the rail, "Sophie, take Pompey and Charley."

"They're not going anywhere," said Cyrus. He moved to intercept them and Mishti slid a throwing ring off her wrist.

Leonardo caught movement through the wooden hatch grate. More pirates, drawn by the noise.

Pinch sheathed his sword and drew his slingshot, eyes on the hatch. Leonardo stepped forward, levelling his sword. Kate advanced on him, her gaze fiercely alive and locked on his blade. Adrenaline dulled the pain in his hand as he placed the tip of his sword below her throat. She made no effort to stop him, a cockeyed grin on her lips.

"Let us go and no one gets hurt," said Leonardo.

"No," said Kate. Her eyes flashed playfully.

The hatch swung open behind her, and Pinch loosed a stone from his slingshot. A pirate cried out, falling back out of sight. Then Kate pushed Leonardo's sword aside. Her blade flashed at his face, and Leonardo reeled back, reversing a swing at her. Kate sprang back easily, laughing.

Leonardo stumbled, his sword slicing through the air.

He recalled Mishti's words; *they're un-vanishable.* He, as far as he knew, was very much vanishable.

Kate came at him again and Leonardo twisted, awkwardly blocking a flurry of blows. She didn't blink, gold-brown eyes glinting in the fairy light.

His mortality pulsed at the forefront of his mind. All six of them could be extinguished at the whim of these ancient kids.

*What were we thinking?*

Pinch's pebbles rattled off the deck, ricocheting in rapid-fire.

Charley and Pompey backed to the rail, the glint of steel reflecting in their wide eyes.

*We're taking too long.* The second the rest of the pirates hit the deck, it would be all over. Leonardo trapped Kate's sword and shoved her away. Kate staggered back, then regarded him appraisingly. Adrenaline or not, the pain in his hand cut through everything, stabbing relentlessly.

She grinned. "You can fight."

A few meters away, Mishti and Sophie hacked at Cyrus, blades and rings clanging as he effortlessly countered their blows. Meanwhile, Pinch's cover-fire on the hatch was losing its effectiveness as more pirates vaulted out of the hole, swords drawn.

Kate lunged, quicker than ever, and Leonardo blocked it on reaction. He gripped his sword two-handed and slashed at her, but she danced out of the way again.

*Shit.* His arms wrenched around with the momentum. He reversed another swing and she dodged it too. *Dammit.* He took a wild swing that she sidestepped easily.

He caught sight of Charley in his peripheral. She peered down the side of the ship, then said something urgent to Pompey.

*Yes,* thought Leonardo. *Jump.*

"Maybe I spoke too soon," said Kate, barely dodging a stone that Pinch loosed in her direction. She tried to sound bored, but Leonardo caught the ragged edge to her tone. She was out of breath.

He whipped his sword around and slashed straight at her.

"That's more like it," said Kate, shifting back a step. Her tone was conspiring. As if this were all some demented game.

Mishti held off Cyrus as Charley and Pompey jumped over the side of the ship and into the water. Sophie lunged at Cyrus, throwing him off balance so she and Mishti could break for the rail. Pirates now flooded freely through the hatch and Pinch backed toward the rail, his gaze flicking from Leonardo to the surge of attackers.

Kate threw her sword in the way of Leonardo's, both of them gripping their weapons two-handed. They locked blades, the edges grinding at the hilts, faces an inch apart. Her eyes flashed, alive with the thrill of battle. Sweat sheened on her skin and she grit her teeth as they fought for control.

She never took her eyes off his, as much a battle of wills as one of force. Like Aleksander. Like Mishti. Like lightning in a bottle. The moment was strangely intimate, charged with the raw, jagged electricity of the fight. It was a split second of nothing but two swords, locked in desperation.

Then Leonardo twisted his wrists and she fell forward, right into the pommel of his sword. She gasped and dropped, winded, to one knee.

Leonardo sprinted for the far rail. He glanced back to see Pinch dive over the side after Mishti, Sophie, and the kids, followed by a pack of pirates. Then Leonardo grabbed the bulwark and vaulted into the air.

He caught a flicker of teal fins below, then he hit the surface and hands yanked him under. Leonardo's body wrenched around as a siren pulled him under the boat and streaked out for the opening to the cave.

Leonardo had a brief, panicked thought that it could be Adriana. They zigzagged through the entrance passage, the siren's nails digging into his skin. Then he was thrust to the surface. Leonardo gasped for breath and twisted to see a siren he didn't recognize. Beyond her, two pirate kids rowed their two-man boat toward the main cave. They faltered at the sight of Leonardo, and one started shouting.

"Take a deep breath," said the siren.

Then they plunged back underwater.

# CHAPTER 23

Charley, Pompey, Mishti, Sophie, and Pinch bobbed in the waves when Leonardo burst through the surface. He coughed, pulling in fresh air and choking on salt as he took stock of their soaked faces, their hair hanging dark and heavy. The sirens tread water around them, attention focused on the mouth of the cave.

"Where's Adriana?" demanded Leonardo.

"She fled," said Thaisa. "We will hunt her down and return her to exile."

"Meaning," said Mishti, her breath ragged, "you never exiled her to begin with."

"Excuse me?"

"Don't play dumb." Mishti twisted in the water to face Thaisa. "You've always had a soft spot for her."

"Watch your tone," snapped Thaisa.

Mishti pursed her lips, then she glanced at Leonardo and the others, who'd all fallen silent.

Leonardo had a sudden memory of the first night his clan arrived in the Cove. The way Mishti had spoken about the sirens, he would've guessed things were tense, to say the least.

Maybe their relationship wasn't as steady as it appeared.

"The pirates are coming," said Mishti, coughing and spitting out more saltwater. "We need to get back to the boats."

"A lot of them jumped overboard," said Thaisa. "It will take them time to get back on the ship."

"They won't wait," said Leonardo. He recalled the pirates leaving Lion Clan's camp after they kidnapped Charley and Pompey. They hadn't hesitated, even though crew members were still onshore.

"Let's go," said Mishti. "Take us to the boats, then you can find Adriana and exile her for good."

Thaisa nodded, curt and icy. Leonardo and the others took hold of the sirens' shoulders, and without another word, the sirens snapped their fins and started back for shore.

***

They sloshed into the boats, wet and bruised, to the relief of the Lions they'd left behind.

"I told you we'd get them back," said Leonardo, as Viola hugged Charley.

"They didn't hurt us," Charley assured them. "They were actually really nice. They told us we could join the crew, but we said, 'No way!' because we knew you'd come and save us."

"Right," Leonardo scanned the river behind them.

"You brought Lion!" said Charley, scrambling over benches to reach the basket.

Moth smiled, watching her. Pinch rolled his eyes.

"We need to go upriver," said Mishti.

"What?" asked one of the girls.

"Their ship is too big to chase us inland," said Leonardo. "It's a good idea."

"This island is massive," said Moth. "It could take all night to find another river to the sea."

"*If* we even find one," said Puck. "There's just as much chance we'll get lost in the jungle."

"We didn't get away clean," said Leonardo. "The pirates are hunting us now. If we don't go upriver—"

"We'll all be captured," finished Sophie.

"And if we don't move now, that will happen anyway," said Mishti.

Leonardo nodded. "Nym, back in the boat. Oars down. Double-time."

Nym yanked the knot loose and threw the line into the bow as the rowers dipped their oars into the water. Nym jumped in and moved to his bench, studying his hands. He frowned, examining something closer, and a spark of fear jumped in Leonardo's chest. But just as quickly, Nym disregarded whatever he'd seen, and Leonardo released his breath.

"Point watch, to your post," he ordered Pinch.

Pinch, still sodden from the swim, clambered to his bench and jammed his hat on his head. He settled into his point-watchman's position, scanning the river ahead. Leonardo wanted eyes on the first possible hint of danger in the dark jungle awaiting them.

They rowed upriver, through the cleft in the cliffs and into the interior jungle that covered the island. Leonardo peered through the shadows along the riverbanks, between tree trunks and dense bushes. It was like being back in the Darkwoods again, except the sounds were different. The frogs were louder, the birdcall strange, and the buzzing of insects more incessant than ever. They swarmed in the muggy warmth of the night, clouding over the boat. The biting ones were the worst—mosquitoes and some sort of tiny red flies, apparently desperate for blood. He swatted them with one hand while gripping the rudder with the other.

That hand on the rudder throbbed with a pain that was becoming harder and harder to ignore. Leonardo finally started to ask Juliet if she had anything left to numb the pain when a swarm of fairies flew around the river bend ahead. They streaked toward the boats, glowing like firelight, and stopped directly over the Lions. A hundred fairies paralleled the boat's movement, the air filled with the high-pitched whir of their wings.

The Lions gazed up at them, and Moth closed his eyes, tilting his head to listen.

"Pirates," he said, after a second. "They're saying *pirates,* again."

*Dammit.* Leonardo turned in a circle, scanning the river.

"Viola?" he asked. "Can you see anything?"

She shook her head, eyes squeezed shut in concentration. "Nothing."

He tightened his lips. "Moth? Are the fairies saying anything else?"

"Just 'pirates'," said Moth.

"The fairies came from ahead," said Puck. "There's no way the pirates could have sailed all the way around to the other side of the island already, is there?"

Just then, a turquoise tail and blonde hair shot past below the surface. Leonardo turned to watch her streak downriver, then flip around and race back under the boats and ahead of them.

"If the sirens can do it..." said one of Lion girls.

*Not the sirens,* thought Leonardo. *Just one.*

And now he knew the pirates were upriver, as impossible as it seemed.

"Do we turn back?" asked Sophie.

Before anyone could answer, an icy wind gusted behind them.

Leonardo ducked, twisting and squinting into a second gust, even stronger than the first. His clothes snapped in the wind and he watched in horror as the leaves tore off branches, filling the air with green confetti. He'd seen this before.

"Forward!" shouted Leonardo. "Now!"

Mishti whipped around from the captain's platform of her boat. "The pirates," she shouted.

"It doesn't matter," he yelled back. His own Lions knew what came with a wind like this, and they gripped their oars, digging into the water.

"Row!" Leonardo shouted at Mishti's crew. "Trust me!"

Mishti swore and grabbed the rudder. "Go! You heard him!"

The wind blasted harder, howling through the treetops. Palm fronds ripped free and took to the sky like giant birds. The trees and bushes downriver now stood as bare as winter, and thousands of leaves pelted the Lions, fighting to row in the gale-force winds.

Around the next bend, they burst into a lagoon, and Leonardo's blood froze. Every tree along the edge stood dead and blackened. Crocodile skulls hung from the branches of every third or fourth tree, and a small island rose in the middle of the lagoon, made of what Leonardo quickly realized were bones. A full crocodile skeleton lay across the pile, a blackened stripe running down the centre of its skull.

"Oh fuck," said Pinch. "Oh—"

"What the hell...?" said Mishti.

"My hands," shouted Nym. Black lines streaked his veins, and he dove to the edge of the boat and plunged them underwater. He cried out and yanked them back as if burnt, stumbling backward into Bates.

"Everyone, calm down!" shouted Leonardo. His own heart pounded so hard it hurt, and every hair on his body stood on end. They'd made a terrible mistake.

"Hard turn. Left rowers up." He yanked the rudder and gasped at the pain in his own hand. He grabbed the rudder with his other hand, twisting to see over the stern.

The mouth of the river was gone. The bank of the lagoon curved, unbroken, as if the river had never been there. A crocodile skull hung from a tree, hollow eyes watching him, where the river should've been. The frothed wake of the boats tapered to the edge of the bank.

"We're trapped," said Moth.

"Fuck," said Mishti.

"There's another river," said Pinch.

He pointed across the lagoon, where a second, wider river opened on the far side of the bone island.

Then the bow of a ship plowed through the opening as the pirates sailed into the lagoon, black sails billowing in the wind.

*Shit.*

Pirates rushed to the rails, gazing around at the macabre skull-filled lagoon. Kate, Cyrus, and the short, chubby, younger pirate Mishti called Pip all stood at the prow. Leonardo looked past them to where the wider river opening used to be and swore. *Used to be,* because, just like the one his own clan had sailed through, the pirates' river was gone.

The lagoon was now a perfect circle, without a single escape route for the three boats trapped inside it.

Then the wind died.

# CHAPTER 24

Silence stretched over the lagoon. The atmosphere shifted as swords slid out of belts on all three boats. But no one looked at the others. Pirate or Lion, all the kids on the water had just become prey of the same enemy.

The sky grew dark and the water dead calm. The shadows lengthened, and the temperature dropped to something frigid. The frogs in the weeds fell silent and the fairies scattered, vanishing into the trees.

"We need to get to shore," said Viola. "This is what happened when the Dark attacked my people's camp. If we stay out here..." She trailed off.

None of them knew what would happen if the Dark caught them. The only person who'd ever been touched by it was Nym, and the condition of his hands didn't bode well for the outcome.

"It attacked me *onshore*," said Nym. His voice was tight with grim focus. "We won't be safe there either."

Leonardo eyed the banks, evenly spaced with crocodile skulls. *Then where* are *we safe?*

"What is this?" called Cyrus from the bow of the pirate ship.

"The Dark," said a voice Leonardo hadn't heard since leaving Raven Clan.

Viola gasped as a dozen canoes materialized on the water, filled with Native warriors.

"Dakota!" said Viola.

At the front of his canoe, Dakota didn't even glance at her. Instead, he rose to his feet, drawing an arrow from his quiver and fitting it to his longbow. His gaze lay fixed on a point across the lagoon, and Leonardo followed it as a shadow suddenly detached from the darkness and came flying over the water.

It looked vaguely human, with long limbs swinging as it charged the boats. Dakota loosed his arrow and it shot straight through the shadow's heart. The shadow jerked, dissipating into smoke. The arrow continued unhindered and slipped underwater.

"More are coming," said Dakota, turning to Viola. His tone was far less hostile than the last time they'd spoken. "We have much to discuss. But we must survive to discuss it."

He looked at Leonardo as he said the last part, and Leonardo nodded.

"Lion Clan." Leonardo turned to his crew. "Form a circle. Nothing gets over the sides of the boat."

"Bring them on," said Puck.

"Pompey, Charley, no heroics," said Mishti. "Stay out of the way and—"

"Don't stop firing slingshots until it's over," finished Leonardo. "We need everyone fighting."

Mishti opened her mouth to argue, but before she could, two more shadows came flying out of the trees.

"Get ready!" shouted Leonardo.

Dakota and one of his warriors loosed arrows and took down the two shadows, just as three more broke from the other side of the lagoon.

The Lions on both longboats scrambled to drag out the baskets of pebbles and fit stones into their slingshots. Leonardo, Puck, and everyone else, including the pirates, gripped their swords and prepared for the first shadows that slipped through the defences.

A bang shattered the air as a row of cannons opened fire from the side of the ship.

Mishti returned her throwing rings to her wrists and drew her boomerang. She stepped across the benches as a pack of shadows materialized from the trees and charged the boats.

She eyed the oncoming mass and hurled the weapon hard into the air. It hooked out over the water and sliced through the shadows, leaving a trail of smoke in its wake. Every slingshot pebble and cannonball that found its mark sent up another cloud, and when one of the shadows took a running leap for the pirate ship, Kate handled it with a slash of her sword.

Leonardo turned in a circle, watching the ranks of shadows destroyed under the fire of arrows, slingshots, and Mishti's boomerang. It was a strange battle. Only one side made any noise. Even when a rock or an arrow hit a shadow, it simply dissipated, silent as a ghost.

The air filled with the rapid breaths of the living, the snap of arrow strings, and the soft whisk of slingshots. One shadow managed to break through the defences, hurtling straight for

Leonardo. Horror jumped in his throat as he sliced through it, sword gripped awkwardly in his left hand. The smoke wisped around him, hot and gritty like sandpaper.

*Holy hell.*

Another streaked in from his right side and he whirled around, shutting his eyes in a mixture of terror and pain as it dissipated, scraping over his skin but leaving him unharmed.

*This is too easy,* he thought. He'd seen what the Dark could do; seen the carnage it left behind. If this was the best it could throw at them—

A boom shook the jungle. The impact threw Leonardo against the boat's stem, and Lions stumbled together between the benches. An icy wind whipped through the lagoon, shredding the last of the shadows into long ribbons.

Leonardo hunched against the force of the wind. Everyone he loved crouched around him, and Leonardo stared down the barrel of a hard truth. Every one of them could be swallowed by the dark in the next few seconds, and he couldn't do anything about it.

One of the shadow ribbons streaked over the surface and hair-pinned toward Leonardo. He spun his sword around and barely managed to intercept the attack.

The shadow split on the blade and one of the ribbons curled around his left forearm. Leonardo gasped, grabbing at it. It burned like a strip of fire until he clamped his hand over it. Then electricity shot through his arm.

White-hot pain jolted through his sea monster bite, writhing like a living thing as it pressed against the dark band on his arm. His fingers curled against his will, digging so hard into his skin that a line of blood ran out from under his fingernails.

The other Lions cried out as black ribbons snaked around them. Up on the pirate ship, swords flashed in a desperate battle with the wind and the terrors waving through it. Cannons boomed in a chaotic barrage, but even they were too slow, and Leonardo flinched at the screams through the portholes.

"Shit!" shouted Bates. "Nym, what are you—holy shit."

"I can't control them!" yelled Nym, as he made a violent grab for Bates's throat. Black veins covered his arms all the way to the elbow, and his fingers opened and shut like something possessed, clawing for his clanmates as they scrambled out of the way.

Leonardo pried his own fingers from the burning shadow on his arm, leaving dark bruises and open scratches. He grabbed a shield from the footwell and ran over the benches at Nym, using it to shove him back as Nym grabbed for Puck.

"I can't stop!" cried Nym.

"Try!" shouted Leonardo, bashing him in the forearms with his shield. Nym staggered back, then lunged at Leonardo again.

"I am trying!"

"Try harder!" Leonardo bashed him again.

A shadow ribbon flew at his head and Leonardo ducked. It snaked past and Viola screamed. Leonardo whipped around as it coiled up her entire arm.

Then Nym came at him again, lunging over his shield. Leonardo grabbed his wrist with his wounded hand, stopping Nym inches from his throat. Another jolt of electricity shot through his fingers and his grip fused to Nym's skin. Nym clawed for him with his other hand and Leonardo threw his shield in the way, beating his fist back while Nym punched the hardened wood.

Their connected arms vibrated, muscles clenched tight with the searing current that coursed through them.

Viola struggled in the meantime, fighting the shadow ribbon on her own arm. She rubbed and scratched at it as Leonardo fought to get to her.

Nym gasped, teeth clenched as his fist continued to pound against the shield. Finally, Pinch grabbed him from behind and yanked him back in a chokehold, ripping his arm out of Leonardo's electrified grip.

While Nym was off-balance, Bates swung a shield around and bashed him in the head, dropping him unconscious. Pinch stepped back, breathing heavy. Then his expression turned to horror as Nym's arms kept clawing. One blacked hand grabbed a bench and pulled him up, head lolling and legs dragging.

Leonardo, Pinch and Bates scrambled back.

"Tie him up!" shouted Leonardo, as Pinch dove for a rope.

"Leo!" yelled Viola. "Look out!"

Her fingers jerked open and her arm lunged for him. Leonardo grabbed her hand, their fingers locking together as he forced her back. A strength she didn't own pushed back against him, black veins spiderwebbing from the black burn on her arm.

Just like when he grabbed his own arm and Nym's, electricity crackled where their palms touched. Their arms shook.

Viola grabbed at her blackened arm and flinched back.

Chaos reigned around them. There was no fighting the fragmented shadows, only suffering at their touch. The crocodile skulls watched from the perimeter as kids and Natives alike fell under the attack.

*The skulls.* Leonardo squinted at the white bone, burnt with stripes of black. Just like the ones attacking them.

"Dakota!" he yelled, still wrestling with Viola's arm. "Shoot the skulls!"

He pointed to the bank and Dakota frowned. Then he whipped an arrow onto his bowstring and fired it over the water. It slammed between the eyes of the crocodile skull. For a second, nothing happened, then the skull cracked, with a shattering sound far louder than it should've been. Another crack split the bone, and another, until the whole thing suddenly exploded into smoke.

Dakota immediately fitted another arrow and loosed it at the next skull, shouting at his men to do the same. Bowstrings snapped, and in a matter of seconds, every skull around the lagoon was under arrow fire. Seconds after that, every skull cracked, in a booming, splintering, explosion of dust.

Except for one.

The Natives turned their fire on the full crocodile skeleton atop the island of bones. Arrows slammed into every inch of the tiny island, bristling along the skeleton's back. The scraps of shadow retreated from the boats, swirling hard and fast around the pile of bones.

Still, the Natives kept shooting, and the Lions added slingshot fire to the attack. But nothing happened. The shadows spun faster and faster, Nym kept clawing, and Viola continued to wrestle with Leonardo. Lions on both boats held down their clanmates, swearing and grabbing for throats.

The arrows weren't enough. He looked to the ship, but all the cannons had gone quiet.

Dread settled in Leonardo's chest as the shadows spun into a wall of blackness, then he caught Mishti moving. She walked across the benches of her boat, sidestepping the clawing hands of her fallen clanmates. Just before she reached the bow, Mishti lifted a ring up over her shoulder and brought it down as hard as she could, sending it spinning toward the arrow-covered skeleton.

In one motion, she hurled her last two rings after it. For a split second, all three rings were airborne, then the first hit. It split the skull in two, with a boom that nearly threw Leonardo off his feet. The following impact was more of a feeling than a sound. The other two rings struck in rapid succession, and the next thing Leonardo knew, he was flying backward, his knee struck the bulwark, then he slammed underwater.

# CHAPTER 25

Leonardo kicked and broke the surface, blinking through a cloud of smoke. Other shapes burst through the water around him. A few feet away, Viola's head of dark hair surfaced. She swam for the boat, rocking in the water, and Leonardo stroked after her.

Lions, Natives, and pirates pulled themselves up over the sides of their boats, grunting and sloshing and calling out to one another. Leonardo straightened in his boat and walked across the benches, squinting through the smoke. As it dissipated, he saw that the island of bones was gone. Every trace of the Dark had vanished, and as if to put a mark of finality on it, hundreds of fairy lights approached through the smoke, pushing back the night.

"Do you believe us now?" asked Leonardo, returning to his captain's platform as Mishti climbed to hers.

"Whatever that was," said Mishti, "I've never seen anything like it. I was stupid not to listen to you."

The kids across both boats struggled back to their benches, tentatively squeezing and unsqueezing their fingers. They'd regained control of their limbs, but the Dark had left its mark. Black bands encircled wrists, arms, hands. Dark veins branched outward from the marks, minimal in some cases and extreme in others. Only a few tendrils extended from Viola's coiled mark, while Nym's arms were almost completely consumed by it. Leonardo eyed his own tightly wrapped shadow ribbon. It encircled his left forearm, halfway between his elbow and wrist. It was the mildest of everyone's, with not a single dark vein extending from it.

"We have much to discuss," said Dakota. His voice carried easily over the water. "Come back to our camp. It is safe there."

He directed this to all parties present, including the pirates. The silence hung for a moment, but no one protested. And after what they'd just experienced, the conflict between pirates and Lions seemed trivial.

The two river openings were once again visible, and the Natives began to paddle for the one the pirates had first emerged through.

"Where did you come from?" called one of the Lion girls, a shade of skepticism in her voice. "How did you know we were in trouble?"

"We are the guardians of the woods," replied Dakota, still standing. "We see what we need to."

Leonardo met the eyes of his crew, shaken and breathing heavy. Solemn fear reflected in Viola's dark eyes, and even Pinch's typical aloofness was non-existent for the moment.

He glanced at Mishti and she ran her hands through her black hair. She was one of the few untouched by the Dark. She looked up at the night sky, searching for something that she clearly didn't find. When she brought her gaze back to earth, she looked uncertain.

"Oars down," said Leonardo.

The two longboats followed the Native canoes to the mouth of the river, followed close behind by the pirate ship.

*The fight is changing,* thought Leonardo. He was half-afraid to find out what that meant.

# CHAPTER 26

Vibrant, green jungle foliage pressed in around the camp, and Leonardo had never been happier to see leaves. The cold, dead, blackness of anything touched by the Dark left a bleak and bitter taste in his mouth. This lush clearing, nestled with glowing tipis and campfires, felt like another world entirely.

Even after they'd destroyed the skulls, the lagoon remained lifeless. Seeing the blackened trees and earth, Leonardo wondered if anything would ever grow there again.

"So that was the Dark," said Mishti.

Leonardo nodded. "That's the worst we've ever seen it."

They stooped through the folded opening of Tokala's tipi, followed by Viola and the four pirate leaders. Firelight danced over the circular shell of animal skins. Leonardo recognized it from his first and only visit, back in the Darkwoods.

"It gets stronger every day," said Chief Tokala.

Leonardo had mixed feelings, sitting before the old man. The last time he'd seen Tokala, the Native Chief had condemned Aleksander and triggered his disappearance. Leonardo now knew it was Aleksander who first let in the Dark—albeit unintentionally—through his refusal to grow up. Sending him away had been for the good of the woods, but none the less, a bitterness rose inside Leonardo as Tokala settled into his spot behind the fire.

"Wait," said Kate, the pirate girl. "You mean it's not dead? It's coming back?"

"We discovered a weakness today," said Tokala. "But I trust it will find a way to remedy that problem. The next fight will be much harder."

"Shit," said the young, chubby one. Pip.

"That boy in your clan," said Tokala, "with the quick eyes. The Dark's hold on him is much deeper."

"You mean Nym?" asked Leonardo. He pulled his lips tight, recalling the black spiderwebs up his arms.

"His affliction lies so far beneath the skin we cannot even see it unless the Dark is present. I wonder if it sleeps when the Dark is hiding, or if it continues to grow inside of him."

The fire hissed and popped, carrying on its own sinister conversation in the heavy silence that followed Tokala's words.

"What is it doing here?" asked Mishti. Her voice lacked the snap she typically spoke with, and Leonardo frowned, studying her. He'd never seen someone look so ill-fitted in their skin.

"It's here to attack," said Tokala. He placed his willow cane across the blankets beside him. He hadn't needed one up north. "It came in through the Darkwoods, and now its heart lies here."

"Its heart?" asked Kate. The space inside the tipi was tight, but the four pirates placed themselves distinctly apart from Leonardo, Mishti, and Viola.

"It's everywhere," said Viola. "It can reach all four corners of the woods, but if we can kill the heart—"

"That's enough, Viola," said Dakota.

Leonardo twisted as he stooped into the tipi, a heavy, bone-handled knife wedged in his belt. Viola crossed her arms.

"Dakota," said Tokala. "Please tend to our other guests, out in the clearing."

Dakota held Tokala's gaze for a long moment, then he nodded. "Yes, Chief."

He backed out of the tipi and crossed crisply to the mob of kids slumped on the ground, just visible from where Leonardo sat. He'd left Pinch and Puck in charge, and both boys' attention was fixed unwaveringly on the group of pirates a few feet away.

"We followed the heart here," said Tokala. His voice crackled, drier than the fire. "It has been hiding, but I fear it will not need to for much longer."

"And then what?" asked Mishti. "It'll destroy the Cove?"

Tokala nodded slowly.

"Unless we stop it," said the fourth pirate leader, the one without a hat. His linen shirt hung off-kilter, his blonde hair dishevelled. John, Mishti had called him.

Tokala inclined his head, slowly. "Correct."

"Then how do we stop it?" asked John.

"We do not know. This is beyond my power."

Leonardo tilted his head, studying the old man. Deep wrinkles etched the years into his face. "Viola said Aleksander caused—"

"You children should take care how freely you speak," Tokala interrupted him. His dark eyes flicked to Viola, then back to Leonardo. "Certain things should not be learned."

"What does that mean?" asked Mishti.

Viola frowned, and Leonardo tried to read the words Tokala didn't say.

*Certain things should not be learned. Like Aleksander letting the Dark in?*

"The woods help us by providing signs," said Tokala. He eyed Leonardo as he said this. "We must solve them."

"Like what?" asked Cyrus, tipping back his elaborate hat.

"Lions," said Leonardo, thinking. "And Viola. And Charley, and Pompey."

"Correct," said Tokala. "And what do they mean?"

"That we're supposed to come together," said Viola, the same as she'd been saying for days.

Leonardo nodded. He saw it clearly now. "When the woods brought you here, Viola was left behind because I already knew her, and the woods knew we'd accept her into our clan. She was supposed to lead us back to you. Then we found Charley and Lion Clan found Pompey. A girl with the boys and a boy with the girls. That was the first sign we were supposed to merge."

"Plus, all the lion signs," said Moth. "The woods *were* telling us to come south and join Lion Clan."

"I think so," said Tokala. "The Dark is not from this place. If we stand together, we can push it out."

"We'll need a lot more ammo," said Pip, running a thumb over his dimpled chin.

"Weapons will not kill it," said Tokala. "We can fend off attacks with swords and arrows, but the only way to truly banish it will require something more powerful."

"Like what?" asked Cyrus.

Tokala turned his slow gaze on Mishti. He regarded her a long moment, and Mishti furrowed her brow, what was left of her smudged bindi dot wrinkling. Finally, he cleared his throat. "Will you excuse us a moment?"

"Pardon me?"

"Some things should not be learned by certain people."

"And I'm one of those?"

"Yes,." Tokala said it flatly, matter-of-fact.

"Only me."

Tokala sighed, heavy and tired. The firelight danced in his old eyes.

"Mishti…" started Leonardo. He had no idea how to finish it.

"So you get to stay, but I don't?" Mishti turned on the blanketed floor to face him. "Not gonna happen."

"Grow up, Mishti," snapped Pip. "The entire world doesn't centre around you."

Mishti levelled a glare at him.

"I will ask you again," repeated Tokala. "Will you excuse us a moment?"

"Fine. Whatever you want." Mishti shoved herself up and stormed out of the tipi.

Tokala watched her go, stoking the fire with a stick. He tossed it into the flames and regarded the six still in the tent.

"The Dark came through a tear in the fabric of this world. Every time a child learns they are dreaming, a little more of the world beyond can find its way in."

*If a dreamer knows he's dreaming, he wakes up,* thought Leonardo. This wasn't a typical dream—more like the place where dreams came from—but it wasn't outrageous to think that its integrity could've been damaged by their awareness of it.

Viola blanched. "Are you saying that when I told Leonardo…and all of them…Oh no."

"What has happened, has happened," said Tokala. "You did what you thought was right at the time."

"What about them?" asked Leonardo, glancing at the pirates. They looked bizarrely out of place in the tipi, all plumes and hats and coloured coats.

John laughed. "We've been here since the woods were first dreamed into existence. Yes, we know it's made of imagination. It's too late for any of us, or you, to unlearn what this place is."

"The fabric has been torn already," said Tokala. "You have all come to terms with the truth, and thus cannot tear it further."

"But if we stop more kids—like Mishti—from learning," said Viola. "Will that seal the hole?"

Tokala shook his head. "I am afraid not. But it will stop more of the Dark from coming in. The larger the tear, the stronger it gets."

Leonardo followed the sewn seams of the tipi up to the peak, where the heavy poles met and smoke escaped through a tiny opening.

"Then how *do* we stop it?" asked Cyrus. "Is there any way to seal the hole?"

"More imagination," said Leonardo. They all looked at him.

"Right?" he pressed Tokala. "Enough concentrated imagination should be able to close the tear."

"It is possible," said Tokala.

"So we need to unite every clan in the Cove," said Leonardo.

Pip barked a laugh. "Oops. I guess we die."

"He's right," said John. "Leonardo I mean, not Pip."

"You're an idiot, John," said Pip, chubby arms crossed. "It's never going to happen."

"Do you want the sea monsters, too?" asked Cyrus. He leaned back on his hands. "How about Demetrius's blue dragons?"

"What about everyone up north?" said Kate. "In the Darkwoods, the Redwoods, the Highland?"

"Exactly," said Pip. "It's impossible."

"That was a serious question," said Kate.

"Oh look," mused Cyrus. "Kate is being serious for the first time ever! We should make a cake."

Leonardo glanced at Viola. Her expression reflected his own thoughts. *This is hopeless.*

Then John stood up, the firelight reflecting on the tips of his boots.

"Ignore these two. I've been here this long; I don't plan on a bunch of shadows taking me out. If you'll accept our apology for kidnapping your kids, we would be honoured to help you unite the Cove."

"And the rest of the woods," added Kate.

Cyrus and Pip looked at each other, then burst out laughing.

"Sit down, John," said Pip.

"Actually, no," said Cyrus. "Let's do it. I look forward to laughing in your face when it fails."

"We'll be dead if we fail," said John.

"Then I'll see whatever is beyond these bloody woods."

Chief Tokala watched all of this through hooded eyes.

John extended a hand to Leonardo. "Will you work with us?"

Leonardo glanced at Viola, then Tokala. They looked so similar that he lost his place for a second. He'd forgotten Viola was Tokala's granddaughter. They both gave the slightest of nods, their faces glowing in the light of the tipi, and Leonardo accepted John's outstretched hand.

"You must go," said Tokala. "All of you. Leave this island and gather all the clans while the Dark still tends to its wounds. Together we will face what awaits us."

***

"You're joking," said Mishti.

They stood on the edge of the clearing, Tokala leaning on his willow cane as Leonardo and the pirate leaders explained the plan, avoiding any details about the dreamworld.

"You saw the Dark," said Leonardo. "The next time it attacks, we won't stand a chance alone."

Lions and pirates alike glanced at the black burns on their skin. Black veins spiderwebbed up Nym's arms, although he appeared to have regained temporary control of them. Mishti was the only one without a single blemish.

"I agree," said Nym, stepping forward. "We need all the help we can get. Chief, did you give Leo some sort of power during the fight? He grabbed my arm, and it felt like…"

*Electricity.* Leonardo hadn't forgotten.

Tokala shook his head. "You were attacked by sea monsters earlier today." He pointed to Leonardo's hand. "That was never treated. The venom is in your blood now. When you grabbed the Dark mark on your arm, the venom stopped the Dark from spreading, and the Dark cauterized the wound on your hand."

"How do you know all that?" asked Mishti. Suspicion salted her tone.

"We are the guardians of the woods," repeated Dakota, just as haughtily. "We can see things you cannot."

A breeze stirred the trees around the clearing, causing everyone to glance up. Fear sparked in Leonardo's nerves, but the leaves stilled and the cooking fires continued to crackle. A few of the other natives paused while crossing the clearing, then resumed their tasks, casting glances at the kids.

"Sea monsters are one of the purest creatures of this place," said Tokala, drawing a long white tooth from the folds of his robe. "They exist nowhere but here. Because of that, their venom has a stronger effect on the Dark than almost anything else."

Leonardo turned over his hand, eyeing the black puncture marks along his skin. He realized the wound no longer hurt. And he'd grabbed Viola's hand and Nym's arm with the same sea-monster-bitten hand, which could explain why Viola's mark hadn't veined out as bad as the others.

"What about you?" Sophie asked Mishti. "You weren't bitten, were you?"

Mishti turned, lifting her hair. Everyone paused, staring at a circular bite on the back of her neck. Every puncture mark was black, and it looked as fresh as the one on Leonardo's hand.

"Why didn't you tell me?" demanded Juliet. "I could've treated you!"

"Getting the clan to safety was more important," said Mishti.

"Damn," said Pinch, grimacing at the bite as he rubbed the back of his own neck.

"Let her treat it once you return to your fortress," said Chief Tokala. He closed his weathered fingers around the tooth. "You will be an important piece in the fight to come. And you as well," he added to Leonardo. "I commend you for making the right choice and coming south."

"Good," said Dakota. "Viola, you'll be staying with us now. Everyone else—"

"What?" said Viola.

"You've returned to us," said Dakota. "Don't tell me you planned to stay with them?"

"I..." Viola hesitated, gazing from her tribe to her clan.

"Viola," said Tokala. "You have been touched by the Dark, my child. And... something strange..." he frowned, his gaze shifting to her shorter left braid, the tip lopped off by Caliban. "You have a gift of sight, yes? You can see things happening which you should not be able to."

Viola nodded.

"It has been strained," said Tokala. "You looked too far."

*Snake Clan. The favour.*

"You must stay so I can rid you of the Dark and this strange magic."

Viola looked at Leonardo, her brown eyes torn.

"It's ok," said Leonardo.

*These are her people.* He should've realized she would return to them at some point. He hadn't expected it to be so soon, but if they could remove the Dark from her, prevent her from becoming like Nym...If they could heal what Snake Clan did...

"You have to stay," said Leonardo. "We'll be back soon. We'll all fight together when the Dark comes again.

Viola shook her head, her eyes darting from Leonardo to Tokala and Dakota.

"It is not your choice, my child," said Tokala gently. "You belong with your people. And you must be healed. A dark magic is still inside you."

"But…" Viola bit her lip, hard.

"We'll be back soon," repeated Leonardo, forcing down the razor-sharp emotion that pierced his chest. If she needed healing, he wanted her to stay and be healed. But Tokala's other words twisted his stomach; *You belong with your people.*

"Now go," said Tokala. "The Dark does not wait."

Leonardo nodded, crisp and curt. He started to turn away, then twisted back as Viola called his name. She took two strides and hugged him, hard and purposeful. Leonardo breathed in the smell of her, the familiar silk of her hair pressed against his cheek.

"Be careful," she said into his shirt.

"I will," he said, stepping back. She squeezed his fingers.

She was the one staying on an island with the Dark. *Stay away from it,* he wanted to tell her. *Don't leave your camp.* But that was impossible. Everyone was in danger, everywhere. The only way to save them would be to do as the chief said.

Next to Leonardo, Charley blinked hard, swallowing as Viola stooped and hugged her. "We'll meet again soon," she promised.

Leonardo turned and led the way back through the trees. Those words would have to ring true if they wanted to survive this.

# CHAPTER 27

Strato was gone. Robin was gone. Viola was back with her people. Leonardo's clan had grown smaller again. But with every member they lost, they gained strangers in the dozens.

Forty-one Lions and fifty pirates crowded the decks of the pirate ship, *The Forever*, full sails carrying them across open water with the two longboats strung on ropes behind them. They'd left the island for the high seas, putting as many miles as possible between themselves and the Dark. Tomorrow, in daylight, they would sail back and attempt to convince Dragon Clan to join the fight.

"Do you really think they've been here since the beginning?" asked Leonardo.

"That's what the stories say," said Juliet.

Leonardo had earned a healthy dose of skepticism about clan 'stories' since arriving in the Cove.

"Who tells these stories?" asked Moth. He yawned, covering his mouth with a fist. Cuts and bruises covered his hands, normally soft and dimpled.

"Everyone," said Juliet. She shook her curls off her face, squinting out to sea. Darkness smothered their visibility a few meters from the rail. "The Lions who were here when I first arrived knew them, and those kids are all old and disappeared now."

In the swinging lantern light, one of the shadow ribbons traced the edge of her neck, stopping precisely where her hummingbird feather lay on its string.

"So?" said Pinch. "According to the *stories* up north, you're all boys. And you don't exist anymore."

"Shut up, Pinch," said Moth automatically, but Leonardo could tell his thoughts were turning.

"I have a theory about that if you want to hear it," said Juliet.

"About how to shut Pinch up?" Moth asked, in the same auto-fire. "Sorry," he amended.

"What's your theory?" asked Leonardo.

"Well," started Juliet. "The Lostwoods play favourites. We know that."

"Mishti said you only earn favour because you're so..." Leonardo searched for the word.

"Devout?"

"Yes. She said any clan could be the same."

"Maybe that's true," said Juliet. "Or maybe not. But no matter what the reason, it's clear to me that the Lostwoods like us more than most clans."

This statement should have sounded conceited, but Juliet's tone was purely academic.

"So," she continued. "It seems to me that if the Lostwoods is playing favourites, it would have an interest in keeping us safe."

"Naturally," said Moth. He scratched his chin, brown eyes deep in thought.

Leonardo began to catch on. "And if the clans in the rest of the woods knew about your fortress, they might try to take it."

"Exactly," said Juliet. "Especially if they knew that we're girls."

"The Darkwoods would be a ghost town if those halfwits knew there were girls down here," said Pinch.

Juliet glanced around, then lowered her voice. "Mishti relies too much on the Lostwoods for protection. We're not helpless, but we wouldn't survive a real war."

Leonardo tilted his head. He'd had the same thoughts about Mishti's clan, but it was different hearing it directly from Juliet.

"So, what is your theory?" he asked. "The woods wiped the memories of all the parties that used to travel south?"

"Not wiped," said Kate, walking up behind them. Lantern light cast her face in an eerie glow. "Altered "

Leonardo and Pinch reached for their swords on instinct.

"Relax," said Kate. "We're a team now, remember. Although you owe me a round two," she said to Leonardo, with a wink.

Moth and Juliet frowned.

"You already fought him once," said Pinch. He rolled the pommel of his sword, chest puffed. "Name a time and place."

"Aren't you the slingshot boy?" asked Kate.

Pinch stopped, affronted.

"Yes, ma'am," said Moth, beaming with dark joy. "Slingshot. Boy."

"I fight with a sword too," said Pinch.

Kate tilted her head, contemplating him. "Nah," she said after a beat. "Boring. Anyway, you're right; the woods—or 'Lostwoods', as you Cove-dwellers call it—alter the memories of any outsiders who visit. And it's not just the Cove; no one from any corner of the woods knows exactly what's going on in any other corner. There are girls in the Redwoods too—I bet you didn't know that."

"How do you know all this?" asked Leonardo.

"When you've been around forever, you learn a few things," said Kate. "Like this."

She took off her hat, and suddenly it wasn't Kate, but Cyrus standing before them.

"What the..." said Pinch.

Cyrus bowed, placing his hat back on his head. Now it was the one with the giant feather plume.

"Don't worry, you'll learn to tell the difference when I impersonate your friends. I'm afraid I'm not a very good actor."

Neither Leonardo, Moth, Pinch, or Juliet responded immediately. Cyrus laughed. He pointed at Leonardo. "She does want to fight you again though. She doesn't lose often, our Kate. It seems she's fascinated with the fact that she did."

He chuckled again, then spun on his heel and strode away. As he crossed the deck, Kate emerged from the stern door between the wooden staircases, flooding the deck with light. Cyrus said something to her and pointed over his shoulder at Leonardo's party.

Kate drew her sword faster than Leonardo could blink. Cyrus vanished, and for a split second, Leonardo thought she'd killed him. But then he reappeared next to her, grinning. He patted her shoulder and disappeared through the door into the ship.

Kate looked in Leonardo's direction, and Leonardo unconsciously closed his fingers around his sword. But she simply slid her sword back into her belt, stuck her tongue out at him, and marched up the steps, coattails flapping behind her.

Nym joined them at the rail, frowning. He looked thin. And he was already the most lightweight member of Leonardo's clan, aside from Charley. His elfish features were drawn as he watched Kate climb the stairs.

"We've come to a strange place," he said.

"Says the kid with demon arms," said Pinch.

Nym displayed his arms, not a trace of black on his pale skin. "Dunno what you're talking about."

Leonardo recognized the twang of unease in his voice.

"We're all...touched now," said Moth, trying and failing to help. He gestured to the black bands on all of their arms. Juliet shifted, letting her curls hide the mark on her neck.

"We're going to chase the Dark out," said Leonardo. "This is our home. We'll beat it."

"Yessir, captain sir," said Pinch.

Leonardo glanced up at the ship's wheel, watching John and Kate speak. If they managed to get the other clans to join, he wondered how many more *captains* could fit on one deck.

"It's going to be tough," said Nym.

"When's the last time we did anything that wasn't?" asked Leonardo. A cold wind snapped the sails, tugging at his clothes like a ghost in the dark. "We'll do it, like we always do."

"There were more of us before," said Bates, joining them.

He folded his arms on the rail, gazing out at the black sea. It was well past midnight, but no one would be catching sleep any time soon. Waves clapped against the hull, tossing up a fine mist that floated over them, frigid and salty on Leonardo's face. He breathed in the rich ocean air, so different from the earthy smell of the forest.

"I miss them," said Moth. "I wish I knew where they went."

"They must be *somewhere*," said Nym.

"Yeah," said Moth and Juliet in sync. They shared a quick smile and Moth nodded for Juliet to continue.

"I mean, we come from somewhere," said Juliet. "Before these woods. We must go somewhere else when we're done here."

It was a point Leonardo and the rest of them had debated enough times that it required no response. They'd already heard every theory. He doubted there was any kid, in any corner of the woods, who hadn't already exhausted the subject.

"I just wish they were still *here*," said Bates. "With us. But thanks to these half-witted *pirates*, they're not."

He cast a dark glare around the deck.

"They could've vanished just as easy in the Darkwoods," said Leonardo. "Or to the freshwater sirens upriver, or to the sea monsters, or the Dark—"

"I know, I know," said Bates. "It's dangerous as shit here. It's still not fair."

He shoved off from the rail and walked away.

Leonardo took a step after him and Juliet placed a hand on his shoulder.

"Leave him. He just needs time."

It reminded Leonardo of something Viola would have said,

and his own bitterness welled up. But Viola wasn't *gone*, and he tried to shove the feeling back down.

*Yet. She's not gone,* yet. Even if they beat the Dark, a fear nagged at Leonardo that his time with Viola might be drawing to a close.

"I think I need some time too," he said, stepping away from the group of them. He crossed the deck and climbed the steps to the bow, and the sloped deck that led up to where the bulwarks met, bracing a long bowsprit tangled with rigging and sailcloth.

*She's with her people again. She's known you for a few weeks at best. Why would she rejoin Lion Clan when she could be with her family?*

He knew she cared about him, but the idea of her forsaking her people because of it made him want to laugh in a bitter, painful sort of way. He'd seen it when Tokala asked her—no, told her— to stay. She'd hesitated, but only for a second.

And why not? If he was in her shoes, would he leave Lion Clan to join her people? He'd left Raven Clan to join Lion, but only because his family—the boys he'd spent years with—had come with him. She would be facing that same decision, and he knew the choice he would make, as tough as it was.

Even if the Natives stayed in the Cove, and Leonardo and Viola made every effort to see each other, nothing would be the same. They could never have a real future anyway; he would grow up and vanish, and she would go on living out her days in the dreamworld.

Whether it was the sheer exhaustion of the day, or the shock of losing so many friends in such a short time, in the few minutes Leonardo stood staring over the bow of *The Forever*, he came to the unshakable conclusion that Viola was as out of reach to him as Strato and Robin.

He blinked the salty wind out of his eyes as a droplet ran down his cheek.

241

# CHAPTER 28

Dawn crested clear and bright to a backdrop of waves sloshing and seabirds screaming in the sky. Leonardo rolled over on the deck, wincing as he pushed himself up from a hard night's sleep. He squinted at the sun, sparkling on the waves and reflecting off everything.

His face felt like stone, caked in salt from sleeping outside. Nym stirred nearby, for once sleeping while Bates served night watch.

The rest of Lion Clan lay scattered around the deck, some sitting up and talking in small groups while others caught a few extra minutes of sleep. There weren't enough hammocks down below, and no one wanted to be split up from their clan, so every Lion spent the night on deck while the pirates kept their regular bunks.

As Leonardo moved to the rear of the deck, the door between the twin staircases swung open and John stepped out, in his typical white linen shirt. A lock of blonde hair flipped over in the breeze.

"Morning," said John.

"Is that your quarters?" asked Leonardo, stretching a pinched muscle in his neck. It annoyed him to think of John sleeping comfortably in his own space.

John nodded. "Cyrus and Kate's cabins are on this level, and Pip's and mine are down below." He held the door open so Leonardo could see a red-carpeted hallway, with a closed door on each side and a staircase leading below.

"I get the impression you didn't sleep well," said John, shutting the door and leading the way to the upper deck.

"I've had worse," said Leonardo.

"I trust you have," said John. "I visited the Darkwoods once; it's a harsh place."

They summited the stairs and John extended his hand. "By the way, I don't think we've properly met. It's Leonardo, right?"

*That's because the first time we met, you kidnapped and killed members of my clan.*

Leonardo shook his hand a little too tight. "John, *right?*"

"Correct." John smiled, easy and amicable. He crossed to the wheel and gave it a spin. "I must apologize for my friends yesterday. Cyrus is crazy, Kate is crazy, and Pip is...well, crazy."

"And you're not?" asked Leonardo. He moved to the rail overlooking the main deck.

*You kidnap children as a pastime.*

"I try to be the voice of reason," said John.

*I see.*

"Why the ship?" he asked instead, gazing around at the heavy bulwarks and black sails.

John shrugged. "Why not?"

"How did you get it?"

"I found it." John grinned at Leonardo's surprise. "I come from the Highland. After the first few generations of kids came and went, I started to realize there was no place for me there anymore. So, I left. I travelled to the Darkwoods, where I met Pip."

They were interrupted by the clanking, grinding sound of a heavy chain being dragged in.

"Anchors aweigh," said John. "They use a capstan belowdecks to crank it in."

He led Leonardo to the side, where a thick, black, rust-spotted chain clanked up through a hole in the hull. After a minute or two, the anchor itself emerged from the depths like a great ruddy-coloured fish.

"Anyway," said John, crossing back to the wheel. "I met Pip in the Darkwoods. He wasn't as bitchy then. We travelled south to the Cove, where we found three things: an empty pirate ship, a lunatic named Cyrus, and a girl named Kate, who'd journeyed on foot all the way down from the Redwoods, because—and I quote—she was bored."

"And the ship was just sitting here, empty?" asked Leonardo.

"The woods like to play little games," said John. "I think we were one of its first."

"So then what?" asked Leonardo. "You decided to team up and start stealing kids?"

John released a breath, quirking his mouth. "We don't do it for fun, you know."

"Of course," said Leonardo. He heard the annoyance in his own voice. "You need to maintain a crew."

"We didn't, at first," said John. "It was just the four of us for a long time. But we grew tired of it; the ship does a lot of the work itself, but it expects us to at least pitch in. So, we started assembling a crew."

"By kidnapping from the other clans."

"We're not a clan," said Pip, cresting the stairs. His tricorn cap fit poorly, and he had to clamp a hand on it against the breeze. To Leonardo's eyes, it closer resembled a sombrero than a pirate's hat.

"No one said we were," said John.

"Good," said Pip. He stopped before Leonardo, pudgy arms crossed. "What're you looking at?"

"You're looking at me," said Leonardo.

"Whatever." Pip procured a sack of cracked hazelnuts and placed one between his teeth, crunching it as he moved past.

"Think of it this way," said John. "Kids are taken into clans without a choice. They're told that such-and-such clan is their enemy, and such-and-such land is their territory. But what if there was another option? We offer that option."

"Which is?"

"Freedom," called Pip, through a mouthful of hazelnuts. "Chance to cut the strings."

"We have no territory," said John. "We don't get tangled in clan politics."

Leonardo glanced back down to the deck. Most of the clan was awake now or in some stage of waking. Moth and Juliet sat near the edge, talking; Pinch used a knife to etch shapes in a deck plank; and Mishti and Sophie spoke rapidly, leaned close together.

"Yet somehow, we've gotten tied up in the very thick of

clan-ness," said Cyrus, joining them on the upper deck. "Good morning, Leonardo."

"Where is Kate?" asked John.

"Sleeping," said Cyrus. "I pounded on her door, but," he shrugged. "Tis not the lady's wish to rise yet."

"Tell her I don't care," said John. "You may not have noticed, but that big island in front of us is getting closer."

"I'm not your carrier pigeon," said Cyrus. "You wake her."

"Pip," said John. "Wake up Kate and tell her—"

"Fuck you," said Pip.

"Well, if you tell her that," said Cyrus. "I doubt she'll be overly inclined to listen."

"Fine," said John. "No one wake her. If she's asleep when we get to Dragon Clan, it's her problem. Leonardo," he continued, "I'd recommend you start getting your clan organized. We'll be rounding the island soon."

Leonardo hadn't realized quite how close to the Turquoise Isle they'd dropped anchor last night. After their run-in with the Dark, he would've expected the pirates to put more distance between them. But instead, the island was in clear sight, close enough to make out trees along the beach.

*They're not afraid enough.*

He should have anticipated that; a group of invincible kids could never truly understand danger. But the Dark's shadow ribbons had burned their arms no different than the other kids.

Leonardo suddenly realized just how vulnerable they all were. Their party now had six leaders, and any number of small misjudgments could throw off the intricate equation that separated survival from vanishment.

*There's no room left for mistakes.*

The ship closed on the island fast, and Leonardo left the leaders to rouse his clan.

"Everyone up," he called, reaching the bottom of the stairs and strolling out onto the deck. He kicked Puck in the leg. "Secoms especially. I need you sharp today."

***

The Dragons again waited around their sheltered waterway as *The Forever* sailed in. Wariness permeated their blue-robed ranks as the pirate ship came to a drift.

Lions, pirates, and Dragons regarded each other for a long moment, then Demetrius spread his hands. He tried to smile through the mask of uncertainty on his round face.

"Come ashore. It seems we have a lot to discuss."

The pirates lowered a wooden dinghy into the water as Leonardo, Mishti, and Kate descended the ship's ladder. Kate climbed atop the rowboat's bow, precariously balancing on the narrow point where the hulls met, then Leonardo took the oars and rowed to the stone wall.

He glanced back as they stepped ashore. *The Forever* floated quiet and docile in the middle of the waterway, crowded with watchful pirates and Lions.

"Welcome back," said Demetrius. "Follow me."

The Dragons guided them through the fig trees and marble columns to the hanging gardens. Little conversation broke the tension, replaced with darting glances and whispers between blue-cloaked kids.

"If it becomes a fight," whispered Kate. "Watch your back."

Leonardo stared at her.

247

"Don't worry." She rolled the pommel of her sword. "The woods wouldn't let me kill you. You're special. Like me."

"We're on the same side, right?" Leonardo whispered back.

"If you want to be."

"What does that mean?"

She shrugged, one eyebrow cocked under her trilby hat.

Demetrius led them to the white curtained, open-air dais overlooking the sea. His Dragons spread out in a sort of perimeter, and Leonardo, Mishti, and Kate moved hesitantly onto the dais.

"You must understand," said Demetrius. Sweat sheened on his brow. His nervous ticks were out of control as he plucked and fixed his robes. "I didn't do anything wrong here."

"You lied to us," said Mishti. The night's sleep had seemingly restored her mettle.

"I didn't lie, per se—"

"We asked you where the pirates were. You said they weren't here."

"Well... I—"

"That's a lie," said Mishti.

Meanwhile, Kate wandered to a platter of dates on a stone table. She took a handful and returned to the group, popping one into her mouth.

"Want a date?" she asked Leonardo. She balanced one on her thumb, eyelashes fluttering under the brim of her trilby.

Leonardo frowned and she winked, then flicked it at him. It bounced off the tile floor, drawing Demetrius's attention.

"Mishti," said Demetrius. "You struck a deal with the sirens. You let them live below your camp. This is no different. I'm a leader, I need to protect my clan."

"This isn't about our deal," said Kate, suddenly serious. "Listen; things are about to get really bad."

They explained what they'd experienced the night before, and Leonardo told Demetrius what the Dark had done up north.

"Let me get this straight," said Demetrius. "You're telling me there's a—what? A giant shadow?—on my island, and it wants to kill everything and everyone here."

"Correct," said Kate.

"It left these on us," said Leonardo. He held out his arm, displaying the black band the Dark had left behind.

Kate rolled up her sleeve, revealing her own marks.

"And you want us to help you fight this...shadow," said Demetrius. His voice shifted a fraction higher. Below the dais, the other Dragons spoke in rapid, hushed voices.

"Everyone in the Cove needs to fight it," said Leonardo. "Together."

"We don't have much time," said Mishti. "Snake and Tiger won't be easy to convince—"

"How many favours are you offering?" Demetrius folded his hands, a brazen cockiness suddenly washing over him.

Leonardo, Mishti, and Kate stared at him.

"You're kidding me," said Mishti. "None. This is about more than—"

"That's what I thought." Demetrius chuckled. "Dragon clan doesn't offer freebies. Sorry."

"Demetrius," snapped Mishti. "We're talking about life and death."

Leonardo was beginning to notice a pattern. Whenever Demetrius panicked, his entire persona switched to one of smug self-assuredness. If it was a façade, he wondered how easy it would be to crack.

"How about this." Demetrius addressed Leonardo, actively ignoring Mishti. "You go talk to Tiger and Snake, then come back here. If they're willing to do what you want for free, I'll consider it."

"That's ridiculous—" started Mishti.

"Ok," said Leonardo.

"What?" Mishti whirled on him.

"Yesterday," said Leonardo, "would you have believed Demetrius if he was the one asking us for help?"

"The Dark is coming!" said Mishti.

"The Dark is here," said Leonardo. *It's everywhere,* Viola's voice echoed in his head. "Until Dragon Clan experiences it—and they will—they won't understand it."

"If the Dark comes here, it will destroy them."

Mishti's tone was lashing, but Leonardo thought he heard a spark of understanding. "Its heart is on this island," she added, her gaze darting to make sure the Dragons around the perimeter were listening. "They'll be the first ones it reaches."

Demetrius frowned.

"I'm sure Dragon Clan knows how to fight," said Leonardo. He struggled to say that convincingly, staring at Demetrius's smooth hands and his clan's complete lack of weapons. "There *might* still be time, but we need to get to Tiger and Snake before it's too late."

Mishti nodded, glancing at Kate. An unspoken message passed between them, and Kate held her tongue. Meanwhile, Leonardo turned his attention to Demetrius.

"If we can convince Tiger and Snake to join us, can we count on Dragon too?"

Demetrius drew a breath, searching for an answer in his clanmates' faces, who'd fallen silent below the dais. Darted glances passed between them; everyone looking for assurance from someone else. Leonardo suspected pride was the only thing barring Demetrius from taking back his words and joining them now.

"We'll send the sirens to tell you once we've united the clans," said Leonardo. "If you can't hold off the Dark until then, come to the Cove. It's the strongest fortress; we'll make our stand there."

"That sounds fair," said Demetrius. He swallowed, scanning the orchard trees beyond the white curtains. Leonardo suspected he'd be jumping at shadows until the sirens arrived. Or he'd give in and bail early. Whichever came first.

"Good." Leonardo extended his hand and shook with Demetrius. The larger boy's hand trembled, though he tried to mask it, pulling away quick.

"Now," said Leonardo. "We need to go. There really isn't much time."

Mishti nodded, grave and sober.

"Of course, of course," said Demetrius. "We'll take you back to your boat."

As they passed between the tall, thin trees, Mishti stepped close to Leonardo. They shared a look of silent victory, her eyes fierce.

It wasn't a win, but it wasn't a loss either. They'd taken the first step in uniting the Cove, and Leonardo felt hopeful, bleak as the situation was.

# CHAPTER 29

L ook," said Mishti. "I need to apologize."

They stood on the bow of *The Forever*, wind snapping at their clothes and hair as they streamed northwest, bound for the Cove.

"For what?" asked Leonardo. He could think of a lot of things, but nothing particularly recent.

"Just listen," said Mishti. "And don't interrupt, because I don't like doing this and I don't want to drag it on."

"The floor is yours." Leonardo gripped the bulwark as they crashed through a trough, throwing spray over the bow. Leonardo winced at the freezing spray on the back of his neck.

"Shit!" Mishti staggered back as cold droplets pelted her face.

Heavy cloud-cover blocked out the sun, and a fierce wind kept them uncomfortable on deck.

"This is my fault," said Mishti, gazing up at the sky. "We didn't praise the Lostwoods at dawn."

For a second, Leonardo thought that was her apology, but then she focused back on him.

"I can't be the leader my clan needs alone, and you can't be the leader your clan needs without our camp and our numbers. I want to work together, as co-leaders. And for real, not just because of a sign."

"You mean that?" asked Leonardo.

Mishti nodded, swallowing hard. "I'm not stupid, you know. I don't just praise the Lostwoods because it's good to us. I'm…well, sometimes I think I'm too afraid of *it* and not afraid enough of the things *inside* it. You've got it the other way around."

*Afraid of the things inside it.* The Dark, Aleksander, his and Viola's future.

Mishti's Lion Clan wasn't the clan of legends, but they had earned the favour of the woods. If nothing else, it proved they could achieve a feat they set their mind to.

*She's not a bad leader,* he thought.

But she wasn't a strong one either. The clans here were more interested in trading favours than blows, and she'd inherited a camp that supplied everything she could need. She'd never had to lead in the face of real danger. Again, Leonardo had it the other way around. Maybe together, they could defeat the Dark and return Lion Clan to its golden age.

They stood facing the wind for a minute, listening to the sails flap and the surf break as the distant cliffs drew nearer.

"It won't be easy," said Mishti. "Any of this. We don't even know what the Dark is."

Leonardo felt a twinge of guilt for hiding it from her, but Tokala's words rang through his mind. *The last time the knowledge was told, it caused a bigger tear to form in the fabric of this place.* The dream world.

He didn't have a choice but to hide it.

"Nothing's ever easy," said Leonardo. "But we keep fighting anyway. And if we fight hard enough, we survive to the next fight."

"Why?" asked Mishti. "Why keeping fighting just to fight again?"

*So that one day, we can end the fight.* That was the choice Tokala had given him before he left the Darkwoods. *Carry on your brother's fight, or let it end.*

Leonardo thought he'd achieved the latter by leaving the Darkwoods, but the reality was, Aleksander's war wouldn't end until the Dark did. His desperate hold on his youth was the thing that first opened the tear.

"I don't know," Leonardo said instead. "But if we win enough fights, maybe we'll find out."

Mishti pulled a face, staring into the spray over the bow.

Leonardo rolled his neck. He wondered how many fights they would have to win before they found what lay beyond the violence. Maybe this one against the Dark would be the last.

*Do you really believe that?*

Only blind faith would justify such a belief. Mishti and her Lions had enough of that for everyone. Leonardo was a skeptic; in luck, in belief—even Viola was gone from him now—but maybe he'd be wrong this time. Maybe this would be the last of the violence.

One way or another, the fight was coming, and Leonardo planned to be ready for it.

# CHAPTER 30

Impatience gnawed at Leonardo as he paced the natural terrace atop Lion Clan's fortress.

*We should be at Tiger Clan right now.*

Instead, they'd sailed here. To the Cove. Because Mishti feared the *Lostwoods* were angry with her and required her to return home and pray. In addition, Juliet felt that with access to her medicines, she could cure the Dark's marks off their arms.

Leonardo eyed the crescent of needle-tooth punctures on his hand.

*The venom is in your blood now,* Dakota said. *When you grabbed the Dark mark on your arm, the venom stopped the Dark from spreading.*

It no longer hurt; *cauterized* as Tokala said, by the contact with the Dark.

Leonardo drew his lips in a thin line and crossed to the balcony. Below, the waters of the Cove glittered in the late afternoon sunlight. The sun itself edged into its final curve for the western sky, where the cliffs broke to give way to open ocean.

*This was a bad decision.* He should have argued harder when Mishti announced they would be detouring to the Cove.

She was persuasive, if nothing else. Her booming orders had left no room for discussion, even from the pirates.

"Penny for your thoughts?" asked Puck, walking up behind him. "Actually, never mind; we don't have pennies here. Apricot pit for your thoughts?"

He took the last bite of his apricot and offered Leonardo the pit, then wound up and threw it out over the Cove.

"Why is the Dark hiding?" asked Leonardo. "We're not even close to ready for it."

"Because the woods are stronger here too," said Kate, coat swishing as she walked up. She climbed onto the stone rail and sat cross-legged, her back to the two-hundred-foot drop. "Did you know the lifeforce of the woods is more present here in the Cove than anywhere else? The Dark has to bide its time. Like a game."

"What kind of game involves killing people?" asked Puck.

"Lots," said Kate. "What is this whole place, if not a big game? How did you play it up north?" She raised an eyebrow.

Puck set his mouth.

"But no one actually dies here," continued Kate. "We just *disappear.*" She made a 'poof' gesture with her hands.

"Where do we go?" asked Nym, joining them now. Leonardo couldn't help but study his hands and arms. Not a single black vein showed itself.

"Hell if I know," said Kate. "I've never been there."

"Is it true you've been here since the beginning?" asked Leonardo.

"As far as I know," said Kate. "And I stopped getting older a few years in."

"Why?" Leonardo had been puzzling over that. "Why you? Out of all the kids who were here when the woods started, why did the four of you never grow old?"

Kate shrugged. "I've been trying to figure that out for a long time."

"What was it like in the beginning?" asked Nym. "You created this whole place, right?"

"Kind of." Kate picked at a fissure in the rock. "Me and all the other 'first kids'. But we didn't just get to snap our fingers and make stuff. It was more like this wild dream, and by the time we all figured out we weren't going to wake up, it was too late to use the magic to make anything new. The woods were created. Our flawed and possessive and beautiful woods. I've spent my entire life trying to understand why it exists."

The five of them stood in grave silence, gazing out to sea. Kate unwound a red scarf from her neck and tossed it over the edge. A gust of wind grabbed it and threw it back into her waiting hand.

She sighed and walked away, tying the scarf around her wrist.

***

An hour later, they were still landlocked, and the minutes ticked away in Leonardo's mind. He stood in one of the stairwells, tapping his fingers in a long slitted window in the rock. Mishti still hadn't surfaced from her prayers. She'd barred the door, last he checked.

*If we don't get to the other Clans in time, no amount of praying will make a difference.*

Leonardo pushed away from the window. They had waited long enough. He would break in with his rock-key and drag Mishti to the ship if he needed to. He wasn't going to sit here idle while the Dark gathered its strength.

Just then, Mishti rounded the stairs, nearly missing a step and stumbling.

"It's getting dark," said Leonardo. "We need to set sail."

"Is too late," said Mishti, heavily slurred "Too danger…not taking my clan out…night again."

"Are you drunk?" demanded Leonardo. He stepped toward her, his spine stiffening.

Mishti shrugged.

"What the hell!" Leonardo felt like he'd entered a twilight zone. "I thought you were praying!"

"I was. At first." She blinked, squinting to focus on him. "Tough times, lately."

"This is ridiculous."

Leonardo turned and stormed up the stairs. He ran into Moth and Juliet around the next corner. Both looked haggard.

"Have you seen her?" he snapped.

"Who?" asked Moth.

Juliet hung her head. "She's drunk, isn't she?"

"What?" said Moth, eyes wide. "Mishti?"

"I'm worried about her," said Juliet.

"I'm worried about *us*," retorted Leonardo. "We don't have time for this."

"Everything in the Cove is supposed to be a luxury," said

Juliet. "That's what we tell ourselves, anyway. But there's a saying here: paradise is only paradise until you figure out why it's not."

"Adriana said that to me," said Leonardo. He didn't have time for riddles either.

Juliet glanced around, then leaned closer to them. "When Mishti is afraid, she freefalls. The Cove's luxuries become a poison to anyone who dips too deep."

"She dips in a lot, I take it?" said Moth.

"More than she should."

"I need her clearheaded," snapped Leonardo. "How are we supposed to talk to Tiger Clan if she's drunk?"

Juliet bit her lip.

"Where is Sophie?" asked Leonardo.

"In Mishti's quarters." Juliet pointed to the door. "Moth and I just told her we couldn't…well…none of my medicines seem to cure the Dark."

Leonardo closed his eyes.

*Everything is falling apart.*

"We're going to keep trying though," said Moth. "Come on, Juliet."

They left him standing on the steps. Leonardo drew a slow breath and centred himself. Sophie sat studying a map when he threw open the door.

"What is Mishti doing?" he demanded.

Sophie blinked slowly. "Trust her, she's been running a clan longer than you."

"This is what she calls running a clan?"

"Trust her," repeated Sophie. "Sometimes being in charge doesn't mean you're the one at the wheel."

"What the hell does that mean?" Leonardo placed his hands on the table.

"It means, I'm about to find a cure for the Dark."

Leonardo stared at her. "What is it?"

"I said *about to*. I need you out so I can think."

"You're kidding."

Sophie looked him square in the eye. "We're on the same side, ok? Get Mishti sober, then we'll save our clans."

*Sometimes being in charge doesn't mean you're the one at the wheel.*

All at once, Leonardo understood how Mishti's clan had managed to survive her turbulent leadership.

"Ok."

"Thank you," said Sophie.

He left the room and walked straight into Kate.

"Oh!" Kate grabbed a fistful of his shirt for balance. She shifted back, blinking brightly in the pink light filtering through the windows. "What's in there?" She leaned to see past him into Mishti's quarters.

"Nothing," said Leonardo.

"Come on," said Kate. "Tell me *something* interesting. I'm desperately bored."

Everything about her, from her eyes to her voice and the lightness of her movements, was like a child. Yet she'd been in the Cove longer than he'd been alive.

"Not now," said Leonardo.

"Come on!" Kate sagged dramatically. "Come with me, it'll be more interesting. I promise."

She grabbed his hand and he tensed.

"Right." Kate rolled her eyes. "Violet, or whatever her name was. Look, I'm not a siren." She stretched her leg for emphasis. *No tail, see?* "I'm just a regular pirate girl who's only half drunk—I found where they keep that punch—and I just want to talk to you. It's important."

She said the last part with a thick accent which rendered the statement somewhat dubious.

Kate started down the stairs, tugging his arm. Leonardo hesitated, then he rolled his eyes and followed her. Maybe he'd learn something valuable.

She led the way through a doorway, then down another stone-chiselled staircase, backtracking when she took the wrong passage. A few turns later, Leonardo realized they were going to the steam caves. He stopped walking.

"Come on," said Kate. "We need somewhere they can't hear us." She leaned closer and whispered, "They have listening holes."

"I know," said Leonardo. But she'd caught his attention now.

Kate led the rest of the way down to the caves and strolled out into the crashing, echoing, fairy-lit chamber. Steam poured off the surface of the pools, silhouetting craggy ledges and the giant stone lion's head high above the largest pool, candlesticks burning in place of its fangs.

"Oh," said Kate. "I thought this was the way to where they kept the boats."

"The lagoon," said Leonardo. "If you wanted to go there, we took a wrong turn at the last landing."

"Oh," said Kate. She splashed her foot in a puddle. "Well, whatever. It's loud enough in here that no one can hear us anyway."

"What did you want to tell me?" Leonardo became very

aware that the last time he'd been alone down here with a girl, it was Viola.

"I know you know what this place is. The woods, I mean."

"The dreamworld," said Leonardo.

"Imagination," said Kate. "More accurately." She glanced over her shoulder at the empty steps. "Back in the Darkwoods, when you felt the woods watching you, did it make you feel safe?"

"No," said Leonardo, after a beat.

"Of course not," said Kate. "Neither did I, in the Redwoods. "We play it different ways, but it's the same game." She leaned close, so their faces were an inch apart. "War," she whispered. The tang of sacred cactus spiked her breath.

Leonardo leaned back, and Kate grinned.

"We're all rats," she said. "The woods hold us by the tail and poke us with sticks."

"You're drunk, Kate," said Leonardo.

"Only a little. Look, Lion Clan is...under an illusion. They think they're the children of some peaceful, golden paradise. You and I both know better."

"Do we?"

She nodded. "Your brother isn't the one who let the Dark in."

"What?" Now she had his full attention.

"I heard some of the boys talking about it. Apparently, you all think he held on so long that a tear opened and the Dark came in."

"That's what Viola told us," said Leonardo. Uncertainty churned his stomach.

"And what are Viola's people? The guardians of the woods.

Their job is to keep the balance. When the woods get reckless, they have to right the ship. The sirens used to be guardians too until they realized what the woods really is. There were guardians in all four corners, but the Natives are the only ones still at their post."

"I don't understand," said Leonardo.

"Aleksander didn't hold on," said Kate. "The woods held him."

"What?" The ground wavered under Leonardo's feet. He placed his hand on an outcropping of rock, staring at the wet surface but not seeing it.

"No one has the power to defy the woods," said Kate. "If anyone did, John, Cyrus, Pip, and I would've left a long time ago. I'm sorry, but your girlfriend is lying to you."

Before he could reply, footsteps echoed down the stairs. A second later, Isabella appeared.

"There you are," she puffed, breathless. "We're leaving. Sophie is calling everyone to the lagoon."

She spun on her heel and sprinted back up the steps.

"Later," said Kate. "When you see that the woods and the Natives are lying, come find me."

She left him standing in the cave, listening to the crashing sheets of water.

"She's lying," said a voice from behind him. The pit hardened in Leonardo's stomach.

"Go away, Adriana," he said without turning.

"She's trying to manipulate you. Think about it; why would the woods let the Dark in?"

Leonardo paused. Kate never said the woods let the Dark in. He furrowed his brow, still staring at the rock.

"And do you really think *we* were guardians of this place? Thaisa can't even banish me, she's such a pushover."

Leonardo eyed her. She brushed aside a lock of blonde hair, pupils dilatated in the darkness.

"I don't know what I believe," he said finally. "But I'm leaving."

Adriana didn't respond right away. Steam drifted past her face as she blinked up at him.

"Don't trust her," she repeated.

"I don't trust anyone," said Leonardo. "Not right now."

# CHAPTER 31

Y ou think the *woods* let the Dark in?" asked Moth.

"Maybe," said Leonardo.

*The Forever* cut through the night. Against Mishti's protests, Sophie, Leonardo, and the pirates all agreed that getting underway as soon as possible was worth the risk. He stood under the single lantern near the bow, with a small cluster of ex-Ravens.

"So…Viola was lying then?" said Moth.

*No.* A flash of annoyance sparked in Leonardo. Viola wouldn't lie. *She can't be lying.* But Moth was only asking the logical question, and Leonardo forced himself to respond rationally.

"Not necessarily," he said. "She might not know what Kate knows."

"What if they're all lying?" said Pinch. "But none of them realize it. If Aleksander didn't let the Dark in, but someone told Viola he did…"

"Then she's telling someone else's lie," finished Leonardo. He was relieved someone else saw it the same way. "And Kate saying she's lying is also a lie. Even if *she* doesn't realize it."

"And Adriana accusing Kate of lying isn't true either," said Puck. "Right?"

"Bingo," said Pinch. "Everyone's lying by accident."

"Not necessarily," said Leonardo. "Adriana might be lying for real."

Out of everyone, her words had rung the hollowest.

*But why? What does she gain? Chaos?* If Lion Clan survived, Mishti would force the sirens to send Adriana upriver, where she would transform into one of the hideous bleached creatures that attacked Leonardo's clan.

*But siding with the Dark can't produce a better outcome, can it?*

Maybe Adriana was rolling the dice.

Nym ran his hands over his face. "We have to get this right. Our survival might depend on figuring out who's telling the truth."

"Dramatic much?" said Bates.

"He's right," said Puck. "If the woods did let the Dark in, we're in deeper shit than we thought."

"Why would the woods do that?" asked Moth. He squinted across the moonlit sea.

"For fun?" Leonardo frowned. "Kate said a lot of things about the woods being reckless, and poking us with sticks, and—"

"Sticks?" said Nym.

"It was a metaphor. I think. But look at it this way: if the woods did let the Dark in, and Viola got the wrong story, then Viola is accidentally lying. Pinch's theory adds up."

"But whose lie is Viola telling?" asked Bates.

That was the easiest question to answer.

"Think about it," said Leonardo. "Who's someone that's lied to us in the past, and is close enough to Viola that she'd believe it?"

"The Chief," said Moth.

"And Dakota," added Nym.

"Exactly," said Leonardo. "I'm going to find Kate."

***

*This is your worst idea yet*, a voice whispered in his mind. He padded softly through the red-carpeted hallway beyond the aft door, where the captains' cabins lay. Aleksander's rock-key pressed heavy in his pocket. Invading the pirates' private space in the middle of the night seemed like a good way to start a fight, but Leonardo ignored his better judgement.

*I can't wait until morning*, he argued. *This is too important.*

*What if you pick the wrong door, and it's John?*

*Or Cyrus?*

*Or bitter little Pip?*

No, John and Pip were downstairs. He recalled that much. But was Kate on the left or right?

He chose left on a whim and lifted his fist to knock.

Just before he could bring his knuckles down, fingers gripped a handful of his hair and yanked his head back. A knife pressed against his throat. A body pressed into his back, shorter than him but unyielding in its control. He swallowed against the cold blade, swearing inwardly.

*Idiot.*

*Stupid, impatient idiot.*

"Looking for me?" whispered Kate. She released him, stepping back and drawing a second knife from her belt. Her smile was

267

bright in the lantern light; somehow both threatening and completely innocent at the same time. Then she frowned, glancing at the door he'd been about to knock on.

"Or are you looking for Cyrus?"

"No," said Leonardo quickly. "I'm here for you."

"Oh good." Kate smiled again. "I hoped so."

She sheathed her knives and crossed her arms, cocking one hip. "Now the question becomes; what are you here *for*? Are you ready to hear about the woods? Or do I finally get round two?" She eyed his sword, uncrossing her arms to half-draw her own gold-handled blade. "Or something else?"

She let her sword fall back into its sheath and took a step toward him. The lantern light flickered in her eyes.

"The woods," said Leonardo quickly, placing a hand on the wall behind him. "I want to know about the lies and the—"

"Oh. Ok sure." She spun the handle of her sword. "Come with me then."

She crossed to the door on the right and swung it open, waving him in with a grand sweep of her arm.

Inside was a room quite unlike anything Leonardo had seen in the woods. Incense burned from lamps, an intricate tapestry hung on one of the slanted walls, and a chandelier of diamonds and candles occupied the centre of the cabin, meant for a much taller ceiling. An inch separated it from brushing the floor.

Exotic plants with giant pink flowers bloomed from gold pots, and a narrow, Roman-style bed in red velvet sat beneath salt-stained floor-to-ceiling windows. Through the cloudy glass, Leonardo made out the ship's wake, silver and glassy in the moonlight.

"Have a seat," said Kate. She nodded to the roman bed, which was somewhat like a lopsided couch. She, in turn, lifted a vase of pink and gold orchids off a side table and placed it on the floor, then sat cross-legged atop the table.

"Where did you get all this?" asked Leonardo.

"I imagined it," said Kate, as if it were the simplest thing in the world.

"How?"

"A bit of leftover magic, I suppose. When John found *The Forever*, I remember hoping it would have a real pirate's cabin, with treasure and jewels and a chandelier. We came on board, I opened this door, and *voila*! Pirate cabin. I dreamed a bit big on the chandelier though," she added, quirking her mouth at the monstrosity.

*Dreamed a bit big.* If she and the other originals really had imagined the entire woods into existence, then it seemed to Leonardo that a chandelier and a room of treasure should be among the smaller dreams she'd had.

"Now listen," said Kate. "The woods is our captor." She said the last three words with emphasis; heavy drama on each syllable.

"Ok..." said Leonardo.

"The woods also loves us," she continued. "Some of us more than others."

"Now you sound like Mishti."

"Shh." Kate put a finger to her lips, tinted deep red. "So, it keeps us captive. It's interesting because it can't directly control us. It can only influence things and watch the result."

"So how does the Dark come in?"

Kate leaned around the chandelier, still sitting cross-legged on the table, and plucked a pair of goblets off the top of an old trunk.

Then she leaned the other way and fished a dark bottle out of a pile of gold-trimmed junk.

"Your brother," said Kate, pouring dark liquid into the goblets. "Want one?"

He blinked. "But...you said earlier—"

"Against his will," she continued, holding out a goblet.

He didn't take it, staring past her as he tried to piece it all together.

Kate shrugged and placed the goblet on the table next to her, taking a long sip from the other.

"The woods get bored of us sometimes. I don't blame it—I get bored of it too—so it finds entertainment. How do you create a hole in dream fabric?" She continued after a beat. "You keep a child in it, and—here's the important part—you allow him to grow old enough that his imagination fades, and he sees through to the outside. Then, and only then, can whatever lives out there come in here."

"So, the woods held onto Aleksander," said Leonardo. If she was lying, he couldn't spot a tell.

"Oh, I doubt he wanted to leave," said Kate. "Very few do, even after they've been here far too long." Her focus wandered a bit on this line, studying the red scarf on her wrist. "But if the woods wanted him out," she said finally, "it would've thrown him out a long time ago."

"What about you?" asked Leonardo. "And John and Cyrus and Pip? The woods have kept you much longer than Aleksander."

"Oui oui, but we never grew old," said Kate. She grinned again, a paradox of wisdom and childish glee. "And we happen to be a bit more imaginative than most kids. Why do you think the woods loves us so much? It can't bear to lose such vivid imaginations. We couldn't see through the fabric of the dreamworld if we tried to, no matter how many times we tell each other it's not real."

"How do you know all this?" asked Leonardo. "What the woods think, what my brother did...?"

Kate shrugged. "I imagine what it would think, and I know that must be true because I helped imagine the woods in the first place. And as for your brother, I've been listening to your clan—they talk a lot—and I've pieced most of it together."

"So, if all this is true—"

"Which it is."

"Then why would the Natives lie about it?"

"The same reason they did last time," said Kate. She took another sip, eyed what was left, then poured a bit from the second goblet into hers.

"This happened before?" asked Leonardo. A cold dread flooded his chest.

"Where do you think the Darkwoods got its name? Luckily, I was in the Redwoods then, but Pip says it was horrible. Not as bad as this time, but still horrible."

"And the Natives lied about it?"

"They're the guardians of the *woods*, not of us." She put down her goblet and leaned forward. "Their job is to keep things balanced through all of the woods' mistakes. Even when it makes the same mistake twice. Letting in the Dark is like jumping off a cliff with no idea how tall it is. You could break a leg, or you could keep falling forever. Either way, the Natives have to clean up the mess, and part of that means making sure we still love the woods once it's over. So they lie, and say Aleksander alone is to blame."

"Shit," said Leonardo. It made sense. He hoped against hope they were right and Viola wasn't in on it.

"The first time, the Lost Boys of the Darkwoods chased the Dark out. The woods had its fun and that was that. Although, I've always believed a little bit of it stayed behind. Could explain why things are so violent there."

Leonardo's horror grew, quickening his pulse. *Were we living with the Dark all those years?*

"This time, however…" Kate downed the rest of her drink, grimacing. "The woods bit off more than it can chew. The Dark is in control now."

Leonardo shoved himself to his feet. He paced the room, fists clenched as he stepped around Kate's piles of treasure. She turned herself on the table to stay facing him.

"How could the woods be so stupid?" said Leonardo.

Kate shrugged. "It's a child's imagination. It makes mistakes."

"This 'mistake' is going to destroy everything."

Kate offered him a goblet. "Want one now?"

Leonardo took it and swallowed a mouthful of the bitter liquid. He scowled at the goblet and placed it on a table.

"The woods isn't powerless," said Kate. "It still has us. All this Lion nonsense, everything with Pompey and Charley, your key, your sea monster bite, your brother…it's paying attention to you."

"What does that mean?" asked Leonardo.

"Depends," said Kate.

"On what?"

"If you can defeat the Dark."

# CHAPTER 32

Waves crashed against the sides of *The Forever* as they plowed south, through the thin darkness of early morning. Seabirds screamed from above, boards creaked, sails snapped, and the shadowed mouths of caves watched from the base of the cliffs.

Leonardo stood near the railing, squinting into each burst of spray. Moth and Juliet slept belowdecks, exhausted from a night of concocting and applying every cure Juliet could imagine. Despite their efforts, the black ribbons on everyone's skin had yet to show a hint of fading.

Nym sat quiet at the base of the main mast, his gaze fixed out to sea. Leonardo chewed his lip, regarding him. Nym had always been quiet, but it was an easier quiet. This was something heavy, something fearful and unsettling.

The Dark was *inside* of him, not skin-deep like the rest of them.

*What happens if we can't get it out?*

He'd been thinking that defeating the Dark and getting it out of Nym would be the same thing, but if Kate was right, then some of the Dark had never left the Darkwoods, even after it was banished the first time. Separating it from Nym might be harder than he'd first thought.

*And what about the rest of us?* If the Dark had always been in the Darkwoods, did that mean each of the ex-Ravens had a bit of it inside them?

Leonardo took a step toward Nym, then changed his mind. Nym had enough to worry about; this new information would only make things look bleaker for him. Leonardo stored it away, next to all the other things he hadn't told people. It felt like he was keeping secrets from everyone these days.

Meanwhile, Bates and Puck lay slumped against a pile of ropes, sleeping. They'd stayed up all night while Moth and Juliet worked on everyone's marks. Bates' marks blended against his dark skin, but they were there none the less.

Pinch emerged from the mid-deck hatch, and Leonardo caught the movement up at the wheel as John noticed Pinch too. It was a strange juxtaposition; Pinch with his cockeyed pirate's hat and John—the pirate—without one. John's eyes followed Pinch across the deck. Leonardo didn't like what he saw in them.

"Morning," grunted Pinch.

"John is staring at you," said Leonardo.

Pinch twisted to look, then frowned when John didn't look away.

"'the fuck?" Pinch gave a theatrical bow, heavy with sarcasm.

"Get your eyes off me, creep-stick," he said so only Leonardo could hear.

"I can't read him," said Leonardo. "Since we've come aboard, he's been watching us."

"What's their deal, anyway?" asked Pinch. "The pirate gig, the boat, living forever."

He turned his gaze forward and Leonardo followed it to Kate, balanced over the water on the narrow bowsprit.

"I don't know," said Leonardo honestly. Despite everything Kate told him, there was still so much he didn't understand. And he still didn't entirely trust her. The situation was too dire for him to blindly believe anyone's story.

"I wouldn't mind if she looked at me like he does," commented Pinch dryly.

"She's insane," said Leonardo.

"How does it work?" asked Pinch. "She's ancient, but she doesn't get old?"

"She's like a child, in some ways," said Leonardo. "And in others...not."

She was a paradox. Both the snake charmer and the snake. Endlessly simple in both aspects, but entirely unpredictable.

Just then, Charley and Pompey ran up. Charley's hamster basket swung wildly in her grip, entirely untended. When she stopped abruptly in front of him, the scrabble of tiny claws jerked the basket.

*Poor thing.*

"Leo," said Charley. "Have you seen the brig?"

"You mean the bottom of the ship?" Leonardo couldn't imagine what reason he'd have had to see the brig. "No, I haven't."

"It's full of beetles," said Pompey.

"They're everywhere," said Charley, as if this were the greatest thing ever. "They're on the walls, in the wood—"

"Oh great," said Pinch. "They have termites. On a wooden boat."

"They're not termites—" Charley shook her basket, staring in at the furry orange bundle. "Stay still. They're not termites," she repeated. "They're big and black and shiny."

Leonardo made a note never to visit the brig.

"Where were you two last night?" he asked. They had promptly disappeared upon reaching the fortress.

"Pompey knows all the secret passages," said Charley. "We went exploring."

Pompey nodded earnestly. His gold Lion robes hung off-kilter, draped on his skinny frame.

Pinch sighed. "Of course they have secret passages."

"They're everywhere!" said Charley. "There're listening holes, and ladders, and tunnels this small." She held her hands in a circle that Leonardo found skeptical even for someone her size.

"More like this," said Pompey, demonstrating a bigger circle.

Charley tilted her head, studying it. "Yeah," she said, nodding. "More like that."

"We should know where those are," Pinch said to Leonardo.

"Can you show us the passages?" Leonardo asked Pompey. "The next time we're back at the fortress?"

*If we get back.*

Pompey hesitated, glancing at Charley. Leonardo couldn't tell if it was loyalty to Mishti, or reluctance to share his secret spaces that held him back. Either way, Charley had no such pause.

"Yes!" she said, excitedly enough to startle Lion the hamster. "Stop," she said when his basket jerked. "We'll all go exploring! But you might not fit in all the tunnels," she mused, studying Leonardo and Pinch.

Before the conversation could go any further, a splash across the deck drew all their attention. A silver shape launched out of the water next to the ship, wet skin gleaming in the sunlight. A dolphin. Another followed it a second later, then another and another. They plunged back into the surf as more leapt after them.

Charley tore across the deck to see them, pursued by Pompey. The dolphins kept jumping, keeping pace with *The Forever* as they crashed through the waves. Charley and Pompey stopped hard against the rail, leaning out almost close enough to touch them.

Ever since their joint kidnapping, the two had become inseparable. Strange and quiet as Pompey was, Leonardo much preferred him to the troublesome Lion Clan girls Charley had befriended in the first few days.

Leonardo's eye was drawn up to the ship's wheel, where he was startled to find John's gaze still fixed on Pinch.

"What the hell?" said Pinch.

"Come on," said Leonardo. He led the way to the nearest of the twin staircases and climbed to the upper deck. A stiff wind tugged at John's white linen shirt and flipped his blonde hair. Pinch clamped a hand on his hat as they crossed to the wheel.

"What do you want?" asked Leonardo.

"My hat," said John.

Leonardo and Pinch both stopped.

Pinch pointed to his tricorn. "You mean *my* hat."

"I mean *my* hat," said John.

"This is *my* hat," said Pinch.

"John," said Leonardo. "Explain, please."

"I lost my hat years ago," said John. He pointed at Pinch's head. "That's it."

"Well, next time, hold on tighter," said Pinch.

John grabbed the highest spoke of the wheel and spun it hard, dropping his arm to let it whirl freely.

The ship jerked suddenly, throwing Leonardo and Pinch against the railing. The rail slammed into Leonardo's stomach and he doubled over it, staring down at Pompey and Charley as they fell to their knees, along with the two dozen other Lions and pirates stumbling across the deck.

"Shit," Pinch swore. Leonardo shoved himself off the rail and grabbed the handle of his sword as John turned the wheel back, rock-steady on his feet.

"Are you trying to kill people?" demanded Leonardo.

"No one dies here," said John.

"Listen here, halfwit," said Pinch. "This is my hat. I'm not—"

John spun the wheel again and Leonardo lost his footing. He hit the deck hard and slid into the bulwarks as the ship cranked in the water.

Pinch slammed into him, driving Leonardo's ribs into the wood a second time. He swore at the explosion of pain. Pinch's hat fell to the salt-stained boards beside him and he snatched it up, jamming it back on his head.

"John," shouted voices from below. "What the hell are you—"

"Come here, you little..." Pinch scrambled back to his feet, and Leonardo staggered up after him, yanking his sword from his belt. John straightened the wheel, barely paying them attention.

Footsteps pounded on the stairs and Cyrus, Pip, Kate, and Mishti ran up onto the deck, hands on their weapons as they took quick stock of the situation. Puck, Bates, Sophie, and a dozen others sprinted up after them.

"What's going on?" asked Mishti. At least she was sober.

"He won't give back my hat," snapped John.

"Oh, boo-hoo," said Pip. "Stop trying to sink us."

"I'm not," snapped John.

Leonard tilted his head. Pip, Kate, and Cyrus wore their own pirate hats.

*What's so special about them?*

"Everyone, calm down," he said instead. Mishti eyed him, a throwing ring in each hand. John continued to steer the ship as if the lot of them were nothing but noisy ghosts.

"It *is* his hat," said Cyrus. "John's, I mean."

"I found it," said Pinch. "So now it's mine."

"He..." Cyrus glanced at Mishti and Sophie and broke off. "Shit."

"He what?" demanded Mishti.

*Imagined it,* thought Leonardo. Which posed a new question, but he couldn't ask it in front of the Lion girls.

"If you lost it," he said instead to John. "Then how did it wind up all the way upriver of the Darkwoods?"

John shrugged.

"If the Lostwoods brought it to Pinch," said Mishti. "Then the Lostwoods must want him to have it."

"The 'Lostwoods' doesn't give a rat's ass about *Pinch*," said Pip. "It's John's hat."

Leonardo studied John, blonde hair flying in the wind, knuckles white on the wheel. Anger radiated from his stiff shoulders.

*What are these hats, really?*

Leonardo thought about Aleksander's rock and Mishti's replenishing rings. He was willing to bet that the hats were magic too.

"I agree with Mishti," said Leonardo, just to see how the pirates would respond. "It's what the woods want."

Kate's eyes darted from Leonardo to Mishti and Sophie.

"The woods shouldn't get a say," said John.

"Why?" said Mishti. "Because you're so powerful you get to do whatever you want?"

"Because it's my hat," said John.

"Did you make it?" demanded Sophie. The question was meant to be sarcastic, but the pirates' expressions confirmed that John and the others had indeed imagined the hats.

John chucked, and Leonardo opened his mouth to steer the conversation away. If Mishti—the most devout of them all—learned that the woods were nothing but a mirage...he didn't want to think about how much damage that could cause. How much more Dark could seep in.

"Don't," said Kate, before Leonardo could speak, her eyes on John.

*Shit.*

"What?" said Mishti and Sophie in unison.

"Nothing," said Kate and Leonardo in sync.

*Shit.*

Now everyone was frowning at them.

*Make something up.*

"They can hear the woods, sometimes," said Leonardo. "Like Moth hears the fairies. They think it's the hats."

Mishti narrowed her eyes.

"This one's broken then," said Pinch, taking his off and peering inside. "Can't hear a thing."

"There," said Leonardo. "Problem solved. Pinch can keep the broken hat and everyone's happy."

No one looked happy.

"Leonardo," said Kate, though she eyed Pip too. "Come with me. We need to talk."

Everyone on the stairs edged out of the way to let her through. Leonardo followed her, and Pip marched after them. Leonardo made eye contact with Nym and Puck on the stairs.

*Stay out of it,* he tried to convey without speaking. *Don't make this bigger.*

Moth and Juliet were just emerging from the mid-deck hatch when Leonardo, Kate, and Pip reached it.

"What just happened?" asked Moth. "Did we hit a wave?"

"Don't worry about it," said Leonardo. "I'll explain later."

Kate was already on the ladder, and Leonardo followed her down. The quarters belowdecks were narrow, but less claustrophobic than he first would've thought. Hammocks swung between supports, and salt-stained portholes let in watery light. A handful of pirates and Lions looked up from where they slept, but Kate, Leonardo, and Pip marched straight past, down another ladder, and deeper into the ship.

When they finally stopped, it was in the lowest confines of the ship, among piles of sailcloth, rope, and endless barrels of food supplies. A shiny black beetle scurried over the top of a barrel, making Leonardo second-guess the quality of their food.

"How much does he know?" demanded Pip.

"Everything," said Kate. She grabbed a fist-sized cannonball and threw it at a beetle on the ground. It hit the boards with a violent crack.

"*What?*" Pip dodged a second cannonball as Kate hurled it at another beetle.

"The Native girl told them," said Kate.

"*All* of them?"

"All the ones from the Darkwoods."

"What do the hats do?" asked Leonardo.

Kate and Pip blinked at him.

"I thought you knew everything," said Pip.

"Not about the hats," said Leonardo.

"So he *doesn't* know everything," said Pip. "Kate, you said—"

"They give us superpowers," said Kate. She weighed another cannonball in her hand and squinted at the wall.

"Kate!" said Pip.

"Superpowers?" asked Leonardo.

"Well, you've seen Cyrus shapeshift," said Kate. She hurled the cannonball at the wall. Leonardo winced as a bang split the air. A beetle scurried up into the shadows, and the ball fell into a pile of sailcloth.

"Why don't you just tell him everything!" snapped Pip.

"That's what I'm doing," Kate said patiently.

"His *hat* let him do that?" asked Leonardo.

"Welcome to your imagination," said Kate. "Anything is

possible. Funny thing is, John is the only one of us who didn't imagine his hat." She eyed up another beetle and Leonardo stomped it before she could throw a cannonball.

"Shut up already," snapped Pip.

"No. He found his hat when he found the ship. The rest of us imagined ours, the same way I imagined my cabin."

"So you can all shapeshift?" asked Leonardo.

Kate shook her head. "Pip can't feel pain. Look." She twisted and punched him in the arm. Pip didn't flinch. He simply rolled his eyes.

"Ta-da," he said dryly.

"And I get whatever I want." Kate smiled sweetly, her gaze fixed on Leonardo. Then she frowned. "Usually."

Leonardo swallowed hard, drying his palms. "What about John's hat?" he asked quickly.

"John's doesn't do anything," said Pip. "I told him to forget about it when he saw Pinch had it. Yet…here we are."

"What's it been, two days?" Kate laughed. "I bet him he couldn't last a week without taking it back."

"Pinch won't give it up without a fight," said Leonardo.

"Let him keep it," said Kate. "I'm getting bored of John. Let's kick him out of the club."

"You're insane," said Pip.

She winked. "I try my best."

# CHAPTER 33

Spires of rock stood sentry over Tiger Clan's territory, looming out of the water as tall as the cliffs around the Cove. Heavy moss and vines hung from the dark stone, tinting the spires a damp shade of green. Hummingbirds buzzed around the vegetation, flitting like fairies from vine to vine. Leonardo watched them as the ship coasted between the towers of stone.

A wispy fog drifted through the waterways, silhouetting an army of more spires in the distance.

"What is this place?" asked Moth.

"I don't know." Leonardo leaned to see along the side of the ship. Dark water rippled where the prow broke the waves.

"Welcome to the Fog Waters," said Cyrus, strolling across the deck with hands clasped behind his back.

"Does every place here have to have its own name?" asked Pinch dryly. "Tiger Clan territory, a.k.a. 'the Fog Waters'; Dragon

Territory, the Turquoise Isle; Snake Clan, the Jungle; Lion Clan, the Cove. And not to be confused with *The Cove*, which is just bloody everything." He made a grandiose gesture, whipping his arms around.

"It's very common to name a place's capital after the place itself," said Cyrus. "When we discovered the Cove—"

"Discovered?" said Pinch. "Don't you mean *imagined?*"

Leonardo flinched, looking around to see if any of the Lion girls were within earshot.

"It's more like discovery than you think," said Pip, joining them. "And shut up. Someone could hear you."

"Don't stress so much," said Cyrus. "We'll survive this. You did last time, so we have experience on our side."

Leonardo read the look on Pinch's face. It mirrored his own thoughts and went, *if Pip is the one leading us into battle, we might as well give up now.*

Not that Pip was a particularly terrible leader, but since meeting him, Leonardo hadn't heard one word out of his mouth that didn't start, lead to, or end in a complaint.

Leonardo stepped around him as a shape materialized in the fog ahead. A red sail cut through the white-grey, followed by the gold prow of a longboat. He started for the stairs to the foredeck, then jogged up two at a time and crossed to the rail, where Nym and Puck already stood.

Charley and Pompey ran up a beat later, and Mishti, Sophie, and a collection of Lions and pirates joined them as the Tiger Clan boat drew closer.

Kate sat out on the bowsprit, suspended over the water on a horizontal beam, her legs dangling. She leaned back to see the party gathering in the bow and straightened to her feet, balance-beaming down the sloped surface to join them.

"Looks like we found Tiger Clan," she remarked as she jumped down next to Leonardo.

"Looks like it," said Leonardo, studying the approaching longboat. It was the same as they'd arrived in for the full moon ceremony, but the young rowers that glanced over their shoulders weren't wearing the chalk-white face paint they'd worn two days ago.

They were wearing the deep red robes, and the girl on the captain's platform stood with the regal dignity he remembered.

Their boldness surprised him. The pirate ship dwarfed their longboat, he knew the pirates' reputation, and yet the Tigers plowed toward them without pause.

Kate turned to face aft, cupping her hands to her mouth. "John!" she shouted. "Hold up!"

A second later, the ship began to rotate in the water. They quickly lost whatever speed they'd been carrying, and the Tigers rowed the rest of the way to pull alongside them.

"Greetings, Tiger Clan," called Mishti. "I was hoping Cleo would be on this patrol."

The Tiger girls studied them. Without their white face paint, they weren't so eerily similar, but a chill ran up his spine regard-less.

"Mishti, Lion Clan," the girl on the captain's platform finally called back. "This is a strange encounter."

"We have news," called Mishti. "We need to speak with Cleo."

This was met with a long moment of uncertainty. The drip of

water off oars and the soft groan of the ship's boards echoed through the waterways.

"If we wanted to attack you, we would have already," called Pip, appearing suddenly from the stairs. "So, let's hurry up and get this show on the road."

"Fine," said the Tiger girl. "Follow us."

The Tigers rotated their longboat and started back through the mist. Above Leonardo, a length of sail dropped with a snap from *The Forever*'s beams. A breeze caught the black fabric and the ship rolled into motion again.

"Politics," said Pip. "I can't stand it."

"I'll do the talking here," said Mishti. "I know Cleo."

"And you hate her," said Leonardo.

"She hates me," said Mishti. "There's a difference."

"Either way," said Moth. "You need to work fast. Juliet is worried about the Dark marks."

"The Dark wouldn't leave these if it didn't plan to use them," said Puck.

"Where is Juliet now?" asked Leonardo.

"Still working on a cure," said Moth.

"Any luck?"

"Actually, maybe," said Moth. "Sophie has an idea that looks promising."

"Oh?" said Nym. Hope flashed in his eyes. A little knife stabbed at Leonardo's heart. The toll of Nym's stress lay bare in his desperate gaze.

"Maybe," repeated Moth. "The only problem is, she doesn't have enough of it to treat the entire crew."

Nym's face fell.

"Well, if it works," said Leonardo, "we'll find her all the ingredients she needs. And let's make sure Nym is at the top of the list to be treated."

"The kids should be first," said Nym. "I'll be fine."

"Finding the ingredients might be tougher than you think," said Moth.

Before Leonardo could ask what that meant, Mishti cleared her throat.

"We can deal with that later," she said. "Listen: When we're talking to Cleo, I'm going to lie."

"What?" asked Leonardo and Moth.

"Don't say anything that could ruin it," said Mishti. "And give me your magic rock-key."

"Why?" asked Leonardo. "What are you lying about?"

"Everything."

# CHAPTER 34

"Welcome," said the Tiger girl who'd captained the patrol. She didn't sound welcoming. "This way, please."

She led the way up a pebbled beach to a stone gate, over which hung the first blossoms of a lush oriental garden. The Tiger Clan longboat and the pirates' two rowboats sat beached on the rocks, just like they used to in Raven Clan.

Leonardo, Mishti, Kate, and Cyrus had come ashore, while the remainder of their mismatched alliance remained on the ship. Leonardo's fingers twitched to grip his sword handle as they passed through the gate, but no ambushers jumped out. Instead, they found themselves at the beginning of a wooden path, nestled between quiet oriental buildings and delicate branches. The faded boards wound into the gardens, arching gracefully over a clear stream, into a world of cherry blossoms, maple trees, ferns, and water lilies. A red-roofed pagoda stood peacefully among the colourful foliage, four storeys high and covered in ornate carvings.

They walked across the bridge, footsteps tapping lightly on the boards. Leonardo leaned over the side as a school of koi stirred the surface, mottled in the shade of floating leaves.

"It's pretty here," said Kate. "I hope it doesn't all die."

The Tiger girl shot her an alarmed look. Kate neither acknowledged her nor offered an explanation. The girl picked up her pace, dipping her head, and they followed her to the pagoda.

Leonardo stepped through the opening and blinked at the sudden change in light. As his eyes adjusted, he found himself in a gold room even more intricately decorated than the outside. A girl Leonardo almost didn't recognize sat on a sort of throne; hands folded in her red robe. Without the white face-paint, she lost the ancient, otherworldly quality she'd possessed at the full moon ceremony. She looked even younger; maybe thirteen, with freckles and dark eyes.

"Cleo," said Mishti.

"Mishti. And her new co-leader," said Cleopatra. A tiger cub slept at her feet, a delicate gold chain around its neck. She ran one slippered foot over its short spine, then regarded Kate and Cyrus. "And you two."

Cyrus' face and body flickered, resembling Cleopatra for a blink, then he was himself again. He smirked at her unsettled expression.

Leonardo gave him a sharp look.

*No room left for error.*

"We need to talk," said Mishti.

"All of you?" asked Cleopatra.

"Have you heard of the Dark?"

Cleopatra frowned. She inclined her head for them to continue.

Mishti relayed the events of both the Darkwoods and the Turquoise Isle. Cleopatra's tiger cub woke during the story and climbed into her lap, watching them through yellow eyes.

After Mishti finished, Cleopatra held silent for a long time, stroking the tiger and studying them.

"And if I don't help?"

"We're not asking for your help," said Leonardo. "We're asking you to join us."

Cleopatra ran a hand through the coarse fur between her tiger cub's ears. It yawned, tiny fangs gleaming in the sunlight.

"Each of us has given up something as a sign of good faith," pressed Mishti.

"Yes?" said Cleopatra.

Mishti nodded. "Leonardo gave me a magical key that can unlock any door, and the pirates gave us the use of their ship."

The lies had begun. An uneasy feeling settled in Leonardo's stomach.

Mishti procured the rock, tossed it in the air, and caught the key.

"Interesting," said Cleopatra.

Mishti returned the key to her pocket. "In return, I gave the pirates my youngest girl, Charley, and Leonardo gave his youngest boy, Pompey."

*Do you really need to lie about everything?* One misstep could blow up the entire plan. Hell, he didn't even know the plan. But so far, both Cleopatra and the girl from the patrol seemed to buy it. The girl plucked at her robes nervously, a smudge of white paint hiding under the edge of her jaw.

"And what do you want from us?" asked Cleopatra.

"Your word," said Mishti. "Nothing but your word."

"Why?"

"Because I'm going to offer you a gamble. Dragon and Snake Clan have taken advantage of Tiger since we first started trading favours at the ceremonies. Their contribution to our little alliance will be to reverse every favour you owe them."

Leonardo recalled what Juliet told him. *Tiger Clan pays a lot for their girls. They are...selective about their recruits.*

"Really." Skepticism coated Cleopatra's words. "They've agreed to that."

Leonardo pursed his lips. He hadn't been in the Cove a week and even he struggled to believe that lie.

"No," said Mishti. "That's why it's a gamble."

Cleopatra scoffed.

"This is about more than favours," pressed Mishti. "If the Dark wins, we lose everything. Demetrius is terrified; he'll agree in a heartbeat if it means another clan joins the fight."

Cleopatra crossed her arms.

Leonardo glanced at Kate and Cyrus. Sunlight cut through a screen in the window, crisscrossing a pattern of shadows on their faces. Both pirates looked as worried as he felt.

*We should have discussed the plan.* All they could do was watch Mishti and hope things didn't go south.

"Why should I care about favours," asked Cleopatra, "if this Dark is so bad that no one else does?"

"Because you're smart," said Mishti. A bead of sweat glistened at her temple. "If we survive this, you'll come out on top of the Cove—well, below me, of course. You'll have to fight the Dark either way. At least this way, you gain something."

Leonardo studied the gold columns and vaulted ceiling. Three girls peered down from a balcony, then shifted back when he spotted them.

Cleopatra drew a slow, deliberate breath. "So I give my word to help, and in exchange, I *might* gain Snake's and Dragon's favours?"

"We told you it would be a gamble," said Kate, speaking for the first time.

Mishti glanced at her.

"Take a risk, Cleo," said Cyrus.

*Careful.* Leonardo watched Cleopatra intently.

She eyed the pirates coldly, intimidating beyond her age.

"Fine," she told Mishti. She folded her tiger's ear and let it spring back up. "What am I giving my word for?"

"The Dark will be attacking soon," said Mishti. "Gather your clan and sail to our fortress tomorrow morning. We'll meet you there with Snake Clan."

"And then we fight this...Dark?"

"Correct," said Mishti.

"Ok," said Cleopatra. "You have my word."

Leonardo released his breath. *It worked.*

"We'll see you tomorrow morning," he said, suppressing the relief in his voice. "Don't be late."

# CHAPTER 35

"What happens when she finds out all those things are lies?" asked Leonardo.

"We'll be fighting the Dark. It'll be too late for her to change her mind."

They stood aboard the deck of *The Forever* again, as it plowed north for Snake Clan territory.

"And if she finds out sooner?" said Leonardo.

"She won't," said Mishti. "Trust me."

"I still don't know why you needed to lie."

"We tried the direct approach with Demetrius. We don't have time to convince everyone that a bunch of shadows are going to kill them. I threw enough bullshit at her that she forgot she had a choice except fighting the Dark."

"She's not stupid," said Leonardo, pacing to a cannon. "She's going to realize that we could be lying about the Dark."

"But we're not."

He gripped the edge of the cannon. "She doesn't know that!"

"Trust me," said Mishti. "She'll show up."

"I need some air," said Leonardo, just to escape the subject.

"You do realize we're outside," said Mishti. "In the wind."

"Yes, I do." Leonardo descended the steps to the main deck and crossed to the hatch. Down below, he found Moth, Juliet, Pompey, and Charley standing around a wooden crate they'd repurposed as a table. Charley rolled up her sleeve to reveal the black ribbon tattooed to her pale skin, as Juliet stirred a bamboo canister with a short stick.

"What's this?" asked Leonardo.

"Voodoo," said Pinch's voice. Leonardo twisted to find him reclined in a hammock, half shrouded in a shadowy corner.

"I think we've found a cure," said Juliet. "It's making the surface marks vanish, at least. But I don't know how we'd safely get it into Nym."

"What is it?" asked Leonardo, slightly alarmed at the word 'safely', when her test subject appeared to be Charley.

"Sea Monster venom." Moth said it quickly, as if that would take the sting out.

"Excuse me?" said Leonardo.

"It was Sophie's idea," said Juliet. "I've mixed it with every sacred plant to the Cove and I'm using a brush of hummingbird feathers to apply it."

"Meaning?" asked Leonardo. Venom was venom, no matter how you dressed it up. The black puncture marks along his hand proved that.

"I've done everything I can to gain the Lostwoods' favour. This should only hurt a little."

"It was you and Mishti who gave Sophie the idea," said Moth. "With your hand and her bite. It made you immune to the Dark, because, as Chief Tokala said, sea monsters are one of the purest creatures of the Lostwoods—"

"Stop saying Lostwoods," said Pinch from his hammock. "You sound like a girl."

"I had some venom with my supplies," said Juliet. "But I was reluctant to use it."

"For obvious reasons," said Moth.

"But you're using it now," said Leonardo.

"Your hand was infected and laced with raw venom," said Juliet. "It has such an intense reaction with the Dark that when you grabbed your arm, the two burnt each other. Your Dark mark is dead, but I think it's like a scar now. The same with your bite."

"And this mixture won't do that?" He eyed the bamboo canister.

"If this works, it should dissolve the Dark, rather than burn it."

"And if it doesn't?"

"I tried it on myself first." Juliet handed Moth the canister and showed Leonardo the side of her neck, bare of the mark she'd had before.

"And you think it's really gone?" he asked. "It's not just..."

"Hiding?" asked Juliet. "I don't think so. Moth told me how Nym was attacked, how all the grass around him was dead. That sounds like a deeper saturation than what we faced on the Turquoise Isle. I don't think there's enough of the Dark in us to hide under the skin like his does."

"But it's just a guess," said Leonardo.

"That's all we can do," said Juliet. "I do have a theory though."

"Which is?"

"I think these marks are like doorways. If we're close enough to the Dark, it can use them to control us. It's different from what's happening to Nym, who has enough of the Dark inside him that it knows to hide."

"So, if we destroy the doorways..."

"We're one step further removed from the Dark," said Moth.

"What does Nym do?" asked Pinch. "Drink the venom?"

"It's too dangerous," said Juliet. "Leonardo and Mishti were lucky the Dark came along when it did. Without something to burn off the venom, who knows what state they'd be in now."

"And you're sure this is safe to use on everyone?" asked Leonardo.

"It didn't hurt me," said Juliet. "Remember, I diluted it down a lot. But I don't have much of it, so I'm starting with Charley and Pompey. We'll need to get more venom before I can treat the entire crew."

"Great," said Pinch. "More spooking around in caves."

"Spelunking," said Moth.

"What?"

"One *spelunks* in caves."

"No, 'one' doesn't."

"Yes, one does!"

"Juliet," said Leonardo. "You can't expect us to go back in those caves. There has to be another way to get the venom."

If Juliet had some stored away, maybe another clan did too.

"There is," said Juliet. "Those sea monsters are too small anyway. I suspect the only reason their venom worked on you was because it festered. This," she said, taking back the canister from Moth, "Is deep-sea monster venom."

"That sounds pleasant," said Pinch.

"It won't be easy to get," said Juliet. "But it might be the only cure. Sophie's been studying maps and she thinks we can find one. Now, hold still, Charley. It might sting a little."

Juliet lifted a thin stick of bamboo from atop the crate. A plume of tiny iridescent feathers formed a brush on the end, and Juliet dipped it into the canister.

Charley held steady as Juliet painted a thin, dark-tinted paste over the bands on her arm. At first, nothing happened, then Charley winced.

"It's ok," said Juliet.

"Ow!"

"You're ok. It burnt a bit for me too."

"It's burning a lot!" Charley looked to Leonardo; green eyes wide.

"Juliet," said Leonardo, lowering his voice.

"Look," said Juliet. The first edge of the Dark began to fade, revealing pink and irritated skin underneath. More dissolved as he watched, and Charley's natural skin tone replaced the inky tattoo.

Charley grit her teeth and Juliet kept applying.

"Hang in there," said Moth. "You're doing great."

Charley gasped and Juliet hesitated. Charley swallowed and drew a breath through her teeth.

"Don't be a wimp," said Pompey. His tone was teasing, and Charley's eyes flashed daggers at him.

"You're next," she managed. "I bet you'll scream like a girl."

"You're a girl," said Pompey. "I don't hear you screaming."

"That's because I'm tougher than you."

Juliet continued applying the salve while Charley was distracted. Based on Charley's expression and the stifled noises she made, Leonardo guessed the distraction did little but take the edge off, but he was grateful for Pompey's presence none the less.

After Juliet painted on the last stroke, it became a matter of waiting for the salve to finish its job. Most of the Dark had dissolved, and Charley was adjusted enough to the pain that she managed better than he suspected she felt.

Juliet started on Pompey immediately. His suffering provided a new distraction and carried Charley through the remainder of her healing.

She cut him no slack and started needling him at the first grunt of pain.

Pompey's ribbon curved down the back of his collar. When he took off his shirt to let Juliet get at it, all five of Leonardo, Moth, Pinch, Juliet and Charley fell silent.

The Dark curved under his arm and wrapped around his skinny torso, winding into a tight spiral directly over his heart.

"Fuck," said Pinch.

"You should start there," said Moth.

Juliet nodded, brow furrowed as she started to paint the salve over his heart, making small, quick strokes with her brush. After the first few rings, she stopped to steady her fingers, drawing a shaky breath.

"That's why we're stopping it," said Leonardo. "We're not letting it go any further."

Pompey's healing was notably more painful than Charley's. He clenched his jaw and balled his hands into fists, knocking them against his legs.

"Here," Leonardo grabbed a rag and rolled it tight. "Bite on this."

Juliet painted on layer after layer of the salve. A few tense minutes later, they all breathed a sigh of relief as the last of the Dark finally faded, leaving nothing but irritated skin.

"That's almost all of the cure," said Juliet, peering into the canister.

"How do we get more?" asked Leonardo.

"Kill a deep-sea monster," said Juliet.

*Right. Naturally.*

"We have cannons," she said, glancing at the nearest one, chained near Pinch's hammock.

"Right." Leonardo drew a heavy breath. If a deep-sea monster was as formidable as it sounded, he feared they could lose more than they gained by going after one. And it could all be for naught if the Dark just latched onto them again at the next attack.

"What do they look like?" he asked. "How big are they?"

"It depends. I've heard of some that look like a serpent. Others look like the ones that attacked us in the cave. Just…" she glanced away. "The size of this ship."

Leonardo stared at her. *Are you insane?*

"How deep do they live?" asked Moth.

Leonardo whirled on him. Moth, who was afraid of monkeys, sounded entirely unfazed at the idea of hunting a sea monster.

"I've only ever seen one," said Juliet, "but it wasn't more than a day's travel out to sea."

"I'm going to find Mishti and the captains," said Leonardo. "There must be another way to get the venom."

He placed one foot on the ladder when he felt the ship begin to turn left. Away from their straight-shot course and toward open sea.

He looked back at Moth, Juliet, and the kids.

"Spooky," said Pinch.

Leonardo climbed the rest of the way up and pulled his shoulders through the hatch. He immediately spotted the reason John had diverted their course, and it had nothing to do with hunting for sea monsters.

A wall of black clouds towered over the horizon, directly in the ship's path. It blanketed the cliffs ahead, moving rapidly over the water as *The Forever* peeled away from the coast.

Everyone on deck stopped what they were doing and stood squinting at the mass of clouds, now shifting to their right side as John angled the ship perpendicular to its path.

Even under full sail, Leonardo could see they wouldn't make it clear in time.

"That doesn't look like a normal storm," said someone near Leonardo.

*No,* thought Leonardo. *It looks like—*

"Everyone belowdecks," called Mishti.

Leonardo swung up out of the hatch and intercepted her as she crossed the deck.

"Where did this come from?"

"Nowhere." Mishti took the steps to the foredeck two at a time. Leonardo joined her at the rail, watching the storm shift and darken as it rolled toward them.

"It was sunny," said Mishti. "Not cloudy at all, and then all at once, this…"

They stood in silence for a few seconds, each processing the weight of another attack.

"Juliet and Sophie found a cure," said Leonardo. "For the marks on everyone."

"Really?"

"Sea monster venom," said Leonardo.

"We already knew that," said Mishti. "That's why you and I are immune. What do they want to do, let everyone get bit?"

"Juliet came up with a way of applying it. But she only had enough for Charley and Pompey."

"Well, at least they're safe." Mishti eyed the approaching darkness. "We should chain everyone else up."

"That could make things worse," said Leonardo.

"I wasn't being serious. But how could it make things worse?"

"I don't know. I just don't like the idea of being immobile."

*Water.* The thought hit Leonardo out of nowhere. When the Dark first infected Nym, the only thing that could hold it at bay was the river. It never cured him like the venom, but Leonardo thought it might be enough to get them through the attack.

"I have an idea," he said to Mishti, already turning from the rail and running to the stairs. "Everyone, we need pails of water!" he shouted at the Lions and pirates still on deck.

Distracted confusion met his request. Everyone who wasn't already down the hatch was either jostling to get down or grabbing whatever loose items were left behind.

"Someone give me a pail," shouted Leonardo, running down the stairs as Puck pressed through the crowd and tossed him a wooden bailing bucket. Kate emerged a second later, carrying two more.

"What are these for?" she asked, one eye on the sky as the Dark drew closer.

"Seawater," said Leonardo. "I'll explain later."

The sea was to the Cove what the river was to the Darkwoods, so Leonardo hoped it would have the same effect. He grabbed the ladder from where it lay stowed and tossed it over the side, then swung his legs over the bulwark and climbed down until water splashed against his ankles, spraying halfway up his leg. Leonardo gripped the ladder rung with one hand and leaned down to fill the first bucket in the violent surf jetting out from under the hull.

Sea spray pelted his face, and Leonardo blinked hard as he started back up the short ladder.

"Give it to me," called Kate, leaning down over the bulwarks. She took the first bucket and handed him another.

Mishti and Puck appeared at the rail, and Leonardo looked up at them as he climbed down to fill the second bucket.

"What are you doing?" demanded Mishti.

"Rags," said Leonardo. "We need rags too."

"Got it," said Puck.

"Tear them into strips and meet me belowdecks," said Leonardo.

He lifted the second bucket to Kate, and she handed it to Mishti, just as Bates and a pirate came running up with three more pails.

"What do I do with this?" asked Mishti.

"Take it belowdecks," said Leonardo.

That was when the first raindrops hit.

# CHAPTER 36

ates cried out in pain, staggering back as a black drop ran down his arm.

"Ow!" Kate dropped her bucket, spilling water across the deck. It flooded through the gaps in the bulwark and sloshed down over Leonardo.

He gasped at the cold.

Panic swept over the ship. Cries of pain punctuated the splatter of inky rain, carried ahead of the storm on a cold wind.

A drop hit Leonardo's skin and rolled down his arm. He didn't feel a thing.

"Get below," he ordered Kate, Puck, and Bates. "I've got the rest of these."

A raindrop hit Kate in the face and she flinched.

"Go!" said Leonardo.

Kate, Puck, and Bates ran for the hatch, and Mishti jumped

to take Kate's spot. More drops splattered against the ship and Leonardo's skin, running like wet paint down the hull.

"It's not hurting you either?" Leonardo asked Mishti.

"I can't feel anything."

More proof of the potency of sea monster venom. And proof that the venom had spread to their bloodstream, or else Leonardo didn't know how to explain their whole-body immunity.

He climbed down two rungs, filled a bucket, up two rungs, handed it to Mishti. Then down two rungs with the next bucket.

John staggered down the stairs from the upper deck, swearing and shouting in pain. The scattered drops of rain became a thin shower, as black as the clouds sliding overhead.

Leonardo filled the last bucket and scrambled over the rail. The streaks of black running down Mishti's face looked like something out of a nightmare. He and Mishti splashed through the dark slicks pooling on deck, and Kate threw the hatch open from below, jumping down the ladder and out of sight as Leonardo and Mishti scrambled down. Leonardo took one last look at the blackness enveloping the ship, then he slammed the hatch.

"Where's Nym?" he shouted.

"Here," Nym pushed through the crowded ranks.

"Give me your shirt."

Nym yanked it off and threw it to Leonardo. Leonardo found the sleeves and submerged them up to the shoulders in water. For the first few seconds, Nym's arms looked fine, then Leonardo caught the first hint of a black vein.

"Here we go," said Nym.

Leonardo wrung out the sleeves and threw Nym's shirt back to him.

"Put this on. Quickly."

Nym struggled into the waterlogged sleeves. "That's nice and freezing," he tried to joke.

"Everyone else," said Leonardo. "Start soaking rags in the water. Tie them over any marks on your arms."

He caught movement in his peripheral and ducked just in time to avoid Puck's blow. Puck made another grab for him, or rather, Puck's arm did, while the rest of Puck shouted in protest. The pile of rags he'd been holding fell to the ground.

Pinch grabbed Puck from behind and Leonardo dove for the rags. He grabbed the nearest and shoved it in a bucket of water, then scrambled to his feet and moved for Pinch and Puck. They were engaged in a strange upright wrestling match, where Puck apologized profusely, and Pinch swore through his teeth.

Pinch threw Puck against the wall of the ship, and Leonardo grabbed his rogue arm. Black veins spiderwebbed out from the shadow ribbon. Leonardo slapped the wet rag over it, struggling to wrap it tight around Puck's entire forearm.

He got it wrapped, then he and Pinch teamed up to overpower the arm. For a good thirty seconds, nothing changed, and Leonardo feared he'd gotten it all wrong. The Dark lent Puck strength, and it took both of Leonardo and Pinch to hold him down. Then, slowly, Leonardo felt Puck's strength falter. Another thirty seconds of wresting and Puck's arm fell limp.

Leonardo and Pinch sagged, breathing heavy.

"Don't take that off," said Leonardo.

"Uh, Leo..." Pinch held up his own arm. His fingers twitched as black veins grew from his Dark mark, zig-zagging across his skin.

"Shit." Pinch dove for the rags, sloshing water out of the bucket as he panicked to wrap his arm.

Sophie tried to do the same and ended up knocking over a bucket as both her arms fought her. She threw herself to the ground, pressing her forearms into the spilled water.

A pirate flew out of the crowd at Leonardo, and Leonardo whirled around. He punched the pirate square in the jaw and sent him reeling back.

Leonardo grabbed the last of Puck's rags off the ground and mopped it through the spilled water, then tackled the pirate and fought to wrap his arm.

The quarters belowdecks were cramped, and Leonardo took more collateral elbows then intentional ones, but they eventually suppressed every rogue arm. He leaned against a support column, gritting his teeth against a hard shot he'd taken in the ribs. Everyone was wet, bruised, and winded, but a sense of respite permeated the space, despite the wall of black water pelting the portholes and drumming on the deck above them.

To Leonardo's relief, the black rain didn't stick to their skin like the last attack. The nightmarish streaks on Mishti's face and his own washed away with spare rags, and within a matter of minutes, everyone was in stable condition.

He had no time to dwell on it. He was just thankful for one less complication.

The ship creaked and rocked in the storm. Winds howled outside, whistling between the boards. As the minutes stretched on, the ship-wide relief began to sour. Doubts took voice, and Lions and pirates shuffled, uneasy.

Leonardo scanned the ceiling boards for cracks. A drop of

black water squeezed through a seam and fell to the ground with a heavy splat, drawing a moment of silence from those around it.

"We're off course," said John. "I never locked the helm."

"What does that mean?" asked Leonardo.

"It means he ran away," said Pip. "And left us to drift. Dammit, John. "

"I didn't see you coming up to help," snapped John.

"What does 'lock the helm' mean?" pressed Leonardo.

"It means," said Pip. "That rather than sailing away from the storm, we're now sailing right into it."

"But what is *locking the helm*?" snapped Mishti.

"You tie a rope around the wheel," said Kate. "It keeps the ship on the same course."

Another black raindrop fell from the ceiling. Mishti looked at Leonardo. Leonardo nodded. "Is there a rope up there?" he asked.

"There should be," said Kate. "But—"

"The Dark can't hurt us," said Leonardo. "We'll be fine."

"Hold up," said Juliet. "Don't go thinking you're superheroes now."

"But you said—"

"*I said*, the venom has made you immune so far." She pointed to a porthole, black with rain. "This is a lot more Dark than we've seen before."

"We'll take our chances," said Mishti. "It's better odds then we have sailing straight into it."

Leonardo didn't point out that any direction might be 'sailing into it' if the Dark shifted with them. Everyone knew that already, but as Mishti said, at least this gave them a fighting chance. However, Juliet had a point.

"If we're wrong," said Leonardo, "Lion Clan can't lose both of us. Stay here. I'll go."

"Set a course due south," said John.

"Like hell," said Mishti. "I'm coming. You get lost up there, we're all screwed."

"Trust me," said Leonardo. "I'll get to the wheel."

They stared at each other in the dim light. Finally, Mishti swore and stepped back.

"Are you sure about this?" asked Moth.

Leonardo met his gaze. He wasn't sure about anything.

"Everyone get back from the hatch," said Leonardo.

"Take my compass." Moth tossed it to him, old and brass and weathered.

"Be careful," said Kate. Under her trilby hat, real concern strained her face.

Leonardo grabbed the first ladder rung and started climbing. Everyone shuffled back as he reached the top.

The howling, pounding of the storm pressed down on the hatch above him, muffled through the wood. Leonardo cast one last look at the crowd below, bunched together in the lantern light, then he threw open the hatch and rolled onto the deck.

***

Leonardo scrambled to his feet in a pool of black water, squinting into the downpour. The world was as black as the deepest night he'd ever seen, the wind screaming as it ripped at his clothes.

He couldn't see the upper deck through the gloom, but he knew its location from the hatch and started toward it, half-running through the black water.

The roar of the storm vibrated his teeth, grit hard against the impact of the rain. The sheer force of it pelted him like flying shrapnel.

*Where is the staircase?* His internal map told him he should've reached it by now. But even if he was off course, he should've reached *something* by now. A railing, a corner...

*Calm down. The deck boards are still under your feet.*

Inky pools sloshed as he stepped through them.

A second later, he fell into the stairs.

He tripped and caught himself awkwardly against the steps. He swore, breathing heavily, braced against the slick wood. The storm was rapidly depleting his reserves. He pushed himself up and started climbing. The rain ran into his eyes, blinding him even more.

So far, the Dark hadn't overpowered his immunity to it. But the longer Leonardo spent in the storm, the more he questioned whether it truly was *the Dark*. It was tainted by the Dark, that was certain, but the Dark itself was more aggressive, more conscious. This storm felt like nothing but brute force.

He reached the top and stumbled, expecting another step.

*It's ok. Keep going.*

Leonardo clamped his fingers on the rail and started for the wheel. When he found it, he fumbled to grip the spokes.

*Due west.* A bolt of lightning flashed overhead, followed by a crash of thunder so loud he flinched.

Leonardo removed Moth's old compass from his pocket and hunched over it, using his body as a shield against the rain.

He wiped the water off with his thumb, but that only smeared more black across the glass. He leaned close to it, squinting in the total lack of light to make out the direction markings.

Another bolt of lightning illumined the needle, pointing north-northwest. That meant they'd drifted nearly a quarter of the compass' circumference off-course.

Leonardo pocketed the compass and turned the wheel left. It spun freely, and he gave it several rotations, concentrating on the feeling of the ship beneath him. He couldn't see the sails, black on black, but he knew they'd be stretched to full capacity in this wind, and he felt the ship plowing through the waves.

He couldn't even tell what was the sound of the waves and what was the storm. It all blended into one ceaseless crash.

This time, he felt the change in their course. Leonardo let the ship come around, then he straightened the wheel and fished out the compass again. A flash of sheet lighting told him he'd brought the ship around to southwest, and it just needed a nudge to come around the rest of the way. Leonardo rotated the wheel twice, waited until he felt the adjustment, then used the palm of his hand to wipe off the compass face. Through the smear of black, he made out a needle pointing due south.

*Ok. Now the rope.*

Water ran freely down his face, and every breath forced him to spit out a mouthful of it. Keeping one hand on the wheel, he crouched and felt along the boards.

*Please be there,* he thought, grimacing at the tremors in his fatiguing muscles. *Please.*

# CHAPTER 37

Leonardo's fingers closed on the rope.

*Thank you.* He hauled it up and tied it to the wheel, lightning and thunder cracking overhead as the storm kept driving down. But no matter how miserable the conditions, he was now certain this wasn't the Dark itself. The next time the Dark attacked, he expected something that took more than a shielding arm to fend off.

He tested the wheel to assure it was immobile, then started for the stairs again. He used the rail as a guide, and when he felt it end, he carefully eased himself down to the first step.

The stairs were a waterfall of black rain, and Leonardo took extra care staying upright until he was three-quarters of the way down and lost his footing. His boots slid out from under him and he went down hard. The edge of the stair drove into his ribs, right where he'd been bruised by the railing that morning.

Leonardo bellowed. The storm ripped away the sound. He

tumbled down the rest of the steps; elbows, hips and the back of his head knocking against the stairs until he sprawled out onto the deck.

*Shit.*

The rain pelted him, and he swore again, pushing himself painfully to his feet. His whole body ached as he started across the open deck.

Leonardo put all his concentration into the geography of the ship. He'd come off the left-hand stairs, which meant he needed to angle right to find the hatch. But not too far right or he'd miss it completely. Every step was a calculated guess, but after what felt like a thousand of them, he kicked a raised piece of wood.

He looked down, then dropped to his knees and felt the unmistakable shape of the hatch.

*Yes.* His victory surged like the lightning overhead. He was getting out of this godforsaken storm.

He tugged, but nothing happened. He tugged again.

*Dammit.*

He pounded on the hatch, water splashing off the wood until it cocked open an inch and a seam of light flooded out. Leonardo grabbed the edge immediately, heaving it open so the water sloshed off. The lantern-lit hole below was the most welcoming sight he had ever laid eyes on.

Whoever unlocked it was gone now; down the ladder and out of danger from the rain. Leonardo swung his legs into the opening and pulled the hatch shut above him.

# CHAPTER 38

His return was met with gasps, and looking down at his body, Leonardo understood why. He looked less like a person, and more like something dragged out of a swamp he never wanted to visit.

Black ran off his clothes, pooling on the floor with the rainwater. Everyone stood back, completely silent.

"Here," Juliet appeared through the crowd with a pair of wet rags. She stopped at the edge of the water and tossed one to him.

"Did you fix our course?" asked John.

Leonardo nodded, wiping the rain off his face. The rag came away as black as if he'd been covered in soot. "Due west and the helm is locked."

The relief through the ship was tenuous. The rivulets of black water running down the walls kept their optimism dampened.

"Great," said Pip. "Except now, the Dark has probably moved to the south and we need to turn north again.

"That's not the Dark," said Leonardo.

"No?" said Pip. He eyed Leonardo up and down, covered in black. "It sure looks like the Dark."

"It's just a storm. It's been touched by the Dark, but we'll sail out of it."

Pip crossed his arms.

"Then I guess we wait," said Kate. "If you're right, we'll be out of it soon. This wind should help us."

Leonardo wiped off the rest of the Dark—or at least, what he could—and edged around the crowd to an open space where he could sit against the hull. Everything was soaking wet, from the rags on everyone's arms, to the pools on the floor and the blackness running down the walls and ceiling, but it was an infinity drier than the world outside. The rain and the thunder were a distant thing now, *out there* while he was in here.

The breath of so many warmed the space, and Leonardo closed his eyes and leaned back against the wood, relieved to be back in the muted confines of the ship.

"What do you think it'll look like?" Charley's voice carried to him from somewhere nearby.

"Big," said Pompey. "I bet its teeth are as long as my arm."

Leonardo shifted, trying to follow the sound of their voices. Lions and pirates milled about, all talking at once and dodging the drips from the ceiling.

"I bet longer," said Charley. "And I bet it has red eyes."

"And spines on its back."

Leonardo leaned to see around a support post and spotted Charley's knee, legs crossed in a shadowed corner.

He pushed himself up, wincing at the bruises in his side, and walked around the support post to find her and Pompey sitting under a hammock, the yellowed ropes swinging freely with the ship's movements.

They were deep in their debate and didn't see him until he eased down against the post across from them. Pompey broke off mid-sentence.

"What are you talking about?" asked Leonardo.

Pompey didn't say a word.

"The sea monster!" said Charley. "What did they look like when you saw them?"

"What sea monster?" asked Leonardo.

"The ones you saw in the cave!" said Charley.

"No," said Leonardo. "I mean, it sounded like you expect us to run into another one. A big one, with teeth as long as your arm and spines on its back."

Pompey and Charley glanced at each other.

"You two talk loud," said Leonardo.

"Juliet is calling a sea monster," said Charley.

*Shit.*

"Calling? And how is she doing that?"

"I don't know. Some sort of magic."

"Right," said Leonardo. "And where is she?"

Charley and Pompey exchanged another look.

Leonardo rolled his eyes. "I won't tell her you told me."

"She's down in the hold," said Charley, quickly, as if that made it less of a betrayal.

"Is Moth with her?"

Charley nodded.

*Of course he is.*

"Thank you," said Leonardo, climbing to his feet again. "They had tentacles," he added to answer her earlier question. He showed them his hand, perforated with black punctures. "If we do see one, don't let it eat you."

Leonardo left them on that, working his way back through the crowd to the hatch that led deeper into the ship. He hoped seeing his hand was enough to give them pause. If they met one of Juliet's deep-sea monsters, he didn't want Charley and Pompey doing something stupid to get a closer look.

***

Leonardo dropped into the hold to find Juliet, Moth, Sophie, and a small fire on the floorboards, in the centre of a ring of red flowers.

"Are you insane?" Leonardo scoured for something to douse the fire.

"It's ok," said Moth. "It's on a piece of slate."

"Right," snapped Leonardo. "Because slate will stop the fire from spreading and burning down the entire ship."

"It's a charcoal fire," said Juliet calmly. "No sparks and no smoke."

"I want it put out," said Leonardo. The flowers around the fire were arranged in a strikingly detailed likeness of the monsters they had fought in the cave. Eight tentacles curled across the slate.

"Who said you could summon a sea monster?" demanded Leonardo.

"I did," said Sophie. She crossed her arms, staring him down. The firelight danced across her face, illuminating a dusting of freckles, like a shadow of war paint on her cheeks.

317

"What happened to, 'we're on the same side'?" he asked, searching for anything he could smother the flames with.

"We need the venom!" said Juliet.

"We need to *live*, too," said Leonardo. He stopped to face her, bathed in the wavering, watery light. "Are we equipped to kill a sea monster?"

"Calm down," said Sophie calmly.

"We have cannons," said Juliet. She glanced at the flower petals, her expression suddenly uncertain.

"Have you fired one before?" he pressed. "You've only seen these 'deep-sea monsters' once. You have no right to risk everyone's safety on an assumption we'll be able to kill it."

"She's trying to save everyone," snapped Moth, surprising Leonardo. He couldn't recall a time when Moth had ever raised his voice at him.

"Yeah?" countered Leonardo. "And how will she do that when she and everyone else is dead?"

"Do you expect us to do *this* every time the Dark shows up?" asked Moth, plucking at the wet rag bound around his arm. "When it attacks, will we be going into battle with these on our arms?"

"Trust me," said Juliet. "This is the only way."

"I'm tired of trusting people," said Leonardo. "I'm tired of secret plans."

"We tried to talk to you earlier!" said Moth.

Leonardo closed his eyes. "Put out the fire," he said, "before you burn down the whole ship. No sea monsters, no secret plans, we talk about everything *as a clan*. Understood?"

"You don't give me orders," said Sophie. She stepped around

Moth and Juliet, shoulders back, chin raised, gold robe glinting as she blocked his view.

"No?" said Leonardo. "How about I go ask the pirates how they feel about this fire?"

No one replied. The fire hissed, flames licking between chunks of charcoal. Sophie blinked slowly, and he could tell she had no good response.

*Did they think through this plan at all?*

"Put it out," repeated Leonardo. "Understood?"

Behind Sophie, Juliet nodded.

"Good." Leonardo grabbed a ladder rung and started up.

# CHAPTER 39

The storm passed shortly after Leonardo left the hold. Black water still ran down the portholes, but beams of sunlight cut through, and Leonardo followed Mishti up the ladder to the hatch.

Outside, they found a sight that was in equal parts optimistic and disturbing. A clear sky hung over them, blue and sunny as the tail end of the storm rolled away. On the flip side, *The Forever* dripped with gallons of thick, black water.

It ran off the sails and the rigging, splattering against the deck, which in itself swirled in sluggish pools, slowly draining through the bulwarks. It dispersed as it met the sea, and only blue, clear waves broke the surface.

The rest of the mixed clan and crew began making their way topside, and Leonardo crossed to the foredeck. He sloshed water off the steps with his boot and shielded his eyes, turning in a circle. They were in the middle of nowhere now; the cliffs a distant shadow beyond the stern. Only waves stretched ahead of them, all the way to the horizon, and Leonardo began to think about how deep it was here.

Juliet had said the last monster sighting was no more than a day's travel out to sea. And with the wind they'd been sailing under, Leonardo guessed they'd travelled much further than they should have in an hour.

*And she was calling them, with the fire.*

He recognized the red flowers from the morning before Charley and Pompey's kidnapping, when the woods left a depiction of two lions in a circle on her table.

*If I don't see another magical thing for a year, it will be too soon.*

"You really don't feel a thing?" asked Kate. She stopped a few feet from him, squinting at the freshly revealed sun.

For a second, Leonardo had no idea what she was talking about, then he realized the rail he leaned on was black with residue from the Dark.

"Nothing," he said. He wiped off a section of rail for her, and she propped her elbows against it.

"You're angry," said Kate, studying him. "At me?"

"No, not at you." Leonardo ran a hand over his face. "Have you ever seen a deep-sea monster?"

"Why?" Alarm tinged Kate's voice.

Leonardo eyed her sidelong, the sunlight splitting her face. This was the first time he'd seen fear in her. The pit in his stomach hardened.

"Because we probably will soon."

He told her what Juliet had done.

"She started a fire?" demanded Kate. "Is she insane?"

"No, apparently that's me," said Leonardo. "Moth fully supports her."

"Then he's insane too. Is the fire still burning?"

"I told them to put it out. But I don't know how these things work. The sea monster could be on its way now."

"At least we won't be on fire when it gets here," said Kate.

"You didn't answer my question before," said Leonardo. "Have you seen one?"

"A deep-sea monster?" She nodded gravely.

"Do we stand a chance?"

She shrugged. "We'll have to."

Leonardo nodded, watching a flock of seabirds wheel past. "We'll have to."

"I'm glad you made it back in," said Kate. "When you went out in the storm, I wasn't sure if I'd see you again."

"There were a few moments, I wasn't sure either," said Leonardo, his mind still on the monster. The ship creaked, the rigging swinging over their heads.

"I'd miss you if you had died."

Leonardo paused. Kate raised an eyebrow. Her skull-and-crossbones trilby was tipped back, and her light brown waves fell around her face, illuminated in the post-storm sunlight. A mixture of childish innocence and wicked intention flashed through her eyes, both intriguing and strangely magnetic.

*Don't think about her that way. Viola...*

Kate read his mind. "Viola is with her people now. It will never work between you."

"I can't..." said Leonardo. But he didn't look away. Something in her gaze was electric.

"Some things happen only for a time," said Kate. "Sometimes the woods give you something to treasure for a few days, or a few months, or years. But very few things are forever."

Leonardo glanced at the ship. *The Forever* and its four captains were 'forever'. He wasn't. He'd disappear just like Aleksander and all the others. He and Viola weren't forever either, for the same reason. Even if they somehow managed to make things work, it would only be until his time ran out. She'd spend her entire life in the woods.

"I stopped doing this a long time ago," said Kate. "It hurts too much when everyone eventually disappears. I don't know why I'm letting it happen again."

"I can't," Leonardo shook his head. "I already betrayed Viola's trust with Adriana. I can't—"

"But would you?" pressed Kate. She leaned closer. "If not for Viola?"

"Why does it matter?"

"Because I like you, and I want to know if you like me too. Even if it doesn't mean anything."

Her youthfulness was showing again. Yet, trivial as the question was, Leonardo couldn't bring himself to answer it. Maybe the answer scared him. Maybe it complicated things in a way he wasn't ready for. And maybe he wasn't good enough at hiding his thoughts, because Kate smiled.

"That's all I wanted to know." She winked. "I'll stop bugging you. For now."

She skipped away, and Leonardo closed his eyes.

He was supposed to care about Viola. He did care about Viola, a lot. But something about the Cove blurred his thoughts.

*Paradise is only paradise until you figure out why it's not.* Wasn't that what everyone kept saying?

It was a place of temptation. For Mishti, that meant getting lost in her cactus punch when they needed her sober. For Moth, it meant Juliet, and vice versa. The woods had tried Adriana with him, and when it didn't work, Kate suddenly showed up.

Or maybe he was a temptation for Kate. He couldn't guess how the magic worked.

He could forgive Moth. The Cove was a powerful place, and he was distracted by Juliet right now. It was fear that drove Leonardo's anger. He wasn't sure about anything, and he was afraid to lose more clan members from a careless mistake.

He wondered where Viola was right now. Were her people fighting the Dark?

*Is she still alive?*

Leonardo drew a deep breath of salt air, watching shreds of cloud inch across the sky. He tried to recall the last time things had been easy. That was a fruitless exercise that carried him back to some time long before Aleksander disappeared.

"You look terrible."

The familiar voice came from overboard. Leonardo swore inwardly.

"The Dark is taking its toll, isn't it," said Adriana. She swam backwards, just ahead of the ship's prow, so she could look up at him. Her fair skin glinted in the sunlight.

"What do you want?" asked Leonardo. *Nothing good*, he could guess that much.

"Do you greet everyone like that?" asked Adriana. "Or just me?"

Leonardo didn't grace that with a reply.

"Fine," said Adriana. "Be hostile, see if I care. I'm just here to see you one last time."

"Are you leaving or something?"

"No," said Adriana. "You are."

"What?" A trickle of concern tainted his disregard.

"All of you are about to be..." She quirked her mouth. "Eaten?"

"Excuse me?"

Fresh dread washed over him. *The sea monster.*

"Well—" Adriana broke off, turning her head to listen for something that Leonardo couldn't hear. After a second, she plunged underwater, then resurfaced a moment later.

"My sisters are coming. They don't like me anymore."

"Is the sea monster close?" demanded Leonardo.

"I'm sure Thaisa will tell you everything." Adriana made a two-fingered salute. "Die valiantly."

Then she was gone.

"Hey!" Leonardo shouted after her. "Shit." He ran his hands through his hair.

*Die valiantly.* Like hell. No one was dying on this boat today.

As promised, the sirens appeared alongside the ship a minute later, their hair and scales shimmering under the surface. When they broke through the waves, Thaisa looked up and spotted Leonardo.

"You need to load your cannons," she called.

*Dammit.* "It's coming, isn't it?"

"Load both sides," said Thaisa.

He stared at her. *How big is this thing?*

"Both sides," she repeated. "Don't stop shooting."

"It can't be that big." Panic pressed at the back of Leonardo's mind.

*Why not? There are no rules here. It could be ten times the size of the ship. Or a hundred times. It could be big enough to swallow an island.*

"Where is Mishti?" asked Thaisa, her tone urgent.

Leonardo turned, gazing unseeingly at the busy deck. All his thoughts were focused on the sea monster.

"Leonardo," said Thaisa. He glanced back down at her.

"We have to go," interrupted one of the sirens.

"Leonardo, tell her—"

"It's coming," said another siren. "Let's go."

Thaisa gazed at Leonardo for a second, her sharp features unreadable, then she tightened her lips and nodded. The sirens dropped below the waves and streaked away.

Leonardo squinted along the horizon out to sea, but only the surf marred the endless line of blue. Whatever was coming was coming underwater.

"What's going on?" Mishti topped the stairs. "Was that the sirens?" She frowned, watching Thaisa flee. Hurt and confusion tugged at her face.

"Come on." Leonardo took her by the shoulders. "Tell the pirates to load the cannons. We're about to be attacked by a sea monster."

# CHAPTER 40

Sea monsters had tentacles. Wasn't that what he told Pompey and Charley?

And then he warned them not to get eaten.

Leonardo stood mid-deck as the first tentacle exploded through the water. He caught his breath as gallons of water dumped off the giant purple limb, covered in suction cups and glinting in the sunlight. The tip curled back on itself, as tall as the mainmast.

The first bang of cannon fire nearly shattered Leonardo's eardrums. The next five left his head ringing. The cannons kicked backward, straining the ropes that held them down.

"Let's go!" yelled Pip. "Reload!"

Pirates and Lions scrambled to ram fresh ammunition down the cannon barrels.

"Head's up!" shouted someone behind Leonardo. He whirled to see a second tentacle looming over the far side of the deck.

*Shit.*

"It's huge," said Puck.

"Fire!" yelled Kate.

Six pirates lowered their torches, and six cannonballs exploded over the water, ripping through the monster's skin.

Leonardo's heart raced, pounding like the gunfire.

*It's ok. The cannons will stop it. It can't—*

"It's going down!" yelled Bates behind him.

Leonardo spun back as blue blood spilled into the air. The wounded tentacle smashed into the water, just as two more whipped through the waves, throwing a curtain of water that crashed over Leonardo and the crew on deck.

It hit him like a wall. He staggered back, gasping.

The first set of broadsides blasted from belowdecks. Leonardo clapped his hands over his ears as a row of shots slammed into the sea, throwing spray twenty feet in the air.

Leonardo, Mishti, and their Lions staggered with the tossing of the ship. They were the second line of defence if the monster got past the cannons. Watching it, Leonardo prayed that wouldn't happen.

*We're supposed to get venom from this thing? Screw that.* Survival was the only priority on Leonardo's mind.

Six tentacles now snaked in the air, and Leonardo ran to the edge as two pirates rammed a sack of gunpowder inside a cannon.

"Leo!" yelled Moth.

Leonardo leaned over the side, peering through the water at a mass of darkness, ringed with long, thin white teeth. Thousands of them, around a circular mouth as wide as the main deck.

Leonardo's legs weakened. He backed up in horror.

The gunners rushed to the ready positions and their cannons blasted off another round, jumping back against the ropes.

"John," yelled Leonardo, watching the shots rip through two of the three tentacles. "We need to move."

John stood at the helm, trying to maneuver the ship so the cannons faced their targets. He craned down at Leonardo. "What?"

Runners sprinted past Leonardo with fresh sacks of gunpowder. He dodged around them and ran up the steps to the helm. "The mouth," he said, breathless. "We need to move."

John's gaze flicked up to the sails, billowing in the wind. "We are moving."

Leonardo stared at him. "Are you kidding?"

John shrugged. "There are oars in the hold if you want to row."

"Its mouth is wide open below us," said Leonardo.

"And it will stay that way until we sink. It can't come above water."

"I saw its teeth. It could rip the bottom of the boat off."

John laughed. "First off, this old boat has survived more than one sea monster. And second, if you saw its teeth, you saw they're too thin to bite through wood."

"Then what, it's just going to swim below us and do nothing?"

"Never said that. Heads up."

John cranked the wheel as two tentacles suddenly swung for the deck, one on each side. The ship pivoted harder than any ship should be able to, and the tentacles loomed over Leonardo, throwing a shower of seawater as they crashed down.

Leonardo dove for the stairs, sliding and twisting knees-first.

He hit the stairs hard for the second time that day and grabbed the railing to stop himself.

The tentacles smashed into the deck behind John, driving the stern of the ship down. They curled, twitching as they slithered across the wet boards.

Leonardo scrambled to his feet and drew his sword, sprinting through the pooled water and raising it two-handed over his head. He brought the blade down on one of the tentacles, three times thicker than his body. The suctioned limb flinched at the impact and blue blood flooded around his sword.

Its skin was softer than he'd realized. He raised his sword and brought it down again, and again, as the tentacles rapidly retreated for the rails. He flipped his blade around and drove the point between suction cups, gripping the handle with all his strength as the monster tried to drag itself free, opening a gash along its slick skin.

*It's too heavy.* Momentum pulled him toward the edge of the ship. He shuffle-stepped, fighting to keep a hold on his sword. Finally, inches from the bulwarks, he braced his feet and yanked the blade free.

The tentacle snapped over the rail, out of sight, and Leonardo heaved for breath, blue blood running down his sword.

"Impressive," said John mildly. "You have spirit, if nothing else."

"Is there no way to go faster?" asked Leonardo. A spray of cannonballs missed the monster. A tentacle coiled back in preparation to crash the deck, but one of Kate's cannons struck it first.

"This isn't our first sea monster," said John. "The woods will bring more wind if we need it."

*Right. Unless the woods are purposely withholding it.* It was Juliet's ritual that called the monster, and if he understood things properly, that meant the woods sent it.

John grunted suddenly; brow furrowed as he regarded the ship's wheel. "Shit."

Leonardo felt the shift as the ship began to rotate. He ran to the edge to see the water swirling in a slow vortex.

A shadow fell across Leonardo, and he ducked as a tentacle whipped over his head, slamming into the main deck. A girl screamed, then cut off abruptly. Leonardo's heart stopped.

*She's dead. She vanished.*

He tore down the stairs as Mishti, Puck, Pinch, and a dozen others charged the tentacle. The tip snapped up hard enough to dislodge a cannon. It flew into three pirates, crushing their screams. All three vanished instantly.

Everyone staggered back, swords drawn.

"Careful," yelled Moth.

"Fight, you cowards!" shouted Mishti. She wound up and hurled a throwing ring so hard it buried itself completely in the creature's flesh.

Leonardo charged in and swung his sword in a long slash that ripped a gash in its skin. Two cannonball wounds bled freely, and he wondered for a split second what good swords could do if cannonballs didn't stop it.

*This is hopeless.*

*Stop it,* he snapped at himself. *Fight, dammit.*

The Lions surged around him, and Leonardo swung his sword as hard as he could, beating the monster until it slithered over the side. The tip flicked at the last second, clipping Bates across the chest and throwing him ten feet. He hit the deck and slid just as far, then gasped, wheezing for breath as he struggled to his knees.

Puck and Nym ran to him, and Leonardo turned to find Mishti standing rooted.

"It killed Celia," she said flatly.

*Celia.* She was the one who'd caught Charley's foot when she nearly stumbled over the balustrade, back on the night of the full moon celebration.

Strato was gone. Robin was gone. Now Celia was gone, and Leonardo had no idea how many more would follow.

Another shadow fell over the deck before he could reply. Leonardo twisted as a tentacle swung toward him. He ducked and it whipped over his head, striking the foredeck. The blow rocked the ship and Leonardo stumbled, staggering into a run. He took the steps two at a time and joined Kate as she hacked at the wet, bleeding tentacle.

It retreated over the side and Leonardo lowered his blade for half a second, then he caught the blur of Kate's sword flying at his head. Leonardo threw his in the way, slashing her backward.

"What the hell?"

Kate grinned, bright and dangerous. "You still owe me a rematch."

She took another swing, laughing as he dodged away.

"Are you serious?" Leonardo blocked another swing. "It's not the time!"

Tentacles coiled up in the water behind her.

"Of course it is."

She tried to disarm him, and Leonardo dropped his sword. It clanged off the deck and Kate stared at him, incredulous.

"You let me win."

"I'm not fighting you right now."

Leonardo picked up his sword and turned for the stairs, just as the cannon fire began to falter.

"What is it doing now?" someone shouted.

The monster's tentacles slipped underwater, stretching out like an eight-pointed star. Across at the helm, John swore, spinning the wheel hard to the left as the bow tugged right.

With nothing to shoot at, the gunners held their fire.

The broadsides kept launching cannonballs underwater, but the angle was too shallow. If they could hit the mouth, they could do some damage, but every shot streaked for the outstretched tentacles in a trail of white bubbles.

*Hit the mouth...*

They wouldn't even need much velocity. A few balls of solid iron down the monster's throat...he didn't care how big it was; swallowing cannonballs had to hurt. And its mouth was gaping open. Hell, it was creating a vortex, it was pulling in water so hard.

Leonardo had an idea. But he needed to act immediately. The ship was almost a quarter-turned now, and rotating faster by the second despite all of John's swearing, wheel-spinning efforts.

Leonardo left Kate on the foredeck and sprinted down the stairs.

"Mishti," he called as he hit the deck. "Tell them to stop shooting. Just drop the cannonballs overboard."

"What?"

"Just do it." He ran to the six cannons on the other half of the deck, and the dozen-and-a-half pirates and Lions operating them.

"Forget the cannons," he shouted over an explosion of broadsides. "Just hit the mouth."

He grabbed a runner by the shoulder, stopping her. "No more gunpowder. Just bring cannonballs. As fast as you can. Tell the others."

She nodded and ran for the hatch. Leonardo grabbed another and told him the same. Meanwhile, the gunners heaved their cannons back and tipped the barrels down so the balls rolled out. The ship continued rotating. It was nearly two-thirds of the way around from where it started.

Leonardo moved to stop another runner when he spotted Pompey on deck, carrying a sack of gunpowder.

*What the hell?*

"Pompey," he snapped, shoving his way through runners. "What are you doing?"

He'd specifically ordered Pompey and Charley to stay belowdecks.

Pompey jumped.

"Where's Charley?" demanded Leonardo.

Pompey looked around.

*Shit.*

"Get belowdecks," said Leonardo. It came out harsh and Pompey jumped again, but Leonardo didn't care. If either kid became a casualty to the sea monster, he'd never forgive himself.

He spotted Charley a second later, lugging a cannonball.

"Charley," shouted Leonardo, running to her.

Now Charley jumped, dropping the cannonball. It hit the deck with a crack and started rolling toward the gunners.

Leonardo jumped to stop it before someone broke an ankle.

"What are you doing up here?" he demanded.

"We...I..." Something splashed in the water and Charley leaned to try and see.

*That's why you're here.*

*Fine.*

"Come here." Leonardo took her arm and led her to the rail. Charley stiffened, looking up at him with big eyes. Now that she was about to see the monster for real, she didn't look so certain about it.

Leonardo knew that if he didn't show her, she'd try again. He'd been exactly the same at her age. If she got an eyeful of it now, he hoped she'd have enough sense to stay belowdecks for the rest of the fight. Pompey ran up and Leonardo ushered them between the cannons.

Pompey and Charley glanced at each other, then peeked over the rail.

"Is that..." started Pompey.

"Those are its teeth," said Leonardo.

"That's its mouth?!" said Charley.

Leonardo's heart raced, having them so close to the creature. The ship completed its first full rotation and started into the second, faster than ever. It was also sitting distinctly lower in the water.

"Ok, now you've seen it," said Leonardo, taking their shoulders and dragging them back. "Now I want you belowdecks."

Both kids nodded, hands shaking, and ran for the hatch.

Leonardo looked overboard, threw Charley's cannonball at the monster's mouth, then ran back up the stairs to the helm.

Dozens of cannonballs splashed into the vortex rotating the

ship. Some deflected off its nest of thin teeth and a handful missed completely, but the majority went straight into its dark hole of a mouth.

For a minute, nothing changed, then eight tentacles suddenly ripped out of the sea, throwing a mushroom of water from all sides. It hit the decks with a wet clap, and Leonardo staggered under the crash.

He spat out water, wiping his eyes, and turned in a circle as the eight massive limbs twitched and jerked in the air, colliding and stiffening.

"It's dying!" shouted someone on the main deck.

All eight tentacles jerked hard, then suddenly began to tip, slowly, inward. Leonardo realized what was about to happen.

"John, run!" he shouted, already racing for the stairs. Leonardo flew down the steps as the eight towers collapsed toward the ship. Pirates and Lions crowded down the hatch, shouting and shoving each other. Leonardo hooked around the bottom of the stairs and ran for the door to the captains' quarters instead, just as Mishti threw it open, yanking a key from the lock. It fell to the ground and transformed into a rock.

*She still had Aleksander's key.*

Leonardo grabbed it and dove after her, followed by John. Kate sprinted across the deck toward them, past the crowd that somehow managed to flood down the hatch, despite the sheer volume of bodies.

Kate looked straight up, then threw herself through the doorway just as the first tentacle smashed into the space where she'd been. She flew into Leonardo and he stumbled into the wall, half-catching her. His head struck the doorframe and he sprawled to the floor, Kate's weight on top of him. Her hat tumbled off and brown hair fanned across his face.

Kate shifted, pushing herself up so she could see who she'd fallen on. She grinned.

"Well, that was a happy accident." She didn't move immediately, her eyes locked on his. Pure energy radiated off her, lips parted and fingertips digging into his shirt.

The moment stretched a second longer and he realized she was about to kiss him. A wall of noise slammed his thoughts; some of it desire, some of it panic, all of it too loud to separate in the split second before his mind said, *Viola.*

He shifted, pushing himself up. Kate blinked, then she rolled her eyes and untangled herself from him.

Leonardo glanced around, but Mishti and John were at the doorway, watching the tentacles slam into the deck. The ship rocked with every impact, and Leonardo flinched as one shook the ceiling over their heads.

"Did everyone get below?" asked Leonardo, his mind still reeling.

"How would I know?" snapped Mishti. Another impact slammed the deck over their heads.

"That's eight," said John. He stepped outside, edging around the tentacle that nearly blocked the door. Leonardo followed him, gazing around at the long purple limbs draped across the decks. Two crossed the helm, one hung over the foredeck, and the other five crisscrossed the main deck, limp and lifeless.

They were heavy enough that they didn't slide overboard. Double rows of suction cups stuck to the boards as pirates and Lions cautiously emerged from the hatch.

Juliet climbed out and regarded the mess of tentacles. She carried herself lightly for someone who'd just called a monster on her clan.

"Help me chain it down," she said. "I need the venom."

# CHAPTER 41

Extracting venom was no simple thing. Especially when they didn't know exactly where the venom was. The safe guess was somewhere near its teeth, but its teeth were still under the ship, and Leonardo saw no easy way to change that.

As he studied the massive creature's dead limbs, he felt someone come up behind him. Kate's boots splashed in a puddle of water as she stopped beside him. Very close. Leonardo waited for her to say something, but she tilted her head instead, regarding the nearest tentacle.

Barely an inch of space existed between her left arm and his right. Leonardo glanced at her, and she winked at him, then went back to studying the sea monster.

"Kate—"

"I know." She grinned at him sidelong. "But making you uncomfortable is fun."

Leonardo ran a hand along his jaw. It wasn't fun for him.

Kate bumped hips with him and strode away without a backward glance. Her coat swished behind her, tattered ends stirring in the breeze.

*Stop looking at her.* He tore his eyes away. He knew exactly what she was trying to do, and it was working. Little questions flew through his mind, casting doubt on his future with Viola. But he chased those questions away with hard resolve. If there was any chance for him and Viola to keep what they'd found, he wanted to try.

Leonardo turned away from Kate's silhouette and started across the deck in search of his clan. They had a venom-extraction problem to solve, and they needed to get moving again.

***

The wind snapped the black sailcloth over Leonardo's head as they streamed past the Cove and further still, their course set on a break in the cliffs.

*The Viper's Tongue,* it was called on Mishti's map; a straight run up a river that burrowed through the cliffs. Once through, it widened and tied into the bigger river which split the heart of Snake Clan territory.

For now, they crashed through troughs and rode swells as they followed the drunken line of endless chalk cliffs. Belowdecks, Juliet and Moth worked tirelessly to concoct a large enough batch of the cure to treat everyone.

The answer to their earlier dilemma lay in the arrival of sharks, drawn by the blood in the water. The sharks had proceeded to rip apart the still-submerged sea monster, splashing and churning the water with startling ferocity. One enthusiastic bite freed several of the monster's long needle teeth, and they instantly floated to the surface, which was the first hint they were hollow. Leonardo had retrieved one of the oars from the hold and used it to pull the teeth over to where Bates could dart down the ladder and grab them.

Juliet found a reserve of venom inside each tooth, contained by a thin membrane. They fished as many teeth as they could from the water, and Juliet started working immediately to collect the venom inside.

Now, the Viper's Tongue came into sight, and Leonardo drew his last breath of sea air as they rounded the corner into the cave opening. *The Forever* plowed into the river and Leonardo leaned over the side, peering down at the sandy bottom. Rocks and boulders lay scattered under the ship's keel as they sailed deeper into the tunnel.

He glanced up at the ceiling, realizing those rocks had to have fallen from somewhere. A splash echoed from somewhere around the next bend and he wondered if everyone should get belowdecks.

The tunnel was dark and humid, and the shaded faces of his clanmates gazed around at the craggy walls, sweat glistening on their skin. Leonardo reached over his shoulder and peeled his shirt from his back, watching the tip of the mainmast barely slide past a stalactite.

Neither Mishti nor the pirates seemed concerned about falling rocks, and Leonardo was forced to trust their expertise, even as the ones underwater grew larger. But contrary to appearances, the tunnel held solid, and ten minutes later, they slipped out into the filtered sunlight of the jungle.

"I still don't understand all the lions," said Nym, as they

passed under a fan of giant palm fronds. He joined Leonardo at the rail, watching the greenery slide past.

"Lion Clan?" asked Leonardo.

"No," said Nym. "Just the lions in general. Why is Lion Clan the woods' favourite? Why did we become Lion Clan too? Why did Moth see a lion? Why did he carve one? Why did it survive the fire?"

"I think, for one, it was to bring us all together," started Leonardo.

Nym shook his head. "That everyone's theory for why they kept turning up. But why lions specifically? See?" He pointed to the trees, and Leonardo caught a glimpse of tawny fur. A second later, a lion pushed through the leaves and stopped to study *The Forever*.

"Why can they vanish and reappear elsewhere?" continued Nym. "Why are lions so important to the woods?"

The lion bowed its great maned head to drink from the river.

"I don't know," Leonardo said slowly. He frowned, studying it.

"Neither do I," said Nym. "But we should find out. It might be important."

"Shouldn't you be with Juliet?" asked Leonardo. "She has more venom than she needs now. She might be able to cure—"

"There's only one cure for me," said Nym.

He held Leonardo's gaze, his eyes solemn, and Leonardo fought a sudden chill.

"That's not necessarily true," said Leonardo. "Juliet's—"

"I'm not drinking venom. And it won't work through my skin. I can feel it."

Leonardo didn't try to argue. He had the same suspicions. "It's rooted too deep."

Nym nodded, his lips drawing into a tight line.

Leonardo gripped his friend's shoulder. Cure or not, the only sure way to help Nym would be to destroy the source.

"We'll defeat the Dark," said Leonardo.

"How do you know?"

"Because we don't have a choice."

A while later, Leonardo was climbing the ladder from below-decks when he paused.

Something nudged at the back of his mind. A piece of a puzzle he didn't know he'd been solving suddenly fell into place, and at once Leonardo changed direction and began climbing back down.

It was the conversation with Nym that had spurred it. Talking about the lion omens, then Juliet, and the Dark, and the inexplicability of it all. He recalled the sea monster depiction Juliet made out of flowers in the hold. The same flowers that the woods had shaped into twin lions in Juliet's quarters back at camp.

The two flower pictures bore an uncanny resemblance, in both their artistry and detail. Reflecting on it now, Leonardo was certain they'd been made by the same person.

"Juliet," he said, dropping into the middle hold of the ship, where she'd shifted her workstation. "What did you say about those lions that you found in your quarters?"

"Lions?"

"The ones made out of flowers. Did you say the woods made them?"

Juliet darted a glance at Moth. For a second, Leonardo thought he was in on it too, then he realized her expression wasn't shared alarm. She didn't want Moth to find out what she was hiding. Well, it was too late now.

"Yes," said Juliet. "That's what I said."

"But it's not true, is it?" asked Leonardo.

Moth frowned at him, but to Juliet's credit, she didn't lie. "No, it's not."

Now Moth turned his frown on her.

"Look," said Juliet. "I knew the Lostwoods brought you all here for a reason. I also knew Mishti wouldn't accept it unless the Lostwoods gave us an undeniable sign—"

"So you faked one?" asked Moth. He straightened from where he'd been kneeling next to a crate of flower petals.

"Sometimes," said Juliet carefully, "the Lostwoods is unable—or unwilling—to act as clearly as we need it to. Sometimes we need to amplify its intentions to those who can't see them as clearly."

"Why didn't you tell me?" asked Moth.

Juliet looked at her hands. "I was afraid." She met his gaze, imploring him to understand. "I thought if I told you, you might tell Leonardo, and he might tell Mishti. Mishti can't know."

"Why not?" asked Leonardo.

"Our entire alliance is built on that 'sign'," said Juliet, her breath coming faster. "If she learns it's fake, who knows what she'll do."

"You don't trust your own leader?" asked Leonardo.

Juliet didn't reply immediately. She gathered herself, a debate playing behind her eyes.

"Let's deal with the Dark," she said finally. "Then we'll talk about Mishti."

A charged silence followed those words, hanging in the close air of the hold. Leonardo, Juliet, and Moth regarded each other, and a silent understanding settled between them. If two clans still existed within Lion, Leonardo had a feeling he'd just witnessed Juliet step across the line.

# CHAPTER 42

When *The Forever* reached the stone jetty in the swamp waters, they found it unguarded. Leonardo and Mishti climbed down, dropping to the mossy landing.

Leonardo stepped away from the ladder and cast one last look up at his clan. Down the rail, Kate blew him a kiss. Leonardo turned away, pushing thoughts of her from his mind. He needed to be fully focused.

They climbed the dark stone steps up the bank, through tangled vines and ferns, and moved out before the giant stone snake that encircled Snake Clan's camp.

They'd left Snake Clan to last for a reason. Caliban was the least predictable leader in the Cove.

*But we need him.* Snake Clan's magic could turn the tides in a fight.

Grey-hooded figures crossed the inner courtyard, but none of them even turned to look at Leonardo and Mishti as they passed under the arch.

"What the hell?" said Leonardo under his breath.

"Welcome back to Snake Clan," said Mishti. "Nothing ever makes sense."

They stopped in the middle of the courtyard, then Caliban's voice came from behind them.

"Mishti, Leonardo. Back so soon?"

"Caliban," said Mishti, as she and Leonardo turned. "Your security could use some work."

Caliban grinned, one eye green and one blue. His grey cloak shaded the contours of his face as he walked toward them, hands clasped in front of him. "Indeed?"

All at once, the Snakes around the courtyard stopped and turned. More flooded out of the stone doorways in the perimeter wall. Within seconds, a loose, staggered formation of Snakes surrounded Leonardo and Mishti. Knives glinted in the folds of their cloaks.

"Right," said Leonardo, eyeing the trap they'd walked into. He swore at himself. Back in the Darkwoods, he never would have strolled into another clan's camp so carelessly.

"We're not here for a fight," he told Caliban. "We need your help."

"And you need ours," added Mishti.

"Do I need the pirates' help too?" asked Caliban. "Or can one of you tell me why there is a pirate ship outside my camp? Last we spoke, they'd kidnapped two of your kids."

"Yes," said Leonardo. "We need their help too."

He and Mishti recounted the events of the past two days.

Caliban's eyebrows raised when they mentioned Tiger Clan's cooperation, then raised higher when they told him about the deep-sea monster.

"You know," he said, scratching the back of his head under his hood, "I would be fully justified to call you liars and throw you out of my camp."

Mishti crossed her arms. "Listen here—"

Caliban held up a hand. "Not to say I don't believe you. I simply mean your story is *almost* too fantastical to believe."

Leonardo placed a hand on Mishti's arm. *Wait.*

She darted the glare she'd fixed on Caliban at him, but she held her tongue.

"As it turns out," continued Caliban, "I do believe you. The Dark has been wreaking havoc with our magic, and it continues to grow."

"What kind of havoc?" asked Leonardo.

Caliban smiled mirthlessly. "Let's just say, it has forced us to completely stop. Any communion with the powers of the Lost-woods is tainted."

Leonardo swore. If Caliban wasn't practicing magic, they'd just lost an advantage.

"The Dark must be expelled," said Caliban. "We'll join you." He extended his hand, letting his sleeve slide back to reveal a shadow ribbon curling up his wrist. "To our new alliance."

# CHAPTER 43

"H e has a mark too," said Leonardo.

He and the ex-Ravens stood clustered on the foredeck of *The Forever*, surrounded by low-hanging vines. The ship was still docked in Caliban's swamp, awaiting the Snakes.

"What?" asked Moth. "Like, from the Dark?"

Leonardo nodded.

"Do you think they're all touched by it?" asked Nym.

"Probably," said Puck. He ran a hand over his pudgy cheeks. "Unless Caliban was out in the woods alone when it got him."

"We have lots of venom," said Moth. "But we don't have enough of the sacred plants to cure the Snakes."

"Who cares about curing them?" said Bates. He swatted away a mosquito. "They're Snakes."

"We care, halfwit," said Puck, swinging his arms at an entire cloud of bugs. "Because if we don't cure them, they turn into Dark zombies and attack us."

"Right, right," said Bates.

"So how do we 'fight' the Dark, exactly?" asked Nym. Filtered light dappled his face, piercing the dense canopy. "Does anyone have any ideas?"

"The same way we've been doing it," said Puck.

"But that's just defending ourselves," said Nym. "How do we *attack* it?"

"We go for the heart," said Leonardo. He plucked a gold flower off a vine, peeling back the petals to reveal a pollen-covered pod.

"Meaning?"

"There has to be a heart somewhere," said Leonardo. "Or something like it. The Dark is intelligent. If we can find that—"

He broke off as Charley and Pompey ran up the steps, breathless.

"Boats are coming," said Charley. "Tiger Clan and Dragon Clan and the Natives..."

"All their boats are here," said Pompey.

"What?" Leonardo, Pinch, Bates, and Puck looked at each other. Apprehension mirrored on their faces.

"Come see," said Charley. She ran back down the stairs, Pompey on her heels. A dozen scenarios played through Leonardo's mind as he followed, but all of them centred on one thought: *something's gone wrong.*

When they topped the stern deck, Charley and Pompey sprinted to the edge, where John stood facing upriver. Beyond him, two longboats preceded a fleet of fast, narrow, canoe-like vessels loaded with what appeared to be every member of the Native tribe.

Leonardo's concern gave way to excitement for a split second as he realized that Viola was on one of those boats. Then Kate's warning tainted the moment.

*Someone's lying,* thought Leonardo. And he had no idea who it was.

He focused in on the two longboats out front; one flying a red sail and the other rowing under a white silk canopy.

Tiger and Dragon.

At the rear of Tiger Clan's boat, Cleopatra's face gleamed in a square of sunlight, painted stark white against the red and black of her lips and eyes.

The iridescent tails of sirens flashed through the water between the boats.

"Why are they coming here?" asked Bates. "We're supposed to meet at the fortress."

"You two," Leonardo said to Charley and Pompey. "Go find Mishti and get her up here."

They nodded and ran off.

"Come on," he told Pinch, Puck, and Bates. "Let's find out what's going on."

***

Viola was in the first boat that reached the ship. She scrambled up the ladder and sprinted to Leonardo. They embraced, her arms tight around him, and Leonardo closed his eyes, breathing in her familiar smell of jasmine and woodland.

"I missed you," she whispered.

Leonardo pulled her tighter, then they separated, and her dark brown eyes followed him as he stepped around her to greet Chief Tokala. Behind Tokala, still in the canoe, Dakota eyed

Leonardo with thinly veiled contempt. Leonardo's heart raced, questioning everything they'd ever said to him. Nothing felt safe anymore.

"Leonardo," said Tokala. "The Dark is coming."

Leonardo nodded. He'd already determined that much.

"The Cove has been consumed," called Cleopatra. "It's impossible to enter."

*Shit.*

"We must act fast," said Tokala. "We were forced to evacuate the Turquoise Island. The Dark may be closing in on us as we speak."

Leonardo's limbs went cold. He'd expected more time. He glanced at Pinch and Moth, standing on either side of him, and squared his shoulders. "We'll fight from here, then."

As he said it, Dragon Clan's boat glided alongside the ship. Leonardo regarded Demetrius in his deep blue robes beneath the silk canopy.

"Have you joined the fight?" asked Leonardo.

"Have you convinced the other clans?" asked Demetrius.

Leonardo rolled his eyes. He didn't have time for pointless pride. "Come on board," he told Demetrius and the others. "We need to start preparing."

Viola slipped her fingers into his as they started across the deck.

"Your shadow mark is gone," he realized, noticing her bare arms.

"Yours isn't," she observed.

"Mine's dead," said Leonardo, thinking about the venom in his blood. "It's just a scar now. How did you heal yours?"

"My people are the guardians," said Viola. "The woods heal us."

*In exchange for lying about its mistakes,* a suspicious little voice chirped in Leonardo's mind.

*That's not true. Necessarily.*

"What about everyone else?" asked Viola. Hope glimmered in her voice. "Did Juliet find a cure?"

Leonardo nodded, forcing a smile. "She healed everyone, including Pompey and Charley. Snake Clan is touched by it too, but—"

"Nym too?"

Leonardo paused, and Viola's face fell.

"It's too deep in Nym," said Leonardo. "There's no safe way to cleanse him."

"Maybe my people can," said Viola.

Leonardo tensed, and she frowned at him.

"How did Juliet do it?" she asked.

"Sea monster venom," said Leonardo. "I'll explain later."

He didn't—he *couldn't*—trust anyone right now. Even Viola, as much as it pained him.

They reached the hatch, just as Mishti summited the ladder. Charley darted around her and ran to embrace Viola, and Mishti crossed her arms as Demetrius and Cleopatra climbed up onto the deck.

"What are you doing here?" asked Mishti.

"The Dark has taken over," said Cleopatra. Her features barely moved under the white paint.

"Everything's dead," said Demetrius. "The entrance to the Cove is just a wall of black."

"This is the worst we've seen yet," said Dakota, pulling himself up the ladder.

"What do you know about it?" Leonardo asked carefully. "How do we defeat it?"

Dakota regarded him a moment before he replied, somewhat impatiently, "If we knew that, we'd still be out there fighting it."

"We don't have time for this," said Mishti. "Leonardo, organize everyone on the ship. I'm going ashore to find Caliban."

As she ran to the ladder, Leonardo contemplated the lot of them.

*We need a plan.* They'd anticipated having time to meet with the other leaders before the Dark arrived. He and Mishti had discussed trying to lure it into Lion Clan's tunnels, where they could limit its space to strike. But nothing was ever perfect in war. Leonardo had the most battle experience; it now fell on him to cobble together a plan in the dwindling moments they had left.

*What would Aleksander do? Stand together or divide it? Face it in the open or try to bottleneck it? Is that even possible here?* Snake Clan's swamp wasn't exactly the fortress he'd been expecting to fight from.

*We'll divide it*, he decided, nodding to himself. They had four clans, the pirates, and the Natives on their side. That certainly seemed like enough fighters to fortify two battlefronts.

*We win or we lose.* It was as simple as that, except that *losing* meant to lose everything. The Cove would cease to exist. The Dark would roll over the rest of the woods, already weakened by its touch. The Darkwoods would fall in minutes if it was still in the state they'd left it.

*We win or we lose.* As simple and as terrible as that.

# CHAPTER 44

We'll split into two groups," said Leonardo. "Lion Clan, Snake Clan, and the pirates will stay here on the ship. Dragon Clan, Tiger Clan, and the Natives will fight from Snake Clan's camp."

"Excuse me for sounding insolent," said Caliban. "But why is my clan not fighting from our camp?"

"Because," said Juliet, to Leonardo's left, "those burns on your arms are like doorways for the Dark. Down here, we can fight it with river water."

"River water?"

*We're wasting time.* In the back of Leonardo's mind, an image of the Dark rolled closer to the jungle with every passing second.

"The plan," continued Leonardo. "Is to divide the attack so none of us face the full force of it. By splitting it between the camp and the ship, we may be able to find a weak point."

"Pardon me," said Demetrius, even sweatier than normal in

the jungle heat. "But the chief has been trying to find a weak point since this all started. Maybe one doesn't exist."

Tokala inclined his head, acknowledging and dismissing Demetrius' point. "I do not have the power that you all have."

"You don't have the power we have," said Cleopatra, skeptical. "And what power is that?"

*Imagination.* So much imagination, it had swallowed them whole. Right out of their past lives and into the woods. Leonardo glanced at Kate. Only the pirates and Leonardo's Lions knew the truth.

"We should start preparing," said Leonardo, to deflect the question.

Cleopatra frowned, and Mishti gave him a quizzical look, but for once she didn't argue.

"We don't stop fighting until the Dark is defeated," he continued. "Understood? Moth, Juliet, Pompey, and Charley will be waiting with medical supplies belowdecks."

"What about Nym?" asked Pip. "That's his name, right? The hopeless case."

Leonardo set his jaw. This wasn't the time for fighting each other, as much as he wanted to knock Pip on his ass.

"He'll be tied up," said Mishti. She, Nym, and Leonardo had already discussed it. "We'll wrap his arms in wet cloths and tie him up for good measure."

"That sounds fair," said Pip.

*No, it's not fair at all,* thought Leonardo. In no world was it fair that Nym got tied up like a prisoner while his friends faced the Dark, but Nym had soberly agreed it was the safest choice.

A splash drew everyone's attention to the water.

"Thaisa," said Mishti. "About time."

*That's everyone,* thought Leonardo. Somehow, miraculously, they had united the Cove.

*But is it enough?*

Leonardo followed Mishti to the edge, where Thaisa and several dozen sirens peered up from the murky water. He scanned the faces, but Adriana was nowhere to be seen.

*Did they finally banish her?*

He hoped so. Enough of the fight rested on chance already. The last thing they needed was her unpredictability.

"We can't stay in the freshwater for long," said Thaisa. "But I felt you deserved an explanation if nothing else."

Mishti crossed her arms. "What the hell are you talking about?"

"We can't fight this war with you."

*What?* Leonardo's stomach dropped.

Mishti gave a single, incredulous laugh. Leonardo stared at the sirens. Their faces were unwaveringly cool.

"You're joking," he said.

"I don't joke," said Thaisa.

"So, you're just abandoning us," said Leonardo.

"Don't bother," said Mishti. She pulled her hair back, sunlight glinting sharply off the throwing rings on her wrists. "When shit hits the fan, Thaisa runs away. Right?" She stepped to the very edge of the ship. "Same deal as the sea monster. Right, Thaisa?"

"I'm not jeopardizing my girls' nor my own life."

"But who cares about me, right?" Mishti chuckled again. "Great. Just fucking great. I should have seen this coming. I knew it—"

"Thaisa." Chief Tokala stepped up beside Leonardo. "You have a duty to the woods."

Thaisa shook her head. "I will *not* die cleaning up another of the Lostwoods' mistakes." She coughed, grimacing at the freshwater. "We need to get back to the sea."

Tokala cracked his cane on the deck. The boards vibrated under Leonardo's feet. "Without the woods, you would not exist."

Thaisa smiled. "I've paid my dues. Now I quit. And I have you to thank; it was only when the Lostwoods brought you here to save the Cove that I realized how little faith it had in my girls and me. You've always considered yourself the guardians of everything, right? Well, now you get your wish."

Tokala narrowed his eyes, the years heavy on his skin, but didn't reply.

"Goodbye, Mishti," said Thaisa.

And with that, the sirens dove underwater, leaving the deck silent as everyone watched them depart. Mishti swore under her breath, eyes locked on Thaisa as she swam away.

"Come on," said Kate. "We have a long night ahead of us."

***

Leonardo stepped into Snake Clan's courtyard, regarding the cluster of kids and Natives getting organized on the cracked tiles. Cleopatra and Demetrius stood before their clans, split into perfect grids of deep red and blue.

*There's not enough of them.* He swallowed a lump in his throat, re-analyzing his decision to split them up. Was dividing the Dark truly their best shot at survival?

*When Raven Clan was under attack, Aleksander split us up to protect the ladders.*

But this was a different clan and a different enemy.

"Leonardo." The Chief's voice came from behind him.

"Chief Tokala," said Leonardo, turning back. "Do you think we're ready for the Dark?"

The more he thought about it, the more he doubted his decision. *Did I just weaken our defences by half?*

Tokala regarded him through slitted eyes. He appeared to weigh his words.

"No one is ever ready to face a nightmare," he told Leonardo. "Yet everyone must."

"And what happens if we're still not ready?"

Tokala didn't reply.

*Win or lose.* Leonardo waited, but the chief's silence ticked on, and his own doubts crystallized into a sudden realization.

*Dammit. We're not ready.*

"I have to go." His plan would only work if the Dark attacked both parties simultaneously. The Dark was too intelligent for that. With the clans divided, it could wipe out half of them before the other half even raised a sword.

He sprinted out of the courtyard and down the steps to the ship, where Lions, Snakes, and Pirates ran around preparing the cannons and lashing shields into defensive walls

"Everyone stop!" he yelled, heaving himself up the ladder from the dock. "Change of plans. We're all going to fight from Snake Clan's camp."

"Why?" asked John. He yanked the last knot, securing a shield to the rigging.

"Because if we stay here, we'll be facing the full force of the Dark. It has no reason to attack both groups at the same time."

"But you said——"

"And now he's saying something else," Mishti cut in. "And it makes sense."

"I agree," said Caliban. "Why would the Dark divide when it could kill us all first, *then* take the rest of them out?"

"Ok," yelled Kate. She jumped onto the stairs. "Let's move it! Stop what you're doing and get up to Snake Clan's camp. Grab anything you need. Quickly!"

"Pinch," Leonardo caught him by the arm. "Let's go find Moth and Juliet."

***

Twenty minutes later, they rushed the last pails of venom into a stone room inside of Caliban's snake pyramid. Juliet and Moth would run their makeshift infirmary from here, with the help of Pompey, Charley, and two dozen younger kids.

"Wait," said Pompey. "Where is Lion?"

Charley gasped. "I left him in his basket. On the ship!"

"I've got it," said Pinch. He rolled his eyes, shoving his pail of venom in the corner and turning for the stairs. "Rescuing hamsters. Jesus, my life is weird."

"You're all set?" Leonardo asked Moth as Pinch ran up the steps. A row of weapons lay propped against one wall, just in case.

"As set as we can be," said Moth.

Pinch's footsteps thumped overhead, followed by muffled voices, echoing through the stone tunnels.

"I should be out there with you, fighting," said Moth.

Juliet looked up sharply at the same time that Leonardo said, "No, we need you here more."

Back in the Darkwoods, Moth would have cowered at the

thought of picking up a sword. He would have done anything to get out of a battle.

*When did he change so much?*

"There are a lot of them out there," said Juliet. "You know you're not a fighter."

Moth opened his mouth to argue, then he sighed. "I know. But still."

Leonardo studied his friend. Moth would never be a strong fighter, but he didn't sound ashamed of it anymore.

"But nothing," said Juliet.

Something unspoken passed between them and Moth nodded. He glanced at Leonardo. "If you're sure?"

"If the Dark gets me," said Leonardo. "I expect top-notch treatment."

"The Dark can't get you," said Moth. "You're immune."

"If it gets anyone."

"We'll be ready," said Moth.

"Good."

Charley hovered nearby, shifting from foot to foot. Leonardo glanced at her. She looked ready to burst with excitement.

"What?" Leonardo asked her.

Charley ran over and waved for him to bend down. Leonardo crouched to one knee and she leaned in to his ear.

"Moth and Juliet kissed," she whispered.

Leonardo raised his eyebrows and Charley stepped back, beaming.

"What did she say?" asked Moth.

Charley ran back to Pompey.

"What did she say?" pressed Moth.

"Nothing," said Leonardo. "Don't worry about it."

*Viola was right after all.* Leonardo was happy for them, though the impending Dark soured his mood. Claws scratched at his insides as a thousand outcomes played behind his eyes.

Moth frowned, glancing at Juliet.

"I'll see you after the fight," said Leonardo. He turned to Nym, sitting with his back to the wall, wet cloth bound around his arms and his hands tied in front of him.

"I'm sorry about this," said Leonardo.

"Kill the Dark," said Nym. "I don't care how long it takes. Just kill it."

"I promise," said Leonardo. And he left them in the humid room, shutting the door behind him. He heard Moth's voice, muffled through the wood. "Charley, what did you tell him?"

*I promise,* he'd said. *I promise I'll kill the Dark.* Could he keep that promise?

He didn't have a choice.

# CHAPTER 45

Viola chose—to her brother's great dismay—to fight with Lion Clan. Leonardo suspected that if Dakota had his choice, Viola would be hidden away in the pyramid with Moth and Juliet.

A part of Leonardo wished for that too, but she'd fought alongside his clan enough times on their journey south that he knew she could handle herself. She kept a cool head, she had good aim, and in truth, he felt better having her near than off elsewhere in the camp.

"Moth and Viola kissed," he said when he found her.

Viola's surprise was only for a second.

"I told you!" She grinned in spite of everything.

"Yes, you did," said Leonardo. He studied the preparations around them. Puck shouted instructions, arms swinging as he directed traffic, but only a handful of kids paid him any attention. Pinch handed Charley her hamster basket at the top of the pyramid, then awkwardly patted her head as she embraced him. Mishti stood above the steps to the swamp, a throwing ring in each hand. Anger radiated from her rigid shoulders. Sophie stood next to her, gripping her bow and arrows like a lifeline.

"These girls aren't fighters," said Leonardo. "Mishti has barely trained them."

"My people are here too," Viola reminded him. "And the Tiger girls look like they can fight."

He shook his head. "It's not enough." Not a single Snake carried a sword or bow. Dragon Clan looked like they'd never touched a sword in their lives. "Everyone here relies on magic. When the magic is gone, they're helpless."

"They'll step up. We're going to survive this."

Leonardo glanced at her. Dappled sunlight painted over her tanned skin, her eyes dark and filled with belief.

"How can you be sure?"

Viola pulled his face down and kissed him.

Leonardo stiffened, then he closed his eyes and let himself fall into her for just a moment. A moment longer, and they pulled apart. Viola blinked up at him, braids—still lopsided from the Snake Clan incident—framing her face. "Everything will be ok. Trust me."

Leonardo held her eye contact, then he shifted his gaze to the canopy. Fairy lights blinked through the branches.

*Get away,* he thought. *Leave before the Dark gets here.*

A clatter of noise drew his attention as Pinch marched across the courtyard, fixing his tricorn with one hand. "John the halfwit just tried to steal my hat."

John followed close behind him. "It's *my* hat!"

"John," snapped Leonardo. "Give it up already. We could die at any moment, and you care about your *hat?*"

John ignored him. "Pinch," he said. "I'll make you a trade. I have gold in my cabin."

"Why would I want gold?" asked Pinch.

"John!" yelled Kate. "Get over here. It's important."

John stared at Pinch a second longer, then he spun and sulked away.

"What a weirdo," said Pinch.

"Have they told you what the hats do?" asked Leonardo.

"You mean that thing about hearing the fairies?" Pinch took off his hat, eyeing it skeptically.

"What are you talking about?" asked Viola.

"Come here," Leonardo pulled Pinch and Viola around the side of the pyramid, away from eavesdroppers. "When Pip wears his hat, he can't feel pain. When Cyrus wears his, he can shape-shift. Kate's lets her get…I don't know, she said 'whatever she wants'."

"They're magic?" asked Viola.

"Then what does this one do?" Pinch took his off, peering inside.

"Nothing."

"What?"

"Apparently, it's never worked."

"That makes no sense." Pinch shook his head. "He must have been using it wrong."

"Kate said John is the only one who didn't imagine his hat. He found it."

"Really." Pinch scratched his chin. "So the woods made it?"

"I guess."

"Wait," said Viola. She closed her eyes, lids twitching. Then she blinked them open. The colour drained from her face. "It's here."

"Now?" asked Leonardo.

"Get down!" said Pinch, a slingshot suddenly in his hands.

Leonardo ducked, and Pinch fired over his head. Leonardo twisted to see a shadow dissipate above the wall. Pinch's shot whizzed up into the treetops.

*The Dark.* Leonardo's stomach clenched. Then he drew himself up.

"Everyone, in position!" he yelled, running back to the front of the pyramid just as Mishti yelled, "Here it comes!"

Leonardo followed her gaze, squinting through the archway as tree after tree disappeared, cloaked by a wall of blackness. *The Forever* was swallowed in an instant, and Leonardo winced.

*That was almost us.*

The pressure changed, and static energy crackled as Leonardo's ears popped. A burning smell tainted the air, rich and putrid.

Leonardo drew his sword and gripped it two-handed as the Dark flooded over the top of the wall, quiet as a whisper. His mouth went dry. *Let us survive this. Please.*

He changed his grip, sword pointed in front of him. But the Dark didn't engage with them. Yet. As it crested the wall, it continued upward, closing like a dome above the stone snake. Total stillness filled the gloom underneath, spiked by ragged, terrified breathing.

"What is it waiting for?" called someone across the courtyard.

"Get ready!" yelled Leonardo. "Stay focused!"

Then a hundred columns of darkness shot toward them. The first screams were cut short in an instant. A fist of shadow drove for Leonardo, like a giant battering ram. He swung his sword through it, reversing instantly to slash away a second attack. Hot, gritty air blasted over him.

Mishti's boomerang whirled past his head, cutting a wide swath through the blackness. A hundred doppelgangers of Cyrus suddenly appeared around the courtyard, drawing the Dark away from the other kids.

Leonardo stared for a second, dumbfounded. *How powerful* are *those hats?*

A freezing wind howled around the pyramid, driving hard into his back at the same time as the hot sandpaper air tore at his face. He struggled to breathe, forcing his eyes to stay open in the on-slaught.

Next to him, Pinch dropped his slingshot and switched to his sword, ducking and slashing as the Dark enveloped them. Boots shuffled and breaths caught, clothing rustling as the clans fought back.

The fight was fast and desperate. Leonardo lost any concept of bearings. He stumbled through the chaos, swinging randomly at the shadows streaming past him. It took every degree of his concentration to dodge the wild swords of his companions, screaming and shouting as they inflicted as much damage on each other as the Dark.

*It's too tight in here*, he thought in horror, watching the mass of bodies weave through the shadows.

Then he shook his head. *Stop doubting your decisions. If you'd stuck to the first plan, everyone might be dead already.* A united front was their best chance at survival, even if it meant over a hundred and fifty weapons were swinging in close proximity.

The fight lasted maybe five minutes, then an explosion shook the jungle and the shadows pulled back, lifting like smoke. The first rays of sun piercing through revealing a courtyard littered with kids on their knees, clutching at wounds. Others yelled the names of clanmates. Some responded. A lot didn't.

Leonardo turned in a slow circle, sword in front of him. No part of him thought, even for a second, that it was over yet. The kids and Natives still on their feet eyed each other gravely, breathing heavy.

To his immense relief, every ex-Raven and Viola had survived the first round.

Then a pirate girl screamed. A tendril of black shot out of the jungle, snaring her leg. She hit the dirt with a choked cry. John jumped to help her, and a second tendril shot out of the trees, striking straight for his heart.

John yelled, falling to one knee as the dark grew like vines, coiling rapidly around him and the girl.

"Help us!" yelled John.

Leonardo was already running. The Dark wound tighter and tighter, spreading until they were almost indistinguishable through the mass of it. Their cries became muffled. Leonardo had no plan; he just threw himself at them.

One second, he was in midair; the next, he fell through a cloud of smoke and crashed painfully into the dirt. Leonardo rolled over as the Dark dissipated. John and the girl were nowhere to be seen.

"Oh my god," said another pirate.

"They're gone," said Kate, stunned.

"How could John be gone?" snapped Pip. "He's—"

"Stronger than the Dark?" asked Sophie.

Before anyone could say another word, a deep groan rumbled through the earth, vibrating Leonardo's teeth. The burning smell returned, heavy and smothering.

"Move it!" yelled Sophie. "Everyone who needs medical help, get into the pyramid!"

"Help them," added Leonardo. "Anyone who can carry—"

Someone gasped, and Leonardo snapped around as a Snake lunged at a Lion girl. The girl dodged out of the way, and a second Snake grabbed her. His sleeves rode up, revealing veins of pure black on his pale skin. He wrenched the girl around, fingers curled like claws.

*Shit.*

Sophie tackled the first Snake as Leonardo ran for the one wrestling the girl.

"Caliban," shouted Leonardo. "Why is no one treated?"

"What?"

"The bindings! They need river water!"

Leonardo grabbed the Snake boy around the shoulders while Caliban grabbed the girl. Fear masked both kids' faces.

"We didn't have time," snapped Caliban. "We had to move up here."

*Shit. Shit,* he hadn't thought of that.

They ripped the kids apart. The boy clawed at Leonardo and he jerked his head out of the way.

"I'm sorry!" the kid cried, scratching his arm hard enough to draw blood. "I don't know—"

He elbowed Leonardo in the ribs and Leonardo gasped, releasing him. Then Leonardo drew a breath and ran at him, catching the kid around the stomach and driving him into the stone wall. The Snake's head struck the wall and he slumped to the ground, stunned.

"We need to get them to the water," said Leonardo, heaving for breath. "Help me."

"I've got him." Dakota pushed Leonardo aside and grabbed the Snake around the waist, then tossed him over his shoulder. The kid immediately started clawing at Dakota's back, but Dakota ignored him, running through the archway and down the steps to the riverbank.

Sophie, Cleopatra, Puck, and Bates followed with the other Snake. He struggled against their grip, but they fought harder, fingertips digging into his arms.

Leonardo ran after them. Both boys screamed and started thrashing when they hit the water. Leonardo stopped a few steps above the dock, ready with the others in case the boys tried to climb out.

"Where is our ship?" demanded Cyrus, shoving his way down the steps to the empty swamp.

"The Dark took it," said Kate. Her voice was quiet. "I watched it happen."

"What?" shock radiated in Cyrus's voice.

Leonardo had bigger problems to worry about.

"Caliban," he asked. "When your camp was attacked, was everyone touched?"

"The Dark never attacked us," said the boy in the swamp, spitting out water and swearing. "He called it."

"*What?*" Leonardo whipped around as Caliban held up his hands.

"What kind of idiot are you?" demanded Mishti.

"He wanted its power," said the boy in the water.

"Shut up already," snapped Caliban.

In his peripheral, Leonardo caught another Snake's arms twitch.

"Get in the water!" shouted Leonardo. He shifted back to make room on the steps. "Every Snake, get in the water."

A few jumped in right away, weaving around Dakota and plunging into the swamp. Others hesitated.

"He said, get in the water!" snapped Mishti.

"You too," Leonardo ordered Caliban.

"I'm fine."

*I'm too powerful to be possessed* was what it sounded like.

Leonardo and Mishti whipped up their weapons at the same time. Sword and throwing ring pointed at Caliban's throat.

Caliban narrowed his mismatched eyes, and for a second Leonardo thought he wasn't going to move, then he shoved past them and jumped off the dock.

A few Snakes still hesitated, and Pip marched down the steps, waving his sword.

"Get in the water, you cowards."

As the last Snakes joined their clanmates, Leonardo regarded the kids still on the stairs and gathered atop the embankment. Their numbers were stunningly depleted.

*Dammit.* He gazed around at the jungle, unnaturally quiet.

*Where is the Dark?*

"What is that?" said Bates.

He pointed as an inky line floated down the mouth of the river, into the swamp water. A second swirl joined it, like an oil spill spreading across the surface.

*It's in the water.* The river was supposed to suppress it.

A hopeless sense of panic washed over him. *Has it gotten that strong?*

"Get out of the water!" yelled Leonardo.

The Snakes, who'd just jumped in, now swam as hard as they could for the dock. A hundred meters away, a dozen white shapes rose through the murky depths of the river.

"Are those…?" Leonardo stepped closer, frowning as a dozen more joined them.

The first Snake boy rolled onto the dock and started up the steps.

"They're croc skulls!" yelled Puck.

"Dammit." Leonardo grabbed the Snake boy's arm and pulled up his saturated sleeve. His skin was free of black veins, though a burn still curled up his arm. He pulled the kid's sleeve back down and wrapped the wet material tight.

"Get into the pyramid. All of you," he called to the Snakes. "Juliet has rags and water."

*Which won't work, if the Dark is stronger than the river.*

*She still has pails of raw venom.* She and Moth would figure something out.

He ran up the stairs after the kid, then stumbled to a stop as everyone froze below the archway.

"Retreat!" someone yelled.

"What is it?" Leonardo shoved his way through the crowd and staggered out into the courtyard.

He blinked at a nightmare scene. Hundreds of crocodile skulls filled the courtyard, piled askew on the cracked tiles. Ranks of empty eye sockets watched them, burnt black and hollow.

*That's how it sees,* Viola told Leonardo an eternity ago.

Behind him, shock turned to panic.

"Retreat!" yelled another kid.

"No!" Leonardo shouted, louder. "We have to fight."

He drew his sword and swung it two-handed at the nearest skull. It shattered, dissipating into smoke. He did the same to the next, and the next, and ten more, as the other kids and Natives joined him. The jungle filled with the shattering, crunching, crack of crocodile skulls being cleaved in two.

Viola stomped on the last one and Leonardo sagged, catching his breath.

"Leo," said Pinch urgently.

"What?" Leonardo jumped, gazing around for another attack.

"I made the hat work."

# CHAPTER 46

W hat?" Leonardo stared at Pinch.

"Watch. Actually, listen first." Pinch whipped his hat off, gripping it in two hands. "Those powers you told me about," he whispered, "they match the pirates. Pip is a bitter little prick who doesn't feel anything. Hence, he can't feel pain. Kate gets whatever she wants…I doubt much was different before she got the hat. And Cyrus is a nutcase. He has a different personality every day—"

"So the hat lets him change who he is," said Leonardo.

"Bingo."

Leonardo glanced around. None of the pirates were listening. Everyone was too exhausted to pay him and Pinch any attention.

"That actually makes sense," said Leonardo. He lowered his voice. "So why doesn't John's work?"

"*Didn't* work. He didn't have the right imagination for it. That's my theory anyway. That's why the woods gave it to me."

"There aren't many of us left!" yelled Puck, crossing the tiles. "We need to make a strategic formation for the next attack."

"Like what?" said Sophie. "It's impossible to fight it."

*She's right. We have no idea what it's going to do next.*

"Tell me more," Leonardo said to Pinch. He kept one eye on the scrambled preparations.

"Think," said Pinch, "if the woods created the hat, it's power would have to do with imagination, right?"

"I guess. Maybe."

"If he found the hat on the ship, that means it was years after the woods were created; after it stopped letting them imagine new things."

Pinch paused with a conspiring grin. "Or so they thought. What if the wearer gets to keep imagining?"

Leonardo furrowed his brow. "You don't think he tried that?"

"John was practical as shit. Even if he tried to imagine things, it would be practical things. Things that already exist in the woods. The hat is for making new things."

Pinch reached inside and pulled out a tiny grenade, no larger than his thumb and covered in spikes.

"What the—" Leonardo winced as Pinch tossed it and caught it. "Where the hell did you get that?"

"I *imagined* it. This is the second one...I shot the first at the Dark."

Leonardo's eyes widened. "That explosion was you?"

"I got the idea to shoot a bomb into the Dark with my slingshot, so I tried imagining it, and it worked!"

"How did you figure out—?"

"I don't know! Maybe the hat makes me brilliant too."

"Brace yourselves!" yelled Mishti. She stood halfway up the pyramid steps. "It's coming back!"

Leonardo and Pinch both looked around, tense. The troops in the courtyard gazed at the tops of the stone walls, backing toward the centre of the space.

Pinch spun his sword. "Come and get it, asshole," he said under his breath.

A hissing, snapping sound filled the air, quiet at first and growing closer with every slam of Leonardo's racing heartbeat.

"What is that noise?" asked Puck.

Up on the pyramid, Mishti stood rooted to the steps, her jaw slack, eyes locked on something beyond the wall. Leonardo and Pinch ran up to join her, stumbling to a halt as they laid eyes on the next wave.

A wall of darkness plowed toward them, bending trees to the ground. The forest flattened before it like a field of grass in the wind. The snapping sound was thousands of branches breaking, the hissing millions of leaves.

*How do we possibly fight that?*

"Watch this," said Pinch. He slammed the hat back on his head and looked around, then focused on the stone head of the snake, directly above them. Leonardo drew his sword, steadying his breath.

Then a fan appeared. Atop the snake's head. An old fashioned, rusty metal fan, with four blades in a wire cage. And it was ten feet tall.

"What the hell?" said Pip.

"A fan?" demanded Leonardo.

"Something that doesn't exist here," said Pinch proudly.

The blades began to spin, faster and faster, with a scream of whirling metal. The Dark surged toward them, flattening the forest as a gale-force blasted from Pinch's fan. They collided a hundred meters from the camp, and the front edge of the Dark dissipated to smoke, like flames doused by a firehose.

The fan began to oscillate, cutting a swath through the Dark and stopping its approach on all sides.

*It worked.* Leonardo stared at Pinch in wonder. *It actually worked.*

Victory flashed through Pinch's eyes, a second before the rest of the Dark surged forward, lower than the wall and out of the fan's reach.

"It's still coming!" yelled Leonardo.

He and Pinch tore down the steps. Pinch loaded his slingshot and fired the second mini-grenade over the wall. It exploded with an ear-shattering bang. Then the Dark fired back. A streak of black hurtled through the archway. Leonardo and Pinch dove to either side, and Leonardo twisted just as Pip was thrown thirty feet.

He slammed into the side of the pyramid and tumbled down, surrounded by tendrils of the Dark, rearing and stabbing at him. Pip grabbed his sword and rolled to his feet, slashing as viciously as if he couldn't feel a thing.

*He can't,* realized Leonardo. *Unless—*

One of the tendrils snapped for Pip's hat. He hacked it away, barely flinching. Then a second caught him in the back of his head, and Pip's hat went flying. Instantly, Pip dropped to all fours, crying out. He covered his head, spasming as the Dark pummeled him.

Leonardo, Pinch, Kate, and Cyrus all ran for him. The whine

of the fan drowned out all other noise as Pip made a desperate grab for his hat, jamming it back on his head just as a second streak of black shot out of the jungle. Pip leapt to his feet and the Dark exploded against his chest, throwing the rest of them backward. Leonardo slammed into the stairs and gasped, heaving for air.

When he blinked across the courtyard, Pip was gone.

Only a black scar remained, burnt into the ground.

*First John, now Pip.*

They needed to end this, fast.

The rest of the Dark flooded over the wall and through the archway. Pinch's fan stopped it from closing over the top of them like before, but enough made it underneath to put them on their heels in seconds.

Leonardo hacked and slashed, gritting his teeth at the hot air. The scream of the fan permeated everything.

"Pinch," he yelled. "You need to imagine something else!"

"I'm try—shit!" Pinch spun and sliced through a long black vine, evaporating to smoke on his blade. Another snapped at him and he cleaved it in half. "The fuck are these?"

"Imagine something!" repeated Leonardo, swinging his sword at a third vine.

"I'm trying!"

A jack-in-the-box appeared in front of Leonardo. The top sprang open, throwing a fireball into the sky. A flaming clown bobbed on a coiled spring.

"How does that help?" demanded Leonardo.

"I don't know! I can't think!" Pinch ducked, hacking at a forest of black vines. "It can't exist here. It has to be new!"

A tendril of the Dark slapped Leonardo across the face, as

sharp as a whip. He cried out, stumbling back, and blindly hacked through it. His eyes watered so hard he could barely see.

*We need to find and kill the heart.* They wouldn't last much longer.

"Viola," yelled Leonardo, squinting through the chaos.

"Here," she yelled back.

He rushed to her, dodging Bates' sword.

"Do you have your ability back?" he asked, grabbing her by the shoulders. "Can you see things, in your mind?"

"Yes." She nodded. "What—"

"I need you to find the heart of the Dark. There must be a brain somewhere in all this, controlling everything."

"Ok, I'll try, but—" she ducked as a column of Dark shot past. "I can't do it out here."

"Right."

He glanced at the pyramid. The snake's mouth was a long way up, but Pinch's fan blasted away the Dark from the top dozen steps.

"Let's go," said Viola.

They took off for the stairs. A blast of hot air snapped at their clothes as Mishti cut through the Dark.

"Mishti." He grabbed her arm. "Cover us."

They ascended the steps, Mishti facing backward as Leonardo and Viola climbed, swords flashing through the Dark. As soon as they reached the fan's protection, all three sprinted through the fierce gusts and threw themselves into the snake's mouth.

"This way." Leonardo helped Viola up and ran past the carved altar, down the steps and into the pyramid.

"What are we doing?" demanded Mishti.

"Shh," Leonardo hushed her as Viola dropped cross-legged to

the floor. She closed her eyes, breathing rapidly. A line of blood trickled down her arm where her sleeve was cut. Leonardo reached out to wipe it away, but she flicked his hand.

"I'm fine. I need to concentrate."

"Right."

He and Mishti stood silently over Viola, gasping for breath, weapons hanging at their sides. The seconds dragged on. The battle raged outside the pyramid. The muscles up Leonardo's sides burned, but he ignored them. Mishti's face was slick with sweat.

Finally, Viola blinked her eyes open.

"It's in the Cove. Over the fortress."

"What is?" asked Mishti.

*Dammit.* He needed the heart to be within reach. *Ok, think. New plan.*

Leonardo got an idea. If Juliet could summon a sea monster, she could damn well summon a lion. "Follow me."

# CHAPTER 47

Everyone looked up as Leonardo burst into the stone room. Mishti and Viola hurried down the stairs behind him. Thankfully, every one of the Snakes was under control as Moth, Juliet, and their army of kids applied the wet rags. Juliet poured venom into the water bucket while Isabella stirred it with a stick. Leonardo staggered to a stop at the sight of Nym; eyes squeezed shut, teeth clenched, sweat dripping down his face as he struggled in his bonds, grunting and swearing under his breath. His sleeves were freshly wet, but the Dark was stronger.

"What's going on?" asked Moth.

"Juliet," said Leonardo, out of breath. "The lions here—the real ones—they can disappear from one place and appear in another, right? Is there any way for a person to use that magic?"

"I…don't know. Maybe, but—"

"Yes," said Caliban. He blinked his mismatched eyes from the shadows. "There is a way."

"What are you talking about?" demanded Mishti, moving into the room behind him.

"How do we do it?" asked Leonardo.

"Well," said Caliban. "It's unpredictable to begin with, and like I already told you, the Dark is wreaking—"

"Havoc with your magic, yes I know. But how do we do it?"

Caliban stood, tilting his head. "We would need lion hair, and I would need the snake pit across camp."

"Juliet." Leonardo whirled to face her. "I need you to summon a lion."

"I—"

"Now. Otherwise, we're all going to be destroyed by the Dark. Listen, if you can summon a sea monster, you can summon a lion."

"Leonardo," snapped Mishti. "Tell me what's going on."

"I'll do it," said Juliet. "Moth, get the flowers, quickly!"

"Leonardo," said Caliban. "Even with the lion hair and my pit, the odds of this spell working—"

"It'll work," said Leonardo. "The woods will help us."

Caliban raised an eyebrow. "Are you sure about that?"

***

"There," said Juliet. She stepped back from a pile of flower petals shaped into a lion. "The lions can move with magic. It will be here faster than the sea monster was."

"Perfect." Leonardo grabbed Juliet's last two pails of sea monster venom.

"What are you doing?" she demanded.

"No time," said Leonardo.

He shoved the second bucket in Mishti's arms and turned for the stairs.

"What's this for?" asked Mishti.

"We're going to kill the Dark," said Leonardo. "We need to get to the Cove."

"You're…" Viola grabbed his arm. "Leo, you can't."

"We have to," said Leonardo. "It's the only way."

"Leo—"

Leonardo tore his gaze away from her. He didn't have time to question anything. "Mishti, Caliban, let's go."

They needed to get outside, *now.*

"This is a suicide mission," snapped Caliban, running behind him.

"We can only survive so long here. We have to try something."

"Can someone tell me what calling a lion has to do with getting to the Cove?" shouted Mishti.

But the boys ignored her and pressed back outside, into the chaos of screams and darkness. Gripping the pail in one hand, Leonardo descended to the courtyard. He barely waited for Mishti and Caliban, sprinting to the archway as the Dark streaked past him. He rounded the wall, into the jungle, just as a hulking shape stepped out of the trees.

Leonardo's blood froze. He staggered to a halt, heart pounding in his throat. The lion moved toward him, streaks of shadow hurtling past it. They flew around Leonardo, slicing his face like razor blades. He didn't feel any of it. The beast bared its teeth, its massive head framed by a mane of rich gold.

*What did I do?*

Leonardo gripped his sword, his fingers white on the leather.

The lion roared, deep and heavy. Leonardo's hairs stood on end. Then the lion looked past him, to the horrors of the Dark. All at once, it shifted backward, amber eyes darting around the nightmare.

*It's going to leave,* he realized in panic.

"Move," snapped Caliban. He shoved Leonardo aside, knife flashing through a tuft of the lion's mane, just as it disappeared again.

Caliban sagged on his knees. He held up a fistful of hair.

*Thank God.*

"Let's go." Leonardo grabbed his shoulder and pulled him up, then raced back through the archway into Snake Clan's courtyard.

"Seriously?" wheezed Caliban.

Silhouettes wove around Leonardo, swords flashing through the swirling shadows, as he sprinted to the doorway in the side of the Snake.

Mishti and Caliban burst after him into the smaller courtyard with the snake pit in its centre. The Dark clouded overhead. Smoke gusted in Leonardo's face, sharp and stinging. He staggered back a step, blinking hard.

"Ok," he yelled. "Do the spell."

"Are you sure?" Caliban looked from Leonardo to Mishti.

"Do the fucking spell," snapped Mishti.

She glanced at Leonardo. He held eye contact with her. *I'm trusting you,* her look said. After everything they'd been through, it all came down to this one gamble.

*Let me be right about this,* he prayed.

Caliban nodded once and stepped up to the pit, shouting words that the shadows ripped away. The Dark descended into the space, nearly blinding them as it whipped around the courtyard. Leonardo and Mishti slashed at it, smoke pouring off their blades. Caliban shouted louder, faster, his hands clenched. His hood flapped behind his head.

Then light burst from the snake eye scar on his forehead.

"It's time," he yelled. "Take this." He pressed a handful of lion hair into each of their hands. He leaned right next to their ears. "Drop it into the pit at the same time and think where you want to go. I make no guarantee—"

"The terrace above your fortress," Leonardo told Mishti.

She nodded, her expression tight. They stepped up to the edge of the pit.

"Wait until I'm gone," yelled Caliban. "I can't predict—" the rest was lost as he ran through the doorway. The Dark swirled around them, harder and harder until Leonardo couldn't see a thing. He got on his knees, feeling for the edge of the pit. Mishti did the same. Then the world started getting lighter, and he tipped his head back to see a circle of blue sky, directly over the pit.

*The woods will help us.*

"Now," yelled Leonardo.

They threw both handfuls of lion hair into the hole, gripping their pails of venom.

The Dark roared like a living beast. The gale nearly threw Leonardo into Mishti, but he grit his teeth and huddled low.

*Nothing's happening.* For a terrible second, he thought it didn't work, then he realized the ground under his knees was limestone, not tile.

*Limestone. We're in the Cove.*

Leonardo felt for the stone rail and climbed to his feet, squinting into the swirling, churning storm over the sea. He struggled to make out anything distinct.

Mishti yelled something he couldn't hear. Leonardo shook his head and leaned closer. She put her mouth up to his ear and yelled, "Look!"

She pointed over the balustrade, and Leonardo squinted, willing his eyes to adjust. For a long moment he saw nothing but black, but then he frowned, stepping closer. A small cluster of darkness rotated over the Cove, even blacker than the surrounding smoke.

*The heart.*

"I can't throw this that far," shouted Mishti, holding up her pail.

*Dammit.* No one could, with any guarantee of hitting it. Cold desperation flooded Leonardo's chest.

*Think. You're this far. There must be another—*

He stopped. There *was* another option. A terrible, unthinkable option. The only way to get the venom to the heart would be to add weight and force. Leonardo met Mishti's gaze through the wind and Dark. Her eyes widened, then she swallowed.

"Come on," shouted Leonardo. "We need a running start." He trekked back across the terrace, forcing each step through blasts that burned his skin like acid. The Dark was getting stronger. His immunity was wearing down. The heavy blanket over Juliet's quarters flapped wildly, and Leonardo stopped with his back against the wall beside it.

Mishti stopped next to him, and Leonardo drew a breath.

"Ready?"

*Don't think. Don't question it.* His friends could die any second.

"Now." Mishti took off and Leonardo ran after her. The wind swung around to their backs, shoving them faster and faster toward the balustrade. The edge drew closer, closer…Leonardo gripped his pail of venom, then in sync, he and Mishti jumped, kicked off the rail, and dove toward the heart.

Leonardo threw his bucket as he twisted in the air. The liquid sprayed out and he fell, tumbling, plummeting through the Dark toward the sea.

The surface flew at him, ten meters away, five, then a shape launched out of the water, slammed into Leonardo, and drove him under.

# CHAPTER 48

Leonardo burst through the water, coughing and gasping for air.

*The Dark.*

He leaned back, kicking to stay afloat as he watched the Dark spin high above, retracting into a tight ball. Streaks of black shot over the clifftops to meet it.

"It's pulling out!" said Mishti.

Leonardo turned to see her treading water. Sodden, but alive. She coughed, pointing to one of the lines in the sky.

"That's from the direction of the island." She pointed to another. "That's from Tiger Clan's territory. And that one—"

"Is from Snake Clan," said Leonardo, as the last of the Dark hurtled over the jungle. It joined the blackness circling the heart, then the entire mass shot through the break in the cliffs, racing out to sea. They watched it until it vanished over the horizon.

"We did it," said Mishti, her voice quiet with shock.

"We survived," said Leonardo. *And we saved the others.*

But they hadn't killed the Dark. A deep knowing filled his gut.

*We have another fight coming.* And something told him they hadn't seen the worst of it yet.

"Who saved us?" Leonardo suddenly asked. He remembered the collision in a blur, a second before he hit the surface.

"I did," said a voice behind them.

"Adriana," said Leonardo. *Of course.* He turned in the water, expecting her typical smugness. Instead, her delicate features were arranged in an expression of dire seriousness.

"I'm ready to help. I'm…I've not always been the type to '*do good*', I suppose. But when my sisters told me they abandoned you all, that the Dark was going to kill you…I realized it might be time to grow up and stop taking life for granted. I don't know anything about fighting the Dark, but if you'll accept it, I'm with you."

Leonardo and Mishti glanced at each other. Adriana was the reason Strato and Robin died, and she'd jeopardized Charley and Pompey's rescue. He had no idea how to receive this new development.

"Think about it," said Adriana. "I have to go, but I'll find you again soon."

She dove underwater, propelling away with hard tail-strokes.

"Leo!" yelled another voice.

*What the…*

Leonardo squinted up at the open-air terrace. Viola leaned over the balustrade.

"I followed you to the snake pit," she shouted. "I must have gotten caught in the spell."

"What next?" said Mishti under her breath.

"Come down," yelled Leonardo, wincing at the pain of shouting. She nodded and disappeared.

"Let's get to the dock," he told Mishti. "Everyone should be here soon." He doubted Viola would be the last surprise awaiting them.

# CHAPTER 49

I t's not dead," said Kate.

"It's hiding," agreed Leonardo, wincing at the pain of talking. He was bruised up both sides of his body. He and Mishti stood on the captains' platforms of their longboats, regarding what was left of their alliance.

"Sophie," said Mishti. "Recite the list of casualties again. Slower this time."

"John," started Sophie, "and Pip." Leonardo glanced at Kate and Cyrus. They kept their faces neutral, but he knew the loss was a blow to them. It should have been the most shocking casualty, and the biggest sign of the Dark's power; to lose two originals was to lose a piece of the woods.

But John and Pip weren't the biggest losses.

Sophie listed a number of pirates, Lions, Snakes, Dragons, and Tigers that Leonardo only knew because he'd heard their names the first time. Then she paused, drawing a breath.

"And all the Natives."

"Except Viola," added Moth.

The rows of kids fell silent. Hearing it for a second time still took the breath away from Leonardo.

*The guardians of the woods, gone.*

Viola was only spared by following Leonardo and Mishti to the Cove. According to all recounts, the Dark targeted her people in the final moments of the fight. That was valuable information if nothing else, but Leonardo didn't feel like celebrating.

Whatever cheap thrill the woods sought from watching its children fight a nightmare, he sincerely hoped it realized its mistake now. The guardians of the woods were gone, for the first time since the woods began, and the future felt deathly precarious.

If the woods continued on this reckless, no one remained to protect Leonardo and the others. They were on their own, more than ever before.

Which was why they currently filled five longboats, watching the jungle walls slide past on the river. They needed help. The Dark would only get stronger, and the collective imagination of the Cove wasn't enough to push it out.

They needed every kid from every corner of the woods.

Leonardo stepped off his bench, into the footwell between Moth, Pinch, Bates, Puck, Nym, Charley, and Viola. No one said anything for a long moment. Leonardo gazed upriver, visualizing the long journey from the Darkwoods.

Finally, he turned to his clan.

"Ready to go home?"

# ACKNOWEDGEMENTS

As always, I have to thank my family. Your support means everything to me. This journey continues to be unpredictable and incredible, and you've been there with me every step of the way.

And again, to my amazing editor Fiona, who gives way more time than any editor should be expected to. Thank you for being consistently fussy and never letting me off the hook. Your fingerprints are all over this book and I wouldn't have it any other way!

To the Dramallamas (and of course, to Supreme-Llama-Leader, King). You're all such a massive part of my life, and I'm constantly amazed by the support. I love every minute I spend in the theatre with you.

To Sofia Soria, artist extraordinaire. You put SO much time and care into the beautiful map at the front of this book. I couldn't have worked with a better illustrator.

To Dan, for creating another spectacular cover. Your ability to pull these images out of my head and into full colour is truly amazing. I can't wait to see this book on shelves next to Lost Boys.

And lastly, to everyone who read Lost Boys and decided to stick around with Leo and company on this second leg of their adventure. Thank you for coming along for the ride. Without readers, there would be no need for writers.

TURN THE PAGE FOR
A SNEAK PREVIEW OF

# THE DARK

BOOK THREE OF THE LOST BOYS TRILOGY

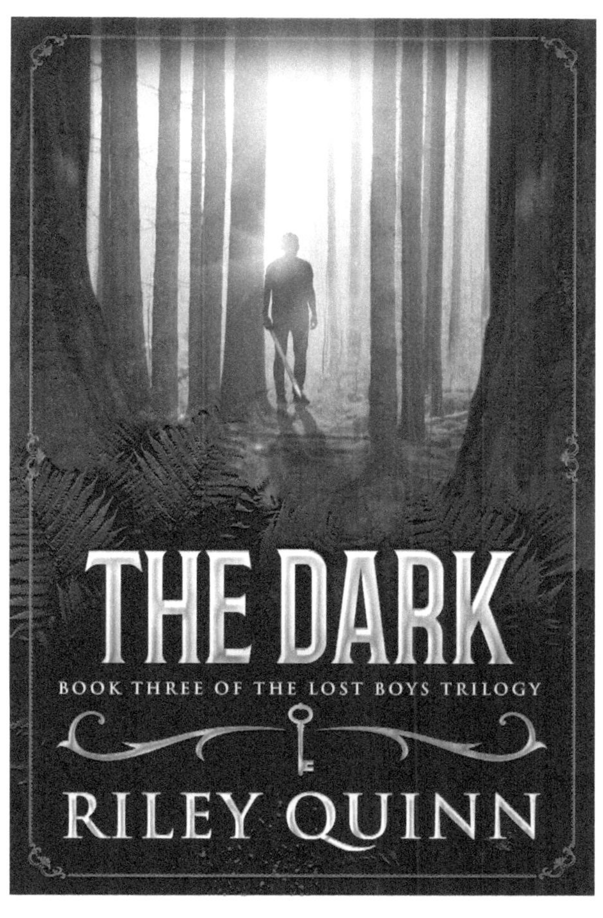

# CHAPTER 1

Tension crackled as Leonardo gripped the stem of his longboat. Oars clunked in precise rhythm, and sweaty faces squinted at the shadows along the bank. Four boats plowed through the river behind them, piled with colourfully robed Cove kids, their expressions tight.

They cut through the Backwaters; a marshland on the edge of the Darkwoods, and not a single living thing broke the silence. It was as if this entire corner of the woods had frozen in time.

"Everything's dead," said Moth, breathless from working his oar. His flushed cheeks turned pale as islands of charred grass slid past.

"I know." Heaviness weighed on Leonardo's chest. He studied a withered stand of reeds, cattail tops drooping for the surface. Around the Backwaters, previously lush aquatic trees had blackened, their branches shrunken.

"Like *dead* dead," said Bates.

"It's so quiet," said Viola softly, her gaze fixed on another island of scorched grass. She glanced at Leonardo. He met her grim eyes.

They had travelled a week to get here, chased from the Cove by the Dark, the all-consuming presence that spent its days ravaging the woods.

"Did you expect green gardens?" Kate sat cross-legged in the boat, a salt-stained coat draped from her shoulders and a skull-and-crossbones trilby resting cockeyed on her head.

"When we left, this place was untouched." Leonardo shuddered. The Darkwoods were never quiet.

"Raven Clan territory was dying fast, though," said Nym, clipped and impatient. "It was only natural for it to spread."

Leonardo frowned at him.

*He's not...right.*

Nym had been battling the Dark inside him for weeks now, but he'd *changed* since the last attack. He was thinner, sunken, bitter. His deterioration was a reminder to all of them; the sand racing through an hourglass.

Leonardo eyed the other three clans of Cove kids, regarding the miles of rotten trees with apprehension. They were all veterans of the Dark, yet they knew so little about it.

They knew the heart of it lay in the Cove. They knew its reach extended across the entire woods. A small group of them knew it was a nightmare, let into the dreamworld by the woods itself. And they knew that sea monster venom could hurt it.

That was all. And they were a long way from any sea monsters.

*We're on our own.* Viola's people—the guardians of the woods—

were gone, and the sirens had abandoned their post as guardians of the Cove.

"The Hawk Clan patrol is still sitting at the border," said Viola, eyes shut as she searched ahead with her mind. "They're not moving."

"Then let's introduce ourselves," said Mishti. Leonardo's co-leader of Lion Clan, she stood atop the captain's platform of her boat, with its gold lion head and silk sail. Days of travel had disheveled her black hair, her gold robes smudged and stained, but the knife-edged throwing rings around her wrists glinted as sharp as her eyes.

A few girls in her boat leaned closer, whispering quickly. Leonardo watched them out of one eye. For all of Mishti's bravado, her clan weren't fighters. Leonardo's boys had told them stories of Hawk Clan's ferocity, and he recognized the hesitation on the girls' faces to confront such a formidable enemy.

*Formidable or not, we have five-times their numbers.*

"I agree," said Leonardo. "But this is only a fly-by. We don't stop."

"What?" Pinch twisted back to look at him. "Why?"

"If we attack a border patrol," explained Leonardo, "we'll have a second fight on our hands, with the rest of the clan. Instead, we'll scare Hawk Clan, let them gather all their numbers, then we'll capture them as one."

He held no illusions that Gallus would listen to logic. He was the new Aleksander, and they would waste precious time trying to convince him to leave the Darkwoods. Tying up Hawk Clan and dragging them in front of the Dark would be the only way to gain their allegiance.

"Imagine when Gallus sees all of us," laughed Bates. "The halfwit's going to curl up and cry."

Leonardo grinned, despite himself. He'd be lying if he said he wasn't looking forward to the expression on Gallus's face. They slipped past a blackened tree, its branches sagging like rubber. The amusement turned sour in Leonardo's mouth.

*We can't waste time here.* They needed the imagination power of all the clans in the Darkwoods, as well as the Redwoods and the Highland, if they wanted to save the woods and survive the Dark.

He eyed the boats beyond his stern, filled with Lions, Tigers, Dragons, Snakes, and pirates. They were weary; tattered from their escape. He hoped they were ready for the fight Hawk Clan would bring.

"There's the river," called Pinch. He pointed over the prow, to where the sprawling delta of the Backwaters narrowed into the mouth of a waterway, laid bare by the flattened, dead vegetation.

*The river.* They'd been on 'the river' for a week, but this leg was different. This was home.

*How much has changed? Has died,* he corrected himself. He wondered if he'd recognize it once they rounded the rocky stretch of Hawk Clan territory and entered Raven Clan's boundaries.

The five boats slipped out of the Backwaters and through the bottleneck of rotten banks, single file, to the steady splash of water sloshing off paddles. The current strengthened, impeding their progress and spraying around the tip of the prow. Leonardo's heart pounded. They were in Hawk Clan Territory now. They had returned to the Darkwoods.

"I never imagined five clans could be so quiet," said Moth. Sweat matted his curls, and a partially healed scab marred his cheek, earned during a fight with demonic freshwater sirens a few days earlier. The journey north hadn't been any easier than the one south.

No one replied, punctuating his point.

Their surroundings became sandier as the banks gave way to large outcroppings of rock. Leonardo tugged the rudder, guiding the boat left, around a bend in the river, and down the final stretch toward where the water funneled through a massive cleft in the Tree Cliffs. The silhouette of pines atop the ruddy stone set his fingers twitching on the dry wood of the stem. Those trees leered down, sinister now. Leonardo had become a trespasser. An intruder in his own woods.

A hawk cry split the air, and Leonardo jumped.

At the far end of the tunnel, a longboat floated near the Raven Clan border. He drew a sharp breath.

*Calm down,* Leonardo told himself. His clan needed him in control.

His clanmates glanced at one another, but they uttered no raven cry in response. They weren't Ravens anymore.

The Hawk boat rotated to face them, and Leonardo wrapped his fingers around the leather grip of his sword. A pudgy figure on the stern platform lifted a hand, shading his eyes.

Viola glanced back at Leonardo, her brown eyes scrutinizing his. It was Gallus's ploy that started Raven Clan's demise. Memories of the ambush played through Leonardo's mind. Of Hawk Clan, Bear Clan, and Fox Clan storming the clearing below the treehouses. Of the treehouses burning as he watched helplessly.

Leonardo's boat passed into the cleft between the cliffs and closed on the Hawks fast, oars churning under anxious hands.

"Oars up," called Leonardo. His clan responded instantly, oars clattering out of the water.

Gallus's face came into focus, all apple cheeks and baby-fat. His mouth dropped open at the sight of the ex-Ravens.

"You!" His gaze darted past Leonardo, to the four packed longboats in his wake. He focused on Leonardo again, his eyes wild. "What the hell are you doing here?"

RILEY QUINN is a Canadian author and musician. He grew up in Western Canada, dividing his time between the Prairies, the Rocky Mountains, and the shores of the North West Coast. When he's not writing, Riley can be found performing and teaching music in his local community.

To learn more, visit: www.rileyquinnofficial.com